Shifter's Sanctuary

A
Legends of Shadow
Earth Novel

Stephanie Kayne

Acknowledgements

Thank you to all who have helped me in this fantastical, wonderful journey that is writing. I've had a tremendous amount of fun creating my worlds and characters. I'd like to thank my husband, Bobby, for all his love and support and 'is the book done yet?' Thanks to Entropy, for hands-on bunny research. Thanks to my weekly writing groups for ideas and inspiration. Thanks to the wonderful folks at the Office of Letters and Light who facilitated my journey into storytelling. Thanks to my editor, Jody Wallace for wading through it all.

Cover Design by Lee Ching of Under Cover Designs

Copyright

Demon's Desire

Shifter's Sanctuary

Shifter's Sanctuary

A Legends of Shadow Earth Novel

Prologue

Two Years Ago

The harsh blare of an alarm propelled Jared from sleep to wakefulness in one abrupt, heart-pounding instant. The screaming siren sent daggers of agony ricocheting through his skull. Pain throbbed behind his eyes in time to the adrenaline-laced beating of his heart.

Fucking bastards.

The sound stopped, leaving blessed silence.

He pressed his palms to his eye sockets in a vain attempt to reduce the pressure.

Deep breaths. Move through the pain. Let it flow out of the body. Deep breaths.

Any moment now it would be back. The horrific sound was calibrated to elicit fear and panic in the test subjects. To make sure they couldn't prepare, it went off at a different time each morning—a test to gauge each person's control over their animal.

Jared opened his eyes and surveyed the area, verifying his location.

Cinderblock walls? Check.

Bars across the front? Check.

Trapped in this fucking hell? Check.

The annoying sound resumed, but this time he used the mental tricks the lab techs taught them to prevent the effects.

He should be used to this shit by now. It happened every…

Single.

Fucking.

Morning.

God damned fucking researchers and their hellish tests.

Jared filled his lungs with cool air, banishing the last remnants of pain. He rubbed his sweating palms against the thin cotton blanket. The blanket provided psychological comfort that surpassed warmth, though he doubted the researchers knew that. The powers that be hadn't argued when the subjects had requested the blankets.

The temperature in the habitat block was strictly controlled. Seventy degrees at night and seventy-eight degrees during the day. Their block consisted of a row of twenty, eight-by-ten cells on either side of a corridor. Cameras in each cell monitored every second of every day. His cell was at the end, closest to the lab and furthest from possible escape to freedom.

Jared stood and stretched. The scrubs they'd been given to wear, pulled across his shoulders. The researches chose scrubs because they were easy to obtain, and easy to get rid of.

Across the hall, others started their stretches, except for one man. He was huddled under the blanket, trying to squeeze himself into the corner. Sometimes the conditioning worked and other times they were reduced to quivering bodies, unable to function until calm.

Jared took a deep breath and waited. The animal hidden within, surged to the surface fighting for control of his body.

Run! Flee! Danger! Hide!

No! I will not flee. I will not hide.

Survive! Hide!

NO!

A brief struggle and the animal retreated to the back of his mind, alert and waiting for the next opportunity to take control—to escape.

It wasn't getting easier as the techs promised. The approaching full moon made it hard to shove the animal back.

The key was to keep calm; to think calming thoughts.

An image popped into Jared's mind. Dr. David Glendale, the Director of Experimental Research for Elaine Pharmaceuticals, the company behind the cancer study, hanging by his wrists from a tall oak, while Jared beat him like a piñata. That image brought a smile to his face. Ah… revenge.

His regulated his breathing to match. *Re*… breathe in… *venge*… breathe out… *Re*… breathe in… *venge*… breathe out.

No fucking good deed ever goes unpunished. This was his reward for volunteering for that cancer research study. Instead of trying to figure out the causes of cancer, the researchers had experimented on the volunteers in horrifically painful ways until the test subjects had been transformed into shape-shifting abominations.

Think calming thoughts. Think… of the bloody husk of the Director swinging in the breeze. Destroyed. Broken. A fitting end to the horror being perpetrated on the subjects of the study.

Jared paced the confines of his cell as the subtle lighting increased in brightness, signifying day. With no windows, they had to rely on this artificial sun. He'd lost track of the days. Had weeks passed? Months? Hard to tell.

If he didn't remain calm, he'd be dead. The myriad of tests they endured had killed off many of the group. And one day soon, it'd be him. The techs warned that if the subject didn't get control of the animal upon waking, the animal instincts overwhelmed the human mind and the subject died. Like the guy across the hall. His shivering ceased and the blanket dropped from unseeing eyes.

His animal had won. His heart stopped scared to death in the name of science.

The far door opened, and two blue-coated lab techs entered the cell block pushing a gurney. They stopped in front of the cell and typed a code into the keypad by the door. With a click, the cell door unlocked and they pushed the gurney inside, loaded the body, and covered it with a sheet.

As the gurney wobbled toward the exit, Jared and the others stood at the bars of the cells, bowing their heads as the body passed—a silent tribute to their dead colleague.

"Another day, another body," one of the techs said. "Why did they pick animals that are so easily scared?"

"Because, idiot, they're readily available." One tech held the door while the other maneuvered the gurney through it.

"I guess, but it's ridiculous how many participants we've lost."

"These guys aren't the final stage of experimentation; they're testing the process."

The door closed behind them.

They're not the final result? They weren't meant to survive this. Fuck.

He had to get out, but how? Ideas churned through his mind—improbable, impractical, and impossible. The longer he pondered a plan, the more outrageous it became.

Jared set his subconscious work on the escape plan while he engaged in morning exercises. His best ideas came while counting reps.

He'd finished sit-ups, jumping jacks, and push-ups, by the time the far door opened. Two different techs entered the room maneuvering a large metal cart.

Ah breakfast. Like Pavlov's dog, Jared's stomach growled at the metal-on-metal squeak of wobbly wheels. He took a deep breath, identifying the contents. It was a game; one he didn't let them know he played. At first, he'd been able to determine the meal when it was something aromatic. Through practice he'd honed his skill and his accuracy had reached ninety-nine percent.

Carrots, apples, broccoli, bananas and water.

"What's for breakfast?" one of the other participants asked.

"The full moon is in three days and you need a vegan diet before your controlled shift."

Sometimes he hated being right.

Jared craved something heartier, more filling. Bacon, eggs, pancakes, French toast. His mouth watered. What he wouldn't give for a large cup of coffee. When was the last time he'd had a cup? According to the techs caffeine was poison for the animal, making it impossible for the human to remain in control.

He waited until all the trays were distributed and the techs left the room before he polished off his breakfast. Pushing the tray through the slot in the bars, he resumed his exercises. If he didn't get protein soon, he'd lose muscle mass.

The physical activity allowed him to escape his thoughts, compartmentalizing them so the researchers wouldn't succeed in their psychological games.

The lab door closest to him opened and two techs, wearing light blue lab coats, stepped into the cell block, their voices hushed.

Jared faced the wall next to where the techs were standing. Bracing his hands on the cool cinderblocks, he did two sets of standing push-ups. His heightened senses allowed him to eavesdrop on their whispered conversation. He was far enough away to assuage any suspicion. Aware the camera captured his every move, he made sure to change the exercises while eavesdropping.

"I've done it! I found the control key."

"Really? That's great news! How?"

"All we need to do is modify the gene splice sequence—"

Control key? What the hell was that? Jared did two more reps as he listened to the tech's methodology.

An explosion rocked the floor and walls of his cell, knocking him off balance. The mortar between cement blocks crumbled to the floor. Alarms wailed, driving daggers of agony through his skull. The high-pitched noise cut off as the white noise machines kicked in.

A second explosion shook the room. Others fought panic and his own animal surged to take command of his body. Jared gritted his teeth, forced his body into stillness, and concentrated on keeping the rabbit contained.

Was this another damned test?

The scent of gunpowder, leather and a hint of something else filled the air along with the smoke.

His foot twitched, followed by his arm.

Flee!

Control. It was all about control.

A high-pitched scream echoed through the room, sounding like a terrorized little girl. The hair on the back of his neck stood up. It was chilling—the sound of abject horror; of certain death.

Damn it, he would NOT succumb.

Heart beating fast, he focused his mind, switching to battle mode. No room for fear, no room for panic.

The far door burst open and a group of men appeared through the smoke as if summoned by a magician. Dressed in black fatigues and masks, with guns drawn, they crept through the room, halting in front of each cell, examining the doors and the occupants.

The techs rushed forward, ordering them to stop. Two shots later and the lab techs slumped to the ground, neat holes in their heads.

One man removed his mask and barked out commands. "Secure the room."

Black clad men took positions at the far entrance. Another group strode to the door nearest Jared. One of the men made eye contact with Jared. "How many in the next room?"

"No idea. They never let us in there."

Two men stood with their backs to the wall, guns at the ready, while two others kicked in the door. A whistle from the other room and the two against the wall rushed in.

The leader stood in front of Jared's cell. "How many are here?"

Jared shrugged. "There are other habitat blocks but I don't know how full they are."

"How many?"

"They never said."

"We'll get you out of here soon." The leader assured.

Jared was skeptical. "This isn't another test is it?"

A horrified expression crossed the guy's face. "No! This shouldn't have happened. We're shutting this down."

Jared frowned. "Who the hell are you?"

"We're a private security force."

Jared had been around enough special forces to let the rest of his questions remain unasked.

Two men walked through the door, yanking a struggling tech. "Area secured."

"Status of the rest of the compound?" asked the leader.

"Secure."

The man in charge turned to the tech. "How many test subjects are there?"

"No idea. I don't work with the subjects." The tech wiped his face with his arm, leaving a bloody smear on the light blue sleeve. He should have been scared, but the guy stood defiant. "You and the Elite won't get away with this."

The leader leaned forward, muttering under his breath. The tech's eyes glazed over.

"Is there a master code for the cells?" the leader asked.

"No. They wanted to ensure no mass escapes."

"Randall, take the tech and see if there are other cell blocks. If he tries anything, terminate him. James, I want a med team ready to examine the patients. Merrick, keypads are all yours."

"Yes, Captain," the man, Randall, responded.

The men leapt into action. The one called Merrick, worked methodically down the block, opening the cells. Other members of the team removed the occupants, carrying them from the room. Jared was the last freed.

A soft click and the door to his cage opened.

Freedom. Jared paused. It was too good to be true. The rescuers treated his fellow test subjects with respect, but he'd reserve judgement.

The rescuers guided them through a complex maze of halls and corridors that led outside.

After the climate-controlled environment, the cold night air was a shock. Jared drew a deep breath of fresh air into his lungs. It hurt, but freedom tasted sweet. For a moment, he stared at the moon and stars. Was this real? Was he really free? He half expected Rod Serling to emerge from the surrounding tree-line.

The animal watched in the back of his mind, ready to take control, but willing to let the human handle things for the moment.

A twig snapped behind him, and he whirled to face a new threat. A few men emerged from the building holding rabbits under their front legs, letting their back legs dangle. The rabbits raked their hind claws along the forearms of the rescuers leaving exposed skin torn and bloody.

Jared hurried over. "You're holding them wrong."

"How should they be held?" one of the rescuers asked.

Another one sneered. "You think you know better? Prove it."

Jared fought the urge to knock the man on his ass. He was helping after all, even if he was being an asshole. Jared took the animal from the man and placed the rabbit's feet against his chest and supported its weight on his arm. With his other hand he stroked from head to tail. The rabbit calmed. The tremors in its small body slowed, decreasing until it ground its teeth in pleasure.

A couple of people dressed in scrubs were escorted from the building by the security force. A few black-clad men emerged awkwardly holding rabbits.

Why were there so many rabbits? The researchers had told them they wouldn't experience their first shift until the full moon, which was days away. Were these rabbits test subjects stuck in animal form or were they non-shifting animals? He had too many questions and there wasn't anyone around to answer them.

Jared squinted at the rabbit in his arms. A faint brown haze surrounded the animal. The same haze, he'd seen around his fellow prisoners. If they couldn't change without the moon, why and how did they get into rabbit form?

The Captain strode to Jared's side.

He was surrounded by a shimmering silver glow. Jared blinked his eyes. Must be seeing things.

"Randall, tell your men to hold the rabbits like that," the man ordered.

Randall, surrounded by a sparkly grey haze, nodded and instructed the others in a low tone.

The Captain held out his hand and Jared shook it. "I'm Captain Jor'dan DúSan. Who are you and what do we need to do for them?"

"Jared Williams." He surveyed the area. "You need a large, covered pen out of the way of noise and anything that would startle them."

"You want to put them in a cage?"

"Not normally, no. Rabbits are easily scared to death. They need to be away from predators to feel safe."

Mr. DúSan waved a few men over and spoke in a language Jared didn't recognize. For a well-traveled man like himself, that was unusual.

The men scattered.

Mr. DúSan faced Jared. "I'm curious. How have you and a few others remained human?"

"No idea," Jared admitted, and even if he knew, it was best to keep information to himself. He didn't know what these people wanted and he'd been betrayed too many times by people pretending to be helpful.

That was enough for Mr. DúSan. He asked no further questions.

Two unfamiliar men approached. Mr. DúSan smiled. "Damien and James, come and meet Mr. Williams."

Jared kept silent, senses on alert. Damien and James were surrounded by a dripping red glow. Jared squinted and the glow disappeared.

Had the techs drugged their meal? Why was his vision screwed up?

"Captain, Merrick needs a consult. We'll escort Mr. Williams to the healer, ah medic."

Jared nodded at Mr. DúSan, dismissing him as a potential threat. He focused on the subtle menace emanating from the two men leading him into the forest.

"Where's the medic?" Jared asked, calculating escape routes in case they turned on him.

They didn't answer. He had no choice but to follow them through the trees. Jared allowed the distance between them to lengthen enough that he'd have a few seconds warning if they attacked. The rabbit in his arms laid its head on his chest and closed its eyes.

Another small clearing held a couple of canopies and multiple pens with a dozen or so rabbits. Everyone walked on quiet feet, not wanting to disturb the animals.

A large tent with a red cross on the side stood in the center.

Still petting the rabbit, Jared approached the medical tent. The two men stopped and the blond pulled a knife from a hidden pocket and used the butt to knock twice on the metal support. He pulled the flap aside and gestured Jared in.

Jared paused a few feet before the tent.

"Who's in there?" Jared sensed some…thing in the tent. Something he didn't want to come in contact with.

An older woman emerged from the tent. Her careworn face smiled in welcome. Golden flames surrounded her. He squeezed his eyes closed for a few seconds and when he opened them, the flames dissipated.

Jared faced a woman shorter than himself, dressed in a white lab coat with a stethoscope looped around her neck.

Adrenaline flooded his system and his inner animal surged—forcing him to take three steps back, closer to the trees and safety.

A frown crossed the woman's face. She spoke in a soft, calm voice. "Thank you, James and Damien. We'll be fine."

"Call out if you need us," Damien said.

The woman rolled her eyes. "I'm perfectly safe."

"He's an unknown, and we're not willing to chance it," James said, crossing his arms.

She put her hands on her hips and stared at Damien. Jared could have sworn flames leapt into the air surrounding her. Her tone was hard. "You forget who I am."

"Sorry, Doctor." The men bowed low before her and left the clearing.

She stepped closer. "My name is Doctor Bar'ella. I'd like to examine you and your friend."

Jared's inner animal forced their body to step back. The rabbit in his arms tensed and pricked his chest with its claws, responding to his rising anxiety.

An expression of concern crossed her face. "What's wrong?"

"Lab coat." Jared knew it was ridiculous to be afraid of a simple piece of clothing, but his animal wanted to hide from the white garment. Too much pain inflicted by those in white coats.

She took off the stethoscope, shrugged out of the coat, and tossed it into the tent. Stethoscope back around her neck, she spread her arms. "Better?"

He nodded, wary. Something about her screamed dangerous predator, though he couldn't put his finger on what it was. He was learning to trust the animal's instinct regarding predators.

"May I examine the rabbit?"

The rabbit trembled.

"It's scared. Do you know anything about rabbits?"

"Not much," she admitted.

"They're easily startled and this one is finally calm."

"Do you know who it is?"

Jared struggled to gather his thoughts. "We weren't encouraged to interact with each other in the lab." He paused, wanting to verify information, but unsure how to ask or if he could trust her answers. "They told us we wouldn't be able to shift without the full moon and in controlled circumstances, yet there are a lot of rabbits. I think some of them shifted, but I don't know how. And I don't know why they don't change back or if they can."

Doctor Bar'ella tilted her head. "It takes a tremendous amount of effort to shift outside of the moon's influence. For natural born shifters, it's theoretically possible, but very, very difficult. As for controlled circumstances, I doubt that."

Wait, what'd she say? "Natural born shifters? You mean people are born like this?"

"Yes. We'll get to that later. Did they teach you how to turn back?"

"The next full moon was to be our first attempted shift, and they were supposed to give us instructions then."

Bar'ella frowned. "This entire experiment shouldn't have been possible," she muttered, her gaze focused on the rabbit.

Jared blanked his expression while he processed the information. That there were others like him, outside of the experiment, boggled the mind. Questions tumbled around his brain. Who were the others? Why did they exist? How was any of this possible? What kind of fucked up world was this?

The more pressing concern was the rabbit in his arms. It needed to become human again. "How can we get them to change back? Do they have to wait for the full moon?"

"I don't know. Come sit with me and we'll figure it out."

She walked over to camp chairs set up beside the tent. "Before we continue, may I check your vitals?"

Jared sat in the chair and placed the rabbit on his lap. His heartrate and breathing were calm; his animal, watchful.

Gold flames surrounded her as she listened to his heart. Shaking his head, he blinked. The fire around her continued to burn. He used his free hand to rub his eyes.

"What's wrong?"

"I'm seeing things."

"What types of things?" she asked, standing up straight.

It sounded ridiculous, but what the hell. She was a doctor helping those rescued. If the techs had drugged him, she'd be able to help. "You're surrounded by gold flames."

Her eyes widened in astonishment. "You can see that?"

Jared nodded, wary. "What is it?"

She leaned forward, stethoscope forgotten in her hands. "Have you seen flames around anyone else?"

"Mr. DúSan shimmered silver, and the two bully boys were surrounded by dripping red."

Bar'ella sat down hard in her chair and shook her head. "Amazing, simply amazing."

"What kind of drug did they use on us?" Jared demanded.

The rabbit perked its ears up, and sniffed the air, looking for predators. Long slow strokes along its back and rabbit released a sigh, snuggling in.

"They didn't give you a drug," Doctor Bar'ella said.

"Then what's going on?"

"I can't answer that question without authorization."

"Who can?"

Doctor Bar'ella smiled. "Would you like to set the rabbit down?"

She pointed to an enclosure behind the tent. The fenced area had a wooden box large enough to accommodate multiple rabbits. Other boxes were being constructed.

Jared spoke to the rabbit on his lap. "Are you ready to go into the hutch?"

It tilted its head to the side as if thinking before shaking its head no.

"I think it's comfortable where it is for the moment," Jared replied

"Very well."

Doctor Bar'ella rose from her chair, took the stethoscope, and placed it against his chest, listening to his heart and lungs. She took his pulse and looked in his eyes, mouth, and ears, while muttering to herself.

Closing her eyes, she held out her hands, palms toward him. A golden glow emanated from her hands and surrounded him before he could move. Soft warmth filled his body, soothing, comforting.

Opening her eyes, she smiled and sat down in her chair.

"What the he... heck was that?"

"I was checking for internal injuries. Both you and the rabbit are healthy."

"You can tell all that from a glow?"

13

"To quote the Bard, 'There are more things in heaven and earth, Horatio, than are dreamt of in your philosophy.'"

"No shit," Jared muttered under his breath.

Mr. DúSan approached. "How are they doing?"

"They're fine." Doctor Bar'ella sat in the chair. "Jor'dan, they need to be integrated."

"What?"

The doctor waved at Jared. "He can see auras."

Mr. DúSan assessed him with a glance. "Interesting."

"What does that mean?" Jared asked.

Doctor Bar'ella glanced at Mr. DúSan, who nodded. The doctor smiled. "Auras surround each living thing. The colors indicate who we are at our most fundamental level."

"And that means what?" Jared asked.

"It means that you can tell what kind of 'person' someone is based on their aura," Mr. DúSan clarified.

Well, that was clear as fucking mud. Jared took a deep breath. *Was it too much to ask to get a straight fucking answer?*

"Let's see if we can get your friend there back to its human form and then we can talk." Doctor Bar'ella stood. "Jor'dan we're going to need clothes."

"On it." He pulled out his cell phone and walked away.

Moments later he returned with a long robe and handed it to the doctor, while continuing to speak in that unrecognizable language.

"Let's go around back. There's more privacy." She led the way around the corner. "Please put the rabbit down."

"Are you ready to resume your human shape?" he asked the rabbit.

It sighed and gave a single nod. Jared lowered it to the grass and rubbed the soft fur between its ears. "Do you want me to stay?"

The rabbit nodded again.

Doctor Bar'ella knelt in the damp grass. "This may or may not work. I don't know if the same rules apply." She took a deep breath and spoke to the rabbit. "Here's what I want you to do. Close your eyes and concentrate on reaching for your human self. Your human self will not allow you to be hurt; you can trust it to keep you safe."

The rabbit glanced up at him.

"I won't let anyone harm you," Jared said.

The rabbit let out a sigh and closed its eyes. For a moment nothing happened, then a swirling black hole enveloped the rabbit.

Jared reached for the bunny but a hand on his forearm stopped him. "Don't!"

"But…"

"Watch."

The black hole popped out of existence, leaving a naked woman kneeling on the grass.

Bar'ella put the long robe over the woman, and Jared gazed at the trees to give her privacy while she dressed.

From around the corner, another woman in jeans and sweater with a red cross on it, stepped forward and led the shifted rabbit away. At the corner of the tent, the shifted woman stopped and turned back.

"Thank you for your help, Doctor," the former rabbit said.

"You're welcome."

The woman smiled at Jared. "Thank you for keeping me safe."

He smiled back. "It was my pleasure."

Doctor Bar'ella struggled to stand. Jared reached out and helped her to her feet.

"Did you get that?" she asked.

"I believe so." He hesitated a moment. "Is that also how we shift into rabbit form?"

Doctor Bar'ella returned to the chairs at the side of the tent. "It takes concentration and a willingness to give up control to your other half. I'll instruct my healers to tell the others how to shift back."

Mr. DúSan approached. It was time to get more answers.

"How do you know how all this works? Who are you people?" Jared asked.

Mr. DúSan spoke. "We're members of a secret world that you and your friends are now a part of."

"What world?"

"A world of magic and wonder. Right now, we need to integrate you into our society."

"Why? Most of us have family and friends waiting for us."

Doctor Bar'ella and Mr. DúSan exchanged look.

Mr. DúSan cleared his throat. "You and the others were reported as killed in an accident while on the way to the lab, a little over two years ago."

"All of us?"

Doctor Bar'ella reached over and patted his hand. "All of you. You can't return to your previous life."

"Why not?" Jared asked.

"Too many reasons to go into now. But if the humans got the chance to examine you, you'll be killed."

"By who?"

"By those of us who are sworn to keep our world a secret," Mr. DúSan said.

"Your world?" Jared asked.

Mr. DúSan held out his hand, "Don't worry. We'll help you find work and adjust to your new life."

With trepidation Jared reach out and shook Mr. DúSan's hand. *What the hell was he getting into?*

"Welcome to Shadow Earth, Mr. Williams."

Chapter 1

Real Earth, San Francisco, Present Day

The Executive Director of Experimental Research at Elaine Pharmaceuticals, Dr. David Glendale, gazed out the window of his penthouse office, down at the teeming masses of humanity. Worker bees for the greater good, a future where both Real and Shadow Earth were controlled by the Alliance.

More than five centuries ago, Shadow Earth was created as an alternate reality by the High Council of Paranormals to provide a safe haven for all paranormal races. Races whose populations had been decimated by the Black Death followed by the Spanish Inquisition.

Paranormals could move between the human world, called Real Earth, and their haven Shadow Earth. Most chose to live and work in Shadow.

It had become apparent there were many opportunities to take advantage of the humans, so the ruling Council set up a police force. The Elite Magical Protection Force was made up of males from all of the paranormal races, and their job was to protect both humans and paranormals from paranormal threats.

As if the Elite, those Keystone Cops, could foil Alliance plans. They kept trying. Occasionally they even succeeded. They'd somehow learned of the last round of experiments and stopped them. David didn't want a repeat of that fiasco, which meant obtaining volunteers in a more covert manner.

The current experiments were proceeding as scheduled, except for one small wrinkle—Jared Williams.

That bastard was the sole survivor of the previous experiments. The Alliance had terminated the others a few months after they'd been freed. But Captain Jor'dan DúSan had conscripted Williams into the Elite, thus protecting him.

David had been willing to leave him be but for one thing. After he'd gone over the security footage, he'd seen Williams interest in the tech's conversation. Due to the white noise generators and subsequent explosions, the recordings hadn't picked up audio of the tech's discovery.

Trying to get Williams into the lab was proving to be more challenging than expected. He'd pry the information from Williams' head or kill him. There were no other options.

The intercom buzzed, pulling him from his thoughts.

"Master Quaid on line one," His executive assistant, Grayson, announced.

The CEO of the Alliance wanted to talk to him? David's breath caught. There were two layers of management between him and the CEO. To have a personal call from him? It was a terrifying honor.

David sat at his desk and took a steadied his breathing. He wiped damp palms on his slacks and picked up the phone. "Good morning, Master Quaid. What can I do for you?"

"What is the status of your project?"

Moisture beaded on his upper lip. "It's going well, sir. We are collecting the last few subjects and we'll be ready to start phase two next month."

"What of the outlier, the successful subject?"

"We're working on collecting him."

"Send me your updated timeline."

"Yes, sir."

Relief filled David until Master Quaid warned, "Don't screw this up or it'll be your last mistake."

"Understood, sir. Everything is under control."

"It had better be. Master Anderson is ahead of schedule and making great strides. I'd hate to be wrong about funding this project a second time."

Master Quaid ended the call.

David put down the phone and placed his palms flat on the desktop, spreading out his shaking fingers. He took a deep breath, then another. He could do this. All he needed was one man. Once Williams was in the lab, David would personally extract all the information required to begin the next stage of the experiment.

Thanks to those meddling Elite, all records from the previous experiment had been destroyed. The only data that survived was from the beginning of the experiments, and those had been his personal notes kept in his home system.

It had taken two long, pain-staking years to recreate the necessary spell work. One piece of information remained outstanding. How to grant control of the test subject to a specified person.

How many times had he wished that idiot tech had written the information down? Too many to count. The Board insisted the control key be put into place before funding had been granted. The last thing the Board wanted was a shifter army not under their complete control.

If he didn't get that information, his funding would be reassigned to Mage Anderson, and his life would be forfeit. The Alliance didn't suffer expensive failures. That he'd been given a second chance after the Elite had stopped the original experiment was a miracle.

Master Mason Anderson was the head of the gryphon research project. He and Anderson had been rivals since college, intent on one upping each other with various projects over the years. David couldn't allow him to win, not this time.

David pushed back from the desk and walked to the credenza. Lifting the carafe, he poured water into the glass, but his shaking hands spilled most of it. After another deep breath he calmed enough to gulp down the water.

How the hell was he going to get Williams into the lab? He'd attempted retrieval before and failed. Williams had to be captured, but how?

Perhaps the answer would come to him as he worked on the numerous reports needed by the Board.

He pushed the intercom button.

"Yes, sir. What do you want?" Grayson was quick to answer.

"What is the acquisition status of the test subjects?"

"The project is short twenty participants."

"How many of the ones in holding are compatible?"

"They're all compatible. I took the liberty of issuing test kits to the acquisition team. The memories of those found incompatible are erased and the subjects are released back onto the streets."

David hand spasmed into a fist as anger surged through him. While it was a great idea and something he should have thought of, Grayson once again exceeded his authority. David wanted to make an example of the man, but Grayson had been hand-picked by the Board. His assistant was spying on him and reporting his every move back to his superiors. He'd come back from lunch early and noticed a report on Grayson's desk, detailing a supposed confidential conversation. His assistant had either phone or office bugged.

"Thank you," He acknowledged through clenched teeth. "How long before the last twenty subjects are acquired?"

"I'll have the team ramp up their efforts and the quota should be filled by the end of next week."

"Let me know as soon as the last subject is picked up."

"Yes, sir."

David released the intercom button and sat back in his chair. His assistant was spying on him, his rival was gaining ground in the gryphon experiments, and his pet project was at a standstill.

The intercom buzzed again. "Your nephew is here."

What was Harold up to now? The boy had spent the last few years looking for funding for one crazy scheme after another. If Harold hadn't been his last living relation, David would have had him barred from the office. He'd denied all his nephew's ideas as infeasible, impractical, and downright improbable.

David sighed. "Send him in."

He sat forward, hands clasped, elbows and forearms resting on the blotter, and watched his nephew enter the room. Harold walked into the room with an excited spring in his step, and enthusiasm on his round face. He hadn't taken the time to make himself presentable. His stained robe was ripped in places and his hair hadn't seen a comb or brush in days.

Harold clutched a wooden box in one hand and a file folder in the other.

"Hello Uncle David. Thanks for taking the time to see me. You're not going to believe what I've discovered!"

David waved to the chair. "Another one of your schemes?"

Harold sat, placing the file folder on the desk and the box on his lap. "Not this time, Uncle. It really works!"

David reached over and opened the file, scanning the notes and documentation. Biochemical formulas were followed by complicated spell work. Had they managed to isolate the chemical reaction that triggered a shifter change? Upon further reading, this formula locked the shifter into his animal form. Would Harold's formula work? He stared at his nephew. "You're sure?"

The young man almost bounced in his chair with excitement. "Yes, I've tested it and the antidote."

"I'd like to see it in person." David pushed the intercom button. "Grayson, do we have any shifters in the building? I need one for a small experiment."

"I believe there are two on the tenth floor. I'll summon them."

"Thank you, Grayson."

David turned back to his nephew. "If this works, it would change the way we deal with shifters."

Harold squirmed. "Yes and no."

David frowned. "What do you mean?"

"I've run into a bit of a production problem."

"How so?"

"When we make a large batch, it becomes unstable. It has to be made in small batches and the shelf life is about a week before it becomes inert." Harold rushed to reassure David. "Don't worry, we're working on how to overcome the shelf-life issue."

"And the instability?"

"I'm not sure we can compensate for that. If you look at the formula on page three, you'll see why."

David flipped to the correct page. They were forcing a chemical bond, but in large enough numbers the bonds would slip and re-bond with other molecules in the solution, thus making it inert.

There was a knock on his door and two shifters entered, followed by his assistant.

"Thank you, Grayson. I don't need you for this."

A flash of annoyance crossed the man's face before he resumed his calm mask. He nodded once and left the room, closing the door behind him.

David looked at the two shifters, both wolves from their auras. "I need one of you for a quick experiment."

The taller one stepped forward. "I'll be your test subject. But first, is it fatal?"

David glanced to Harold, who shook his head and said, "No, it will be uncomfortable for a few moments, nothing more."

The shifter nodded.

Harold took a syringe from the box and approached the man. Looking to his partner, Harold asked, "Please hold him after he shifts."

The other shifter agreed.

Harold injected the serum, and within a few moments, a swirling black hole enveloped the shifter. With a flash of bright light, a wolf stood in his place. The second shifter grabbed the wolf around the neck with one arm and clamped his free hand over its muzzle. The wolf snarled, an enraged growl that filled the office.

He tried to lunge at Harold, but the second shifter held him with one arm locked around his neck and one around his torso. Harold took two hasty steps to the back of the desk. "Let me administer the antidote."

"Hurry, he's pissed." The shifter fought to hold the squirming wolf in place.

Harold skirted the desk and approached the wolf from the back. He quickly administered the antidote and within seconds the man turned from wolf to human.

The tension in the office dissipated.

David raised an eyebrow. Harold's serum worked.

The clothed shifter helped his naked friend up from the floor. "What was it like?" the shorter shifter asked.

"Hell. I never want to go through that again. I couldn't shift. My wolf was out of control."

"Thank you, gentlemen. You may go now," David said. He waited for the two to leave the office before David held out his hand. "Congratulations, Harold. It worked."

Harold beamed with happiness and grasped David's hand in both of his own, shaking vigorously. "Thanks, Uncle."

David needed to get Williams into the lab, and what better way to do so, than as his animal? Williams as a man, had proved difficult to capture, but as a rabbit? It'd be

"How long does the serum last?" he asked.

"We're not sure. So far, we've had to administer the antidote because the shifters wouldn't calm down. Since they're volunteers, once they've had a dose, they don't volunteer again. It's getting hard to find any willing test subjects."

A plan formed in David's brain. A perfect way to get Williams into the lab and use him to further scientific discovery. "I have a subject for you, and don't worry about causing him irreparable damage. The bastard deserves it."

Harold grinned. "Excellent. When can we have him?"

"I'll want enough formula to fill this ring." David handed him a box. "I need him for a few days and he's all yours."

"I'll get you a dose this afternoon."

Harold left the office and Grayson entered. "What was that all about?" his assistant asked.

"Nothing. Just another side project Harold is working on."

"It wouldn't have anything to do with your project would it?"

"No." David waved his assistant away. "Dismissed."

He could see the temper in the other man's face and didn't care. After a long moment Grayson bowed his head and retreated to the outer office. Probably to go and tattle.

David reclined in his chair fingers steepled. Now to figure out who would administer the drug to Williams. There was one possibility—the mole. The man owed him a favor. He pulled out a burner phone from his desk. He didn't want Grayson know about this.

David sent a quick text. *Calling in my favor.*

The response came a few moments later. *What do you need?*

He texted back. *Williams brought in.*

How?

I have it all worked out. Meet at Angelini's at two.

Confirmed.

Chapter 2

Jared Williams sat in his office in the Elite Magical Protection Force headquarters, in San Francisco, contemplating the piles of files littering his desk.

Paperwork sucked.

What would happen if he ran screaming into the hills to escape the endless flood of files and forms? Someone else would step in, someone who might not fight for the forgotten—the paranormal outcasts. Those who didn't fit in either world, Real or Shadow.

With people like him in mind, he huffed out a breath and grabbed the nearest file, determined to conquer Mount Paper.

His phone beeped and he checked the text. It was from one of his contacts. *Experiment starting again.*

A shiver of dread filled him. His body flushed hot and then cold. His inner animal fought to run, hide, anything to get away from the news. That wasn't an option.

Details? he texted back.

Homeless off the streets, new cannon fodder.

Shit, shit, shit. Those fuckers weren't going to get away with this, not if he could help it.

Previous location in Marin? Jared asked.

No. Lab abandoned. Believe new lab in SF. Will try to locate.

Keep me posted.

Will do.

The lure of a controllable shifter army was too enticing for the Alliance to resist. In the past two years, he'd made it his mission to learn everything he could about the experiments from the confiscated records. They'd been destroyed after he'd finished with them, by order of Captain Jor'dan DúSan.

Jared pulled up the encrypted software on his phone. He'd been planning for such an occasion, creating a sleeper virus that once uploaded into the Alliance system, would corrupt all data pertaining to any genetic modification program. The last remaining detail was how to introduce the program into their system. Physical copies would be as easy to destroy as setting a fire.

The Elite code forbade personal vendettas regardless of the reason. Most of the time, it kept the Elite from fighting among themselves. But for this? He was going to make sure the Alliance didn't succeed. There'd be no more experimental half breeds, not if he could help it.

Jared closed the files on his phone and tried to concentrate on the file in front of him. But his brain refused to let it go. He closed the paper file and sat back.

He had plenty of vacation time saved up. He'd use the time off to take care of the matter, and if he was fired over it? That was a price he was willing to pay.

The office phone buzzed. "Yes?"

"My office, now," Captain Jor'dan ordered.

"On my way." Jared replaced the file on the top of the stack and sighed. A temporary reprieve from Mount Paper.

Jared walked into the Captain's office to see his partner, Randall Jennings, waiting for him. His partner was dressed in all black, but unlike his own jeans and T-shirt, the mage wore designer clothes. The Elite dress code specified one could wear anything as long as it was all black and the emblem of the Elite was clearly visible. Each of officer preferred a certain style of dress and this allowed freedom of choice.

Captain Jor'dan spoke. "Head down to Fisherman's Wharf in Real."

Jared frowned. Why hadn't Captain Jor'dan told him that over the phone? Why the personal meet?

"What's going on?" Randall asked.

"Two shifter groups are causing problems."

"We'll check it out." Randall responded. He opened the door and glanced back at Jared. "Coming?"

"I'll meet you there."

"See you in a few."

Once the door closed, Captain Jor'dan shook his head. "You and your paranoia."

"It's justified," Jared replied. The captain referred to his preference for driving by himself in his specially modified vehicle. Less chance of an ambush that way. He'd been targeted more than once for being an abomination. Jared didn't know if being an Elite made the situation better or worse.

Captain Jor'dan sighed. "Unfortunately, yes. What do you need?"

"I'd like time off."

Captain Jor'dan was silent, a frown crossing his face. "You? Take vacation?"

Jared tried not to squirm at the intense look. "Yeah."

The captain shrugged. "You have the time saved up. Going to relax somewhere?"

Jared shook his head. "No. I'm pursuing an independent investigation."

"What's going on?"

"There are rumors the Alliance is experimenting again."

"Why do you need time off for that?"

Jared met the Captain's eye. "I'm going to stop them, no matter what it takes."

Captain Jor'dan ran a hand through his hair. "Damn it, you know that's against the rules."

"I know."

"You're determined to do this?"

"Yes. No one will experience the horror I did, not if I can help it."

"Can I convince you to do this officially?"

Jared shook his head. "The Alliance mole on staff will let them know what's going on."

"You're a good agent, I'd hate to lose you." The captain sighed, and came to a decision. "Do it on the clock and tell no one. I want daily updates. After you clear up the shifter mess, you're off active rotation for the next week."

"Thank you," Jared replied in relief. He'd never expected the Captain to allow the investigation, let alone support it.

"Going dark will keep the mole off your back."

Jared stopped. "Do you know who it is?"

"I have a good idea. I'm building the case and I want to make sure there are no loopholes for him to sneak through."

"Did you ever think I was the mole?" Jared asked, curious.

"Never."

"Why? I'm the newest Elite, and I wasn't raised in Shadow."

"The last thing you would do is sell out others to the organization who made you."

That was true.

Jared was dismissed and left the office. Stopping by his desk, he grabbed his black bomber jacket with the Elite patch. Jared headed to the garage and got into his modified SUV. Paranoid he might be, but he hated letting anyone into his havens. Both SUV and apartment were modified with the latest magical and technological security.

His SUV moved at a slow crawl and it took longer than anticipated to find a place to park.

He met Randall at the corner.

"What took you so long?" Randall asked.

"Traffic."

"Should have gone into Shadow. Streets were clear."

Jared shrugged. "I didn't think about it." Even after two years of learning Shadow, he often forgot about utilizing the alternate reality.

They walked around the corner and stopped. Two groups of shifter teens were fighting in the middle of the street, drawing human attention.

The two groups were known rivals—Tigers and Wolves. Growls and howls filled the air.

Jared sent a quick text to the tech gurus at Elite HQ to scrub any videos that may have been uploaded. They pushed through the human crowd and Jared heard Randall mutter under his breath. A wave of magic pulsed in an expanding circle. Jared's animal lurched at the use of magic. He soothed the rabbit and it calmed, but remained watchful.

The humans cleared the area. Randall must have used a revulsion charm, and shifters weren't affected by spells.

The shifters turned toward them, growling. "Fresh blood."

His inner rabbit sniffed. How dare these kits pull this attitude? They needed to respect authority, regardless of who that authority was. The rabbit was on board with teaching them a lesson.

The energy of the fight changed. No longer focused on each other, both groups faced the new threat, the Elite.

Randall stood next to Jared and braced for an attack.

The leaders of the shifter packs glanced at each other and smirked.

"Look who we have here. Elite swine. A puny mage and a freak. Think they can handle us?"

Members of both groups laughed.

The Tiger leader sneered. "Nah, they wouldn't belittle our abilities like that."

"Then I'm wondering why they're here, sticking their noses into our business," The Wolf leader retorted.

Out of the corner of his eye, Jared saw Randall shake his head.

"Where do these punks learn manners?" Randall asked.

"It's clear they didn't." Jared addressed his next comment to the shifters. "You're in violation of Shadow Law. Cease and desist or face punishment."

The Tigers and Wolves looked around, uncertainty in their expressions. "What do you mean? Which law?"

"You're using your shifter abilities in Real Earth in full view of the humans." Jared replied, his voice filled with soft menace.

The leaders of the rival shifters exchanged a glance, but their followers weren't as difficult to read. A few licked their lips and twitched their fingers. From their body cues, they knew they were in trouble.

The Wolf leader spoke with hands raised and palms out. "Hey man, we didn't realize we're in Real."

"You didn't know where you were?" Randall scoffed. "I don't believe it." He leaned forward. "Here's what I think went down. You're itching to fight but your packs won't let you. What better way to go behind their backs than to take it into Real?"

Jared stared at Randall. What the hell? The situation had been controllable up to that point.

"What the fuck are you doing?" Jared whispered. "You're making it worse."

"Someone needs to teach these cocky assholes a lesson." Randall's voice was filled with condescension.

Anger vibrated in the air as the insult registered. Shifters crouched, hands out, ready to fight.

"Just try," The Wolf leader growled, before lunging at Randall.

Jared placed his hand in his pocket and pressed a two-digit code for back-up on his cell and joined the melee.

Fists and kicks connected with flesh. Shifters dropped to the ground and it was clear that none of them knew how to use their speed and strength against an experienced opponent.

It didn't take long to subdue the teens. Jared and Randall restrained them using specialized cuffs made to negate shifter strength. A short time later a van with darkened windows pulled up. Three Elite exited the van. Mage Merrick grinned at the pile of groaning teens. "Nice job. No permanent damage."

The Elite threw the kids into the back of the van, heedless of their complaints.

Randall shared his version of events, and celebratory back slaps were given to both Jared and his partner.

Jared gasped as a sharp stinging pain radiated from one of the slaps on his shoulder. He examined their faces, but didn't know which one of his coworkers had done it.

Merrick dusted his hands together. "Tidy. New orders from the boss. Shifter Jared and Mage Randall, report back to the office. Shifters Glen and Nigel check out Golden Gate Park for suspicious activity."

Merrick got into the van and headed back to Elite HQ, where the teens would be placed in holding cells beneath the office until their respective Alphas could bail them out.

The others popped into Shadow, leaving Jared and Randall alone.

"Well, that went well," Randall boasted.

Jared turned to him. "What the hell were you doing, trying to pick a fight with them?"

Randall raised an eyebrow. "It got the job done."

Jared's vision wavered, like he was looking at an underwater world. The rabbit began to panic, flooding his system with adrenaline. *Run, hide, find a safe place!* He tried to obey, but his limbs refused to work. "Whas goin' on?"

Cotton dryness filled his mouth as words slurred and his tongue felt ten sizes too big. Dizziness made the world tilt. His body contorted, pain filling him until each nerve screamed in agony.

Randall reach for him. "Are you okay, Jared? You don't look good. Hold on, I'm calling for help." The words moved like maple syrup, slow and oozy until the world went away.

§

Chuck got out of the car, motioning for Benny to grab the item from the back seat.

"Why'd it have to be pink?" Benny complained.

Chuck fought not to roll his eyes. "Because that was the last one they had, dumbass. Like he's gonna know the difference anyway."

"I guess." Benny carried the pink pet carrier to where their contact was waiting.

Chuck nodded at the guy who was careful to keep his face averted. Chuck picked up a small unconscious bunny and loaded him into the crate. After making sure the door was secured, he addressed the guy. "We'll take him from here."

"Don't fuck up," the guy warned.

Chuck shuddered. "No, sir." He motioned for Benny to follow him back to the car.

"Put the carrier in the back," Chuck instructed, and for once Benny did what he asked without his usual complaints.

Once they'd driven three blocks, Benny spoke up. "He was a scary ass motherfucker, don't you think?"

"Yeah. Not one to cross. Call Dr. G and let him know we're on our way."

"Right." Benny pulled out his phone and placed the call. "Hey Doc, we'll be there soon."

They drove for a few blocks before the car sputtered and died. There was enough momentum to get them to the curb and out of traffic. "What the hell?" Chuck checked the gauges. Fuck, they were out of gas. Furious he turned to Benny. "Why didn't you get gas?"

Benny gave him a sheepish expression. "I forgot."

"You idiot! How the hell are we going to get him to the lab?"

"The bus?"

Taking a deep breath Chuck gritted his teeth and counted to ten. Needing another ten, he released the steering wheel. "Alright we'll take the bus. You carry him." He got out and slammed the door, glaring at Benny over the roof of the car. "You get to explain to the Doc why we're late."

Color drained from Benny's face. Perhaps this would be the scare Benny needed to use his brain. Somehow Chuck doubted it. There was a reason Benny was the muscle.

While Benny placed the call and grabbed the carrier, Chuck surveyed the area. Damn Benny. He'd run out of gas at the Civic Center. Too many official types around for them to escape notice. And oh shit, four Elite were approaching. If Elite saw them, they'd be locked up in half a heartbeat. Not only for their role in today's caper, but for a handful of outstanding warrants with the human cops.

Shit. Shit. Shit.

They needed to hide and fast.

Chuck looked over at City Hall. Too much security. Same with the Courthouse. There wasn't a performance at the Civic Auditorium so that was out as well. That left the library, where plenty of humans going in and out of the building would provide cover.

"Benny, come on."

"Why?" Benny finished the call and gave Chuck a confused look.

"Elite."

"Fuck."

They dashed across the street with the carrier, dodging traffic.

"Act casual," Chuck ordered in a whisper.

Benny gasped for breath. "What's that supposed to mean?"

"Never mind. Come on." Chuck led the way through the double doors into the building.

"You know this is insane right?" Benny whispered.

"Why?"

"Are you nuts? We're in the wrong part of town to be pulling this shit."

"We have no choice, thanks to your ineptitude." Chuck said. Another paranormal approached them. Fuck, now what? A second later he recognized the uniform of the mage.

It was the Guardian of the Library. Each major human library housed a magical book depository in Shadow. Access to the magical libraries was severely limited and an enterprising group of paranormals had entered the human library and popped into Shadow, bypassing paranormal security. They stole a rare and dangerous book, which pissed the mages off. From then on, all human libraries with a Shadow counterpart, had a high-level mage acting as a guardian in Real to make sure the incident was never repeated.

"Go hide him, quick!" Chuck hissed. "I'll stall the guardian."

Benny hurried over to the elevators and in their first piece of luck of the day, the door was open. His partner got in and ducked out of sight.

Chuck turned to the guardian.

"And what are you doing here in Real?" the Guardian asked.

While being mage would give him a bit of leeway, it didn't count for much. He thought fast. "I'm avoiding the Elite patrol out front."

"Bah, those idiots."

Chuck nodded his agreement.

"Are you involved in anything nefarious within these walls?"

Chuck felt the subtle magic of a truth spell. "No," he answered. For once, not having to lie.

"Very well, you may stay until those swine Elite have passed and then you must leave. My leniency goes only so far."

Chuck bowed. "Yes, sir. I'll be gone as soon as they are."

"Good."

The Guardian moved away and Chuck released a sigh of relief. That was close.

The elevator dinged and Benny walked back to his side, hands empty.

"Where'd you put him?" Chuck asked.

"In one of the rooms on the top floor. No one will look there."

The Guardian glared at them and Chuck grabbed Benny's arm. "Let's go. We'll come back later to retrieve him."

Outside the glass doors the Elite paused to chat. Fuck. Chuck grabbed Benny's arm and pulled him into the alcove between the double doors. "Shadow." Chuck ordered.

They popped into Shadow and left the library, avoiding all Elite entanglements.

"Hey Chuck?" Benny asked.

"Yeah?"

"Why didn't we hide the little dude in Shadow?"

Chuck sighed. "Two reasons." He pointed to the groups of Shadow citizens walking around the Civic Center grounds. "First, we'd have never escaped detection by them. Second, how do we know the guy can Shadow?"

A frown crossed Benny's face. "What do you mean? He's a shifter, of course he can Shadow."

Chuck tilted his head in exasperation. "He's a created shifter. That means he might not be able to get into Shadow since he started out human."

"Huh."

Chuck held up a hand, forestalling the next question. "I'm not sure if the doc even knows if he can Shadow."

"Okay."

Chuck led Benny around the building. While it appeared to be an impenetrable fortress from the outside, he'd spotted a few ways they could get in. He'd glanced at the library hours. They'd come back after the library closed, avoiding the guardian and unnecessary explanations.

Chapter 3

What the hell happened?

Jared woke with pain ping-ponging inside his skull, in time to the beating of his heart.

Couldn't have gotten drunk. He avoided booze, not willing to give up control. A small rebellion against his alcoholic family.

How long have I been out?

Damn, he'd never passed out like this before. The military conditioned him to be on guard at all times, a lesson further reinforced by his animal. Jared never slept deeply unless his environment was secure and even then, he kept an ear open for noises and threats.

Think.

What happened?

Yesterday he... Pain stabbed behind his eyes, sharp and intense. What day was it?

Breathe through it.

Fuck... the memories were...blurred, hazy. A bunch of kids fighting in Real Earth, then what happened?

Damn. He had no idea.

Lifting his head, the throbbing intensified.

Don't move. Got it.

Jared lowered his head, expecting the softness of his pillow. He jolted when he hit a hard surface. Hard surface? He lay on his side on... what?

Where was his pillow? Where the hell was his bed? Where the fuck was he?

Don't panic. Assess the situation and go from there.

Jared opened his eyes, his vision blurred. An image in shadows on the far wall. Boxes of light in a square pattern.

It took a few moments for his synapses to snap on-line. Those were bars...

Bars?

He was back in the fucking lab.

No. Oh fuck, no.

Panic, that monstrous beast, grabbed at his mind and swirled through his blood, potent and frightening.

He's going to kill me this time.

The director, David Glendale, had promised a torturous death for his role in destroying the original study.

Had the mole in the Elite delivered Jared to the Alliance experimental lab?

Which begged the question, why hadn't the mole warned the Alliance of the raid two years ago? Multiple answers flitted through his mind. Perhaps the mole had been out of town? Or perhaps he'd not known about the raid until too late? It didn't matter at this point. The most important thing he had to do now was figure out how the hell to get out of here. He'd escape or die trying.

Death no longer scared him. Not anymore. Not after the shit that had been done to him and the others in the name of science. Science ha! It had been a horrific experiment that spliced human and animal genes, forcing people to become animals.

Fuck. Fuck. Fuck.

Dizziness assailed him, and his breathing became choppy, pulling him out of his thoughts and back into the physical reality.

Calm down.

If he didn't, he'd end up dead, like so many of the other test subjects. Did it matter? The thought made him stop.

What if he didn't survive? Would anyone care?

The answer was no. No one would give a damn, with the exception of Captain Jor'dan. Dying sounded attractive. No more pain, no more condescension from most paranormals, no more working for people to be grudgingly paid for his work.

But the bastards were experimenting again. And he couldn't let them torture anyone else. He had to stop them, he had to make sure others didn't suffer his fate. To do that, he needed to be on the other side of these damned bars.

First, regain control. Of his breathing, of his heart rate. Control was key. It was that simple, that complicated. A switch turned on in his brain and he began the calming exercises the techs had taught him when he'd been in the lab the first time. Command the animal before it commands you.

Breathe in... Re. Breathe out... Venge.

Repeat. Re-venge.

What a beautiful word. Revenge. Using his favorite imagery, Dr. Glendale as a piñata, helped him relax.

His heart rate slowed, the pounding in his head receded and his breathing returned to normal. Now for the next battle. Tension infused every muscle while he waited for the animal to take possession of their body.

Nothing. No urge to flee. No instinct to hide. *What the hell?*

Puzzled, he searched the corner of his mind where the animal resided and found it devoid of its spirit.

Jared stifled the quick surge of hope.

It was a trick. It had to be. Doctor Bar'ella had confirmed that what had been done to him and the others was irreversible. He was stuck being a shifter for the rest of his life.

But what happened to the animal?

Jared took a deep breath. Something wasn't right.

The overriding aroma that filled his nose wasn't that of the lab; antiseptic and sterile. Instead it smelled dry and musty, like old books. What the hell were books doing in the lab? Wait... maybe he wasn't in the lab after all.

Colors became clear. The far wall resembled plastic. Pink?

Reaching out, he froze. The hand he extended wasn't a hand—it was a paw.

Fuck.

He was the animal.

The sound of approaching footsteps froze him in place.

§

"Attention. The library is now closed." Lara Adams didn't pay any attention to the rest of the announcement. She inhaled the soothing scent of books. Finally, they were closed. It had been a hellish day from the moment she'd gotten to work.

Most days, she enjoyed helping the public at the reference desk. The things people came in to the library to research, fascinated her. But something about today made the patrons short tempered and extra pushy. The belligerent college students who demanded she do their research for them, had taken every drop of patience she possessed. She was more than ready to put the day behind her.

There was one last thing to do before she could head home to a hot bath and book. The nightly walk through. Each member of the library staff was assigned a different area to check, making sure no patrons remained.

Tonight, Lara had the study rooms on the 5th floor.

Following the others up the stairs, Lara grinned. All she had to do was go up and down the stairs a few times to get a workout without having to pay the outrageous gym membership fees.

Arriving on the correct floor, she checked the stacks, reading nooks, and study crannies. No one loitered. She checked the study rooms, her mind wandering.

On the table was an old parchment with symbols drawn all over it. Stepping into the room to take a closer look, the slamming of the door whirled her around, gasping in surprise. A handsome man in a brown leather jacket and fedora stood near the door. He reached for her hand

and pulled her into his arms before placing a steamy heated kiss to her lips.

"I need you." His rough voice filled her with delight as the whiskers on his jaw rubbed over her cheek. She sighed in pleasure and...

Considered the empty study room. Darn it. She had to stop day-dreaming at work. She got caught up in her dreams and didn't notice time passing. Lara had to catch the last bus otherwise she'd have to walk home, yet again.

She moved onto the next room. A reference book was left on the table. A history of the founding families of California. The book triggered bitter memories. Preston searched for his family history. They had poured over the pages, finding an interesting mix of wealthy landowners and highway bandits. Preston Garrett the Third. A pretentious name for an egotistical criminal defense attorney. Too bad it had taken so long to discover his true colors.

Preston had been sweet at first. Wining and dining her, interested in her day and friends. They'd been dating for a while before the first time he turned into an Edward Hyde. He'd gotten mad and demanded she alter her wardrobe and eating habits. Thank heavens, Lydia had pointed out what he was doing. It had forced Lara to wake up and leave him. With her family gone, she was emotionally vulnerable and he'd taken full advantage.

No. Stop it. Stop thinking about him. It was a trap, wondering how he was doing, if he wanted her back.

I wasn't good enough for him before. Nothing had changed. Closing her eyes, she repeated her mantra. *I'm a caring and wonderful person. I'm not going to modify who I am to please a man.*

Repeating the mantra over and over helped her to focus on the now, rather than the past. Preston was firmly in the past, where he belonged.

One room to go and she'd be finished. Opening the door, she flipped on the light. The room was clear. Lara began pulling the door closed when she heard a scratching sound.

What was that?

Hopefully, it wasn't mice. That was all the financially strapped library needed, a pest problem.

Lara stepped into the room, moved the chair and peered under the desk.

"What the heck?"

A pink pet carrier sat in the far back corner.

An occupied carrier, from the slight movement of the shadows within.

"Hello?" Lara kept her voice soft to keep from startling whatever it was.

She reached under the desk, grabbed the carrier, and lifted it onto the desk to get a better look.

"How in the world did anyone manage to smuggle you into the library? I can see it now." Her tone dreamy. "A man in dark glasses, a dark fedora pulled low, and a long gray trench coat, walks into the library. He blends in with a group of people, the carrier smuggled under his coat, looking pregnant."

Lara laughed at the image, turning her attention to the carrier.

The animal had brown fur with a small head and long ears that twitched with every sound and movement she made.

"Hey, little bunny, how'd you get here?"

As if it could tell her.

A throat cleared behind her. Lara jumped around to face the door, hand going to her heart. "Doreen! Carp! Don't sneak up like that!"

"You and your fishy curse words." A grin stretched the older woman's face. "Sneaking up on you is the only fun I'm have. Why haven't you finished your walk through?"

Lara stepped aside and pointed to the pink carrier.

"What's that?" Doreen asked.

"It's a pink pet carrier with a bunny inside." Lara tried to stop the sarcasm, but didn't think she succeeded. She did manage to stop her eyes from rolling, though it took effort.

"Where did it come from?"

Lara lifted one shoulder. "How should I know?"

The frown on Doreen's face turned into a glare with the narrowing of her eyes. "We are *not* an animal shelter."

Lara looked at carrier. "What should we do with it?"

"It can't stay here."

"Of course not." Lara's tone placated, trying not to incite her boss's temper. All the signs were there—the narrowed gaze, the pursed lips, the fists on the hips. Doreen was close to losing it.

"Well?" Doreen demanded.

"What do you want me to do about it?"

"Take it to the animal shelter."

"What if it's someone's pet?"

"Then they shouldn't have left it in my library."

"I'll take it home. That way if anyone comes looking, it'll be safe with me. It'll keep me company on my days off."

Lara peered through the bars. The bunny hopped forward as if interested in what was going on. "Do you want to come home with me?"

Brown eyes met hers. The rabbit nodded once, slow and deliberate.

"Overactive imagination again," she muttered. There was no way the bunny had understood her question.

Doreen glanced back at her, one eyebrow raised. "What did you say?"

Lara tried to smile. "Nothing. Just talking to myself."

Doreen grinned. "Hop to it, we need to lock up."

Lara groaned at the bad pun. "Please tell me you're not going to start with the bad bunny jokes."

"Why not?" Doreen led the way down to the break room. "I've got a hare trigger."

Lara picked up the carrier and followed her boss, shaking her head and trying not to laugh at the terrible puns. Lara didn't want to upset her boss further by laughing. The puns she was making were so bad, that she caught Doreen laughing at them. Whew. Doreen was over her bad mood. The woman's temperament was erratic at best. One moment cheerful and laughing, the next ready to chew someone's head off. Lara had yet to figure out why.

Once in the break room, it took a few moments to gather her things. Coat, scarf, purse, carrier.

"Let me walk you out. It's pretty foggy out there," Doreen said.

"Sure." The others had left, and they were the last two in the building.

Doreen's cell phone rang as they were about to leave. "Janelle forgot her keys. She's at the front door. I'll be back in a few minutes."

Lara shook her head. "Don't worry about it. The bus stop is around the corner, and it'll be here soon. I'll be fine."

"Call me when you get on the bus, so I know you're safe."

"Okay."

"Fur Pete's sake, you'd better hop along. You don't want to miss the bus." Doreen grinned as she left the break room.

Lara shook her head and left the building, letting the heavy door close behind her. She waited for the electronic click as the lock engaged.

Turning toward the street, she walked at a brisk pace, heading for the bus stop. Within a few steps, the ubiquitous San Francisco fog thickened. Visibility dwindled until she could no longer see the street lights ahead of her, only a faint glow.

A malevolent gaze pierced the fog to track her movements.

Goosebumps pebbled her skin. "It's my imagination. Fog makes everything creepier," she said, reassuring the bunny as well as herself.

It felt like someone was watching her. Any minute now, the bad guys were going to emerge from the fog. Where was a hero when you needed one? She should sign up for those self-defense classes. That way she wouldn't need a spandex-wearing good guy to come to her rescue.

"Don't worry, little bunny. I won't let the bad guys get you."

The muffled crunch of approaching footsteps sounded deliberate, gauged to elicit the maximum amount of terror.

She whirled around and a dark figure emerged from the swirling fog, hat pulled low, a gun in one hand, pointed straight at her.

"Give me the carrier."

Chapter 4

"This isn't real, is it?" Lara whispered. "Please tell me I'm imagining things."

The guy stepped forward. His squinty eyes were close together and he reminded her of a Hollywood typecast mobster—heavy set, no neck, went by the name of Guido or Tony. Was there a Mafia presence in San Francisco?

It took a couple of seconds for his request to register. He didn't want her purse? What kind of hold-up was this?

She shook her head. "I'm sorry, could you repeat that? I thought you said you wanted the carrier?"

The gun never wavered. "That's what I said. Give me the carrier."

Lara retreated, hand clutching the handle of the carrier in a tight grip. "Why? What are you going to do with it?"

What would the mob want with an innocent little bunny? Drugs? Was this bunny a lab experiment to test out a new street drug?

"None of your business. Now hand him over."

She shuffled back to put more distance between her and the gun. If she got far enough away, the heavier-than-normal fog should conceal her. Where was the closest place to hide? The library was behind her. What was ahead? The topography of the immediate area dribbled from her mind. Carp. *Come on, think!* Gnarled trees and a few benches in the park. Unfortunately, he stood between her and safety.

"Don't worry, I won't let him have you," she whispered.

Guido advanced a step, matching Lara's movement backward.

"Hand him over. This is your last warning."

Lara opened her mouth to stall him somehow. She needed to create enough distance so he'd lose her in the fog.

A black figure dropped from the sky and landed on Guido. She heard a metallic clank that sounded like the gun hitting the pavement. Thoughts of it accidentally firing made her drop to her knees and hunched protectively over the carrier. Any moment now, she expected to feel the burning sting of the bullet as it pierced her flesh.

She flinched at the sound of a loud bang. Did Guido have a second gun? Another bang, but this time it was accompanied by the sound of squealing tires. She sagged in relief. A car backfired.

Through the bars of the cage, she saw the bunny tilt his head as if in inquiry.

"Stray bullets."

The bunny nodded. Wait, it understood her? She was losing it. It was reacting to her tone of voice, nothing more.

The black thing stood over Guido as he stumbled to his feet. Did the figure in black have a cape and mask? Was there a sidekick nearby, waiting to lend a hand? Didn't most superheroes have them?

Fog churned as the two began to fight an eerie battle. Punches and kicks were exchanged in silence, at a speed too fast for her to follow. The swirling movement of the fog revealed then concealed the fight. The action was unreal. Did people fight that quietly? Where were the moans and groans? It was like watching a fight movie on mute.

Lara looked at the bunny. "Time to get the heck out of Dodge."

Once again it nodded.

She got to her feet, keeping an eye on the raging battle. On silent feet, Lara tip-toed toward the street and safety.

The fog thickened like primordial soup, murky and hazy, obscuring everything in her path. She put her hand out in front of her. What the heck was going on with the weather? The fog was never this thick. She whirled to face the threat. Her eyes strained, peering through the heavy mist, but she couldn't see a darned thing.

She imagined Guido's hands coming out the swirling grey to grab her. *Nope, don't think about it. Time to leave. Wait, which way to the street?* Her sense of direction wasn't the best. Throw in the fog and she was disoriented.

Holding her free hand in front of her, she took a few careful steps toward where she thought the street should be. The palm of her hand smacked into the concrete of the building. Stinging pain radiated through her fingers, and she bit her lip to muffle gasp of pain. Shaking her hand to dull the sensation, she trailed her fingertips along the wall and crept toward the street.

She glanced back at an agonized moan. A break in the fog allowed her to see Guido lying on the ground curled up. The black figure stood over him with hands on hips.

Lara took another step, kicked a rock and sent it tumbling over the pavement.

The figure glanced toward her and approached.

"Carp. We're busted," she whispered.

The dark figure—a female, based on the form fitting body suit, halted. She was dressed in black with a full mask over her face, concealing her identity. Lara tucked the carrier behind her.

"The word you're looking for is crap, not carp," the woman said.

"I say carp because I don't curse. What do you want?"

"Just lending a helping hand." The figure gripped the bottom of the mask and pulled upward, revealing a familiar face.

"Cyn! What are you doing here?" Relief filled Lara at the sight of her friend. They'd met many years ago, when Cyn had come into the library researching ways to play a practical joke on a friend who loved ancient torture devices.

"I had a bad feeling, so I thought I'd come and check on you. I'm glad I did."

"Me, too," Lara said, feeling giddy. "For a moment I thought you were a comic book hero come to save me. Leaping from the top of building in a single bound."

"Really? Cool." Cyn struck a pose. Her hip cocked, and her hand curved into the shape of a claw, swiping the air. "Purrrrfect."

Lara fought back a laugh. "Heroine, not villainess."

"I know, but heroes are goody- two -shoes. It's the villains that have all the fun. They party, have minions and get to play with all the interesting toys."

"True, but they also get caught."

"Hmm, I'll have to work on that." Cyn checked out the surrounding area.

"Where did you learn to fight like that?" Lara asked.

"It's just one of those things a girl picks up here and there."

"At super villain school?"

A look of interest crossed Cyn's face. "There's a school for that?"

Lara shrugged. "I don't know, but it would be fun, wouldn't it?"

"I'd sign up. Do you think they'd offer night classes?"

"I don't see why not." Lara thought about her friend's extreme photosensitivity. The poor woman couldn't be exposed to the tiniest beam of sunlight without hissing in acute pain and breaking out in third degree burns.

Cyn's gamine grin was clearly visible. Wait a minute. The street, park and everything she couldn't see before was now visible. "What happened to the fog?"

Cyn surveyed the area. "I guess it decided to lift."

"There wasn't a breeze."

Cyn shrugged. "If the weather here was normal, we wouldn't be living in San Francisco."

"True" Lara admitted. "Guido's gone!"

"Who?" Cyn asked.

"The guy you pounded into the pavement."

"His name was Guido?"

"I don't know; he seemed like a Guido to me."

"What did he want?"

"Someone left a bunny in the library, and he wanted it."

A frown crossed Cyn's face. "A bunny?"

Lara held up the carrier.

Cyn stilled. "Oh shit."

Lara swore recognition crossed the other woman's features. "Animals aren't allowed in the library, so I'm taking him home until we can locate his owner."

Cyn crouched, her face at cage level. "Jared? Is that you?"

The carrier moved when the bunny shifted.

"What the hell happened?"

"You know him?" Lara asked.

Cyn glanced up at her. "I know of him. He belongs to a friend of a friend. Jared, can you...?" She waved her hand.

The carrier rocked again.

"I thought not. That'd be too simple, I suppose." Cyn sat back. "Do you want me to call someone?"

Lara leaned over and caught the bunny shaking his head. "What's going on?"

Cyn stood. "You know there are certain things I can't tell you about, right?"

"Yes, but I thought that had to do with your classified work."

"It does, and Jared is part of it." A thoughtful expression crossed Cyn's face.

"What's wrong?"

"I'm not sure." Cyn came to a decision. "Do me a favor. Keep Jared with you."

"Shouldn't you take him home to his owner?"

Cyn shook her head. "Right now, he's safer with you than with me." She grabbed Lara's arm and tugged her toward the street. "I want you to take a cab home. The bus isn't safe."

"Okay." Lara winced at the cost. As if reading her mind, Cyn pressed a couple of bills into Lara's hand.

"I can't take your money, Cyn."

"Don't worry. Jared's owner will reimburse me for the expense."

Lara frowned at the other woman. "Are you sure?"

Cyn glanced down at the carrier. "Trust me. His owner would pay *anything* to keep him safe. I'll stop by tomorrow night."

Cyn frowned at the trees of the park. "I think someone is coming, go now."

"Wait." Lara called. "Can you tell Jared's owner I have him?"

Cyn waved in response. Lara hurried to the street, and hailed a cab in less than a minute. She got in and slammed the door. "Where to lady?"

Lara gave the address and tried to pierce the shadows beside the library. Should she call the police? No, Cyn had an aversion to authority, and Lara didn't want to screw up the other woman's work by bringing in the cops.

I can always call the police later.

§

Chuck waited at the side of the library for Benny. What was taking so long? It should have been easy to find a way into the building to retrieve the damned cage.

A scuff of a shoe against the pavement and Benny limped around the corner holding his arm to his ribs.

"What the hell happened?" Chuck demanded.

Benny grimaced in pain. "I don't know. I was scoping the place out, when the back door opened and a lady left with the carrier."

"You didn't try to take it from her?"

"I did, but I was jumped. Cut the fog. Maybe we can find her."

Chuck muttered under his breath and waved his hands in a complicated pattern. He reversed fog spell he'd cast earlier. The fog dispersed until no more remained than what Mother Nature had provided. It was great being a mage. The problem was that each spell he cast demanded a large amount of energy. If he'd continued his education and gained in power, such simple spells would not tire him. But he'd dropped out and exhaustion loomed like an unstable brick wall, ready to collapse and pound him into slumber. He had an hour at most before succumbing.

They peeked around the corner, in time to see the woman with the carrier get into a cab.

"Damn it," Chuck cursed.

"Don't look now, but the bastard who got the drop on me is over there."

Chuck watched the lithe feminine figure walk around studying the ground.

"You got beat up by a girl?"

"Girl? What do you mean?"

Chuck waved toward the figure. "That's a woman, lady, person of female persuasion, and her aura reads vamp, if I'm not mistaken."

"She sure doesn't fight like a chick."

"How do chicks fight?" Chuck asked.

Benny shrugged. "I don't know. All girly and shit. Afraid to throw a punch so they don't break a nail."

Something nagged at Chuck's mind about the vamp's behavior. "Does she seem odd to you?"

Benny nodded. "Besides the fact she fights and we're in Real? Hell, yeah. Maybe she was banished and beats up people for kicks?"

Chuck shook his head and lead the way to the car. "The Council won't banish a female for fighting."

"Why not?" Benny limped to the passenger door.

"Didn't you learn anything at Mage School?"

"As little as possible. I know some basics but that's it."

"The Council would send her for Reconditioning so fast you'd get whiplash."

"Why?"

Chuck fought from rolling his eyes. "You're an idiot. The female's job is to reproduce. Full stop. Occasionally one'll get permission to teach or work. But they're not allowed to fight. Ever."

"That's stupid. Looks like this one didn't get the memo."

They got in the car, and the female vamp caught sight of them. Shit, time to get out of here. He threw the car into gear and squealed the tires. He didn't want to experience getting his ass kicked.

"Do you think she recognized Williams?" Benny asked.

"Why?" Chuck asked.

"His aura was weak, but recognizable."

Chuck glanced at him. "What do you mean?"

"I saw his aura when the woman brought him out of the building."

"The shot was supposed to suppress that."

"Well, it didn't work. What are we gonna do?"

"Let me think." Chuck concentrated on driving.

"Hurry it up will ya?"

"I'm going the speed limit, don't want to get pulled over." Chuck retorted.

"That's not what I meant. Think faster."

Chuck's hands clenched on the steering wheel. "I wasn't the one who fucked up."

"What do we do now?" Benny asked.

Chuck let out a deep breath. "Nothing. We're gonna lay low."

"What about the fighting chick?"

Chuck drove around, thinking of a plan. "Call the Elite on their anonymous tip line. That should teach her to mess with things she shouldn't."

Benny grinned. "But what about the bunny?"

"We're going to find out who grabbed him, get him back, and make her pay for her interference."

Benny's cell phone rang. "Shit it's the boss."

"You screwed up, you take the heat." Chuck said.

Taking a deep breath and wincing, Benny answered. "Yeah boss? Um. No, there was a slight… yeah, I know. But…"

He held the phone away from his ear, and Chuck could hear the yelling coming through the phone.

"One of the librarians took him home… Yes sir."

He disconnected the call and looked at Chuck. "We're to meet with his contact to find the lady."

"Shit."

§

Cyn searched the area for anything that would give her a clue as to what was going on. Guido's auric signature was that of a mage. Regardless of what she'd told Lara, the fog wasn't natural. Too many questions arose. Why was the mage in Real? Why was he after Jared? What was the Elite doing in rabbit form?

Her sensitive hearing picked up the low murmur of voices from around the corner. She skulked to the corner. She heard two car doors slam. The car carrying the mage she fought and his accomplice, sped away. Ready to follow on foot, she stopped as her cell phone rang.

"Hello, Hans."

"Where are you now?"

"I'm in Real at a library. Why?"

"Cut short your research. I need you to check with Carlos. Homeless people are disappearing off the streets."

Chapter 5

Cyn located Carlos via a specialized tracking app on her phone. He was within easy walking distance and it didn't take long for her to meet up with him.

She found him crouched behind a dumpster. He waved her over. "Where have you been?" he whispered.

"Saving a friend. What's up?"

The young human pointed to a black van driving well under the speed limit. There wasn't enough traffic to explain why the van was cruising so slow.

"Watch."

Two homeless men were curled up in old sleeping bags near cement steps leading into a dilapidated apartment building. The van stopped yards from the men. Three males with the auras of mages, exited the vehicle. *What the hell?*

Two were dressed in jeans and leather jackets, while the third, was dressed in an emerald green shirt with black jeans and loafers, directing the others. Must be the leader.

Emerald shirt's hands moved in a series of complex gestures while the other two waited. A greenish glow traveled from the mage's fingers to surround the sleeping men. The spell caster motioned to his two accomplices who rushed to retrieve the two sleepers.

"Only eight more to go," one of the peons commented.

"Indeed," replied the man wearing emerald.

They dumped their cargo in the back of the van and drove off.

"What the hell was that?" Carlos asked.

"You saw the glow?"

"Yeah, I did. What was it?"

Cyn bit her lip. How to explain. "I think the in the green shirt had one of those hypnotic lights."

"The kind they've got at the Tech Fair?"

"Yeah, and they're using it to kidnap people."

"Why?"

"That's an excellent question."

Carlos shrugged. "You and Hans will figure it out."

Cyn placed her hand on his shoulder. "Yeah we will. Spread the word and keep an eye out. We want to make sure everyone stays safe."

"I'll do that." Carlos stood and leaned against the wall, hesitating.

"What's wrong?"

"They got Uncle Jack."

"Fuck."

"You'll get him back, won't you Cyn?"

Cyn sighed, not wanting to disappoint him. "When did they take him?"

"Two nights ago. I tried to follow them, but they were too fast for me."

"I'll see what I can do." Cyn pulled him into a hug and then released him before anyone saw. She didn't want to get his hopes up. "Uncle Jack may not be recoverable."

Carlos kicked a rock. "I know. It's just, we were close, ya know?"

She squeezed his shoulder. "I know. But life sucks…"

"And then ya die," he finished.

"Exactly. Better leave in case they come back."

Carlos nodded and headed out.

Cyn checked her watch. Lara should be home by now.

She texted a quick message. *I'm fine, but Guido got away. Will stop by tomorrow night.*

Stay safe, Lara replied.

Will do.

For the next several hours she scoured the city, but found no trace of the van or its occupants. None of her contacts had seen them since the sighting with Carlos. They must have given up for the night.

Time for a break. The Tech Fair should still be open.

Cyn pulled out her phone and texted her honey, James. While he was Elite, he also made her laugh. She thought about him often and his kisses rated almost as high as a new pair of shoes. *Busy tonight?*

Yeah in a work meeting, rain check?

Sure.

Well that sucked. She didn't enjoy going solo, but it was too late to invite anyone else, so she'd go alone.

James loved the tech stuff. His apartment was filled with all the latest greatest tech toys. They'd been dating for about a year now, and he'd been hinting at a more permanent relationship. She'd have to think long and hard about committing to him. He was Elite, and she was… breaking the law. Could she give up her crusade to be with him?

Cyn walked the last two blocks and came to an abrupt halt.

"You son of a bitch," she muttered.

Cyn dashed into the shadow of the closest building, to avoid being seen. Elite James Kirk, her boyfriend and rat bastard, escorted a laughing, redheaded human out of the Tech Fair.

They passed by her, close enough to overhear their conversation.

"Shall we go to dinner?" the redhead cooed at him.

Sharp points of pain registered in Cyn's palms as she clenched her fists. *Must not punch the hussy, must not punch the hussy.*

"Sure, I know a nice little restaurant on the pier," James replied.

That rotten two-timing, mother-fucking, son of a bitch! Cyn seethed as he helped the redhead into his car and whistled as he walked around the hood to open the driver's door.

They drove off into the night.

Eyes filling with moisture, Cyn refused to let a single tear fall. "He's not worth it, the bastard."

Closing her eyes, she took a deep breath, and another. The pain in her chest felt as if a twenty-ton weight was sitting on her rib cage. If she were still human, she'd think it was a heart attack. But vampires didn't have the same types of aliments humans had.

She pressed a fist to her chest and bowed her head.

So be it. If the mother fucker wanted to play around, he was more than welcome to do so. Life had thrown her too many sour lemons for a tasty lemonade. It was a wonder she'd let him in as far as she had. No more. Unlocking her phone, she blocked his contact info.

Cyn walked the streets in a daze as she tried to absorb the emotional blow.

She placed a call to her best friend. "Deidre, the rat bastard is cheating on me."

"Meet me for coffee and we'll plan the best way to eviscerate him."

Cyn gave a watery chuckle and headed to Angelini's.

§

Jared stood in a dark space. It smelled sharp—antiseptic and metallic. The room was covered in once white tile, splattered with reddish-brown stains. A chain hung from the ceiling with a single shattered bulb in the light socket. Wicked looking stained instruments decorated a metal tray pushed against one wall.

A metal gurney was parked above an iron grate in the floor. A discolored white sheet covered an object on the table.

Drip.

Drip.

Drip.

Dread filled him. His heartbeat pulsed loud in his ears as he discovered the source of the sound.

Deep crimson blood dripped from a corner of the table, splattering on the floor in a macabre pattern before joining other drops to run down the drain.

Something bad had taken place here. Something horrific.

56

Leave now!

Instinct screamed at him to hurry away, to save himself. But compulsion made it impossible to turn away. Morbid curiosity won over caution and he approached the gurney.

A trembling hand reached toward the sheet. The white cotton crumpled in his fist as he pulled the sheet back.

The body on the table was covered in cuts and holes, some seeping red, others mottled with yellow-green bruising. A scream of horror rose within him. Willpower locked the sound in his throat. He glanced at the head, and gazed into his own face.

Lara stared at the man in the center of the room. Somehow, she knew it was a man, even though his body was concealed by a dark swirling cloud of pain.

Weird things happened in dreams.

"Do you need help?" His pain called something insider her. The need to soothe, to heal, rose, unstoppable. Taking two steps forward, she touched where she thought his arm should be.

A jolt of energy arced between them, jerking his body. The sharp spark sent a tingling sensation up her arm. The dark miasma drained from his body like water flowing down glass. He stiffened under her hand before turning to face her. She jerked her hand away from him.

Oh my! Thank you, subconscious.

Before her was a fabulous specimen of manhood. Her gaze wandered up his body. From his bare feet to his jean-clad, well-muscled legs, this was a man worth dreaming about. The best part was the tucked-in white Oxford shirt with the sleeves rolled up, exposing muscular forearms.

Her eyes met his. Dark and turbulent, they flashed with intensity before cooling with suspicion.

"Who are you?" His voice was deep.

She retreated a step, feeling threatened.

"Well?" He closed the gap between them, invading her space. His hand reached out and circled her throat. She grabbed his wrist in both hands, but didn't have the strength to pull him away.

"Your name?"

The expression in his eyes made her feel like a small rabbit trapped in the clutches of a ravenous hawk. And not in a sexy, hot way. In a you'll-taste-good-with-barbeque-sauce way. Except hawks didn't enjoy barbeque, did they? What sort of sauce would they prefer?

This wasn't fun.

Wake up. Get away from the scary killer.

She needed to leave, now. Wake up. WAKE UP!

"Answer me!"

She tried to kick him, but grabbed her shoulders, lifting her from the ground, removing her leverage.

Why couldn't she wake up? What was wrong with her subconscious that she made her dream man a killer? Her bad luck with men followed her into her dreams. "L... Lara, my name is Lara."

A frown crossed his face. "That name's familiar. Why?"

Who the hell knew? Why was she dreaming about a crazed hottie? Probably her subconscious trying to work through the stress of being held at gunpoint.

"Why is the hot guy a deranged serial killer?" she mumbled.

He jolted back and the threatening vibe cut off in an instant. "I'm not a serial killer."

Lara snorted. "As if you'd admit it if you were."

"I can't argue that. But I'm not." A puzzled look crossed his face. "Did you rescue a rabbit?"

How did he know? "Y- yes. L-let me g-g-go."

The scary guy lowered her to the ground and released her. His fingers caressed her shoulders before lifting from her. She stepped back, away from him.

He held both hands up, palms out. "Easy, little rabbit. I didn't mean to frighten you."

As if she believed that. She lurched away, putting more distance between them.

His eyes warmed as his gaze roamed up and down her body. "You're a courageous rabbit."

Yeah, right. "How so?"

"You saved Jared from a fate worse than death."

Why was she dreaming in clichés? Wait, she didn't save him, Cyn had. She'd better play along so she didn't end up another one of his victims. "I did?"

"Yes, and he's grateful."

"Jared, the bunny, is grateful?"

He nodded.

"Who are you? How do you know Jared?" She held up a hand. "Wait. My mind is making you up, so of course you'd know the bunny."

He gave her a small bow. "My name is Jared Williams, I'm not a figment of your imagination, and I own the bunny."

She was a sucker for old world manners. Damn. He grinned revealing a dimple. Double damn. She was such a sap. He had a bad boy vibe that sang a song of temptation, irresistible now that he wasn't threatening her.

Serial killer, remember?

Wait a minute. "You named your pet after yourself?" That was a ludicrous thing for her dream man to do. No more cheese before bed; it reportedly gave you weird dreams. This was by far the strangest dream she'd ever had.

He shrugged. "That way I don't have to remember his name."

"Oh."

Despite the earlier scare, she felt drawn to him. Looking into his dark eyes, she saw sensual promise in his gaze. Oh yum.

"Perhaps we should adjourn to more comfortable surroundings?" His deep voice set off effervescent explosions in her body.

This was her dream and it had to conform to her desires, right? Oh, the things she wanted to do to his delectable body, if he were tied down, of course. There was no way she'd be brave enough to do half the things she wanted if he remained free. He'd take over and she wouldn't be able to explore, to discover.

A bed surrounded by gauzy material popped into the room. Leather restraints hung from the posts at each corner. Large feathers, a blindfold, and gold-foil packets in a large brandy glass, topped the bedside table. The soft glow of hundreds of lit candles provided romantic illumination.

Jared raised an eyebrow. "A bit soon, don't you think? But if you insist." He captured both of her hands in his, brought them to his lips and placed nibbling kisses on the tips of her fingers.

Heat rose in her cheeks. Oh my god. What was she thinking?

She bit her lip. "That wasn't... I didn't mean..."

"Apparently your subconscious does."

Lara glared at the bed. Now was NOT the time for sexual fantasies. Though she could see him tied up at her mercy... no! Bad Lara! Control yourself!

The bed vanished to be replaced by two comfortable armchairs arranged before a crackling fireplace. A hot cup of tea steamed on a table next to her chair.

The wicked grin on his face made her reconsider the disappearance of the bed.

Lara tugged at her hands; he placed a soft kiss on each palm before sliding his fingers along her sensitized skin. Then he released her and held out his arm. It took her a moment before she realized what he wanted. Darn. Old world manners again. Placing her hand on his arm, he escorted her to the chairs, holding her hand as she sat in the closest one. She sank into its comforting cushions and picked up the cup, gazing at him over the rim as she sipped. He sat down in the opposite chair. The flames snapped and popped sending flickering light through the room.

"Why are you here in my dream?" she asked, curious.

His smile warmed her. "Are you sure you're not in mine?"

If she was in his dream, how had the bed materialized? Maybe it was his fantasy? She'd never met him before; she'd have remembered. If they'd never met, how could he be imagining her? How could she think *independent thoughts? Her brain hurt at the Nietzsche-esque ideas. Was she real? Was he real? What the heck?*

"You're a figment of my imagination. You've got to be. I'm under too much stress."

He smiled again, and her panties grew damp. Damn, her dream man was potent.

"Thanks for saving Jared," he said.

"Cyn saved Jared, I brought him home." How ridiculous to be having this conversation, when all she wanted to do was summon the bed back and indulge in her fantasies. No. No. No. No dream sex, at least not without a little get-to-know-you chat first.

"You faced down a gunman. That took courage."

"Yes, but I was scared the entire time. Why was he after the bunny instead of cash? Drugs? Too many questions and no answers."

Jared shrugged, "The bad guy wanted the rabbit for a heinous experiment. I doubt he would have survived."

"Poor little bunny."

For the first time in too long, Jared was fascinated by a woman. A human one at that.

His luck remained shitty as always. It'd been so long since he'd felt interest, or even found someone to be interested in. Paranormals didn't let him chat with their women, and most human women he'd met recently were of the criminal variety.

Something about Lara triggered his protective instincts. She was a breath of fresh air in a stagnant room. He'd been lonely for so long. Not fitting in, in Real or Shadow. Her warm, compassionate nature soothed him, and from the appearance of the bed, she had hidden, sensual depths.

Too bad he hadn't met her years ago. He'd like to start something, but everything he'd have to hide from her because of Shadow and their laws would be a problem. If he sought permission to tell her about Shadow or to court her, he'd be denied by the Council as his existence was barely tolerated.

That didn't mean he couldn't indulge here in the Dreamscape. He grinned. Perfect. Now if she'd call that bed back, they'd have a stimulating time.

Lara sipped the tea.

She'd saved him twice now, once as a rabbit, and now from his nightmare.

He needed to repay her kindness. She could have walked away in both cases, and if it had been any of his acquaintances, they would have. Lara deserved a suitable reward for her good deeds.

Jared's gaze roamed her body. Her brown hair was loose around her shoulders, soft and touchable. Quite a change from the ponytail she'd worn at the library. The loose shirt hid her curves, but the leggings hugged her like a lover's hands. He had quite a few ideas about the bed she'd summoned earlier. A night of passion was a fitting way to pay her back.

He shifted in his seat, trying to keep his growing enthusiasm hidden.

Until he felt her gaze. Watching her eyes roam his body felt like an erotic caress and it took willpower not to cross the small distance, pull her into his arms and ravish her delectable mouth. The blush staining her cheeks and her deepened breathing indicated her own rising desire.

She hid behind her cup of tea. Mint by the scent. "So now what?" she asked.

"We get to know each other," he replied.

"Why?"

"Why not?"

"You're doing the question with a question thing. What are you hiding?"

Too much. "Many things, but I want to get to know you."

"Once again, why?"

"Because you're selfless and a brave little rabbit."

The skeptical expression on her face was too delightful to resist. Jared stood and removed the cup from her hand, setting it on the table. Reaching down, he lifted both of her hands in his, her pulse fluttered beneath the skin of her throat. He pulled her out of the chair and into his embrace.

"What are you doing?" she asked.

"Thanking you for saving Jared." he whispered, brushing her lips in a feather light caress. A slight tremor shook her body, and her lips parted.

He was tempted to deepen the kiss; to take things further. But he kept his lips soft, his touch reverent. He'd frightened her before and he didn't want her backing away. In her own way she was as timid as a rabbit, hiding the heart of a lioness beneath an insecure exterior. He'd be gentle for now, until she got to know him. Jared pulled her flush against his aroused body at the feel of her tongue against the seam of his lips.

In the distance a beeping sound intruded. Soft at first, it gained in volume until she broke the kiss. Her dark brown eyes were filled with desire, that cleared as the beeping registered.

"What's that?" she asked, her soft voice, hesitant.

Jared opened his mouth to answer, and she disappeared from his arms.

§

Jor'dan DúSan, Captain of the San Francisco branch of the Elite Magical Protection Force, perched on the corner of his desk, and dialed the phone for the tenth time.

His finely-honed intuition told him Jared was in trouble. The phone went into voicemail, again. Damn it.

Randall, Jared's partner, might know what had happened, but both men were late for their check in. Merrick had brought in the shifter teens hours ago. He texted Randall's phone and waited. No response.

A knock on the door interrupted his worrying.

"Enter."

Regina, Oracle of L'Dan, and general pain in his ass, entered the office. She was dressed in her signature red suit with matching heels.

Why she chose the color red when she was an air elemental, Jor'dan didn't know.

He picked up the phone. "Please have tea service brought to my office."

"On it," one of the Elite replied.

Jor'dan waved Regina to a seat. "To what do I owe the honor of your visit so late in the evening?"

"You can cut the bullshit. I'm here to help."

Jor'dan didn't bother to hide his snort of derision. "With convoluted sayings that can be interpreted in so many ways, they hinder rather than help?"

A grin stretched her lips. "Of course. It's my job, you know."

"I can't think of a more perfect fit for you."

Her light, airy laugh filled the office.

There was a knock on the door and an Elite carrying a silver tea service entered and put in on the corner of his desk. "Thanks Merrick," Jor'dan said.

"You're welcome." The mage bowed to Regina and left the office closing the door behind him.

She accepted the cup Jor'dan handed to her and inhaled the steam. "You don't need to worry about him, you know."

"Who, Merrick?"

Regina stared at him. "No, Jared."

Jor'dan narrowed his eyes at her. "Perhaps not, but he's one of my men, and I worry about all of them."

"You're such a mother hen." She put the cup down.

"If it keeps them alive, so be it."

She sat back in her chair, eyes closed, and became as still as a statue. In an otherworldly voice, she intoned, "Safety is assured for the moment. Predator becomes prey; the hunters shall be hunted. Success maintains status quo. All is not what it seems."

Out of long habit, Jor'dan wrote down her words. Sometimes she remembered her visions and other times she didn't.

It was a long moment before she woke from the trance. Jor'dan stood, walked around the desk, and refilled her tea cup. She accepted it with a small smile. Both hands wrapped around the mug, and she inhaled the soothing fragrance.

Jor'dan leaned against his desk, ankles crossed and palms on the flat surface.

"Feeling better?"

"Yes, thank you. That was a rough one."

"Do you remember what you said?"

Regina raised an eyebrow. "Of course. I remember visions given for the greater good, just not the ones for private individuals."

"Can you clarify?"

Regina sighed. "Sorry, I speak them as I get them; usually the meaning is no clearer to me than it is to you."

"Usually?"

She grinned and drank the tea, not answering the question. But then again, he hadn't expected her to.

Another knock on the door.

"Come."

Vampire Damien Alexander entered his office and closed the door behind him.

"Where's James?" Jor'dan asked. It was rare to see the two vamps apart.

Damien rolled his eyes. "He says he's 'cultivating a new source of information'." He used his fingers to air quote. "Whatever the hell that means. Has Jared reported in yet?"

Jor'dan considered the tall, dark vampire. "No. Why?"

"I found his truck off Market. He's not answering his cell or home phone, and the tracking chip in his phone led me to his car."

"Real or Shadow?" Jor'dan asked, pulling on his bottom lip.

"Real. Have you spoken to Randall?"

"No, he's not answering his phone. But I wonder…"

Maybe Jared had gone off grid to pursue his investigation regarding the experiments by the Alliance. That seemed a plausible scenario, but doubt niggled in the back of Jor'dan's mind.

Damien's phone rang and he answered it as Regina reached over and refilled her cup.

Damien's face registered shock. "We have a problem," he reported.

"What now?" Jor'dan asked.

"An anonymous tip came in saying there's a female vampire beating people up in Real Earth."

Jor'dan pinched the bridge of his nose, feeling the warning pressure of an impending headache. If he didn't ground soon and regain his center, he'd be down with a migraine and low energy for days.

"Is the witness sure?" he asked.

"The tip said there were two witnesses and they're both sure it was a vampire."

Jor'dan paced from the window, to the bookcase and back. He stopped behind his desk and moved the mouse, waking up his computer.

"Don't bother," Regina said.

He and Damien both stared at her. "Why not?"

"Because whoever it is knows what she's doing."

"She's breaking Shadow Earth Law." Damien reminded her.

"Perhaps. But if she's captured now and Reconditioned…" Her breath caught and the color drained from her face. The teacup slipped from her hands and fell to the floor shattering into pieces. "Blood spilled, spirits undone." The scratchy rasp of sound emerged from her mouth. "Leave the vampire alone to do what must be done."

Jor'dan shared a glance with Damien. "That's that, I suppose."

Damien nodded. "I wonder who it is?"

Regina slumped into the chair, perspiration along her brow. Jor'dan picked up a napkin, wet it from the water carafe on his desk, moved to her side, and dabbed her face. Damien opened the door and spoke to someone in the hall. Soon the mess was cleaned up and a fresh cup of tea was placed in the Oracle's shaking hands.

She glanced up at him, devastation in her gaze. "Don't do it Jor'dan. Don't pursue her."

He knelt next to her and grasped one of her hands. "You know who it is, don't you?"

"Yes, but I'm not going to tell you."

Jor'dan paused for a long moment. "I give you my word. I won't go after her," he promised. He had his suspicions, and if he was right, he would do whatever he could to protect her. No one deserved Reconditioning, no matter what the Council decreed.

Regina's body slumped in relief. "Thank you."

Jor'dan kissed the back of her hand and placed it gently on her lap before rising and leaning against his desk.

Damien cleared his throat. "What are we going to do about Jared?"

"I want you to find James and swing by Jared's apartment. Check on him as friends. I don't want to make this official, not yet."

"Why not?"

"The less amount of attention we call to him the better." His intuition demanded he keep this quiet as long as possible. He didn't want the spy in the Elite to discover Jared's mission. If the shifter fell into Alliance hands, he was dead.

Chapter 6

Jared woke, once again not recognizing his surroundings. Bright sunlight filtered beneath a two-inch gap where a grey ruffle didn't reach the ground. He reached for the high heeled shoe that lay on its side and batted it with his paw. Damn, still in rabbit form.

What was a woman's shoe doing here? Wait. Where was here? The low ceiling was comprised of thin fabric and wooden slats. He sneezed as a dust bunny tickled his nose.

How the hell had he gotten under the bed? Memory returned from last night. Library, librarian, gunman, right.

Concentrating, he reached for his human form and stopped. He'd better get out of this confining space before trying to shift.

He nudged aside the ruffle and hopped from beneath the bed.

Jared heard a noise, and one shapely feminine ankle then the other descend from above.

Lara stood up, and his ears flopped over. She wore a pale purple tank top with a matching pair of low riding pants decorated with white flowers. She was an oh-so-tempting package that he wanted to unwrap and rumple. His back foot thumped on the floor. Inside, he grinned at her startled jump.

"Jared, you scared me!" Her hand rose to cover her chest, as if trying to keep her heart from bursting through her ribcage.

She appeared well rested for someone who'd spent the night flopping around as much as she had. It was something to keep in mind when he regained his human form.

Lara knelt and rubbed her finger between his ears. "Good morning."

Oh yeah, right there. That was the spot. His eyes crossed at how good that felt.

"Let me jump in the shower and we'll scrounge for breakfast."

Hmm, she was going to shower? He should go and keep watch. To protect her. Though how he'd protect her, he didn't know. Nibble ankles?

Jared hopped through the open door of the bathroom and settled down on the rug, waiting for the show to start.

Lara walked in, lifting the bottom of her tank top and stopped. Uh-oh... he didn't like the look on her face.

"I'm not going to strip with you here." She pointed to the door. "Wait in the bedroom."

Jared sat where he was, not moving a muscle.

She bent, hands reaching out.

His ears laid back and he hunched down further.

"Okay. Be that way."

She huffed out a breath and left the room. His ears lifted at the sound of drawers opening. Lara entered the bathroom a few minute later dressed in a robe and pink fuzzy slippers.

The slippers... mesmerized him. In his human brain, he knew what they were, but these were outside of his animal's experience. The rabbit was so fascinated by the slippers that Jared missed Lara getting into the shower. One slender arm appeared from behind the opaque shower curtain and draped the robe on a nearby hook.

But the fluffy pink slippers sang a siren's song of lust.

One hop later and his little hips pumped in and out as he mounted the soft fuzzy slipper.

A gasp of surprise couldn't pry his attention away from the primal instinct to reproduce.

"Jared, what are you doing?"

The frenzy of mating had him in its grip.

Two seconds later, he was lifted in the air, hips still thrusting, and deposited outside the bathroom door. It slammed closed behind him.

Lara returned to the shower, shaking her head. She felt the heat of embarrassment in her cheeks. "Was that normal behavior? I can't believe he did that!"

She didn't know, which meant that she needed to research domesticated bunnies. The info should be available online. Lara hurried through her shower. What was Jared getting into on the other side of the door? Was any more of her footwear in jeopardy?

Shower done, she headed into the bedroom wrapped in a towel. Lara grabbed her clothes and dressed as fast as possible, keeping any eye out for Jared.

He was on the other side of the room looking out the sliding glass door that led to her miniscule balcony. Good.

"Shall we have breakfast?"

At the sound of her voice, he hopped over, and she reached down and rubbed the spot between his ears. He made a grinding noise with his teeth. "Hmm is that a good sound or not?" His ears flopped over and his eyes were half closed. "Good, I think."

Lara entered the kitchen hearing thumps as he followed her. Opening the fridge, she gazed at the contents. While she didn't have any carrots on hand, maybe he'd enjoy celery? She took it out and chopped it into bunny-sized pieces and put them on a paper plate on the floor. Lara popped a couple of pieces of bread into the toaster for herself and started a pot of water for tea. She prepped her mug with honey and Earl Grey.

Breakfast consumed, Lara wandered into the living room and powered on her laptop. "Now let's see what I should be feeding you and find out if more of my footwear is in danger of bunny lovin'."

While waiting for the computer to finish booting, Lara frowned at the phone and the blinking light indicating messages.

Lara picked up the handset and grabbed a pen and notepad. Jared hopped over and rubbed her ankle. She bent down and scratched behind his ears, and played the first message, putting it on speaker.

"Hello, my name is Preston Garrett the Third, and I'm a criminal defense attorney in San Francisco. I want to talk to you about the future of our city."

Lara jolted at the sound of his voice, flushing hot, then cold. How had he managed to find her new number? She'd changed it a few times since they'd broken up. Carp, she'd have to change it again. Maybe this time, she'd drop the land line and go cell only.

Why would Preston leave a political message on her phone? Wait, he was running for mayor? She tried to listen to the rest of the message, but his voice threw her into a whirlwind of anger, guilt, and embarrassment. She'd been so stupid over him, and his stalking her hadn't helped matters. Then what he was saying registered.

It was a generic political message sent out to everyone in the city.

How could she have been so gullible to believe his lies?

Her hand shook as she stabbed the delete key, cutting off his voice, mid-spiel.

"It was poisonous, my relationship with him." A deep sigh left her. "I hope to God he doesn't win. His narcissistic tendencies would be bad for the city."

She felt sharp pain on her bare foot and glanced down. Jared stood on his hind paws resting his front paws on her shin. If she didn't know better she'd think he was asking to be held. Better make sure. "Did you bite me? I don't think bite-y bunnies get to snuggle."

Jared tilted his head at her.

"Weak as water," Lara mumbled. "Fine, but just this time. You nibble on me again, and you'll be left on the floor."

She lifted him, careful to support his feet and put him on the couch next to her. He hopped onto her lap and settled in. She ran a hand down his back, stroking his soft fur. The repetitive stroking motion soothed her.

"He's such a bastard." Stroke. "I can't believe he's running for office. I left him months ago. He cheated on me, knowing I'd be home at a certain time. Doreen says it was nothing more than a game of manipulation. And she's right. It hurts, knowing that I was weak, gullible. But hurtful habits are difficult things to break."

"One more message." She took another deep breath, feeling much more at ease. Perhaps there was something to having a pet. Jared seemed to be making her anxiety disappear with each slow stroke of her hand.

The message was from Doreen. "Hi, Lara. We got a call from a man named Charles Rich. The rabbit belongs to his boss, Dr. David Glendale. Mr. Rich said something about a practical joke going wrong. He wants the rabbit back before Dr. Glendale's daughter notices her pet is missing. Please give him a call." She rattled off the number and Lara wrote it down.

Lara frowned and studied Jared. "Strange. I thought Cyn said your owner was unavailable?"

Jared stiffened in her lap, claws digging into her jeans, his little body shaking. Could it be fear?

"Shhhh. It's okay." She petted his back, long, soothing strokes from ears to tail. It took a few moments, but she felt him relax against her. For good measure she rubbed the sweet spot between his ears.

A few more strokes and she said, "I'd call him back, but Cyn said she knows your owner. This whole thing feels weird. I think I'll wait for her."

He nodded once.

"I almost believe you understand me."

He ground his teeth.

"Time to find out more about you."

Lara picked him up and walked to her desk, putting him in her lap as she logged into the computer. "Let's see what Google knows about bunnies."

§

Chuck cringed as he and Benny met with Dr. Glendale. The man was pacing back and forth in front of them, yelling and shouting. Yeah, they'd fucked up, but calling their parentage into question wasn't helping anything.

The doc ended his rant, took a deep breath, and faced them. "How are you going to find him?"

Chuck and Benny exchanged a glance. "I don't know, boss. I've tried calling the library to get the name of the librarian, but they don't give out that information."

Dr. Glendale pinched the bridge of his nose. "Idiots, the both of you."

Chuck clenched his teeth, but didn't respond to the barb, and instead asked, "How do you want us to proceed?"

Dr. Glendale sat down in his chair and picked up his phone. "The same mage who gave you Williams will meet you at Angelini's at seven. Don't screw up this time."

Chuck hated to ask, but the more precise information he got, the better. "Real or Shadow?"

Dr. Glendale typed into the device. "He says Real." He gave them a look. "Don't fuck up."

Chuck took that to mean they were dismissed. He grabbed Benny and left.

Chuck and Benny arrived at the coffee shop a few minutes early. Chuck was grateful they had, because it was strangely busy at that time of night. He recognized more than a few Paranormals scattered throughout the human population. All the tables were taken. Near the back three people gathered their things and freed up a table. Chuck was quick to claim the space. At the next table, two women chatted. A vampire and one whose aura he didn't recognize.

He and Benny sat down with their overpriced coffee drinks.

"Can you believe this place? Who knew there were fifty different ways to make coffee?" Benny asked. "Why the hell does it cost so much?"

Chuck shrugged. "I don't know. I make mine at home."

"Yeah me too. Hey did you check out the hot chick next to us?"

"The vamp or the other one?"

"Bah, I don't care about the vamp. The other one, she's smokin' hot."

Chuck saw a flash of an impressive amethyst ring when she waved her hands. "She's smokin' taken."

"What?" Benny glanced at her. "Damn, check out the rock. Maybe she'd be in for a little piece on the side, know what I mean?"

"Doubt it. We need to finish the job before you can play."

Benny sighed. "Bummer. Think the vamp is taken?"

Chuck glared at him. "The fuck? I just said keep it in your pants until the job is done."

"I like to check out possible lovelies." Benny frowned at the vamp. "She seems familiar somehow."

Chuck took a closer look. Yeah there was something familiar about her, but he couldn't put his finger on what it was.

"Never mind, here comes the meet," Benny announced.

§

Cyn leaned forward and whispered to Deidre. "The two at the next table are checking you out."

Deidre fluffed her hair behind her. "What's new?" There was a distinctive twinkle in her violet eyes.

"Does it bother you?"

"Nah." Deidre leaned in. "The attention raises their lust; it's a tasty treat."

"I thought you weren't imbibing anymore?" Cyn raised an eyebrow.

"I'm not going for the full meal, just a light snack."

"Do I need to leave you to feed in peace?"

Deidre waved the question away. "Nah, I absorb the ambient lust." She paused, "Crap."

"What? What's wrong?"

"It's what's his face. That Elite mage Damien and James work with."

"Merrick?" Cyn asked.

"No, one of others. Can't remember his name."

Cyn glanced over her shoulder and frowned. "What's an Elite mage doing slumming here?"

"Don't know but he's headed this way."

"Let's ignore him, pretend we don't recognize him."

"We don't," Deidre responded.

Cyn and Deidre sipped at their drinks. Cyn tried to suppress a shudder when he walked behind her and sat at the next table. Was that one of the goons from last night? No way to tell.

"What are we going to do about the rat bastard?" Deidre asked.

Cyn was about to answer when she heard "Jared Williams," from the next table. She held up her finger.

"What's up?" Deidre asked.

Cyn leaned closer and in a soft whisper that didn't go past her bestie, said, "The guys at the next table said something about Jared and he's in trouble."

The smile slid from Deidre's face. "What happened?"

"I'll tell you later, once I figure out if these guys are responsible."

They sipped their coffees as Cyn wished her hearing was as sharp as a shifter.

"…I can track him, but you two need to come with me. You're in charge of recapturing him." The condescending Elite's voice grated on Cyn's nerves.

One of guys spoke up. "Okay, how're you going to track him?"

There was a rustle of clothing. "I'm going to use this."

Cyn glanced over out of the corner of her eye and saw the Elite remove a charm from his pocket.

Shit. "Can you do me a favor?" Cyn whispered to Deidre.

"Sure. What do you need?"

"Can you stall the goons? I've got to hide Lara and her pet."

Deidre winked. "Leave them to me."

"Will Damien be upset?"

"What's a little flirting between friends?" Deidre grinned. "Plus, he knows I love him."

"Okay. Thanks."

"Let's meet tomorrow and you can give me all the deets."

"Drinks on me." Cyn said, then weaved through the tables and out the door. Glancing over her shoulder, she saw Deidre get up from the table and saunter over to the Elite's table.

Cyn didn't have much time, so she popped her and her car into Shadow and broke speed limits getting to Lara's apartment.

§

Jared hopped after Lara as she entered the kitchen to make dinner. He enjoyed watching her cook. He'd spent a nice afternoon napping next to her on the couch while she read.

An urgent knock sounded at the door.

He followed her out, recognizing the auric signature of vamp on the other side of the door.

"Cyn! Just the woman I wanted to see," Lara said.

Cyn hurried into the apartment and shut the door. "I've got horrible news."

"What? What's wrong?"

"We need to move Jared to a safer place. The bad guys are coming."

"What? How'd they find us?"

"I don't know, but a friend and I overheard their conversation at the coffee shop."

How had they discovered his whereabouts? Shifters were immune to magic, and to the best of his knowledge, no one should have been able to track him. They needed to get to a secured location. The best place was his condo, but how to communicate that?

Cyn grabbed Lara's arm. "Go pack a bag. We need to stash the two of you somewhere safe."

Lara hurried down the hallway. "Does this have anything to do with the was a message on my machine from the library? His owner called and wanted Jared returned."

Cyn frowned and called to Lara. "Jared can't call, he's out of touch."

"The guy's name was Dr. Glendale, not Jared." Lara responded. "Wait, Jared's owner's name is Jared?"

"Did you say Dr. Glendale?" Cyn asked.

"Yep," came the reply from Lara's room.

"Shit, they want Jared back in the experimental lab." The vamp knelt in front of him. "What the hell is going on?" she asked in a whisper. He couldn't answer in his current form, even if he knew what was happening. Jared shook his head to indicate he couldn't speak.

"Damn it. I forgot you can't talk." Cyn rubbed her temples. "Yes or no questions."

Thus began the bobble-head session.

"Are you working undercover?" Head shake no.

"Is Lara in danger?" Head tilted to the side, possibly.

"Can you shift?" Head shake no.

"Jared, are you in trouble?" Nod, yes.

"Okay. Do the Elite know where you are?" Head shake no.

"Do you want me to call them?" Empathic head shake no.

Jared had no idea if anyone in his office was behind this, so it was better to be cautious. The ones who'd welcomed him in the beginning had been the vampires and the Captain. He didn't trust any of the others. He expected betrayal. It was something any of the Elite were capable of; prejudice ran deep and for many of them, his creation made him an abomination.

"What about Bar'ella?" Cyn asked.

He hesitated a moment. The healer, Bar'ella, worked with the Elite, and while she was considered the go to person for any and all medical questions, how much he could trust her? She was a Dragon, after all. On the other hand, she was the only one who could figure out how to get him back into his human form.

If he didn't get help soon, he'd be stuck as a rabbit for the rest of his life. Not a pleasant prospect.

Jared nodded his head once with great reluctance.

"Let me call now while Lara is packing."

He settled himself in a comfortable position, and from the half of the conversation he heard, he guessed the healer was unavailable.

Cyn ended the call. "She's dealing with a deadly outbreak of some virus. She'll be back in a couple of days and fix you then."

Jared's ears picked up the zipping of a bag.

"Meanwhile where shall we stash you?"

Home was the safest. He hopped into the carrier, looked at her. The expression of confusion on her face made him repeat the action a few more times. Enter the carrier, look at her, sigh, hop out.

"Ah, I think I got it. Home? You want to go back to your condo?"

Jared jumped with enthusiasm.

"Okay." She pulled out her phone and did a quick search. "Is this the right address?" She rattled it off. He nodded again.

"Real or Shadow?"

Jared tilted his head. Either would work. He was lucky enough to own the apartment in both Real and Shadow. That way he had all the bases covered in case anyone tried to hunt him down. Magically or otherwise. By owning the space in both, no one could enter his home in Shadow and pop over to Real or vice-versa.

"Let's do Real so Lara can stay with you until I figure out what's going on," Cyn decided.

"Who are you talking to?" Lara asked as she came into the room with a small bag.

Cyn cleared her throat. "Um, bouncing ideas off Jared. I know where you can stay for a while."

"Your place?"

Cyn shook her head. "No, I'm in a studio, remember?"

Jared's fur tingled and a slight tendril of magic filled his nose. He pushed his senses out as far as they would go and inhaled the scent again. Someone had entered the building. Someone of the paranormal persuasion. Two male mages. Shit. It was the thug from last night and one other. There was a hint of one more person, but he couldn't pinpoint who it was. As if they knew of his sensory abilities and blocked him.

Fuck! There was no way to prevent them from getting into the apartment. Instincts humming, he hopped up and down and darted into his carrier. They needed to leave, now.

"I wonder what's gotten into him?" Lara asked.

Cyn gave him a look before her eyes unfocused. "Shit! Bad guys are coming." Cyn reached for the bag. "I'll take the bag. You get his carrier. Hurry!"

Cyn open the apartment door and stuck her head out. "It's clear. Come on, we've got to move."

"How do you know they're coming?" Lara whispered.

"I can feel them." Cyn replied as she led the way to the stairwell door.

"Magic?" Lara was amazed at what she was learning from her friend.

"Let's call it a heightened sense of danger." Cyn paused at the door, "They got here sooner than I expected. Hustle, they're coming up the elevator."

Cyn pulled the door open and gestured Lara to go first. "Down we go, hurry!"

Lara dashed down the stairs, trusting her friend's unusual skill-set to guard her back. When she reached the bottom, she heard a door open. "She could have taken the stairs." A male voice echoed down the stairwell, filling her with dread.

Cyn nudged her back, and held a finger to her lips. Got it. Be quiet. Lara silently opened the door. Cyn held the bar and eased it closed, making it as noiseless as possible.

"Is there a side entrance?" Cyn whispered.

"Not that I know of."

"We'll run for it. My car's out front. Let's go."

They hurried through the lobby, Cyn pointing the key fob at the black two-seater parked at the curb. The trunk popped open and she threw the bag in the back, while Lara strapped in and secured Jared.

Cyn leapt into the driver seat and revved the engine. "Fuck."

Lara glanced in the side mirror. Three men ran out onto the sidewalk, one of whom was Guido from last night. Had it been last night? It seemed like he'd held a gun on her forever ago.

One of the men was dressed in all black with a strange symbol embroidered on the breast pocket of his coat. His pressed black pants and shirt looked expensive, but it was the cold expression on his face that frightened her. Scary, scary man.

Cyn sped away, and Lara watched in the rearview mirror as Guido reached into his jacket. The man in black shoved Guido's arm and the goon yelled something. The man glared at Guido.

"Was he going to pull out a gun?" Lara asked.

"Probably." Cyn replied as traffic cleared and she careened around the corner. "Shit. Shit. Shit."

"What's wrong?"

Cyn glanced at the carrier before focusing back on the road. "It's one of the Elite. But I don't remember his name. It's on the tip of my tongue. Damn it."

Lara remained silent letting Cyn figure it out.

"Randall!" Cyn exclaimed, startling Lara. The carrier on her lap bounced.

"Sorry, Jared," Lara said. "Who's Randall?"

Cyn bit her lip and then sighed. "Jared Williams owns Jared bunny. Randall is Jared's partner." She took another turn, glancing in the rearview mirror.

"Wouldn't he know where Mr. Williams is? Maybe we could have him take us to Jared's owner."

"Bad idea. Randall was with the goons from last night. I'm pretty sure they work for Dr. Glendale. I don't think the bunny's well-being is their top priority."

"That's horrible! Why would Jared's partner want to abduct his pet bunny?"

"I don't know, but I have a feeling it has to do with money."

Lara sighed. "I don't get how people can do that to innocent animals." She patted the top of the carrier. "Don't worry, Jared, Cyn will keep us safe. Where are we going?"

Cyn smiled but concentrated on the road ahead. "Somewhere safe, but I want to make sure we're not being followed."

Chapter 7

Cyn pulled into an empty parking space in front of a gleaming glass and metal apartment building.

"Who lives here?" Lara asked. The light reflecting in the glass took on a surreal quality as the building glowed in the fog.

"Jared Williams."

"You've talked to him? He's home?"

A brief hesitation from the driver's seat. "Not exactly."

"Then why are we here?" A dull throb pounded behind her eyes. Lara rubbed her temples to ease the pain.

"This is bunny Jared's home. He'll be safer here than anywhere else," Cyn explained.

"Won't they track us here as well?" Lara asked, looking with suspicion at everyone who walk by.

"Maybe, but I'm not worried."

"Why not?"

"You'll see," Cyn answered at her enigmatic best.

The passenger door swung open, and a startled gasp escaped Lara. The doorman from the building gave her a polite smile and he held out a hand. Lara remembered to unbuckle her seat belt and allowed him to assist her from the car.

Lara held the carrier at her side and accompanied the doorman to the building. He waved her inside. She fiddled with her purse strap, waiting for Cyn.

Cyn retrieved the bag from the trunk and strode into the building.

At the far side of the wide lobby, a security guard sat at a desk, expression disapproving.

"All visitors need to sign in," he said in a gruff voice.

Lara took a deep breath as she crossed the ornately tiled floor. She could do this. She'd faced down a gunman yesterday, so a security guard should be easy, right? She glanced down at the beautiful tiles; the golds, oranges, and reds of the complex pattern caught her attention, slowing her steps. The guard cleared his throat and a wash of heat rolled up her neck.

She put the carrier on the counter, wiping sweaty palms on her jeans. The guard's attitude made her feel like she'd been caught breaking curfew.

Lara glance around for Cyn, who'd stopped to chat with the doorman.

She grabbed the pen, and wrote down the pertinent information in the visitor's log. The security guard took the clipboard and glanced at it.

"Welcome to the building, Ms. Adams."

Lara smiled. "Thanks." Oh carp, she should've falsified her name. Didn't spy types always have a couple of aliases handy? Too late now.

He glared at the carrier. A hostile scowl flitted over his expression before an impassive mask slipped over his face. "Welcome home, sir." He glanced at her. "Elevators to the left."

"Thank you." She'd navigated that gauntlet.

Lara grabbed the carrier and went to wait at the elevators. Cyn hurried to the desk and quickly scrawled on the paper.

Cyn stepped into the elevator and the doors slid closed. There was one button on the panel, L for lobby. "How are we going to get to Mr. Williams' place?" Lara asked as the elevator rose.

Neither she nor Cyn had pressed a button, why was the elevator moving? This was something out of either a horror movie or cheesy sci-fi flick. "How…?"

"Programmable elevators," Cyn said. "The security guard set it to the correct floor."

"Weird. What were you chatting with the doorman about?" Lara asked.

"I was wondering if Mr. Williams had any recent visitors."

"Besides us?"

"Yeah."

"And?"

"We're his first visitors in months."

"I'm surprised we didn't have to provide fingerprints and retinal scans."

"It won't be long before those measure are put in place. This place caters to the security conscious, paranoid types."

"Mr. Williams is one of those?"

"Yes. From what I've heard, he has more than a few enemies."

"That's why you're not worried if the bad guys find us? Because they can't get by security?"

"Yep."

"But what if they sneak in the back?"

"They can't. According to the doorman, the back door has more security than the lobby."

The elevator stopped and Lara took a step toward the door, Cyn caught her arm, stopping her. "Wait, I want to make sure it's clear."

The other woman left the elevator and skulked down the corridor. Lara held the elevator doors open and watched. "Clear of what? I thought it was a super-duper, high-tech security area?" Clandestine maneuvers and spy chases were interesting on TV, but in real life, they were hard on the nerves.

A man in a dark trench coat with fedora pulled low slunk along the corridor darting from shadowed doorway to shadowed doorway, a briefcase chained to his wrist. "Don't worry about him. That's Mr. Smith on his way to work."

Cyn came back. "All clear. Let's go."

"Answers, need some," Lara grumbled, following Cyn down the hall. Each alcove they passed had a door with a number beside it. There were no doormats, plants, decorations, or anything that would hint at the people who lived beyond the doors. It felt more like a hotel than a condo building.

At the end of the hall they rounded a corner and faced a single door.

"How did you know which one was his?" Lara asked.

"The doorman told me," replied Cyn. "Set the cage down and let Jared out."

"Are you sure that's a good idea?" Lara studied the area, scanning for possible bunny escape routes.

"Yes, he's not going to run away."

Lara set the cage down, opened the door, and held her hands out, ready to catch Jared if he hopped the wrong way.

The bunny crept from the cage, his little nose twitching as he sniffed the area. He winked at her before hopping over to the door. Did bunnies wink, or had it been a blink?

"Open the door," Cyn instructed.

Lara reached for the door handle, grabbing it at the same time Jared's nose touched the door. A jolt of electricity snapped at her fingers and she jerked her hand away, shaking the sting out. "What the hell was that?" Darn it, now she was cursing. Blowing on her fingertips, the pain eased.

Surprise crossed Cyn's face. "I don't know." She pulled a thin leather driving glove out of a hidden pocket and put it on before twisting the handle. The door opened, and Jared hopped into apartment.

"The door was unlocked?" Disbelief filled her tone. No one left a door unlocked in the city. That was asking to get robbed. "That's not very secure. Or does he leave the door unlocked because there's so much security getting up here?"

Cyn was unconcerned. "I think it's a new technology keyed to Jared's touch."

"That shocks people?" Lara thought about it for a moment. "It wasn't a very big shock."

Cyn gave her a look. "Would you touch it again?"

"No."

"Most others wouldn't, either."

"Why didn't you get shocked?"

Cyn shrugged. "Maybe there wasn't time to rebuild the charge."

Lara followed Jared into the apartment.

Cyn set the carrier and bag inside, closing the door behind her. Jared hopped to the door and sniffed, touching it with his nose. Very strange.

"Are you sure this is a good idea? Does Mr. Williams know we're here?"

Cyn smiled. "He knows, and it's not a problem."

"How does he know? I thought you said he was out of touch?"

"He is, but trust me, he'd prefer Jared bunny was secure at home rather than being locked up in a science lab, experiencing unspeakable horrors."

Lara shuddered at the thought. She could imagine a lot.

"Let's explore." Cyn bounced on her toes like an excited child.

Lara put her hands on her hips, arms akimbo, and frowned at Cyn. If Lara didn't push for answers now, she'd never get them. Cyn excelled at distracting Lara from any questions she might have.

"What's going on? Who were those men chasing us? What did they want?"

"They want Jared to experiment on, but I don't know why."

"Cyn…"

The other woman sighed. "Really, I don't know."

"Then we should go to the police, get them involved."

"No. Not police," warned Cyn.

"Why not?"

"They're not going to be able to help."

"Are you sure?" Lara narrowed her gaze at the other woman. Something wasn't quite right here. She'd always trusted her intuition about Cyn before, but the other woman's evasiveness was beginning to make her suspicious. "Just whose side are you on, anyway?"

With a cocky grin, Cyn replied, "My own, of course."

Doubt must have shown on her face because Cyn put a comforting hand on Lara's shoulder. "Have I ever given you a reason to doubt me?"

"Well, no, but…"

"I need to find out what's going on. Until I do, please, don't call the police."

"But what can you do?"

"I'll gather information and act on what it tells me."

"Will you tell me?"

"If I can."

Lara knew that some of the work that Cyn did was classified, but not everything she was involved in was top secret, hush-hush, or was it?

"Tell me what you can, when you can."

"As long as you give me time to figure it out."

Lara sighed. "How long? Twenty-four hours?"

"Give me forty-eight"

"You promise to explain?"

"Yes."

Lara gave in. "All right. But I want answers."

"Deal. Now, let's explore." An expression of glee crossed Cyn's face, as if she were hoping to uncover secrets.

Lara's focus shifted from Cyn to the apartment. A large screen TV hung from the wall on the left with a black cabinet beneath it, housing electronic equipment. Tall bookcases with cabinets on the bottom stood on either side of the tv. On the right side of the room, an oversized black suede couch was backed against the wall, with a glass coffee table in front. The wall opposite the entry was a bank of floor to ceiling windows. A desk and chair sat before the left window. The arch to the left led to a kitchen gleaming with stainless-steel appliances. To the right a short hallway ended in three doors.

A couple of picture frames sat on the far bookcase. Other than that, there weren't any knick-knacks to clutter the space. Yet the condo had a homey feel, welcoming. Unlike Preston's place, which he'd had professionally decorated, where she'd been afraid to sit on the furniture lest she smudge or mark it somehow. In contrast, the leather couch with its colorful throw invited a snuggle.

"Quite the bachelor's pad," Cyn commented as she walked toward the bookcase. Jared hopped after her. Squatting down she opened one of the cabinet doors and petted Jared; his back foot thumped on the floor. "Ooh, I haven't played this game yet," she remarked.

The more Cyn poked around, the faster Lara's heartbeat. Sweat pooled at the base of her spine. Why was Cyn invading Mr. Williams' privacy? This wasn't right. A deep breath and Lara managed to unclench her fists. "Games?"

"I play when I have time."

Cyn browsed through the bookcases. Rolling her bottom lip between her teeth, Lara crossed her arms, hands cupping her elbows. Her stomach churned like river rapids after a heavy rain.

Breathe, come on, breathe. Lara tried to do the calming exercises she'd found online, but they weren't working. *In and out, there's plenty of air, in and out.*

A sharp pain on her ankle and she glanced down at Jared. Was that an expression of worry on his face? Nah couldn't be.

She reached down and ran a shaky hand over his back.

"What's wrong?" Cyn asked, concern filling her tone.

Lara hugged herself tighter. "You're searching a stranger's house, and I don't know if Mr. Williams wants us here, and we're hiding from bad guys, and Guido held a gun on me, and…"

Putting a comforting arm around her shoulders, Cyn led her over to the couch. "Sit."

Lara pressed the fingers of her left hand against her right wrist and concentrated on calming her body, trying hard to fight off a full-blown panic attack. Cyn went into the kitchen. Cabinets opened and closed and a faucet ran. Jared hopped onto her lap, startling her.

Having had a gun pointed at her last night and being chased tonight would send anyone into a panic, right?

Cyn returned from the kitchen with a tall glass of ice and water. "Here."

Lara accepted the water with both hands and absorbed the coolness of the glass. She sipped the cold liquid, easing the tightness in her throat. She took a hand from the glass and cupped it around the back of her neck. It felt so good. She drained the glass in a series of sips, not wanting to down it all at once. With care, Lara placed the empty glass on the coffee table.

Jared twitched in her lap. As she stroked his soft fur, the tactile sensation calmed her. Heart rate and breathing slowing, Lara leaned back to rest her head on the couch cushion and continued to pet Jared.

Cyn sat next to her. "Too much for you, huh?"

Lara gave her a shaky laugh. "Just a little. Does this happen to you a lot?"

"Being chased by bad guys?" At Lara's nod, Cyn patted her leg. "Now that you asked, yeah, I guess it does happen often. Thank goodness for night classes at super-villainess school."

"I don't think I'm cut out for the life of a super-villainess. I think I'd do better as the trusty right-hand woman who makes sure the plans get put into effect."

"Cool, you can be my HHIC."

"HHIC?"

"Head hench-woman in charge."

"Sounds fun, as long as I get to stay safe in your gun-proof, bomb-proof, hero-proof, natural disaster-proof secret lair."

"Deal."

They sat in silence for a moment. Lara's mind fussed over recent events, specifically the men from her apartment, and a salient fact jumped out at her. "You said Mr. Williams and Randall are partners? What do they do?"

"They work for a specialized police force."

"A rent-a-cop?"

A startled expression crossed the other woman's face and she laughed. "Rent-a-cop? Oh good one. I'll have to remember that. But no, it's a task force."

If Randall were a cop, then he was a good guy, right? Was the bunny harbinger of doom? Was he going to upend her life more than it already was? Or could he be a fugitive from justice? An escaped pet of a criminal kingpin, making her an accessory. She took a deep breath to combat the sudden lightheadedness. "Am I in trouble for aiding and abetting?" Lara could see it now...

Locked in plastic wrist cuffs and a tacky orange jumpsuit, she stood in a courtroom full of faceless people. The judge sentenced her to twenty years for harboring a fugitive. Two cops appeared and led her down a sickly green hallway through a heavy door and into a holding cell.

"No." Cyn's voice pulled her from her vivid imaginings.

Lara rubbed her wrists, feeling the phantom pain of the restraints. "What?"

"No, you're not committing a crime."

"So why was the cop after me?"

Cyn hesitated. "I think he's on the take."

"That's why you don't want me to call them?"

Cyn nodded. "I'm not sure if it's just him or if there are others involved."

"Why didn't you just say so?"

"Because I wasn't sure the best way to sum up."

"...But the Inquisition's here and it's here to stay!" The chorus sang out, breaking the silence.

Lara smiled. It must be Cyn's torturer friend.

"Hello Hans," Cyn answered.

Lara grinned down at Jared. Was she good, or what?

"Okay. I'll meet him at the golf course clubhouse." Cyn hung up and glanced at Lara. "I've got to go."

"What's wrong?"

"Another project I'm looking into." Cyn got up, patted Jared on his head and walked to the door. "I'll be back tomorrow night. Promise you'll stay here, and don't let anyone in, other than me."

"I promise," Lara assured.

"Good night." Cyn slipped out the door, closing it behind her.

Now that Cyn was gone, the energy in the room drained away. "I feel like Alice down the rabbit hole. This is all so confusing. And I'm talking to myself again." She felt the prick of nails on her lap. "Sorry Jared, I'm talking to you, not myself." He nodded, his eyes half closed as she scratched behind his ears.

What was she supposed to do now? The two framed pictures on the bookcase tempted her. It wasn't as if she were going through his personal things, since they were in the open.

A deep breath for courage and she shifted Jared into her arms, supporting his feet against her body. She felt silly for needing him with her, but he kept the panic away. Lara wandered to the shelf before she chickened out, curiosity getting the better of her. One picture showed two young boys, the taller one with an arm slung around the smaller one's shoulder. The small one was thin and gaunt as if he was sick while the taller one seemed familiar. She glanced at the second picture and squeezed Jared.

Oh. My. God. It couldn't be.

It was the man from her dream.

§

Cyn left the apartment, pulling the door closed behind her, and testing to make sure it was locked. The door handle didn't move, Jared had locked it behind them. She neared the elevator and felt the faint psychic trace of vampire becoming stronger as the elevator neared the floor. Damn. She knew who was coming, Mr. Player himself, the very last person she wanted to see.

Sprinting to the stairwell, she eased the door closed behind her as the elevator dinged.

Feeling like the hounds of hell were on her heels, she raced down the steps, relying on her vampire speed, sure that any moment the stairwell door would open and she'd be caught. The last thing she needed to do was answer a bunch of idiotic questions about the situation. Plus, Jared didn't want her contacting the Elite. It'd be best to avoid them.

Exiting the building she rounded the front of her car and saw a note under the windshield. Shit!

"What the hell are you doing here? Call me. – J"

James, the cheating rat bastard. How dare he!

Cyn crumpled the note in her fist. While she'd love to rip the bastard a new one, she was still too raw from the pain. It'd have to wait until she calmed, perhaps in a couple of centuries? A grin lifted her lips imagining him frustrated for that long.

She had to get moving, Carlos was waiting.

Traffic in Real wasn't bad and she made it to Golden Gate Park in a half hour. She pulled into the parking area and drove to the side so her car so it wasn't visible from the road. Getting out, she met the teen as he motioned to her from behind a tree. She crept into the shadows to join him.

"What's going on?" she whispered.

"I saw the van again and followed it. I'll show you where I lost it."

He led her though the area that separated the golf course parking lot and the archery range. They skirted the back edge and through the trees. He stopped at the trail, knelt and pointed to tire tracks.

Cyn squatted down. It was a wider wheel base than most of the park vehicles, but that didn't mean anything.

"Will this help you find Uncle Jack?" Worry filled his tone.

She put her hand on his shoulder. "I don't know, but he's been missing for a couple of days. Don't get your hopes up."

"Can I help?"

"No, thanks. You've done a great job finding this." She squeezed his shoulder. "I'll take it from here."

"If you need me, you'll call, right?"

"Promise."

He nodded and melted into the trees. Most humans couldn't hear the minimal noise he was making, but her heightened senses traced him back to the parking lot.

She followed the tire tracks down the trail until they headed into a dense cluster of trees. Whoever they were had done a good job of covering the impressions made by the wheels, but a few bent sticks and twigs hadn't been covered up. She followed the trail deeper into the trees. The trail stopped abruptly. There weren't any tire tracks backing away from the area. What happened?

Cyn popped into Shadow to make sure they hadn't transported the vehicle there. The area was clear, no impressions left in the damp ground. She popped back into Real and searched. Where had the van gone? Taking a step, she saw a small red light in the crook of a tree. Surveillance cameras, out here? What was so important about a bunch of trees that someone went through considerable expense to monitor the area? Wildlife camera was the first thing that came to mind, but they weren't pointed at any nesting areas that she could find.

A metallic grinding had her ducking behind a tree. The deep-throttled roar of an engine clanked and groaned. The ground in front of the tire tracks rose to reveal a subterranean passage, wide enough for a vehicle to drive down. Very James Bond-esque.

Cyn crept toward the opening and stopped, ducking for cover as she saw two people walk up the ramp, carrying a heavy burden between them.

Damn. They carried what looked to be a body, wrapped in black plastic. After they cleared the secret entrance, they tossed it into the underbrush. "The clean-up crew will dump the body in the bay later tonight."

"I don't envy them their job. These bastards are heavy."

"One might call 'em 'dead weight'."

They both laughed and walked back down the ramp.

Should she follow the guys down or should she check out the body? The motor engaged and the access hatch closed, further limiting her options.

Avoiding the cameras, she crept toward the discarded corpse.

Had they noticed her and Carlos? No. If they had, they would have waited until the area was clear to dispose of the body.

Cyn knelt on one knee and pulled her out her pocket knife. She cut the black plastic over the face and bit her lip at what she saw.

Uncle Jack's face, bruised and bloody, stared up at her with sightless eyes.

Fuck.

Cyn left the body where it was and returned to the dirt track. She sent a quick text to Hans detailing her discoveries and shut off her phone. This was the first solid lead she had to the disappearances around the city. If she found a way into the villain's secret lair, the chances of finding the others was high. There had to be another way inside. All she had to do was find it.

§

Lara sat on the couch, absently petting Jared. It was impossible, wasn't it? How did a man she'd never met, show up in her dream?

Unless shared dreams were real?

"I'll admit, I have a vivid imagination, but to think I met your owner? I don't know."

Though it would be neat if it were real.

Someone pounded on the front door, startling her.

"Police, open the door," a voice commanded.

Jared wiggled and she realized she'd tightened her hold on him. Police. Crap.

Years of unconscious law-abiding habits had her moving toward the door to open it.

A sharp sting on her arm and she stopped a few steps from the door. "Did you bite me?" she asked in a shaky whisper.

Jared huffed out a breath.

She examined the sleeve of her shirt. The material was intact – no blood.

"Open the door!" At the command, her body flushed with heat followed by cold chills.

Lara walked toward the door and felt sharp nails dig into her skin. "I'm just going to see who it is," she whispered, gazing through the peephole.

The two men on the other side appeared scarier than goons who'd chased her. Their clothing matched Randall's; all-black with a decorative patch on the left side of their coats. The taller one had dark hair and his eyes flashed red. The shorter one had blond hair and appeared less menacing than his friend. Even if they were the good guys, deep down, they terrified her. How did she know they weren't going to hurt Jared? She didn't. She promised Cyn not to let anyone in.

She backed away from the door, keeping her eye on the door knob, waiting for them to bust in. The coffee table hit the back of her calves and she stopped. She looked around the apartment trying to find a place to hide. There.

Lara crept to the sliding glass door. There was enough space between the couch, the end table and the curtains to offer her a safe place to hide. She moved the table a few inches, allowing her enough room to squeeze behind. Lara sat and Jared was a soft weight between her chest and her raised knees. "I'll keep you safe," she whispered.

Jared responded with a soft lick to her cheek.

Two men in dark glasses and black suits opened the door. "You know too much, you need to come with us, Ma'am."

The knocking continued and the door knob wiggled.

Tension held her in an unshakeable clawed grip. She was sure they were going to break down the door at any minute.

After a long moment, the knocking stopped.

Was this a trick to get her to open the door so they could pounce? She'd give it ten minutes and go check.

"Why is it that time slows to a crawl when you want it to fly by? And speeds up when you need it to slow down?"

Lara sat with Jared, petting him as the time laboriously passed. After what seemed like ten hours, twenty minutes had gone by. She lifted Jared and set him on the floor, before emerging from her hiding spot. She crept to the door. A look through the peephole showed the empty hallway. "But that doesn't mean they're not around the corner, ready to pounce if I open the door."

Lara plopped onto the couch, a yawn overtaking her. She'd rest for a moment. "All this running and hiding is more stressful than books led me to believe." Her eyelids felt as if heavy bags of concrete were weighing them down. "Just a few winks…"

Chapter 8

Captain Jor'dan sat behind his desk listening to Damien and James give their report on Jared.

"Conclusions?" he asked.

Damien answered. "Jared is safe for now. The security on his building is top notch. Security didn't let me view the log of visitors, but we do know a human woman and vamp entered the building. While we were on our way up, the vamp fled the scene. The human is still in the apartment. We put the building under surveillance, and we'll grab the human when she leaves and bring her in for questioning."

"What about the vamp? Do we know who it is?" Jor'dan asked.

Damien grinned. "You'll never guess."

A scowl crossed James' face.

"Miss Madison?" Jor'dan asked, trying not to smile. He'd had a suspicious feeling about her the first time they'd met a couple of years ago. Not that he'd do anything about his suspicions, but he kept a close eye on her. Regardless of the relationship between her and James, he didn't want anything untoward to happen to her.

James' phone buzzed. "Hey doll... Oh, sorry about that. I thought you were someone else... Really? Thanks for keeping an eye on it for me... Can you do me a favor? Find out who... thanks... Yeah it was fun. We'll have to do it again sometime." James ended the call.

Jor'dan raised an eyebrow. "What was that about?"

"Jared's case files have been remotely accessed, but not by Jared."

"By whom?"

"Randall Jennings," James answered.

Damien frowned. "Who the hell were you talking to?"

"Clarice Jeannot."

"The human computer guru?" Jor'dan glared at James. "What makes you special enough to gain her services? I have to jump through miles of red tape with the human police for a simple request."

James looked uncomfortable.

"What did you do?" Damien asked.

"Last night I took her to the Tech Fair."

Damien cleared his throat. "Did Cyn know about this?"

James shook his head. "No, but Cyn's not into tech stuff."

Jor'dan rested his heads in his hands and took a deep breath. Was James that obtuse? "Let me make sure I understand. You're romantically involved with Miss Madison, and yet you took another woman to the Tech Fair?"

"Yes, why?"

"How old are you, James?" Jor'dan asked.

A frown crossed James' face.

Damien grinned, showing a hint of fang. "Two centuries."

Jor'dan shook his head. "How long have you been dealing with women?"

James was looking a bit confused. "Almost as long. What's your point?"

"Do you want to tell him, or shall I?" Jor'dan asked Damien.

"Go ahead. He might believe you. I still get to tell him, 'I told him so.'"

Sometimes running the Elite was worse than trying to herd cats. "James, women are very prickly when their men take other ladies out."

"But it wasn't a date." James hurried to defend his actions.

Damien smirked. "Do Clarice and Cyn know that?"

"I don't know about Cyn, but Clarice should know."

"How? Did you tell her?" Jor'dan asked, curious. James was reported to be a lady's man, who had such a way with women that even his ex's spoke fondly of him. That he was having trouble with Cyn meant she'd gotten under his skin in a way no one else had.

"Yeah, I told her it was great to go to the tech show with someone who appreciated technology," James said.

Damien clapped a hand on James' shoulder. "You're toast."

"Damn." James pulled out his cell phone, dialed, and after a brief pause, left a message. "Call me babe, I can explain. It wasn't what you think."

He hung up and Damien rolled his eyes. "As if she'd believe that, especially in that tone of voice."

"How the hell did she find out?"

Jor'dan sighed. "It doesn't matter. They always find out."

"But I didn't cheat! It was the Tech Fair and dinner."

"Don't tell me, tell Cyn," Jor'dan replied.

James tried texting, "Damn it. She blocked me. How could she block me? I've left her dozens of messages."

He appealed to Damien. "Can you see if Deidre will give her a message for me?"

"I can try." Damien pulled out his phone. "Hey love, James has a message...." He pulled the phone away from his ear and they all heard the yelling.

"... lying, cheating, no good, son of a bitch! Bastard son of J'kala, may the hounds of Dar'kirm feast upon his genitals..."

Jor'dan winced before turning away to hide his grin, coughing behind his hand. That was one pissed off succubus. Minutes later the profanities wound down, allowing Damien to speak in a soothing tone.

"Did she say how Cyn found out?" James asked.

Damien repeated the question and after a one-sided conversation, Damien hung up. "Cyn went to the Fair and saw you and your new flavor leaving."

James ran a hand through his hair. "Fuck."

"Deidre isn't going to help. And I quote, according to the bestie handbook, chapter seven, page two hundred, section four, subsection fifteen, paragraph one, states: If a boyfriend is caught lying, cheating, or otherwise behaving in an inappropriate manner and abusing his lady's affections, the aforementioned lady and best friend are entitled to burn him in effigy, create voodoo dolls in his image, and do everything within their power to make his life a living hell. Unquote."

"Damn it," James replied.

While this was amusing, they were getting far off topic. Two questions needed answers. Why was Randall accessing Jared's files, and why was Cyn at Jared's condo?

Jor'dan would take care of the first, and as for the second... "Damien, see if you can hunt down Cyn and bring her here. I want to know why she was at Jared's."

Damien winced. "It's going to be a cold day on the couch for that."

"It's important."

"If I can get the info without bringing Cyn in, would that work?"

Jor'dan preferred to question her in person, but she wasn't comfortable with him or the Elite in general. "Yes. Will you have Deidre ask her?"

"I'll try. Not sure if it'll work."

"Try it." If it didn't work, Jor'dan would sneak out to have coffee at Angelini's and accidently run into them.

"I'll bring her in," James offered.

Jor'dan shook his head. "No. You are to stay away from her, and that's an order."

"Why?"

"Because she's avoiding you like the plague, dumb-ass." Damien cuffed James on the back of his head.

"James, check out a disturbance in Golden Gate Park. Glen and Nigel found a dead body but the scene was scent free. Read the aura and find out what happened." Jordan turned to Damien, "How long to get the information from Deidre?"

"A couple of days. I'll have to convince her, and it's not going to be easy."

"I want to know as soon as you chat with her. No matter what time of day."

Damien nodded.

"Dismissed."

§

Lara stood in the center of a dimly lit room. Smokey hands reached out from the shadows, fingers grabbing, trying to capture her. Lara ran, holding her screams inside. If she uttered a sound, they'd her location, making her easy prey. Being trapped in this nightmare wasn't her idea of a good time. A horror fan, she was not.

An image appeared in front of her. A wavering picture of a little girl with golden ringlets hovered in the air. Tears streaked down her cheeks. "Please, please give me back Mr. Sweetums."

The image multiplied, surrounding Lara on all sides. Voices chimed in, echoing in the cavernous space. "Return my bunny."

First cajoling, then pleading.

"Mr. Sweetums, where's my Mr. Sweetums. I miss you."

"Return the bunny, give back the bunny." The whispers grew louder until they were screaming at her. Lara had to cover her ears to try to drown out the sound.

This was a trick. Lara knew better than to respond to the guilt trip; to the manipulation of her emotions. She wouldn't give Jared up. She had to protect him.

She'd learned not to give in, but it was hard, so hard, to resist the pictures of a little girl with tears in her eyes.

"Where's my bunny? Please I need my bunny," the little girl cried. If she spoke, if she gave in, Jared would die.

Hands grabbed at her clothing, tugging on her hair, jerking her toward the walls where skeletons and rotting bodies hung like macabre decorations. She ran, dodging the grasping hands, fleeing from pleading little girls.

"Give us the bunny and you'll go free," the voices whispered. A seductive enticement in a horrific scene. Flashes of rotting corpses surrounded her. Some reaching, others smiling maggots filled their mouths.

Lara ran, but the scenery never changed. She was trapped; there was no escape. And it all boiled over, the fear, the panic, everything was too much. Lara tucked her chin to her chest and put her arms over her head. "Leave me alone!"

Two hands grabbed her from behind. A scream ripped from her throat.

Caught!

"NO!" Lara kicked, scratched, jerked, anything to escape. It pounded through her brain, through her blood. Run, escape, run, escape.

"Shh. Lara, it's okay. It's me."

She struggled for a few moments until the voice penetrated the fog of terror.

"J-Jared?"

"Yes."

She turned and found herself in his arms. He pulled her to his chest. Surrounded by his strength, she felt safe, protected.

Lara wrapped her arms around his waist, hugging him tight. "What are you doing here?" she mumbled into his chest.

"Saving you from your nightmare."

A small laugh escaped her. "Thanks. I guess we're even."

He squeezed her. "Come, there's a cup of tea waiting for you."

Lara turned her head and checked the area. The room had changed. Gone was the dark, cavernous, body-strewn landscape. In its place, her cozy room from the last dream. The two armchairs had been replaced by a large overstuffed chair facing a fireplace. Flames crackled over the wood in a soothing, hypnotic dance.

Jared lifted her into his arms, carried her to the chair and sat with her sideways in his lap. On the end table was a steaming hot cup of tea.

He stroked a hand down her spine and she melted into him, resting her head on his shoulder.

"Mmm, this is nice," she whispered, tension seeping out of her muscles with each stroke of his hand.

"Want to talk about it?" His voice echoed deep within his chest.

Tension crept into her muscles as she fought the terror and panic that threatened to pull her under. She tried to burrow closer, to lose herself in his strength. To wash away the feeling of those ghostly hands.

"A teary little girl and hands, millions of hands. Wanting the bunny."

"What did you do?"

"I ran." Her voice was small as she considered her act of cowardice. She should have stood up to them, but her courage had deserted her and her only thought had been escape.

"Why didn't you give them the rabbit?"

"I'd promised Cyn I'd protect him. I'm... getting attached. If something happened to him because I made the wrong decision? No, I just couldn't do it."

He hugged her close and reached for the cup. "Here, drink."

Lara inhaled the soothing scent before taking a sip of the hot tea.

"Better?"

"Much. Thank you."

"It was the least I could do after you refused to give up Jared."

She sat sipping her tea, content to be held by him.

Long moments later he spoke. "What do you want as a reward?" His grip on her tightened, making his lap a bit uncomfortable. His grip on her tightened.

Lara didn't like his tone. Why was he insistent about this? Did he think she'd only saved the bunny for an accolade?

"I told you last time I didn't save Jared for a reward. I did it because it's the right thing to do."

Another chair popped into the room and Lara struggled in his embrace. Enough of this. She felt battered and beaten, and instead of comforting her, as a proper dream man, he was demanding and huffy, and it was simply too much.

She'd drink her tea and then wake up.

The chair disappeared. What the heck? She closed her eyes and concentrated. A small pop and the chair appeared again. She struggled to get off his lap. "Let me go!"

"No. You don't need that chair." With a wave of his hand, it disappeared.

Her temper spiked. "I don't know who you are or where you come from, but I know what I need, and that's not to be sitting with some well-behaved serial killer, who's ready to believe the worst of me! In fact, you can just poof yourself out of my dream. I want a different dream man!" Lara crossed her arms and glared at him.

He pulled her back into his embrace and his body softened on his exhale. "You're sweet, kind, protective, and funny. There's something wrong. You're too good to be true." She heard his mutterings, almost as if he were speaking to himself rather than her.

"I'm just me. Let me go."

"No. A sweet thing like you would be gobbled up in the cold, cruel world. You need a protector."

Lara turned to him and tried to arch an eyebrow. It was so hard to do when there wasn't a mirror. "You're applying for the position?"

"No, I'm taking it."

"Why?"

"Because you're too…"

Lara narrowed her eyes. "Too what?"

"Too sweet."

"Uh-huh."

She huffed. Gentle pressure from his hand and she found her spot and snuggled in. Why did he have to be so moody and smell so good?

"There must be something you want. What is it?" Jared asked.

Should she? Was she brave enough?

"Well?" His tone grew impatient. "You do want something. What?"

Lara bit her lip. This was it. Kiss or die. She looked at his face, and red heat filled her cheeks. Darn, this was awkward. Focusing on the unbuttoned top of his shirt, she whispered. "I'd enjoy one of those scorching hot kisses."

He went still. Maybe he didn't want to give her one? Where was a large hole to disappear into when you needed one?

A circular void appeared behind the fireplace, swirling and consuming everything in its path.

Jared waved his hand. "You don't need that."

"If I want a black hole, then I'll get a black hole."

"I thought you wanted a kiss?"

"Not if it takes you that long to work yourself up to it," she complained.

"You misunderstood. I want it too much."

"Really?"

He tilted her chin up and placed a chaste kiss on her lips.

"How's that?" he asked.

Lara frowned. "That's not funny. Now do it right."

A grin crossed his lips and a gleam entered his eye. "My pleasure."

He kissed her and time stopped. Suns spun, universes formed, and she knew nothing but the taste of him. The deep thrusting of his tongue, the nibbles of his teeth on her lips. He broke the kiss and she looked into his eyes, breath uneven. "How was that?"

She opened and closed her mouth. He'd fried her brain and expected her to answer? "Perfect," was all she could say. From his smug expression, that was the response he wanted.

Lara leaned her head against his shoulder. This was a dream. Of course, her dream man's kisses were perfect. That's what dream men did.

The crackling fire filled the silence. It was nice to be held by him. The twinges of awkwardness that she'd experienced around most men were non-existent. She could relax, be herself, and not have to worry about what he was thinking.

"You're cute, Mr. Dream man."

"I told you, my name is Jared, and what do you mean, I'm cute?" He sounded offended.

Lara lifted her head and smiled at the irritated look on his face. Her hand touched the stubble on his jaw, cupping his chin. "You're my dream man. Of course you'll say what I want to hear. That's all part and parcel of the whole dream man gig; saving fair maiden from nightmares and vowing to stand as a shield between her and adversity."

"I'm as real as you are."

"Right. I daydream a lot, and that's exactly what my subconscious would have you say."

He was sweet, this figment of her imagination.

"I have an idea."

"Okay." Lara needed more tea and maybe a couple of cookies as well.

She'd finished the thought, and a fresh cup of tea and small plate of sugar cookies appeared on the end table. Smiling, she lifted a cookie and bit into sugary, buttery goodness. The empty cup disappeared from her hand.

"You've summoned cookies, so that means everything in your dream is under control, right?"

"Sure," Lara agreed.

She heard the grin in his tone. "How did I save you from your dream?"

Lara shrugged. "My subconscious conjured up a handsome dream man to save me."

"You don't believe I'm real?"

"Nope."

"Make me do something, or change what I'm wearing," he said.

Lara paused in her nibbling. "Like what?"

"Anything."

She put the half-eaten cookie back on the plate. "Okay."

Lara closed her eyes and imagined what Jared would look like in one of those hoop dresses from the 1800's. He'd have blond ringlets, with dark stubble on his cheek... She giggled. Oh, and the dress would be pink with matching shoes and a wide-brimmed hat, secured with a band of chiffon tied in a large bow under his chin.

She opened her eyes to see him still dressed in a white oxford and blue jeans.

Hmmm, maybe she hadn't concentrated hard enough? Narrowing her eyes and staring at his chin, she tried again. Nothing.

"What's wrong?" His deep voice pulled her from her internalizations.

"It's not working."

He smiled. "That's because I'm as real as you are and we're sharing a dream. You can manipulate the environment, but you can't manipulate me."

"Or it could be because I'm touching you," Lara replied.

Jared squeezed her. "You're fine where you are."

Lara wiggled. "No. I need to test this to see."

He sighed and loosened his arms.

Another chair appeared with side table and steaming cup of tea. Reluctant to leave his embrace, she crossed to the chair and sank down into the welcoming softness.

Jared grinned at her, raised an eyebrow, and spread his hands. "Well?"

Lara closed her eyes. This time she imagined him in a hot pink flapper dress with matching fascinator. Heels, pearls, and silk stockings completed the outfit. A giggle escaped her as the vision appeared in her mind's eye.

"What's so funny?"

She opened her eyes and he hadn't changed. A picture in a frame popped into her hand. Looking at it, she burst out laughing.

"What?"

Tears streamed down her face. There he was in the flapper dress with stubble and built shoulders. She couldn't speak, overcome with hilarity. Lara held it up, showing him. The scowl crossing his face added to her mirth.

"That's wrong on so many levels," he complained. "I would have shaved at a minimum."

"S... s... sorry." Two deep breaths later and she was able to regain control of her giggle fits.

"Now do you believe I'm as real as you?"

"If you are, what are you doing in my dream, and how did you get here?" The giggles subsided and skepticism filled her. Her imagination was working overtime tonight.

"I don't know." Jared shrugged. "Is it important?"

"You're not curious?"

"About many things, yes. You being in my dream or me being in your dream? Not really."

Jared snapped his fingers and glass, dripping with condensation, appeared in his hand. It was filled with amber liquid, topped with white foam. Why would her dream man drink beer? Shouldn't he have a more sophisticated palate? Perhaps scotch on the rocks.

"You drink beer?"

"Yep."

"What about scotch?"

"Not a fan."

Wait a minute. "Do you watch sports?"

"Of course. What red-blooded American man doesn't?"

Why was her dream man doing this? Unless... he was right and they were sharing a dream? Panic rose with sharp talons, clawing away at her relaxed serenity. She needed to wake up. Now.

"Wake up. Wake up. Wake up," she chanted. Perhaps if she closed her eyes? She repeated the chant with her eyes closed. She lost touch with the chair. Her eyes popped open. He'd lifted her out of the chair. She grabbed at his shoulders.

"What are you doing?"

"Getting comfortable."

"But I was comfortable in my own chair." She protested as he sat with her in his lap.

He traced the curve of her cheek with one finger. "Isn't this better?"

"Maybe. But you shouldn't be here. I shouldn't be here. This is impossible!"

"There are many unexplained things in life. Consider this one more."

"But..."

"Shhh, you were doing so well before."

He pulled her head to his shoulder and resumed the soothing strokes down her back. By slow incremental steps, Lara felt herself relax into his embrace.

Jared reached over and brought her tea and the half-eaten cookie. She accepted both, her thoughts tumbling like playing puppies. If he was real, then she shouldn't be on his lap.

Lara tried to sit up and he pulled her back. "You're fine."

"But if you're real, I shouldn't be sitting here."

"Why not?"

"Because."

"You make a pleasant lapful."

What did that mean? She harrumphed and put her head back on his shoulder and nibbled on the cookie.

She offered it to him. "Want a bite?"

"Sure." He ate the last of the cookie.

Another thought intruded. "Do you own bunny Jared?"

"Yes."

"Is it okay to stay at your apartment?"

"Yes, Jared is more comfortable at home, plus I want you both to be safe."

"Where are you? Are you in trouble?"

"I'm safe for the moment."

"Safe? That's it?"

"Yes."

"Explain."

Jared took a deep breath. "Your friend Cyn can't tell you things because they're classified, right?"

"Yes."

"Much of what I do is classified."

"But I thought she said you were a rent-a-cop?"

Jared squeezed her in retaliation. "I'm on a special task force and that's all I can say."

Lara thought about that for the moment. "Okay. But can you tell me one thing?"

"Maybe."

"Are you one of the good guys?"

"Yes. I am."

"What about your partner?"

"He's supposed to be, but I'm not sure what he's up to."

She took a sip of tea as her mind dealt with what he was saying.

"We should go to dinner in person," Jared said.

Whoa, where did that come from? Talk about a jump in the conversation.

Out to dinner with him? If he was this forceful, dominant and sexy in her dream, how would he be in real life? It'd be better if she didn't find out. Plus, men were off her list.

"Um…"

"You're thinking too much," he whispered taking her tea cup and putting it back on the table.

His hand tilted up her chin and he lowered his head, softly touching her lips with his.

Lara's eyes fluttered closed as she gave herself up to the mastery of his kiss.

He broke the kiss and rested his forehead against hers. "Say yes, please."

Lara wanted to, but what if this was another manipulative trick? "If I say no, will you try to kiss me into submission?"

His grin melted her insides. "No, but it's a great idea."

"Oh." How was she supposed to resist him?

Jared fused their lips again. Instead of a sweet gentle caress, this was the kiss of a marauder, a pirate, and she couldn't help but immerse herself in her favorite fantasy. His mouth plundered hers, demanded her passion with strength and will that left her breathless.

His hand stroked over her shoulder, and brushed the side of her breast. She moaned, loving the sensation of his strong hands on her body.

She wrapped her arms around his neck and held on. Dear god, he kissed like all her favorite fantasies rolled into one. She might not survive. But then again, this was a dream, wasn't it?

Jared's hand nudged her breast before kneading it.

"I want skin," she mumbled.

Jared winked, and her hands trailed over heated male flesh, shoulders and chest. She could spend hours petting him.

"Get rid of your top."

Lara glanced up at his face and bit her lip.

"It's only fair. I'm topless," he replied.

Lara sighed and closed her eyes. Calloused fingers on her bare breast had her pulling in a gasping breath.

His eyes heated as his gaze raked her body. "Now, where were we?"

She wrapped her arm over her chest. The heat of embarrassment rose from her neck to her cheeks.

"Why are you hiding?"

"Because I know how I look and what my faults are."

Jared tilted her head up with the edge of his hand and kissed her nose. "Who put that poison into your head? The prick who called today?"

"Um, yes?" Wait. "How do you know about Preston?"

"I have my ways."

Lara opened her mouth to protest, and he placed a finger over her lips.

"What else did the bastard tell you?"

"How about we not discuss this?"

"No. I need to know what shit he fooled you into believing, so I know what I have to overcome."

Lara imagined a T-shirt to cover herself and it appeared on her body "I'm not comfortable talking about it with some stranger from a dream."

"Who better to help you get it off your chest?"

"Maybe, but not now."

He heaved a huge sigh. "Fine, but don't think you're going to get out of telling me."

We'll see.

"Since you won't talk, what shall we do now?"

Lara smiled. What she wanted to do and what she would do were two different things.

"This," *she whispered as her hands wandered over his chest, sculpting the firm muscles. She delighted in the reactions it brought to his face.*

Jared lifted his hand. "May I?"

Lara kept her gaze down and reluctantly nodded. He nudged her face up and his eyes locked to hers. He lowered his hand, placing it on her breast. He waited a heartbeat before, he rubbed her nipple between thumb and forefinger, sending shivers of sensation through her body. She gasped as streaks of electricity sparked through various her erogenous zones. Wicked and delightful at the same time.

Fiery heat filled her cheeks. His intense gaze never left her eyes, but still, this was... uncomfortable.

He kissed her again, tongue surging into her mouth. He tasted rich, decadent, like expensive chocolate.

Aching emptiness consumed her. She needed him now. Lara arched into his touch encouraging him to take things further without embarrassing herself by asking.

Jared trailed kisses along her jaw, down her neck, to her collarbone and then over her breasts. The heat of his tongue and the warmth of his mouth made her wish they were both naked. But it was too soon.

"No naked. Not yet," *she said in a hoarse whisper.*

He sucked on the nipple, dampening the cotton, alternating between teeth and tongue, keeping her on edge. What sensation would come next?

Jared switched between breasts and it felt as if her body was zipping down a rapid filled river, causing small zings of pleasure that locked her breath in her lungs.

A shift of her body and she lay across his lap. With one hand, he continued to play with her breasts. With the other, he unsnapped the button of her jeans.

She grabbed his wrist, stopping him. "What are you doing?"

"Playing."

Uncertainty filled her as old insecurities began to rise. What if she wasn't good enough? Would he be disappointed? Would she?

"Shh, let me play."

"But, what if—?"

Jared placed a finger over her lips. "Trust me."

Lara nodded.

"God, you're so responsive," he praised as he slipped his hand beneath the waistband of her jeans. He stroked her through her silky panties. Light, teasing touches, heightening her arousal until she was incoherent with need.

A finger slipped beneath the elastic, stroking and rubbing. Her hips tilted, inviting further touch. He petted her, brushing the edge of her opening before inserting a finger inside.

Oh, that felt good!

She arched within his embrace, wanting him deeper.

"Please!" Lara demanded. Though what she was begging for, she wasn't quite sure. "Don't stop."

"I won't. I'm not a bastard."

He bent and kissed her, his hand stroking, caressing, until molten lightning coursed through her body, burning every memory of another's touch, leaving only him, only Jared. She screamed into his mouth as the sensation turned into an explosion of glorious fulfillment.

Lara drifted like a feather on the breeze, floating down to a languid sea of relaxation. His fingers withdrew and she missed the connection. Lara opened her eyes. "Thank you."

Jared rose with her in his arms and carried her to the bed she'd imagined last time. He laid her down and crawled into bed next to her, pulling her into his side, her head rested on his shoulder, his arm cradling her.

Mmm, this was nice. She missed cuddling. She realized, Jared hadn't... Well he'd not orgasmed.

Lara tried to move but his arms tightened, holding her in place. She tilted her head, looking up at him.

"What about you?" she asked.

"What about me?"

"You didn't orgasm."

"This was for you."

"But—"

He squeezed the breath out of her.

"Not all men are greedy assholes."

Lara leaned up and placed a soft kiss on his lips. "Thank you."

Her lassitude lasted until a jarring noise intruded.

"What's that?" Tension pulled at her.

"Time to wake."

Chapter 9

The shrill scream of fire engines yanked Jared from sleep. He jolted up, rabbit instincts urging him to hide. *Shit, not again.* He automatically started his breathing exercises. Long moments later, his heart rate returned to normal.

Jared stretched paws instead of hands. Damn it, he was still a bunny. Concentrating, he reached for his human form. Nothing. *Fuck.*

Blanket-covered legs twitched in front of him. The hollow created by the curve of Lara's legs made a comfortable nest. She'd fallen asleep on the couch and started shivering during the night. His attempt to pull the throw from the back of the couch had failed and had woken her up long enough for her to flip the blanket over herself before falling back to sleep.

Jared leapt over her ankles and hopped down to the floor. In the corner between the entertainment center and his desk, was a litter box for the times he spent in rabbit form. After taking care of business he hopped back to the couch to wake Lara. A wave of premonition ruffled his fur. Something bad was going to happen today, something that involved Lara. Damn it. How the hell was he going to protect her?

Lara pushed back the blanket and stretched. He stared, transfixed. Man, he could watch that all day. "Mmm. I had a fabulous dream last night. About your owner. It ended much too soon," she said.

She sat up and he hopped over. She bent down and scratched behind his ears. Oh yeah, that felt goooood.

"You know, it's funny. Part of me wants him to be real, because wow, can that man kiss. On the other hand, dealing with the complications of a male ego would get tiring fast."

I don't have an ego. I just know what's right. His back teeth ground together, as she hit a spot.

"Today is going to be a great day."

Disbelieving, he tilted his head to the side and stared up at her.

She smiled at him. "It's got to be better than yesterday, right? I'm being positive."

Was she one of those cheerful morning people, an optimist seeing the world through rosy-hued vision? The past two mornings she'd been cheerful, but was that her standard, or was it a defense mechanism against the stress she'd suffered? He tended to be a grouch before vanquishing the morning vapors with hot coffee. If this relationship was going to work, she'd have to drop the chipper cheerfulness… wait.

What the hell?

What relationship? There wasn't a relationship. Yes, he was attracted to her, but all he needed was a hot night of steamy sex and she'd be out of his system. There wasn't any permanency here. *But there could be,* his inner voice suggested. *Weren't you wishing otherwise?*

Lara's stomach rumbled. "Breakfast first. Do you think Mr. Williams would mind if I raided his pantry?"

Jared shook his head no. He had no problem with her eating whatever she found.

He hopped after her as she walked into the kitchen to scrounge for breakfast. "Tea. The man doesn't have tea," she muttered while peering into the fridge and cupboards.

Jared didn't have tea. He drank coffee, not boiled twigs.

A bowl of cereal for her and a plate of leafy greens for him. Man, he was starting to miss real food. Bacon, eggs, sausage, and coffee. His mouth watered thinking about it. But this form was vegetarian. He'd found out the hard way. Rabbit digestive tracks couldn't handle animal proteins. He'd been sick for days, even as a human. Eating meat as a man wasn't a problem. It was when he tried to eat it as a bunny that he'd become ill.

Jared watched, amused as she hand-washed the dishes then wiped down the countertops and sink.

"Now for a shower," she announced.

He hopped down the hall after her, enjoying the smooth glide of her walk and getting a good view of her ass. Mmmm, that ass. He imagined the feel of it pressed against him as he took her from behind. The urge to mate became a haze across his vision. Seeing her naked was a treat he didn't intend to miss a second time.

Lara stared at him. "I don't think so. Today I'm showering alone. You can wait out here."

Lara closed the door before he could hop into the bathroom. His breath huffed out. Damn it. His system, energized from the dream last night, was primed and ready to go. His thoughts weren't helping matters. The water started, and he pictured her naked, water beading on her skin, sliding down her body as she soaped herself, caressing her skin with soft hands.

Jared's hips twitched, once, twice. He clenched his entire body to keep his hips still.

Breathe through it; control the mating urge.

He was the master of his body. Lust didn't control him. It took a while but he was able to hop without humping air. The water stopped.

Visions of Lara caressing her body with a soft towel, rubbing it over her lush curves, had his hips pumping again. Fuck. He needed to think about something else, anything else, to get his body to behave.

She'd said she wanted tea. Not a good idea for her to leave the apartment when he couldn't protect her. How could he get her to stay inside, now that she'd been keyed into the security system?

He settled down in front of the bathroom door and began to brainstorm.

Could he reverse the permissions? Maybe, but the answer was in the paperwork he'd been given when the security system was installed. That information was in the locked drawer of his desk. There was no way to access it in this form. And if he were human? He had other options to keep her occupied. The first of which involved tangled sheets and a long sweaty day in bed.

His little hips thrust once. Damn it. Stop thinking about taking her to bed. Think about other things. Like how the hell was he supposed to change back?

Jared concentrated again. This time he felt a small flicker, but it died, leaving him stuck.

Fuck.

The door behind him opened, jerking him from his thoughts. A foot to his side sent excruciating pain radiating throughout his entire body. He screamed before he could control the sound.

Lara crashed to the floor in front of him.

A cry of pain escaped her. Damn it, she was hurt. The urge to care for her overrode everything else. Until he tried to hop. His body protested, and a sharp twinge sent electric currents of agony to his limbs. Damn, it hurt to breathe. With great care, he lay flat on his belly and drew shallow breaths waiting for the worst of it to pass. He'd trained his brain to ignore pain while in the military, and needed to work on ignoring the pain in this form.

The throbbing eased so he took a hesitant step toward Lara. He reached her and licked the back her hand, worried that she wasn't moving.

A soft groan and her hand swung out, he jerked back to avoid the blow. Fuck! The agony was intense. He collapsed to his side and focused on breathing.

Lara opened her eyes. She was on her side on the floor. What happened? She'd left the bathroom and tripped on something.

"Ouch." There was a tingle in her hands and knees from the impact. She rolled to her back and when no other body parts protested, she pushed herself into a sitting position against the wall. Lara sucked in a deep breath as her pain pulsed in her right wrist with every beat of her heart. Okay, she'd hurt her wrist, but was anything else wrong? It was hard to get past the pain, but she managed. Rotating her various joints assured her nothing besides her wrist was injured.

Jared was laid out on the floor, breathing labored.

"Oh God! Did I hurt you?" She scrambled on her knees to his side. At the last minute, she remembered to reach out with her uninjured hand. She stroked his side and it didn't feel like anything was out of place. He shook his head, relaxing as she petted him. She kept her touch light to avoid further injury.

"Why were you sleeping in front of the door?" Lara shook her head. "Why do I expect you to answer me? Can you hop?"

Jared got to his feet, each movement slow and deliberate. He tried a small hop, but stopped.

"You're hurt. Let me get some ice and we'll figure out what to do next."

Standing was difficult without the use of one hand. Tucking the injured wrist against her chest, she went into the kitchen and began her search. Finding baggies in one drawer and an ice maker in the freezer, she filled two bags with ice. One went over her swelling wrist and she carried the other back to the bathroom.

The bunny wasn't where she'd left him. "Jared?"

His little tail disappeared into the bathroom. "What are you doing? You shouldn't be moving. Stay right where you are."

She entered the bathroom and put the second bag on the counter. "What were you trying to do?"

Jared stared at the cabinet door.

"You want something from there?"

He nodded once.

Lara sighed. Now she was imagining that he was communicating with her. Giving into her flight of fancy, she opened the cabinet and saw a familiar box with a red cross on it. "Perfect."

She bent to retrieve it became momentarily dizzy as the blood rushed to her head. Sitting on the toilet she waited for the vertigo to stop. There was a soft weight next to her foot. Jared leaned against her, resting his chin on her toes. She leaned down and scratched behind his ears.

He gingerly hopped away and Lara knelt on the bathroom carpet. She wouldn't have as far to fall if she lost her balance. She reached into the cabinet and grabbed the first aid kit. Inside there was a long bandage, perfect for wrapping her injured wrist.

Wrapping it, however, proved to be a challenging endeavor. After several minutes of tugging and rewrapping, she managed to wrap the ice pack so it was secure against her wrist without her having to hold it. "It isn't pretty, but it'll work." Her wrist felt better with the ice and support.

In the first aid kit, were packets of individual doses of popular over-the-counter medications. She removed a couple and put them in her pocket.

Jared took several test hops, seeming to get stronger as he moved, but it was hard to tell. "Dang it, do you need to go to the vet?"

Jared shook his head.

"Okay, but if you're not better later on, I'm risking it." Lara pulled her lip between her teeth. "You shouldn't be hopping, and I don't want to risk injuring you further by picking you up. I guess that leaves creative problem solving."

Using the toilet and the cabinet door to gain her feet, she stood for a moment to check if the dizziness had passed. No vertigo, great!

Lara grabbed one of the oversized bath towels and spread it out on the floor. She set the second bag of ice in the middle of the towel and covered it with two smaller hand towels. "Your magic towel is ready. If sir would care to hop on?"

He stepped carefully onto the towel and lay down on the ice.

Lara clutched the two corners of the towel in her good hand and tugged him out of the bathroom, down the hall, and into the living room, providing a smooth tension for an even ride.

"That's about all the oomph I have in me today." She bent over and bunched up the towel so it made a nest. There were so many things she didn't know, and not having access to the mass of information that was the internet drove her crazy. Examining the books on the shelves, she didn't see anything that would help her. No books on bunnies, or basic rabbit care.

Lara sat on the couch. "You know, for having gotten a good nights' sleep, I'm exhausted."

She used the arm of the couch as a pillow and stretched her legs out. "I'll just rest my eyes a bit."

It was early afternoon before she woke. Her entire right side, from wrist and shoulder to hip, ached. Over the counter meds to the rescue.

There was a thump on the floor. "Jared?" She sat up, wincing at the movement. "Are you feeling better?"

Jared hopped around the chair, cocked his head and nodded.

"It looks like your hop is stronger," Lara said.

She tried to rotated her right hand, but there was too much pain and swelling. "My wrist still hurts. I hope it's only sprained and not broken. I need more drugs."

Jared whipped around to stare at her.

Lara smiled. "Drugs of the pain-relieving kind."

Heading to the bathroom, she popped pain meds and brushed her teeth. It took longer than normal because wielding the toothbrush was difficult to do left handed.

She removed the water-filled baggie from around her wrist and dumped the water in the sink. Lara grabbed Jared's baggie on her way to the kitchen. "Do you need more ice?"

Jared shook his head.

Lara refilled the ice, re-wrapped her wrist, and resumed her seat on the couch. "Ever notice how you can stay home, whiling the day away doing nothing, but as soon as you're stuck at home, there's a bunch of errands you need to run, places you need to be?"

Jared hopped up onto the ottoman, then to the couch and settled himself on her lap.

Lara pet him with her good hand. "What shall we do this afternoon?"

He focused on the TV.

"You want to watch something?"

He thumped his back foot.

She reached over to the remote, and through trial and error, managed to turn everything on. Keeping the sound on low, she dozed off and on for the rest of the afternoon.

Lara woke to darkness. The clock showed a few minutes after five. She yawned and stood, stretching her good arm above her head. Napping helped, but her throbbing wrist made deep sleep difficult.

The ice had melted and she dumped it in the kitchen sink.

Back in the living room, she glanced out the window into the foggy night. A rumble from her belly reminded her she'd skipped lunch. "What requires minimal effort, and can be eat left-handed?" A simple meal of cheese and crackers worked for her, with more leafy greens for the bunny.

"I wonder if Cyn will be by?"

Jared froze in place. In small degrees, he maneuvered to stare at the door. Perhaps he'd heard something.

"What is it?" Like he could answer her. But he'd done well enough with yes or no questions, so she tried that. "Is it Cyn?"

He shook his head.

Damn. "Is it dangerous?"

Jared nodded once.

"Can they get in?"

He shook his head, and she released her pent-up breath. "As long as I don't open the door, we're safe, right?" He nodded again.

Jared snuggled into his nest and watched her with an air of expectation.

She sat down, studying the remote and finding the channel selector. After a couple of passes up and down the channels, she settled on the local news.

A heavy knock sounded at the door. "Not going to answer it, right?" she whispered to Jared.

He thumped in agreement.

The knock sounded again, somehow instilling urgency, demanding to be answered. Now.

Palms sweaty, she rubbed them on her jeans before taking a couple of calming breaths. With each knock, her heart rate rose, until she jumped up and paced to the window and back, anything to work of the nervous energy filling her system.

Maybe it's a door-to-door salesman or a pizza delivery guy. She didn't think so, but she was trying to stay positive, right?

Peeking out of the spy hole in the door, her breath caught. It was the guy from yesterday, the one who had chased her from her apartment. "What did Cyn say his name was, the guy bad guy? Randall?"

He knocked again and she backed away from the door. *We'll outwait him.*

With that affirmation in mind she waited. The silence lengthened. No more knocking. Tension locked her muscles. This was killing her. The fear threatened to turn her into a sobbing ball of incoherency. She checked the door again. This time the hallway was empty. Relief filled her like warm water, melting away the panic. Safe. She felt safe again.

Lara collapsed onto the couch. "I'm not cut out for spy games. I prefer reading about it instead of experiencing it." Reaching down, she petted Jared.

The newscaster's urgency drew her attention.

"Two people were shot this afternoon at the main branch of the San Francisco Public Library, sources confirmed. Both victims appear to be employed by the library and are being treated at local area hospitals. No word yet on their condition. Police are canvassing the area searching for two men in their mid-thirties. Witnesses say two Caucasian men were seen with the victims before the shots were fired and screams were heard. If you have any information, please call the police hotline number on your screen. We'll bring you more information as it becomes available. Now, onto the weather…"

Lara jumped to her feet. "Oh my God! That's my library!"

She stared at Jared in horror. "Could they have been looking for you? How could someone do that?"

Her thoughts careened into each other like bumper cars. "I need to find out if they're all right. Doreen would know. I'll call her and get the story."

"Now where did my purse go?" She found it on the floor, pushed toward the back of the couch. She peered in all the usual pockets for her cell. "I put it in here yesterday, didn't I?"

The last time she'd used it, it had been beeping at her as it ran out of juice. Dang. It was at home on the charger. "Carp, it's at home. There should be a phone here somewhere, right?"

She searched the kitchen, both bedrooms, and ended in the living room near the desk. "It figures your owner wouldn't have a land line. How do I call Doreen?"

Lara looked out the window and surveyed the street below. "I didn't think those existed anymore." The phone booth was the answer to her problem. "I wonder how much a call costs nowadays?"

Digging in her purse, she pulled out a handful of change. "Hopefully this will cover it." She smiled at Jared. "I'll be right back. I need to make a quick phone call."

Jared hopped up and down, protesting her decision.

"I know I promised Cyn I'd stay here. But I have to make sure my friends are all right. I know you'll be safe here. I'll be back in a couple of minutes. It shouldn't take me that long to contact Doreen."

She hurried from the apartment. Thank goodness, the elevator arrived within a few seconds.

Lara rushed through the lobby, ignoring the security guard and darting out the door, narrowly avoiding two men dressed in black. "Excuse me." She tried to step past them and a hand grabbed her arm, swinging her around.

"What have we here?"

Chapter 10

In a van with blacked out windows, parked down the block from Jared's apartment, Damien monitored the live feed from the security system on the twentieth floor. Behind him, James rummaged around making coffee.

The interior of the van was separated into three parts. The cab where the driver and passenger sat; the surveillance section; and the transportation section for prisoners and persons of interest, that was isolated from the rest of the van by a thick steel wall.

The surveillance section was filled with flat panel screens mounted to the walls, electronic bits and pieces secured in a small cabinet next to a mini fridge with coffee maker on top. Four chairs, two on each side of the van, finished the interior. Very high tech and incomprehensible to Damien. Not that he couldn't understand it, he chose to leave the techno-babble to James.

The entire van had been imbedded with a variety of complimentary spells and medallions, making it theft-proof, water-proof, ice-proof, fire-proof, magic-proof, curse-proof, elemental-proof and proof against all other abilities of Paranormals. Hell, it was even RPG-proof. All in all, a damned expensive piece of equipment.

"How do you think Cyn and the human got in?" James asked slumping in the second swivel chair. "What the hell was Randall doing there?"

"No idea, but that's one of the questions I'm going to ask him."

"Do you think Cyn's involved in something nefarious?" James asked, concern coloring his voice.

"Maybe. How well do you know her?"

James grabbed his hair in frustration. "That's the problem, I don't. I believe she's hiding something, and I didn't press the issue, because she's nervous around the Elite. I know lots of things about her, but it's all surface stuff."

"Like what?"

"Her favorite food, her favorite color, and her unhealthy love of shoes. Shit like that."

"What about her family?"

"Every time I ask, she evades. Didn't seem right to push it, and I'll find out eventually. What about Deidre. Does she share?"

"No, she keeps her secrets. As for Cyn, you'll need to grovel. You fucked up."

"Think that'll work?"

Damien sighed. He was the last person to be giving advice on difficult females, even though he was involved with one of the most contrarian of them. "What do you think?" he said, the sarcasm heavy.

A worried expression crossed James' face. "I don't know. Has Deidre heard from her?"

"Not that she's said."

"Is Deidre going to chat with Cyn about Jared?"

Damien stared at the monitor. "I forgot to ask."

"What? Why?"

"Because we were busy doing other things," Damien said.

"All the things I'm not," James grumbled.

"You got it."

"Of the two of us, I never imagined you'd be the first to settle into domesticated bliss."

Damien hadn't thought so, either. "I never thought either of us would settle down." He admitted.

James frowned at him. "Why not? I love the ladies."

Damien didn't want to get into this now, but clearly James was floundering. "You might love the ladies, but you never take them seriously. It's all surface shit. You never let them in past a certain point. And if you're frustrated with Cyn not sharing deeper stuff, what makes you think she's happy with the distance you've been keeping?"

James was quiet for a moment. "It's hard."

"Trust me, I know." Damien rubbed at his chest and the phantom pain where an ex tried to cut out his heart.

James toyed with a couple of buttons on the keyboard.

Damien clapped a hand on the other Vamp's shoulder. "Is Cyn worth it, in the end? Because if you can't open yourself up to her, don't bother trying to get her back. She'd be better off without you."

"I'm lost without her."

"Then you need to grovel and mean it. Now, how does all this shit work?"

James patted the equipment with a fond hand. "It's the latest in surveillance technology. Clarice and I worked on it for a month to get the bugs out. It's able to tap into an existing security system and provide a live feed without security personnel knowing anything about it."

"Sneaky."

James grinned. "Yep."

Damien was getting warm. He removed his duster and it clanked when he threw it on a chair. What the hell was in his coat? "Did you ever tell Cyn you were working with the human?" He dug though the pocket and rolled his eyes. Deidre didn't. Yes she did.

"No."

Damien pulled a Slinky from his pocket. "That was your first mistake. No wonder Cyn thinks you're cheating on her."

"But it's not like that. It's a work relationship. I didn't cheat."

Damien set the metal spring toy on the counter. "You've never treated a woman so badly before. What's the deal?"

James sighed. "It's stupid. Cyn was being secretive and shy. Clarice was open and genuine in her appreciation."

"Your ego fell for it."

"Yeah," James admitted.

"How far did it go?" Damien started to play with the toy to keep his hands busy so he didn't smack his friend upside the head.

"Nowhere. It's the damnedest thing. We went to dinner, had drinks, and that was it. She tried to kiss me and I turned so it was a peck on the cheek."

"Let Cyn go."

"I can't. I'm fascinated by her, I want to learn all her secrets, damn it."

Damien shook his head. "Are you sure that's what you want? Why? She's not exactly your ideal." One James had spouted off about on more than one occasion. A biddable, sweet woman, willing to let James make all the decisions, the total opposite of Cyn. "Didn't you want…" He held his hands out in front of his chest. "…large tits?" From what he'd seen of Cyn she was a B cup at best.

"My ideal changed when I met her." A serious expression crossed James' face and he glanced away. "She's funny and witty and has a smart mouth that begs to be kissed." In a soft voice he added, "The days are cold and lonely without her."

"Well, you fucked it up good. You broke her heart, and her trust, and neither are easily mended."

James looked at him. "How did you rebuild trust with Deidre?"

It was Damien's turn to sigh. "I haven't, not completely. She's still wary, and it's something that I have to live with. It's getting better, but fuck, it hurts."

James' phone rang. "Hello, Captain. The only visitor in the last twenty-four hours was Randall. No, he didn't get in. We haven't seen anything on the monitors yet…"

Damien grabbed his arm and pointed to the screen.

A door slammed via the speakers on the hidden camera. Watching on the main feed, they saw a young woman running down the hall toward the elevator.

"Hold on. The human is leaving Jared's apartment…okay, we'll bring her in." He beamed at Damien. "She's in the elevator. Let's go."

128

Damien led the way out of the van. He stopped within feet of the entrance to the building. "Be ready in case she heads the other direction."

The woman rushed out of the glass doors and glanced around. Her wide-eyed look indicated alarm.

She spotted something behind them and moved to walk past. "Excuse me."

Damien caught her arm, pulling her to a stop. "What have we here?"

The woman struggled. "Let me go!"

"We want to ask a few questions." He had to give her credit. She didn't cower.

"Not now, it's an emergency. Let. Me. Go!"

The woman twisted her arm in his grip at the same time she kicked his shin. Surprised, he let her pull free and she escaped.

Within two steps, James grabbed her wrist, swinging her around to face them. He twisted her arm behind her so she couldn't flee.

§

Lara screamed. The brute grabbed her right wrist, the one she'd injured earlier. Waves of agony flooded her system with sharp shards of pain traveling up her arm and spreading until it filled her body. Black and white dots obscured her vision, narrowing until the world turned to shades of gray. She stumbled, losing her balance. With her wrist locked behind her there was no way to brace herself. A firm arm around her waist prevented her from hitting the ground face first.

Arm trapped between her and the goon behind her, she was lifted from her feet and carried down the sidewalk. The men spoke, but she didn't register what they were saying—she was too busy concentrating on not throwing up, on breathing through the pain.

Ahead of her, the rear doors of a van opened up and she was thrown into the cargo area, landing against the unyielding metal floor. Thankfully she landed on her left side, sparing her right wrist from further injury. More bruises. The doors slammed, shutting her within absolute blackness. The lack of light was disorienting as well as frightening.

Darn it, the bad guys captured her after all. She should've stayed in the apartment and had Cyn call Doreen. Carp! Doreen! With much groaning and wincing, she rolled to her knees. Her arms were free. Thankfully her abductors hadn't secured them with handcuffs or other restraints. The van jerked forward and she fell on her side.

Lara rolled to a sitting position. She felt around with her free hand, tucking her right against her chest. Smooth metal met her questing fingers; maybe there was a handle or something she could use to open the doors.

Acceleration of the van smashed her into the rear doors, face, shoulder and bad wrist hitting at the same time. A small scream escaped at the intensity of the pain. Bastards! They drove like maniacs, turning corners, stopping and accelerating as if they were racing the Indy 500. She felt like a human pinball, bouncing from side to side, doors to walls. It was giving her the mother of all migraines.

The good news? Her wrist didn't hurt as bad. The bad news? Her entire body was one agonizing ball of pain.

Think Lara. Think. How was she going to get out of this?

Escaping into her own mind, she imagined her dream man coming to save her.

Gunshots fired and echoed in the still night. The van lurched then slowed. More gun shots were fired. Muffled sounds of fighting seeped through the doors. Just when she thought all was lost, the back doors opened and she was lifted into strong arms.

A gentle hand brushed the hair from her face. "It's all right love. I've punished them for hurting you."

He held her in his arms and the two men who'd attacked her were lying on the pavement, unconscious, blood dripping from their noses. Police surrounded them, praising Jared's quick action. Paramedics arrived, and Jared cradled as they examined her. Once they returned to his apartment, he laid her down on the bed, bathed each scratch, and kissed each bruise, until the remaining sensation was the pleasure of his touch.

§

"Shit, shit, shit," Chuck cursed under his breath.

He pulled out his phone and called Glendale. "The librarian has come out of the apartment, as you planned. But there's a problem."

"Now what?"

"The Elite grabbed her before I could."

Chuck held the phone away from his ear as the string of curses increased in volume. Once Glendale was done ranting, Chuck spoke.

"Do you want me to watch the apartment or follow the girl?"

"If Williams is still a rabbit, there's no way he can get out of the apartment. Follow the girl. S..ee where they take her and report back," Glendale said.

"You think they're working with your spy?"

"Doubtful. I'll let him know. Maybe he can get her away from them and use her as leverage to retrieve Williams."

Chuck hung up and followed the van. It pulled behind Elite HQ, and he wasn't going any further.

§

The van came to an abrupt stop, knocking her into the sidewall, pulling her out of her fantasy. No gunshots. Darn. Two doors slammed closed. The double doors opened, letting in a rush of air. One of them reached in, grabbed her upper arm in a punishing grip, and jerked her from the cargo hold.

Lara blinked at the sudden light. She stumbled to the ground and her muscles screamed as her legs collapsed under her. Her hip hit the ground. Her body was covered in bruises, what was one more?

Fear shivered up her spine. What were they going to do to her?

She was yanked upright. On unsteady feet, she searched for help or a way to escape. Steel and concrete towered high into the sky. They were in a deserted loading bay devoid of witnesses. No one to recognize her predicament, or to come to her rescue if she screamed.

She opened her mouth and took a deep breath. Perhaps the sound of her yells for help would echo among the buildings alerting someone to her kidnapping. A hand clamped over her mouth, fingers pressing hard against her jaw.

"There's no one to hear you scream." A dark whisper in her ear. "Now are you going to cooperate or shall I knock you unconscious?"

The hand lifted.

"I'll walk." Lara tried to hide her fear, but her voice came out high and shaky. Desperate, she glanced around, hoping for something that would help her escape. Cyn could rescue her; anytime now.

"Good."

A shove at her back pushed her up concrete stairs to the loading dock, where she tripped on the top step and fell. Darn it, she was getting tired of being hurt. She lay where she was. Hopefully, they'd decide she wasn't worth the trouble. Nope, the dark-haired man picked her up and slung her over his shoulder.

Heartbeat echoing in her ears, she tried to breathe through the threat of her earlier meal of cheese and crackers making a reappearance. The shoulder in her stomach wasn't helping. Her vision dimmed, and she felt her muscles go limp. She was tired. So darned tired. Lara embraced the darkness as it enfolded her in comforting arms.

§

A stinging slap to the face propelled Lara into a waking nightmare. She tried to move, tried to get away from that slapping hand, but something prohibited her body from cooperating. Lara opened her eyes. Carp. Coarse rope secured her body to the chair, with her wrists locked behind the chair. Her injured wrist throbbed in time to the pulse of pain in her head.

"You're awake." The dark one, she'd call him Tony, walked to the table.

Carp, it was the police guys who were at the door yesterday. Tony and the other guy who looked like a Crazy Joe.

In front of her was a wooden table with two chairs on the opposite side. On the wall behind the chairs was a darkened window. Probably a one-way mirror. Who knew how many bad guys were hidden behind it?

The cinderblock room was small and dark, the only illumination coming from two lights hanging from the ceiling. It resembled an interrogation room from a gangster movie.

And her without her super spy gadgetry, darn it.

Lara bit her lip and took a deep breath and froze. Ouch. Her ribs protested. She'd have to take shallow breaths from now on.

She shifted in her seat and the dull ache of pain that had been in the background surged through her veins, leaving burning agony behind. *Would it kill them to offer a Tylenol?* With her luck it'd be some hallucinogenic drug she'd be allergic to.

Her two kidnappers, Tony and Crazy Joe, sat behind the table.

"Now that you're awake perhaps you'd care to answer a few questions," Crazy Joe said.

Not bloody likely. Lara remained silent, knowing if she opened her mouth, she'd bawl like a baby. How did those strong silent types deal with the pain? She rolled her lips inward and bit them to keep the pain and the words locked inside.

"What is your name?" Tony asked.

What is your quest? What is the air speed velocity of a swallow in flight?

She tried to suppress a giggle, which put pressure on her ribs. She panted to get enough air.

Where was a brave knight when you needed him? She'd even take the not-so-brave Sir Robin at this point.

Crazy Joe and Tony exchanged a look. "I don't think she's ready to cooperate," Tony said.

Crazy Joe smiled at her. Yeah right, as if that were in any way reassuring. She held her ground and her tongue, not knowing what would happen next.

Tony raised an eyebrow. "It'll go better for you if you cooperate."

A voice spoke inside her mind. *"Just answer the questions, and you're free to leave."*

Lara mentally snorted. Bad guys never kept their promises.

"Answer our questions."

"I'm not telling you anything. You're just a crazy voice my mind has invented in order to help me deal with this. Go away," Lara thought back at the pushy intruder.

Tony frowned and rubbed his temples.

Crazy Joe glanced at his friend, then back at her. "We just want a few answers."

"Why should I answer your questions?"

"You're a person of interest in an ongoing case," Tony said.

"What case?"

"We can't answer that," said Crazy Joe.

They were still pretending to be cops. "You've kidnapped me, caused injury to my person, and now you want information? No."

"Answer the question," the mental voice commanded.

"Screw. You."

"Why were you in Jared's apartment?" Crazy Joe asked again.

Lara kept her mouth shut and concentrated on breathing. The rope tied around her torso put pressure on the bruises on her ribs and she focused on the pain.

"How did you get into the apartment?" Tony asked.

Lara shook her head, stopping when the room waved in and out. Too bad the sensation triggered nausea. She wiggled her fingers, which had fallen asleep. The sensation of pins and needles was uncomfortable, but not unbearable. Great, her hands were losing circulation.

"Look, could you undo these? They hurt."

"Not until you answer our questions. Where is Jared Williams?"

134

That's what she wanted to know. It'd be best to play dumber than she was, for now. "Who?"

"Jared Williams, the man whose apartment you were in."

"I don't know who you're talking about," Lara responded.

"How'd you get into the apartment?" Crazy Joe asked, looking meaner by the second.

"The front door." Lara bit her lip. She hadn't meant to say that. Oops.

A small smile flit across Tony's face before he become stern. "There's no need for sarcasm."

Lara snorted. *Yes, there is*.

Crazy Joe slammed his hand on the table startling her into jerking back. Which sent the low-level thrum of pain into high frequency, and their words buzzed, incomprehensible, in her ears.

"This isn't getting us anywhere," Crazy Joe complained.

"We don't have time for this shit." Tony stalked to the metal door, jerked it open and with a last glare at her, left the room.

Her wavering attention snapped to Crazy Joe.

"All we need is your cooperation and you're free to go."

If she believed that, they had some lovely beach front property in Reno they'd sell her.

Silence stretched between them. While she appreciated his trick, she was feeling too horrible to succumb to that form of manipulation.

The door opened again. What the heck? Tony entered the room with by a tall, thin man with straight blond hair that reached halfway down his chest. Eyes the color of ice chips. Did he have pointed ears? The elf double grinned, but it didn't reach his eyes.

"Has she answered the questions?" Legolas asked.

"She's being uncooperative," Crazy Joe replied.

"The hard way, then." Legolas approached and cupped her face in both his hands. Electricity slammed into her mind. Screams filled the room. Whoever it was needed to stop it right now. Images and memories flashed before her eyes. A burning sensation built in her brain before it was all too much. Painful darkness engulfed her.

§

Jared hopped back and forth in front of the door.

Where the hell was Lara? It didn't take this long to go to the corner to make a phone call.

He concentrated on shifting. A small tingle meant something happened, but it faded as his concentration waned, leaving him rabbit-bound. Damn, in this form the door knob was two feet out of reach, leaving him stuck.

What the hell should he do now? There was nothing to do, except wait. *I hate waiting.*

Vampiric energy penetrated the door as the knob turned. He stretched his senses, but Cyn was alone. Where the hell was Lara?

Cyn opened the door, looked down, and grinned.

"Hey Jared. How's it going?" she paused for a moment, leaned down and scratched behind his ears. "Sorry, forgot about the yes no thing. Did you have a good day?"

He shook his head, *hell no.*

Cyn closed the door behind her and sat cross legged on the floor. "Is Lara around?"

He shook his head again.

"Damn it! Where is she?"

Jared faced the TV where the news was repeating the top stories.

"Crap. She wanted to check on her co-workers?"

He nodded.

"Why didn't she call?"

There was no way he could answer that question so he didn't try. Jared didn't have a landline and Lara didn't have her cell. He wished he had the ability to communicate mind to mind, but rabbit vocal cords did couldn't make human sounds.

Cyn pulled out her phone and dialed. Jared sighed. She wasn't going to get an answer.

"Call me asap." Cyn left a message and put away her phone. "She doesn't have her cell phone, does she?"

He shook his head.

"I'm going to go look for her. Do you have any idea where she might be?"

This bobble-head stuff didn't make him sick, but it got old. Jared nodded, hopped to her, and pawed at her phone.

"She went to find a phone?"

Bobble nod again.

"You don't have one here?"

Head shake.

Cyn pet him for a bit and his legs thumped on the floor as she hit a good spot. "I'll find her and bring her back."

Her cell phone rang, startling them both. Cyn checked caller id. "It's Bar'ella. Hey, how's the outbreak? Good. I'm with him now. Elite HQ? Why there?" Cyn sighed. "That's the last place I want to be. I know, yes, fine. It'll take us a half hour to get there."

Cyn put her phone away and scratched between his ears. "Okay, we're headed to the office. Bar'ella wants to meet us there. But if that rat bastard is there, I'll stake him and you can nibble his jugular until he bleeds out."

Jared cocked his head in a questioning manner. "You want to know who? That two-timing cheating son of a bitch, James."

Jared rubbed his face against her leg, trying to offer sympathy. She pet his ears. "Enough about him. Do you have clothes you want me to bring?"

Jared hopped to the hall closet door and scratched at it. Cyn followed, and pulling out a small duffel bag. "This it?"

Jared hated to leave in case Lara came back, but once he regained his human form, he'd look for her, himself. *Hold on for me.* He hopped over to his carrier and got in. He didn't appreciate being caged, but his animal felt comfortable in the enclosed space.

Cyn picked up his bag and the carrier. "Let's go."

§

The human female slid to the floor as Luesar released the bonds holding her to the chair

"Bring her here," Damien said, patting the wooden surface.

Luesar lifted the human with ease and placed her on her side on the table.

"She'd be more comfortable without the restraints." Luesar said, releasing the handcuffs. Damien peered at her hands. One wrist was swollen twice the size of the other. "Damn. We broke her wrist."

The phone rang, and James answered. "Right. Be right there. We need a healer... okay."

"It's not well done to break your toys," Luesar commented without inflection.

James shrugged. "It gets the job done."

"I forgot how fragile humans are," Damien said.

"You're wanted in the Captain's office. The healer Bar'ella is on her way," Luesar reported.

"What about you?" James asked.

"My presence has also been requested."

Damien picked up the human, careful not to add to the myriad of bruises blooming across her delicate skin.

James led the way through the underground maze of corridors, intentionally set up to confuse anyone who escaped their cell. They'd become lost in the twists and turns and be easily recaptured.

Damien took extra care passing through doorways, falling behind the others.

When he got to the Captain's office, pandemonium reigned.

Chapter 11

The carrier jostled when Cyn removed him from the car. Jared's senses were on high alert as they entered Elite headquarters in Real.

"Damn it, I don't want to be here," Cyn complained in a whisper.

That made two of them. Predatory energy permeated the air, putting the rabbit on edge.

Cyn stopped at the reception desk and put the carrier down on the floor. "I'd like to see Captain Jor'dan, please."

"Purpose of your visit?" the man at the desk asked in a bored tone.

Jared missed Cyn's response, focusing on the approaching threats. One saving grace that protected him from the predators was the Elite had to be on their most secretive behavior. The office was located in one of the rare nodes. It existed in Shadow and Real at the same time. Which meant there were always Elite around to take care of any problems, along with humans wanting their problems solved.

He sensed a Tiger shifter approaching. The rabbit, relying on instinct, froze.

The view outside the cage shifted when Cyn lifted the carrier and walked toward the security enhanced steel door.

Once through the door, Cyn whispered, "Are you as uncomfortable as I am here?"

Yes, but how to answer her?

He thumped his back foot against the bottom of the carrier, once.

"One thump for yes, two for no?"

Jared thumped again.

"Here we go. Hope the Captain is in and the rat bastard is out," she said.

The door to the Captain's office was closed.

"I don't like the feel of this. I should put you down, knock on the door, and leave. You'll be safe here, right?"

He thumped hard twice. There was no way he'd be safe here. And if he didn't miss his guess, Randall was sneaking up behind them.

Cyn knocked on the door, and Captain Jor'dan's voice bid them enter.

Randall reached them. "What the hell are you doing here?" he demanded.

Get into the room, get into the room. If Randall captured him, he'd be delivered to the lab within minutes.

Cyn opened the door, put the cage and duffle down, and pushed them into the room.

"I have an appointment with the Captain. What are you doing here?"

"I work here," Randall said, condescension filling his tone.

"Really? I thought you were a bad guy." Jared grinned at the sarcasm dripping from her voice. "If you'll excuse me?"

"Does James know you're here?"

"No, but I expect you to rush off and tattle." Cyn entered the office. The door slammed and he heard Cyn's sigh of relief. "That was too close, Jared."

"Jared?" Captain Jor'dan asked.

Someone lifted the cage and placed it on the desk. He froze.

"Miss Madison, why do you have him? Are you responsible for his condition? What were you doing tin his apartment?" Captain Jor'dan began his interrogation.

Cyn snorted. "If I was responsible, would I be stupid enough to bring him here of all places? Wait, don't answer that. I was in his apartment to keep him from being bunny-napped and returned to a lab for experimental purposes. Don't look at me as the villain here. Look to your own."

"That's enough, Jor'dan." Bar'ella said. "You can finish questioning her after I check Jared."

Cyn peered through the bars at him. "The room is clear. It's only Bar'ella, your Captain and myself."

Jared let his senses flair out. No enemies near. Randall stood in the hallway outside the door, and after a moment, he strode away.

He hopped out of the carrier and onto the desk. Being the center of attention unnerved, him and he had to force himself not to hop back into the carrier.

"What's going on with Randall?" the Captain asked Cyn

Cyn glanced at Bar'ella who gave a slight nod. "I believe Randall is responsible for Jared's condition."

"How?"

Cyn shrugged. "I don't know. This is his third attempt to capture Jared that I'm aware of."

Bar'ella approached the desk. "Jared, can you change into human form?"

Jared closed his eyes and reached for his human body. Once again there was a slight flicker, then nothing. Disappointed, he stared at Bar'ella and shook his head.

"Hmm. Let's see what's going on."

The healer extended her hands and a soft golden glow surrounded them. He felt the glow like a soft ouch along his fur as she stroked her hands over him.

"Interesting."

Jared glanced up at her and tilted his head in question. She grinned. "Sorry. Talking to myself."

"What is it?" asked Captain Jor'dan.

"I can't get Jared to change. Something's wrong."

Reaching down out of sight, she lifted a black medical bag from the floor and put it on the table. Bar'ella opened it and dug around inside. "Damn assistants, nothing is where it needs to be. Ah here it is."

She pulled out a couple of items, but he couldn't get a clear view of what they were.

"Jared, I need to draw blood."

He inhaled twice and flopped an ear forward.

"Will you remain still?"

Jared reined in the instinct to jerk away. He was in a secured location and should be able to hold still. He nodded once.

Bar'ella stroked a soothing hand down his back, and his body relaxed. It wasn't as calming as Lara's touch, but it worked.

"Is there anything we can do?" Captain Jor'dan's question seemed to come out of the blue.

"Yes, sit here and pet Jared. Long slow strokes down his back."

Cyn sat in one of the visitor chairs. He was deposited on her lap and she began petting him. Jared was able to ignore the slight sting of the needle as he concentrated on the hand stroking over his fur.

Pressure was exerted on his ear and then eased. Bar'ella moved back to her bag. "I need to get back to the clinic to run the blood work."

Cyn continued the slow strokes. "How long will it take?"

"I'm not sure. It depends on what I find." Bar'ella paused. "Cyn, can you stay?"

"That's a bad idea," Cyn protested.

Bar'ella re-packed her bag and picked it up, turning to Cyn. "I want someone in the room with Jared at all times. That'll be hard for Captain Jor'dan to do."

Having Cyn here would be a good idea, and until he could defend himself Jared had to rely on others. And from what he'd seen, Cyn knew how to fight.

"Are you sure he's in danger?" Captain Jor'dan asked.

Bar'ella turned to him arms akimbo. "Jor'dan DúSan, you know very well he's in danger. He's not safe here among the predators. Someone did something to lock him in this form and until I can get him back to human, Cyn can guard him."

"What can she do against my Elite?"

Bar'ella raised an eyebrow. "More than you think. The least she can do is call for help."

The Captain backed up a step and held out his hands, palms up, in a gesture of surrender. "I'm sorry I asked."

Bar'ella gathered her things and headed for the door. "I'll return as soon as I can."

Cyn continued to stroke Jared's fur, but there was a slight hesitation, as if she were now uncomfortable.

"You handle him well," Captain Jor'dan said.

"I've never pet a bunny before. It's nice."

Captain Jor'dan sat behind his desk and leaned forward with elbows and forearms flat on the wooden surface.

"How did you find Jared?"

Cyn stilled. "A friend found him, and I helped her out."

"Where is this friend?"

Jared wanted to know the same thing.

"I don't know. She went missing a couple of hours ago. I'll find her once I'm done bunny sitting."

Captain Jor'dan paused before asking, "Why didn't you bring Jared here when he was first found?"

Cyn scratched him behind the ears before answering. "He was safe where he was until Randall found them."

"Why didn't you call and tell me about Randall?"

Cyn snorted. "I hate to break this to you, but the Elite are the last people I'd call. Let's just say I've run afoul of your help before."

"Does it have anything to do with James?" Captain Jor'dan asked.

A deep breath left her. "It's complicated. But even if he and I were on good terms, I still wouldn't have called."

Captain Jor'dan spoke softly. "He'll find out you're here and come looking for you."

"I know. If I had any other option, I wouldn't be here right now."

"What are you going to do?"

"I'll think of something."

Captain Jor'dan tapped the pen on his desk. "I don't want to interfere, but I think you should hear him out before doing anything rash."

"We'll see." Cyn hesitated. "There is something else…"

When she didn't continue, Captain prodded. "What?"

"Has anyone said anything about humans disappearing off the streets?"

Captain Jor'dan shook his head. "No one has brought it to my attention. Wouldn't this be a SFPD matter?"

"Not if they were being abducted by paranormals."

Captain Jor'dan's eyes narrowed. "Tell me."

"I've seen the kidnappers in action."

"And why didn't you report it?"

Cyn scoffed. "Like you'd make a case of disappearing homeless humans a top priority."

A tingle of knowing went through Jared. This matched what he'd been told by his snitch. He hopped a couple of times on Cyn's lap.

"I think Jared is trying to tell us something," Cyn said.

"Does this relate to your investigation?" Captain Jor'dan asked Jared.

Jared tilted his head to the side. *Maybe.*

Captain Jor'dan fiddled with his pen. It was something he did when thinking hard about something. He looked at Cyn. "Do your hostile feelings toward the Elite mean you can't work with us?"

"It depends on who my liaison is." Cyn said.

"Are you willing to work with Jared?" the Captain asked.

Cyn paused in her petting. "Work with him, how?"

"That'll be up to him." Captain Jor'dan looked at Jared. "When you regain your human form, I want you to look into the disappearances."

Jared nodded once.

"I have one last question for you." Captain Jor'dan addressed Cyn.

"Will it piss me off?" she asked.

"Probably."

"You can ask, but I can't guarantee I'll answer."

The Captain stood up and went to the window with hands clasped behind his back. "I've heard rumors of a street fighting paranormal female. Have you heard anything about her?"

Cyn froze beneath Jared. "I... I've heard of this person. That's all I can say."

Why was Cyn lying to the Captain? She hadn't done anything wrong... oh. Jared thought back to the night Lara found him. Cyn fought with a stealth and cunning most Elite couldn't hope to match. Which, from what he remembered from the rules of Shadow Earth, was illegal.

It broke one of the greatest taboos in Shadow Earth. Females were allowed to mate and reproduce, and that was it. Few were allowed to work, but each had to be approved by the Council through a rigorous process beforehand. Jared had to wonder how the paranormal women stood it, considering their human counterparts enjoyed freedoms denied them.

"Can you pass a message to her?"

"I can try."

"Tell her to be careful. Her actions have been noticed and reported."

"Are you interested in finding her?" Cyn asked, her hand gripped Jared's fur, before relaxing.

"Not at this time. However, if further reports are made, I'll be forced to bring her in."

"I'll pass the message on."

Captain Jor'dan returned to his desk. "Thank you." His phone rang. "Yes?"

"I'll be right there." Captain Jor'dan switched his attention back to Cyn and Jared. "I'll return soon. Lock the door behind me."

He left and Cyn stood with Jared in her arms. She placed him on the floor and locked the door. "And just to make sure no one comes in..." She propped the chair they had been sitting in under the door knob.

Jared tilted his head. *I don't think that'll work.*

Cyn shrugged. "Hey, it works in the movies."

She sat on the floor and he hopped over to her, settling in her lap and getting pets.

"I need to leave soon. I'm worried about Lara," Cyn said.

That made two of them. The first thing he was going to do when he regained his human form, was to check on Lara.

A knock on the door startled him. He could feel tension invade the Vamps body.

Judging by the auric signature, Randall had come to visit. Fuck. A small burst of magic meant the locked door wasn't an effective barrier.

"Shit, I don't think the chair is going to hold after all."

The chair slid against the tile floor as the door pushed open.

"Yeah, I didn't count on a spell," Cyn whispered. "Go hide."

He hopped off her lap and studied the room. Under the desk appeared to be the best hiding place, but he couldn't get there without crossing Randall's line of sight. The shadow next to the bookcase would have to do for now.

He hid himself and settled to watch the confrontation.

By the time Randall entered the room, Cyn was leaning against the desk, her arms crossed.

"Captain, I have a report…"

"He's not here," Cyn said, stating the obvious, "but you knew that didn't you?"

Randall arched an eyebrow. "I admit nothing."

Jared watched the mage scan the room, eyes widening when Randall saw him.

"Jared. There you are! We've been looking all over for you." Randall approached Jared, and Cyn stepped in front of Randall. The unexpected obstacle stopped him.

"Out of my way, vamp." Randall sneered.

Cyn put her one hand on her hip, shifting her weight to the side in a belligerent pose that shouted challenge. "I don't think so."

Randall scoffed at her. "You're out of your league."

"Maybe, but you're not getting Jared."

Randall lifted his hand and backhanded Cyn. The expression on the mage's face when she dodged the blow made Jared wish for a camera. Cyn struck back with a kick to the stomach. The fight was on.

Punches and kicks were exchanged with lightning speed as the fight ranged around the office. Jared couldn't help but be impressed by Cyn's speed and skill. Both of which seemed to enrage the mage.

146

"Fighting is taboo for females." Randall grunted when her foot connected with his ribcage.

"Yeah, and the Elite are supposed to be upstanding members of the community, not backstabbing assholes, but you don't see me complaining."

"I'll take great pleasure delivering you to Reconditioning."

"You and what army?" Cyn taunted.

A sound in the hallway distracted Cyn for a moment and Randall took advantage, pinning her against the wall, his arm pressed against her throat.

"You lose. This should teach you to go up against your betters."

Cyn smiled. In the space of a heartbeat, she was no longer under Randall's arm but behind him. He bent over, gasping for breath. She'd used her knee, and Randall never saw it coming. Jared wanted to cheer. She swept the mage's feet out from beneath him.

Randall crashed to the floor.

The office door swung open and bounced off the wall.

James entered, stun gun drawn. "What the hell is going on here?"

Randall wiped a thin trail of blood from his lip and got to his feet, wincing.

"Restrain her. She attacked me as soon as I entered the office."

James glared at Cyn. "Is this true?"

Cyn crossed her arms over her chest, leaned against the desk, and remained silent.

Randall grabbed her arm. "You're under arrest."

Captain Jor'dan entered the room. "What's going on?"

Chapter 12

Captain Jor'dan walked into mayhem. Randall was bleeding from his lip, James was pissed, and Ms. Madison glared at them both.

Bar'ella pushed James out of the way, scowling at Randall until he released Ms. Madison. Cyn and the healer exchanged a hug and began catching up.

"What happened?" Jor'dan asked.

James and Randall spoke over each other. Cyn and Bar'ella's voices added to the rising cacophony. Jor'dan shook his head unable to identify individual words over the noise.

Luesar entered the room, followed by Damien carrying a battered and bloodied human woman.

Jor'dan rubbed his temple, feeling the headache build. He'd reached his limit. If he didn't get things under control soon, he'd be down for a week dealing with the physical repercussions of stress.

Cyn rushed over to Damien, yelling at him. James grabbed one of her arms and Randall grabbed the other. The noise level rose.

"ENOUGH!" Jor'dan yelled. Silence filled the office. "Damien, who's that?"

"The human from Jared's apartment."

Cyn opened her mouth, and Jor'dan held up a hand. "Ms. Madison, you'll get your turn." Jor'dan focused on Damien. "What have you done to her?"

"She got hurt on the drive over."

"Put her on the couch for now." The vampire lowered the woman to the soft cushions and stood, leaning against the bookcase.

Bar'ella knelt near the woman, putting her bag on the floor. One thing down, many others to go.

Jared's aura was between the bookcase and the wall; he was safe for the moment. Next on the list was Randall, James, and their captive.

"Release Ms. Madison, both of you," Jor'dan ordered. The angry expressions on their faces paled in comparison to the rage on Ms. Madison's. "Do it."

They released her and she rubbed her arms. She marched to the couch and crouched down, taking a damp cloth from Bar'ella, cleaning the wounds on the human's face.

"Randall, what happened?" Jor'dan asked.

Randall narrowed his eyes in anger at Cyn. He pulled a linen square from his pocket and wiped the blood from his face. He stood at attention. "Sir. I'm placing this vampire under arrest. I came to interrogate her, and she attacked me."

Cyn squawked in outraged but subsided at Jor'dan's look.

"Why did she attack you?"

Randall shrugged. "I don't know."

Jor'dan studied Cyn. "Did you attack Mage Randall Jennings?"

Cyn's eyes widened, and an innocent expression crossed her face. "It was self-defense."

"Liar," Randall accused.

"Stop," Jor'dan ordered. "Randall, what are the charges?"

Randall ticked them off on his fingers. "Kidnapping an Elite with intent to harm, aiding and abetting a known criminal, obstruction of justice, physically attacking an Elite, and illegal use of physical combat."

One of Jor'dan's eyebrows went up. That was quite a list. "What do you say to that?"

"The mage can shove the charges up his ass."

Randall stepped toward her, face contorting with fury.

Bar'ella hid a snicker behind her hand and nudged Cyn, who sighed. "Fine. I'm innocent of all charges."

"Do you have a witness who can testify on your behalf?"

A beautiful smile crossed her face. The vamp had a plan. "Of course I do."

Randall scoffed. "Her partner in crime."

Cyn sneered at Randall. "Not at all. In fact, my witness is unimpeachable."

"Who is it?"

"The same man you're after, Mr. Jared Williams, of course."

James grabbed Cyn's arm and yanked her to her feet. "Jared? Where is he? What have you done with him?"

Cyn jerked her arm out of his grasp, rubbed her shoulder, and glared at him. "I'm not telling you a fucking thing."

The situation was spiraling out of control. Jor'dan put a halt to further conversation. "Silence! Randall, you're dismissed. I want a full report on my desk before you leave today."

The mage stared at Ms. Madison. "What about her?"

"I'll conduct the interview myself."

Randall glared at Cyn and left the room, muttering under his breath. Jor'dan recognized a shimmer around the door. What spell had the mage had cast? Was it for the vamp, for Jared, or both?

Jor'dan looked at Luesar. "What do you have to report?"

The elf straightened away from the doorway and stood at attention. "I probed the human's mind. She found the bunny and took him home, treating him like a spoiled pet."

"Did she have anything to do with him being trapped in rabbit form?"

"No."

"Thank you, Luesar." The elf nodded and left the room.

"How is she?" Jor'dan asked Bar'ella.

"Stable for the moment, I need to do a further check to make sure I've located all her injuries."

Now to untangle the rest of the mess. "Have you found a cure for Jared?"

Bar'ella glanced around. "Yes, but where is he?"

Cyn detoured around James to the bookcase. She picked Jared up, holding him protectively in her arms. She rubbed his head between his ears.

Jor'dan patted the wooden surface of his desk. "Bring him here."

Jared's ears flattened out. "You want to see her?" Cyn asked.

Jared nodded once. Cyn carried him to the couch and set him down next to Lara. "You beat her up?" Cyn turned to James, an expression of anger on her face.

James shrugged. "She got a little banged up, she'll heal."

Cyn snarled. "She's human; they take longer to heal. She's going to hurt for a long time, asshole."

"I'll heal her when I'm done with Jared. Please bring him to the desk." Bar'ella moved to the remaining visitor chair.

Jared shook his head.

"Before?" Cyn asked.

Jared nodded.

Jor'dan cleared his throat. "That's not a good idea. We'd have to blindfold her to keep our secrets."

Jared tilted his head, patted Lara's hip with a paw, and hopped to Cyn.

"Damien, shut the door. We don't want others watching the process," Bar'ella ordered. "James, go get him something to wear."

"Yes, ma'am." James glared at Cyn. "Stay here."

Cyn crossed her arms over her chest and raised her eyebrow. "Why, are you arresting me?"

James glared at her. "Not yet."

"Then I'm out of here."

"Stay."

"Fuck. You."

"Don't tempt me, sweetheart."

Jor'dan cleared his throat. "James," he warned.

James scowled at Cyn and left the room. Ms. Madison gave the door a one-fingered salute, and picked up a duffle bag by the door.

"What's that?" Bar'ella asked.

"Jared's clothes," Cyn replied.

"Why didn't you say something before?" Damien stepped away from the bookcase.

Cyn rolled her eyes. "Because I'm sick of his bullshit and I don't want him anywhere near me." She knelt next to the human on the couch. "I'm worried about Lara. She hasn't woken up yet. Did the elf do something to keep her unconscious?"

"I don't know." Damien answered.

Bar'ella pulled a syringe and vial from her bag.

"Are you sure this will work?" Jor'dan inquired.

Bar'ella filled the syringe. "I hope so."

§

Oh God.

Lara hurt. From the soles of her feet, to the tips of her fingers and everywhere in between. There wasn't an area of her body that wasn't sore.

Dull pain pulsed through her with every beat of her heart.

What happened?

Memories returned in a haze. Some elf wannabe had messed with her brain, and it felt like it was two sizes too big for her skull. She'd been kidnapped, thrown into the back of a van, and used as a human pinball.

Whispering voices tempted her to open her eyes. Should she play possum and wait for a moment of weakness to escape? Was movement even possible?

She cracked one eye open. She was in an office rather than the interrogation room. Great, they'd moved her, and who knew what else. One of the kidnappers was leaning against the wall to her right and an older woman with white hair approached the desk with a syringe in her hand.

On the desk was Jared. How had he gotten here? Last she remembered she'd left him safe back in Jared's apartment. The old woman grabbed Jared by the scruff. No!

152

She had to save him. *Come on adrenaline do your thing!*

Lara leapt from the couch and stumbled toward the desk. Arms wrapped around her from behind, stopping her.

"Stop! Leave him alone!" Her hoarse shout didn't travel far.

Lara kicked and squirmed, but the arms tightened and lifted her off the floor, removing all leverage.

She hissed at the stabbing pain in her ribs. *Carp, please don't be broken.*

Her wrist was trapped between her ribs and the arms that held her. Agony. Could she endure it? Black spots swam in her vision. A few blinks didn't seem to help. But she had to save Jared.

The thought became a mantra. *Save Jared.*

"Be still." A deep voice spoke next to her ear. It sounded like Tony. Carp, carp, and double carp.

She struggled. Jared was her priority.

"Damien, release her."

That voice. "Cyn?"

The guy, Damien-not-Tony, dropped her to her feet and she stumbled away from him.

"I'm here," Cyn replied. Her friend put her arm around Lara's shoulders, supporting her weight.

"Cyn, what's going on? Don't let them hurt Jared!"

"B hold up a moment," Cyn said. The woman with the white hair stopped, her gaze moving between Lara and Cyn.

Cyn lifted Lara into her arms and carried her to the couch, setting Lara on it. Cyn flopped next to her. "It's going to be okay. They're going to help Jared."

"Is he still hurt? He didn't want to go to the vet." Guilt filled her. She should have taken him in the moment she'd been able.

Cyn grabbed both of her hands. "Lara, look at me." Lara considered her long-time friend, and the expression of sincerity etched on her face. "I promise you, it's going to be okay."

Tears gathered in Lara's eyes, blurring her vision. "They hurt me, Cyn. I didn't do anything wrong, and they treated me like a criminal. Are you sure they're not going to do the same to Jared?"

Cyn squeezed her hand. "They're not going to hurt him. Trust me."

"But they're bad guys, aren't they?"

"Only some of them."

Lara leaned in. "Like Tony over there?" she whispered.

Cyn whispered back, "Who's Tony?"

Lara pointed at the dark-haired kidnapper sporting an amused expression on his face.

"His name is Damien and he's a good guy."

"I think he needs to re-check his definition of good guy."

There was a snort from across the room. Cyn grinned. "Probably but he thought you were a bad guy."

"Even bad guys deserve better treatment."

"I know. I'll make sure to pay them back with interest for you, okay?"

"Okay."

"Now, let's let the doc...uh...vet, help Jared."

"Why didn't you tell me she was a vet?"

Cyn bit her lip as if trying not to smile. "You never asked."

The white-haired woman arched an eyebrow. "I've been called many things before, but that's a new one." She injected Jared with something and stepped back.

Twinkling lights surrounded Jared. "What has she done?" Lara whispered.

"You'll see." Cyn whispered back.

The lights engulfed the bunny, hiding him from view. They coalesced into a vortex. Black night filled the center of the void and expanded two feet away from the center. The spinning increased. Lara fought the hypnotic effects of the swirling lights being sucked into the heart of the vortex.

The next instant a blinding flash of light filled the room. Lara squeezed her eyes closed and still saw red dots on the inside of her eyelids.

"Lara." Wait. That voice sounded familiar. What was Dream Man doing here?

Lara opened her eyes. Jared sat on the edge of the desk. Dear Lord have mercy, he was naked. Lara's gaze ran over his well-defined shoulders and chest. Down to… yes well.

"Jared? You're real? Not just in my dreams?"

"You've dreamt about him?" Cyn visually examined him head to toe. "Very nice."

Lara elbowed her. "Hey, no ogling my dream man."

Jared hopped from the desk and strode toward them.

Her eyes roamed. He was delectable, very naked, and very happy to see her. He snagged her hands and pulled her up into his arms. The pain in her body became nothing more than background noise as he held her in a gentle embrace.

"What is going on? Am I dreaming?" she asked. It was the only explanation for such strange events. How often did bunnies change into humans? Or maybe that was their secret power? Lara fought a giggle. Now was not the time for hysteria.

The stroke of a finger-tip along the side of her cheek pulled Lara away from her wild imaginings.

"It's not a dream," he assured her.

Right. If she believed that he had beach front property in Las Vegas to sell her?

"I'll explain, but first, I want Bar'ella to examine you."

Lara held her hand up in protest. "No thanks. I'll go see my doctor. I don't think a vet can help."

"She is a doctor."

"Uh-huh. I'm at my limit. I can't deal with anything else," she said in a low voice.

Jared hugged her. "Please, let her look at you, and then we'll go home."

Lara wrapped her arms around his waist and breathed in the scent of him. It was the same as her dream. "Not yet."

A throat cleared behind him. "Get dressed while Bar'ella checks out your young lady."

Lara peeked around Jared's shoulder. A man wearing grey slacks and shirt, leaned against the desk. Amusement lurked in his chocolate brown eyes.

Lara held on to Jared. He was her safety. Her world was spinning out of control faster than she could deal with it. Jared may have sensed her rising panic because he began to pet her. His hand stroked down her spine, firm and somehow comforting. If only he weren't so happy to see her, everything would be okay. The hard length against her belly, on top of everything else, was simply too much.

Cyn stepped into her line of sight. "Let your hottie go. Bar'ella will make sure you're healed, then you can take him home and play doctor," she winked.

Heat flashed into Lara's cheeks and she ducked her head, tucking it into his chest, getting an eyeful in at the same time.

Dang it, where was a hole to disappear into when you needed one? Lara waited for the hole to appear like it did in her dream.

As Lara shuffled to the couch, all the previous aches and pains blasted her with their presence. Cyn sat next to her. "Your dream man has a fine ass," Cyn remarked as they watched him catch a pair of jeans, bend over to slip his feet into them, and pull them up over his very squeezable backside.

"Yes, he does."

Jared glanced over his shoulder at her and winked.

Lara squirmed at the wink then hissed in pain. It reminded her of all the ways she shouldn't move, ever.

The woman, or doctor, or was she a vet, named Bar'ella smiled and sat on the other side of Lara. "He does have nice ass-ets," she grinned.

Lara squirmed closer to Cyn. "I'll go see my own doc."

"Nonsense, I'm here now. Regardless of what Cyn may have told you, I'm a doctor, not a veterinarian."

Cyn shrugged. "Hey, you work on animals as well."

"Ms. Madison," the man who sat on the other side of the desk, chided Cyn.

Cyn grinned at Lara. "Sorry, Captain Jor'dan."

The dark one, Damien, paused at the door. "Don't forget to erase her memory."

"Damien." Jared, now clothed, addressed the other man.

"Yes?"

"You're responsible for her bruises?"

"More or less."

Jared punched Damien in the mouth. It happened so fast that he fell back against the door. Lifting his hand up to his mouth, he wiped away a smear of blood.

"What the hell was that for?" Damien glared at Jared and stood away from the door.

"You hurt her."

Damien was silent for a moment and bowed his head. "Fair enough." He left the office, pulling it closed behind him.

Jared grinned at Lara, "Now let's see about you."

A hum came from Bar'ella, and her hands glowed.

"I must be imagining things," Lara muttered.

The doctor gave her a startled glance. "What were you imagining?"

"Sorry, I have an overactive imagination. I thought I saw a golden glow coming from your hands."

"No need to be sorry. What hurts?"

A snort of laughter escaped Lara's control. *Ow, no laughing, either.* "The question is, what doesn't hurt?"

The woman smiled. "Okay. What doesn't hurt?"

"Nothing."

Jared knelt in front of her, incredibly sexy in his white button-down shirt and faded jeans. He captured her hands in his until she gasped at the pain in her wrist.

"Wrist still paining you?" he asked.

Lara frowned. "How did you know I hurt it?" Then her brain provided the answer. Jared bunny had been there, so Jared human would know about it? Maybe?

"I'll explain everything later," he assured her.

Cyn patted her shoulder. "Bar'ella will fix you right up. She's healed me many times. It's been nice catching up with you and everything, but I need to get going before the rat bastard gets back." She glared at Jared. "Take care of her. She's a friend."

"I won't hurt her."

"There's hurt and then there's hurt," Cyn warned.

"She'll be safe in my care," Jared promised.

Her friend bounced to her feet and left the office before Lara could protest.

Jared sat in Cyn's place and put his arm around her shoulders.

Bar'ella leaned over and grabbed her black bag, opened it, and began rummaging around. Lara halfway expected to see a lamp, a bowling ball, or some other odd thing come from the bag.

Eyes feeling like they weighed a ton, Lara closed them for a moment, letting Jared support her.

§

Jared hugged Lara to him, accepting her weight and trying not to touch any of the colorful bruises blooming beneath the collar of her coat.

"Lay her down. I need to make sure I get every injury," Bar'ella said.

"What did you do?"

"I put her to sleep. I don't want to cause her further pain when I heal her."

Jared stood and positioned Lara so she was supine along the length of the couch and stepped back.

"Multiple bruises, most bone deep, fractured right wrist, hairline crack in three of her ribs," Bar'ella recited as she traced Lara's body with her glowing hands.

Captain Jor'dan's voice came from behind the desk. "Anything life threatening?"

"No."

"Please, heal her," Captain Jor'dan requested. Bar'ella raised an eyebrow and he continued. "She was hurt by members of this office. The least we can do is to make sure she's returned to optimum health."

"I'll send you the bill," Bar'ella promised.

The glow from her hands intensified, and spread to encompass Lara. The bruising faded and Jared released the breath trapped in his lungs.

"Jared."

He glanced over his shoulder. "Yes, Captain?"

"You're on leave for the next week."

Jared was prepared to argue, but Bar'ella's hand on his arm trapped his protest. He turned back to her. "Jared," Bar'ella said. "I want you to take it easy. I don't know how long the drug will remain in your system or if there will be side effects. No shifting for seventy-two hours. Call me immediately if anything happens, and I'll see you at the clinic in two days."

"Yes ma'am."

Captain Jor'dan spoke. "What caused your shift?"

Jared ran a hand through his hair. "I don't know. The last thing I remember was breaking up the fight between the wolves and the tigers. Randall and I subdued the kids, there were congratulatory backslaps, then a sharp sting in my shoulder, and I woke in a pet carrier in the library."

"Stay away from Randall. Take your lady and go rest for a few days" Captain Jordan ordered.

Now that was a task he'd enjoy. But first. "I need your computer for a minute." The Captain agreed and Jared logged onto the machine and navigated to his personal cloud where all his research was kept. He copied the specific files to Captain Jor'dan's computer. "This is the information I've been gathering. It's not complete, but if anything happens to me, you'll have it."

"Thanks."

"Don't thank me yet, not until you've analyzed it. You're not going to like it."

Jared glanced at Bar'ella. "Will she be okay?"

"She'll be fine. With a bit of rest, she'll be as good as new." Bar'ella gave Jared a steely look. "I've put her out for a couple hours. Let her rest."

"Yes ma'am."

Her eyes narrowed. "Have I told you how much I hate being called 'ma'am'?"

Jared tried to keep his expression innocent, but a grin slipped through. "I figured it out on my own."

Captain Jor'dan spoke again. "If the human says anything about today's events, her memory will be wiped."

Shadow Law forbade humanity from learning about paranormals and the fact the captain hadn't already wiped her memory, surprised Jared. "Why haven't you ordered that yet?"

The Captain gave him a small smile. "I have my reasons."

Jared lifted Lara into his arms.

"Damien brought your vehicle in. It's in the garage," Captain Jor'dan said.

"Thanks." Jared carried his precious cargo from the room.

§

Bar'ella stared at the closed door. "Why didn't you erase her memory?"

Jor'dan smiled. "Did you notice Jared's aura?"

Jared appeared calmer than the last few times she'd seen him.

"When he's with her, the anger and pain inside him, are softened, tempered. It's because of the human. If something should happen and they should part, then I'll order her memories removed." Jor'dan paused. "Jared deserves a chance at happiness."

"I didn't realize how much of a romantic you are. Why haven't you found a woman to settle down with?" Bar'ella asked.

160

"Because I don't think she'd understand what it's like to rein in the Elite. I swear they're worse than children." Jor'dan complained.

Chapter 13

Cyn left the Captain's office and felt the tingle of magic settle over her skin. Fucking mage Randall. What'd he spell her with? Hopefully, nothing more than a tracker. If it were anything else, she'd already be suffering the effects. The first thing she needed to do was have the enchantment removed. She'd visit Hans and get it taken care of.

Glancing into an empty office, she read the clock on the wall. It'd be dawn soon and she needed to get home. There was no way in hell she'd stay in the vampire day rooms in the basement of the Elite offices. That was asking for trouble. That also meant she didn't have time to get the spell removed before the sun rose.

Cyn strode down the hallways, anxious to leave but not wanting to trigger the Elite impulse to take down fleeing prey. While she could hold her own against one or two, she wasn't strong enough to take on the entire office.

"Cyn, stop," James ordered.

Fuck. She didn't have time for his bullshit.

She sped up, but he caught her wrist, swinging her around to face him.

Cyn yanked her hand. "Let me go!"

James snarled at her. "No."

She twisted and broke free. There was little chance he'd let her leave. It'd be best to hear him out. She leaned against the wall arms crossed.

James took a menacing step toward her.

"What the hell are you involved in now?" he asked.

"None of your business."

"That's where you're wrong, babe. I consider everything about you, my business."

"Well think again. You have no rights, nor any say, in what I do."

"Bullshit."

James ran a hand through his hair. Cyn concealed her pleasure at the frustration evident in his every movement. He paced back and forth in front of her as if trying to control his temper.

"Fine." James scowled. "Then tell me why the hell you're not answering my calls or texts."

Aw poor baby, he feels neglected. Tough shit, asshole.

"I've been busy."

"Too busy to go see a movie?"

Cyn felt herself weakening. While he wasn't enamored of seeing modern movies, he'd made an exception and gone to the theater with her. But no, she had to be strong. She wouldn't, couldn't, let him walk over her and treat her like a dirty secret while seeing another woman.

"Sorry, had a better offer."

His dark eyes flashed. "What the hell is that supposed to mean?"

"I went to see the new adventure flick with a friend."

"A male friend?"

"I don't see how that's any concern of yours."

He leaned forward, the delicious heat of his body surrounding her, turning her on.

Stay strong. Remember he took another woman out on a date.

"Guess again."

"Back off. Now." Steel infused her tone, and her expression.

James paced to the other side of the hallway, frustration evident in the set of his shoulders. His angry stride took him down the hall to the next office door and back again. He resembled a duck in a shooting gallery. One who was pissed off, and her without a BB gun.

"I can't believe you're ignoring us."

"I'm not the one who's ignoring us. You're the one who destroyed our relationship."

The distinctive notes of the song "The Inquisition" echoed through the hall.

Perfect timing, Hans.

Cyn reached for her cell phone. "Hello?"

"Are you busy?" Hans' deep voice filled with concern.

"Not at the moment. What do you need?"

"I need you to stop by first thing tonight. Suspicious activity has been reported at the southeast corner of Golden Gate Park."

"I'll be there."

Hans was silent for a moment. "Do you need a rescue?"

"Not yet, but keep an ear open."

Hans laughed. "Readying the cavalry now."

Cyn grinned and ended the call. "Excuse me, Mr. Kirk, I have to go."

The flash of pain in James expression was quickly masked, but she'd caught it. While it tugged at her heart, she needed to remember he was the one who cheated on her, not the other way around.

The click-clack of heeled boots broke their argument. A human woman approached. Her red, chin-length hair was tipped in jet black. Black framed glasses emphasized her green eyes. An oversized sweatshirt and leggings tucked into boots completed the outfit. Cyn recognized her as the woman James had taken to the Tech Fair.

An expression of delight crossed the human's face when she spotted James.

"I've been trying to get a hold of you for hours!" the woman exclaimed, coming up to him and wrapping her arms around his waist.

Cyn raised an eyebrow when the woman looked at her. "And who is this?" the chick asked.

Animosity rolled off this woman like waves from the ocean.

James cleared his throat. "Clairice, I want you to meet Cyn Madison. Cyn, this is Clairice Jennot."

"James and I have been working on security software," Clarice gushed.

"How long have you two worked together?" Cyn asked. Just how long had he been cheating on her?

Clairice smiled up at him. "For about a year now, and it's been wonderful."

James paled, and it took extraordinary willpower to keep Cyn's polite mask in place. A year. A. Whole. Fucking. Year.

She gave James a brittle smile. "Fuck. You." Cyn stalked down the hallway.

"Cyn, wait." James called.

She ignored his cheating ass. Feeling like there was a lead weight in her chest, she left the Elite offices, fighting tears.

Time to get the hell out of town. Running into him again would remind her of what a fool she'd been. Sometimes escaping the pain was better than facing it, at least at the beginning. She'd reevaluate once the gaping wound in her heart scabbed over.

A deep breath of the salty night air was followed by water leaking from her eyes. She had such hope. That he'd be the one. That he was different than all the others. Lesson learned, James was like all the rest, faithless. What was the quote? *Men were deceivers ever…to one thing constant, never.* She thought he'd be different as he affected her as no one ever had. Thanks to his philandering, she'd make sure no one would get close enough to hurt her ever again.

Vision marred by tears, she made it home without trouble. She entered her room as morning light filtered through the clouds. Thank heaven for the torpor of day-sleep. Where she wouldn't be plagued by foolish desires and pointless dreams.

§

Randall Jennings sat stewing in his office with the door open, watching his fellow Elite walk by. He wished he'd had cast a much stronger spell, but the tracker was spur of the moment thing. The vamp, Ms. Madison, stomped by the door, anger radiating in every step. James had complained many times that she was a hard person to track down. The tracker would make it impossible for her to hide. Unlike James, Randall wouldn't lose her. The bitch was going into Reconditioning if it was the last thing he did. No mere woman would get the best of him he'd make damned sure of that.

Jared strode by the door carrying an unconscious human woman in his arms. How had Jared regained his human form? Had the serum stopped working? Jared carried woman from the library; his rescuer. The care with which Jared held her revealed the shifter had deep feelings for the human. Interesting. Jared's attachment could prove useful.

Randall's cell phone rang. He touched the small bust of Beethoven on the desk which when activated, created a null zone, rendering any listening devices, both magical and technical, inoperable.

"Hello?"

"It's Glendale. What's going on?"

"Williams is human."

"Fuck. How?"

"Healer Bar'ella was with him, so either the serum wore off or she's figured out how to counteract it."

"Shit. He needs to be in the lab, no later than Friday."

"There may be a way to capture to him. He's very protective of the woman who saved him."

"The librarian? Can we grab her?"

"I don't know. I'm being watched. I'm laying low for now."

"Understood. I'll put Benny and Chuck on it."

"Are you sure you can trust those two? They're not competent."

"Up to now they've been very reliable."

"Your call."

The red light on his desk phone blinked. "I've got to go."

"Thanks for your help."

Randall hung up the phone, and thanked Beethoven. The spell bubble collapsed back into the bust. He answered his desk phone. The captain summoned him to his office. Randall stood at attention in front of the desk.

"What can I help you with sir?"

Captain Jor'dan motioned to one of the chairs. "I've interviewed Ms. Madison and as of now, no charges will be brought against her."

"What? Why? She attacked me."

"Because she's providing this office with intel regarding another matter."

"That takes precedence over attacking me?"

"In this instance, yes. The charges against her have been dropped."

Fist clenched, Randall bowed his head hiding the flash of rage. "If she attacks me again, I'll take care of her."

"Understood. What's going on with the Findley matter?"

Randall gave his report on a relatively routine assignment. He left the Captain's office and headed home. Before he went to bed, he loaded the vamp's coordinates into his computer. The location pinged as her apartment. She'd gone home for the day. Excellent. He'd catch her tonight when she emerged from day sleep, and escort her to the Reconditioning center.

The normal process for reconditioning required approval by two different Council members, he was owed enough favors by the mage who ran the center, that he'd get her in and reprogramed before anyone knew what was going on.

§

Lara opened her eyes on a familiar scene. Two comfortable armchairs sat before the roaring fire. Seeing no one else, she sat and grabbed the hot cup of tea on the end table. She'd arrived before her dream man.

She thought about the events of the past few days. Were Jared bunny and Jared man one and the same? Impossible, wasn't it? What if it were true though? That'd be the coolest thing ever.

Jared was hot and desirable, and she wanted to ride him like stallion. The problem was handsome men like him didn't pursue women like her. If only she were brave enough to make the first move.

Perhaps she could do that here? In a safe place? What would be the harm of summoning the bed and ridding herself of this overwhelming desire for him?

Lord knew Preston hadn't been the most imaginative or passionate man in bed. More along the lines of missionary with the lights out. Which was fine sometimes, but she wanted more. She wanted to explore her sexuality, and if she felt comfortable doing that in her dreams? She'd do it. Maybe.

It'd been a few minutes now. Where was he?

What if he didn't show? Now that she'd made her decision, it'd be her luck that he'd invade someone else's dream. Darn it, Dream Man where are you?

"Right here."

Lara almost spit her tea in surprise before narrowing her eyes. So you can read minds too?

Jared smiled before scooting the other chair closer so they shared the table. Their legs were within touching distance.

"There was a little thought bubble over your head, like one of those comic book characters. So, I'm your dream man, huh?"

"Only in that you're a man and you're in my dream. Not in the you're-my-ideal-mate-for-life type of way."

A warm expression crossed his face. "What if I want to fill that position?"

She took a sip of tea. "That's a different fairytale. You'll have to fill out an application, go through a review board and compatibility test and if you pass all that... maybe."

Jared threw his head back and laughed.

168

With sudden insight, Lara understood that he hadn't had much laughter in his life and a small burst of happiness filled her. For a brief moment, she'd lightened his burden.

He was devilishly handsome, dressed as usual in jeans and white oxford. She didn't know what it was about his style of dress, but it turned her on. He was her ideal of masculine perfection. Not too buff, not too skinny. Strong without being overbearing.

Once he regained control of himself, he gave her a heart-stopping smile that filled his eyes.

"Thanks for that. I haven't laughed like that in a long time."

"Glad to be of service," she said.

The shadows crept into his eyes and the lighthearted moment was gone. Reaching out he took one of her hands in his, rubbing his thumb along her knuckles. "What can I do to repay you?" His voice, was a mere whisper of seduction.

Should she? Could she, ask for what she wanted? Now that the moment was here, hesitation stopped her. What would he think of her requests? Did it matter? With a deep sigh, she realized that it did.

Jared spoke. "Don't look so serious. It's not as if I'm asking you to plan a detailed expedition into ancient Mesopotamia."

Biting her lip, she glanced at him, then away. "Perhaps a kiss?" She didn't want him to feel obligated to kiss her, yet at the same time, the feel of his arms around her made her stomach jump in anticipation.

He stood and used her captured hand to pull her to her feet. "Your wish is my command." His deep voice seemed to resonate in the room. Effervescent bubbles of delight rose from her toes spreading throughout her body.

Cupping his hand at her nape and stroking his fingers over the sensitive skin at her hairline, he leaned down. The contact of their lips shot her into a river of need.

Lara found her arms wrapping around his neck, pulling his hard body flush to hers and it still wasn't enough. Hunger replaced delight. Hunger for him, for his body, for the pleasure she knew he could give her.

The change in her kiss knocked Jared off guard. Where before he'd had to coax a response from her, she wrested control of the kiss, and sought her pleasure. An activity he fully supported, but not when he'd been taken by surprise.

Regain control. Keep it light. But it was too late. She'd shattered his restraint and a part of him didn't want to regain it. To stop himself from taking her to the floor, he slid his free hand down her back, along her spine to the sweet curve of her ass, and squeezed.

She broke the kiss. "Did you just grope my butt?"

"Yes." He squeezed it again. "What a delightful butt it is."

"Oh, if it makes you happy."

For that bit of teasing, he swatted her. Not hard enough to hurt, but hard enough to get her attention. Her eyes blanked with shock and then filled with heated desire. Oh damn. She liked a little kink. Just thinking of all the possibilities made him harder than he'd been before.

Until she grabbed his hair in both of her hands and plundered his mouth.

Jared broke the kiss and pulled back trying not to succumb to her allure.

"Is this enough for you, or would you like to take it further?"

"Mmm." She tried to kiss him again.

He wanted this, Lord how he wanted this, but he needed her clear-headed consent. "How far can I go?"

She leaned away from him. "What do you mean?"

His grin felt wicked. "I want you. But I don't want you to feel pressured into sex."

Her eyebrows wrinkled in a cute frown before her smile turned radiant. She peered over his shoulder and red filled her cheeks.

He glanced behind him. It was the bed from the first visit. "I like your style." His grip shifted, and he lifted her into his arms, carrying her to the bed. There was a moment of frustration trying to find the opening of the light, diaphanous curtains.

"Why do they make beds with these gauzy things?" he asked, fumbling to find the opening while trying not to drop Lara. There was a way in somewhere, he had to find it. He first tried to shoulder the sheers aside, but it tangled around his feet. Jared tried to grab the silk with the hand under her legs and missed.

Lara hid her face in his neck, her body shaking. A few deep breaths later and she released his neck and pulled aside one of the troublesome sheers.

"Because women find it romantic." A giggle shook her body.

"Inconvenient if you ask me." He placed her on the soft and fluffy comforter and stood back. The damned curtains fought to trip him up. He ripped the material off his feet and sat on

Lara lay sprawled on the bed, a lovely feast for his eyes. The longer he looked, the more flustered she seemed to become, so he joined her on the bed, lying beside her, head on resting on his left palm, right hand on her stomach. The muscles quivered and jumped under his palm.

"Are you okay with this?"

Lara bit her lip. "Yes."

"You don't seem sure."

"I want you, but I'm nervous."

Jared reared back. "You're not a virgin, are you?"

Lara laughed as he'd intended. "No, but my previous experiences haven't been as exciting as advertised."

"A challenge. I accept."

Panic crossed her face, and she tried to sit up. "Wait, what do you mean challenge?"

"Let me show you what all the fuss is about."

She rolled her bottom lip between her teeth, then came to a decision. "Okay."

He slid his hand beneath her top, skin against skin. He wasn't sure what she was expecting, but whatever it was, held her still. Jared knew better than to tell her to relax, so he'd let his touch soothe.

171

Sliding his hand around her belly, he traced the dips and contours with his palm, making sure to stay away from her breasts and waistline for the moment.

"It might help if you took off your shirt," she said.

"You want to see my chest?" he asked, a knowing smile crossed his face.

She nodded.

If it distracted her from being leery of his touch, he'd strip to the skin right now. But that'd make her anxious for another reason, one that had become hard as a rail spike behind his zipper.

Jared sat up and began to unbutton his shirt. Her soft hand on his arm stopped him. "Slowly."

He raised an eyebrow. "You want a show?"

"Who doesn't like to watch a man unwrapped a hint at a time? I've heard it heightens the antici..."

How long would she wait before she finished the word?

It took four buttons.

"...pation."

Jared grinned and finished unbuttoning his shirt. He untucked the right side. Lara rolled onto her knees and untucked the left, running her hands up his abdomen and chest. Her tongue slipped between her lips and she bit down, her expression focused. The softness of her hands caressed his skin as she pushed the material over his shoulders, following it down his biceps to forearms and off.

"You're a very sexy man," she muttered as her hands explored his body.

"Thank you."

Jared wanted to return the compliment, but she was absorbed in tracing his body.

"So strong. So hard."

"You haven't reached the hard part yet."

Lara glanced up in shock, her mouth falling open. It was too much to resist. Jared bent and covered her lips with his own, taking advantage of her open mouth to thoroughly taste her.

172

His taste exploded on her tongue, rich and wild. Untamable. Addicting. She could kiss him for days.

Hands crept under her shirt and caressed her, pulling her into his chest. Oh yes, this was fabulous. His arms tightened around her, and the kiss changed from gentle and exploratory, to passionate and hungry.

A conflagration of desire heated her body. She wanted more. More of him, more of this delicious feeling.

He shifted, lying down on the bed and pulling her over him, not breaking the kiss. A man of many talents, this one. With a thought, she vanished her shirt and bra, feeling the hair on his chest against her breasts. His hands stroked over her naked back and a distinctly feline urge to arch into his touch consumed her. But that meant exposing her smooshed breasts to his gaze, and that was something she wasn't comfortable with.

"Let me see you," he whispered, tone reverent.

"Um, I'd rather not." Lara admitted.

"Why not?" He rubbed his hand down her backside.

Lara opened her mouth and closed it. How to explain?

He pulled her down and kissed the protest from her lips.

"It doesn't work like that, you know," Jared remarked.

"What?"

"Women getting hung up on their slight imperfections."

Lara bit her lip. "It's not slight to us."

"But I don't see it."

Lara tilted her head. "What do you see?"

Jared rolled to the side, spilling her from his chest. His hand cupped her breast, brushing a finger over the distended nipple. "I see a beautiful, courageous woman. A voluptuous Venus with dangerous curves. One I want to make love to as often as she'll let me."

She smiled. "You mean that?"

"Yes." The sincerity in his expression gave her pause. She wanted desperately to believe it, but experience made her hesitate.

"Can we take it a little bit at a time? So I can get used to you?"

"I'll hurt the bastard for what he did to you."

"Shhh, no, don't bring him here. Go slow, okay?"

Jared nodded. "You're in charge."

Delight bubbled inside of her. "Really?"

He nodded. "Right here, right now, it's all you."

Jared flopped onto his back, hands behind his head. With a wink, he closed his eyes.

Lara leaned up on her elbow and traced his pecs down to his abs. As she stroked over his hip bones, she realized he'd gotten rid of his jeans. He was laid out for her in all his full naked glory.

A quick glance at his face. Eyes were still closed. Good. She'd never been allowed to touch a penis before and curiosity drove her to reach out and fondled his hard erection. A gasp from him, and she stopped. The muscles in his arms clenched.

"Am I doing something wrong?" she asked, her voice hesitant, but she didn't release him.

"No, you're doing it right. Harder."

"Like this?" She tightened her fingers.

"No, this." One hand came covered hers, forcing it to grip him hard.

He moved their fists up and down. His muscles clenched and his breathing became erratic.

"Are you sure this doesn't hurt?"

"It's heaven and hell," he replied.

Lara beamed. He guided her strokes a few times, then replaced his hand behind his head. She gripped him tight, and on the upstroke, pressed her thumb against the head. Based on the hissed breath, it was a good thing. Lara smiled and did it again. After a few pumps, he grabbed her wrist. "Enough."

Lara glanced at his face. His eyes were squeezed shut, and sweat trickled from his temple. She pouted, "I was enjoying myself."

He opened one eye. "If you keep going, I'll be done."

Lara opened her mouth to tell him that was okay by her. Jared pulled her across his chest and took her mouth in a steamy hot kiss.

"My turn," he whispered.

"But I wasn't finished."

"Maybe next time."

Lara snorted. If there was a next time.

He tugged at the snap of her jeans. Lara leaned up a little bit. "What are you doing?"

"Removing your jeans."

"Why?"

"I'm naked. You should be too."

Lara bit her lip. The problem was he looked good in the buff. Her? Not so much. He pulled her back into the kiss. If it was meant to be a distraction, it was working. She didn't pay attention to the tugging of the material as he pulled it over her hips. Lara lifted her butt to make it easier for him.

He pulled her pants and underwear down over her hips and off her legs. He tossed them over the side of the bed. She didn't pay much attention to his hands stroking down her body and cupping her full ass.

Jared rolled her onto her back, not breaking the kiss. This time his hands roamed over her chest, rolling her nipples. While it didn't do anything for her lust levels, it seemed to excite him. His mouth traced a path from her lips to her jaw and down her collar bone to her breasts. There he spent time licking and lavishing each with attention.

"Is this doing anything for you?"

Lara smiled and ran her fingers through his hair. "Not really."

"I'll just have to find your triggers then," he teased as he kissed a path down her belly.

"Um, not necessary."

"Oh, it's very necessary. I want you to enjoy yourself."

"I am."

"Not enough."

She frowned. "But I'm feeling better than I have with anyone else."

"That's not good enough."

He kissed the top of her mound. Lara grabbed at his shoulders. "Please don't."

Jared glanced up. "What's wrong?"

175

Lara bit her lip. "I don't like that part."

He quirked an eyebrow. "Then whoever you've had in the past was incompetent."

"Please, just don't."

Jared nodded. "For now. But we'll revisit this later."

"Can't we just forget it?"

"Not a chance."

Maybe this wasn't a good idea after all. How adventurous could she be if she couldn't handle oral sex? Disappointment filled her. She closed her eyes and conjured a robe to cover her.

Lara sat up and tried to escape Jared.

He removed his hands from her body, giving her space. "Where are you going? We're not done yet."

Tears blurred her vision and she held the robe in front of her, covering all the necessary bits. "I'm sorry," she said, voice soft.

Jared sat next to her close enough that she could see his erection still pulsing in his lap. He cupped her cheek, tilting her heads so they were face to face.

"Talk to me. What's wrong?"

"I... I don't want you to be disappointed."

"I won't be."

"So you say now."

"You're worried I'll be disappointed and then what?"

"I don't think we should talk about this anymore."

"Honey, I'm not that bastard."

"I know that in my brain, but the rest of me..."

"Is going to take some convincing," he finished.

"Yeah."

"We'll work on it."

Lara glanced up at him again. "I don't know..."

"That's okay. Let's see if we can get you back to feeling good." Jared leaned toward her, and she fell back against the pillows, fluffy robe still clutched to her chest.

He lay on his side next to her and slid his hand under the fabric, running his palm over the inside of her leg.

Lara tensed, whether in anticipation or alarm, not even she could tell.

He leaned over and kissed her, which distracted her from what his hand was doing. Until he pressed inside her.

Lara broke the kiss. "What are you doing?"

"Playing."

He hit a spot that sent pleasure flashing through her. "Oh my," she gasped as he did it again.

"You like that?"

"Um, yes!" And then her world imploded in a shower of body pulsing fireworks.

Lara drifted on a sea of lassitude.

"Feeling okay?" Jared asked.

"Mmmm."

He slipped the robe down, exposing one breast then, peered her. She felt so good, so fabulous, that she didn't blink when he pulled the robe away, exposing her.

Jared bent over and kissed her. "Are you ready for round two?"

Lara lifted her hand and waved it.

He took that as permission and began kissing her. There wasn't a way for her to feel more, was there?

The more he kissed and nibbled, the more her body sang with sensation. She was thankful that he kept his kisses above the waist.

Her breath caught. He positioned himself over her, hips resting between her legs, weight propped on his hands. "Are you with me?"

"Where else would I be?"

"Just making sure." He levered himself up and thrust into her body.

"Oh, that feels wonderful," Lara moaned.

He paused, resting his forehead against hers, panting. "It feels fucking amazing."

Lara agreed. He filled her up and it was wonderful. This was where they both belonged, a part of each other.

"Are you ready for me to move?"

Lara wiggled against him. "Please!"

Jared pulled back and thrust again. Oh wow, that felt even better. His hips shifted, and he hit that spot. The one that had her seeing stars. Dear Lord that was fantastic. "Again!'

He grinned down at her. "As my lady demands."

Repeated caresses made her body tighten around his. She felt more wound up than a spring. With one final thrust, the tension burst, and she flew to the heavens. His shout of completion, vied with her own scream.

Jared collapsed on top of her. Lara felt surrounded, protected, and it was comforting. So that's what it was all about. She could see how sex with him could become addicting. He lifted away from her and touched his forehead to hers.

"I'm satisfied. How about you?" Jared asked between light kisses.

"I'll let you know when I can feel my arms and legs."

He rolled to his side, pulling her against him, snuggling with her.

Lara floated on a sea of sated bliss, wrapped securely in his embrace.

Wow, just wow.

Chapter 14

Dr. David Glendale paced from the windows, past the bookcases lining one wall, to the door, and back again. Anger suffused him and he fought to keep from grabbing the nearest object and hurling it at the wall. That bastard, Jared, was human again, holed up in his impenetrable apartment. Damn him! With the Director calling every day demanding progress reports, he felt the pressure of an imagined noose growing tighter and tighter around his neck. To further add to his stress, the gryphon experiment was nearing completion, the creatures having passed the benchmark tests.

How the hell was he going to get Jared out of that damned apartment?

His cell phone rang; it was Chuck.

"Yes?"

"Hey Boss, we followed bunny boy to his apartment. His lady friend is with him."

"Lady friend?"

"Yeah, the chick from the library. The one who took him home."

David's thoughts churned. There might be a way to get Mr. Williams into the lab. "Keep an eye on the place and if you see an opportunity to grab his lady friend, do it."

"Will do, Boss. How long do you want us to watch?"

"Forty-eight hours. If you can't grab her by then, it'll be too late. Bring her to my lab office when you get her."

"Sure."

He hung up as the door opened, and his assistant, Grayson, peeked his head around the corner. "Master Quaid wants an update. He's on line one."

"Thank you, Grayson. Hold my other calls."

David inhaled, preparing for the call. All the news he had to share was summed up in two words; no progress.

§

Lara woke and stretched under the sheets. Man, she felt good. Relaxed and energized at the same time. She wanted to lounge in bed all day and enjoy this feeling. Too bad she had stuff to do. First on the list was a shower then tea.

Her eyes opened to a light-filled room. She glanced at the clock on the nightstand. Ten a.m.? She must have needed the rest, because she never slept in so late.

The unexpected knock at the door startled her, but it wasn't enough to break this wonderful mood. The door opened, and Jared walked in.

Holy heck. He was real! Dressed in well-worn blue jeans and a white button-down Oxford with sleeves rolled up, he looked like he'd walked straight out of her dreams. Unless she was still dreaming?

Lara pinched her arm and hissed. Ow, that hurt. Okay, so she wasn't dreaming. She bolted upright, the covers sliding down to pool in her lap. Oh good, she wasn't naked, either. Her sweatshirt was torn and bloody in places, though the skin beneath was unbroken and unbruised.

Lara raised her right hand and stopped. Wait. Looking at her arm, she murmured, "I could have sworn the wrist was broken." She rotated it, slowly at first, in case of pain. Taking inventory of her body, she realized she no longer hurt.

"Good morning, sleepy head."

Her attention was drawn back to Jared standing next to the bed with a warm expression on his face. Jared grinned. "I told you I was as real as you."

Lara opened her mouth and closed it again, unsure what to say. She focused on her surroundings. The walls of the room were gray with sparse furnishings, and a big screen TV against the far wall. The room was familiar, but not her own.

Jared sat on the bed at her hip. A teeny tiny part of her wanted to grab his shoulders and pull him into a steamy, hot kiss. Heat rose in her cheeks. Dang it, she had to stop thinking of him in a sexual way. "What happened? Why am I in your apartment, in your bed?" Lara asked.

"You needed to recover, and this is the safest place. You went into shock, and the healer, uh doctor wanted you monitored."

He should stop grinning. It made her want to do naughty, naughty things. He mentioned a doctor. She remembered an older lady with a medical bag, but it was hazy, dreamlike. "I was hurt, right?" From the state of her clothes, she'd been in a war zone.

"Yes. The doctor fixed you up."

"How long have I been out?"

Jared glanced at the clock. "You've been asleep since two a.m."

Completely healed in eight hours? There wasn't any lingering pain. "She must have serious drugs. I'm not even sore. But why am I here?"

"Your place isn't secure."

"Are the bad guys still after me?"

His strong shoulders shrugged under the crisp white cotton. "I like to be prepared."

"This is kind of weird."

"What?"

"Being here with you. Before it was with the bunny, and that was okay... Oh my God! What happened to bunny Jared? I can't believe in all the hassle I forgot about him." Lara tried to get out of bed, but Jared gripped her arm and with a gentle touch, settling her back against the pillows.

Jared gazed into her eyes. "Do you believe in magic?"

"What does that have to do with bunny Jared?"

"It's a complicated story. Will you listen?"

"Is he safe?"

"Yes."

"Okay, I'll listen."

Jared rubbed the back of her hand in circular strokes with his thumb. It had a soothing effect, and by the easing of his shoulders, she wasn't the only one calmed. He looked away. "A few years ago, I volunteered for a cancer research study. Instead of attempting to find a cure for cancer, they used us as human guinea pigs. Long story short, the researchers spliced our genes with that of rabbits to try to create shapeshifters."

Lara gasped, "How atrocious!" It sounded like something out of a B movie. "People do such terrible things?"

"It's not the movies, I'm living proof."

She didn't know what to think. That people did this sort of thing was incredible, cruel, and evil.

He sighed. "It was hell. The pain was indescribable. The others have died over the years and I'm the remaining survivor."

"You're able to change shapes?"

"Yes, into a rabbit."

"You and bunny Jared are the same person, animal, um being?"

"Yes." Jared seemed to be waiting for something. The circles on the back of her hand slowed and stopped. Was he expecting judgement? Condemnation? What had been done to him was terrible, a travesty of science. But it was as if he walked straight out of one of the books she'd loved to read. He was a real, live shapeshifter.

How to answer? Best go with the truth. "While that was horrible, it's kind of neat too."

"Neat?" His tone was incredulous. "You think turning into an animal is neat?"

Lara smiled. "Yes. Think of all the things you can do as a bunny that'd be hard as a man."

Jared arched an eyebrow. "Like what?"

"I don't know, but there has to be something, right? You could slip through small spaces, creep into the bad guys' lair via the duct work. That sort of thing."

"You don't think I'm a monster?"

"Do you turn into a slavering, eighty-foot-tall creature bent on sharpening your fangs on the buildings in San Francisco?"

"No."

"Then you're not a monster. Why do you think you are?"

"Because I change shape."

Lara shrugged. "It's an asset."

"Asset?" The expression on his face was incredulous.

Heat filled her cheeks. Dang it, now he was making fun of her.

"You're one of those glass half-full types, aren't you?" Jared asked.

"Yes," she said, turning serious for a moment. "The world is filled with so much negativity and hate. I can't handle it. I'd end up on the floor in a fetal position rocking my life away. I look on the brighter side to control the dark."

"Huh."

Well, that was non-committal.

"How'd you end up in the library?" she asked.

"I don't know. The last thing I remember was a sharp prick on my shoulder after subduing a group of teens."

"Do you know who wanted to bunny-nap you?"

"No. I've heard rumors the same people who ran the experiment the first time are doing it again."

Lara gasped, her hand covered her mouth. "They need you to help them?"

"I'm not sure."

"You have to hide and stay safe!"

Jared lifted her hand to his mouth and kissed the back of it. "Don't worry, this place is more secure than Fort Knox. I've got time off, and there's no reason for me to leave, thus no opportunity for them to grab me."

"But what happens if they manage to kidnap you?"

He removed his watch, slid the back off, and showed her the secret compartment that held two small white pills.

A shiver pebbled her skin. "What are those?"

"Insurance."

"For you or for them?"

"Either.

"But what if they confiscate your watch?"

"The idea is to take them before they get me to the lab. I won't go through that again." He shuddered. "I can't."

Lara reached over and hugged him. She held him, trying to give him hope, anything to combat the desolation in his eyes. The growling of her stomach interrupted the tender moment, and heat filled her cheeks.

Jared chuckled. "Grab a shower, and I'll make breakfast."

"Are my clothes still here?"

"Yes."

"My purse?"

"Still here. You didn't take it with you, remember? You grabbed the pocket change and left."

She petted the white cotton over his chest, thinking of what had happened yesterday. She'd broken her wrist, there was that story on the news, and... "Doreen! I can't believe I forgot about her!"

"The woman from the news?"

Lara pushed at the covers and tried to get out of bed.

"You can call her after your shower."

Lara glared at him. "No, it's too important."

"Here, it's charged." Jared held out her cell phone.

"How...?"

"I swung by your place and picked it up on the way home."

Jared got up to leave and she put her hand on his arm, stopping him. "I don't mean to sound ungrateful. Thank you, for everything."

He leaned over and placed a quick kiss on her lips. One that ignited every erogenous zone in her body. She leaned into the kiss, but it ended too soon.

"Make your call." He winked and left the room. Lara couldn't help but ogle his jean-clad butt. Was he as good in person as he was in her dreams? Wait, what was she thinking? Lara shook her head, trying to clear it of lustful thoughts. Doreen, right.

She placed the call. "Hi Doreen, it's Lara."

"Are you okay? We went to your place, and there's police tape over the door," Doreen replied.

"I'm fine. A friend got me out in time."

"Why didn't you answer your phone?"

"I forgot to charge it. Is everyone okay? I saw the news story last night."

"Everyone is fine, but I'm worried about you. The creeps wanted to know where you live and if you still had the rabbit. No one told them anything."

"Good."

"You still have it, right?"

How should she respond? "No. I found his owner, and he's been reunited with his family."

"That doctor guy wasn't the owner, was he?"

"Nope. The doc wanted take the bunny to experiment on it."

"That's awful."

"Yeah, but the little guy is safe now."

"Make sure you stay safe as well. I spoke with management, and they think it's better if you take additional time off. You're on a week of administrative leave. By that time, the cops should've caught those scumbags, and you'll be cleared to come back to work."

Jared appeared in the doorway and walked to the bed. He leaned over and nibbled her ear lobe. Shivers raced over her skin, and it wasn't due to the ambient room temperature. "Breakfast will be ready in twenty," he whispered, and then left the room.

"Who was that? He's got a sexy voice."

"He's the friend I'm staying with."

"He isn't gay, is he?"

After all he'd done to her in her dreams? "No, I don't think so."

"Why the hell didn't you tell me about him?"

"It's a long, unbelievable story."

"Try me. I'll be at Angelini's at three tomorrow. Meet me there."

"See you then," Lara replied and ended the call.

Lara entered the bathroom and took a quick shower.

§

Jared went back into the kitchen, stretching his arms over his head. He woke up a short time ago and needed a shot of caffeine to get his day started. He pushed the power button on the coffee maker. God, he'd missed the bitter brew. Too impatient to wait for the pot to fill, he inserted a cup under the drip and replaced the pot when the cup was full. He inhaled the acidic aroma of Columbia's best. The first sip tasted of ambrosia.

He'd been so exhausted this morning, it was all he could do to tuck Lara into his bed. He'd collapsed onto the couch and shared that erotic dream with her. He needed real food, not the vegetable crap he'd been forced to eat. He craved a rare steak with fried onions and mushrooms. A baked potato loaded with butter, chives, bacon and sour cream. Damn. His stomach rumbled, but for now, bacon and eggs would do for brunch. Dinner would be soon enough for the red meat he craved. While he'd love to show Lara his favorite steak place, he didn't trust Randall and his goons not to grab them, so they'd order in.

The shower started and his thoughts went to Lara standing naked beneath the spray. Droplets of water flowing over her soft, smooth skin, caressing every curve. He longed to chase each drop with his tongue, sipping the nectar of life from her body.

A short, agonizing time later, the water shut off.

On his third cup of coffee, she entered the kitchen, smelling of damp Lara and vanilla. She had on jeans paired with a shirt and sweater. Even the socks on her feet turned him on. He'd never seen anything sexier.

To take his mind off what he wanted to do, he grabbed a box from the counter and put it on the small table with a hot mug of water.

"Breakfast?" he asked, voice rough from the lust coursing within him.

Lara gave him a look. "Are you all right?"

He inhaled trying to clear his head, and breathed in her scent. Shit, this wasn't what she needed from him. "I will be. Breakfast is almost ready."

Lara sat at the table, staring at the box and mug of water. "I didn't know you had any tea."

"I didn't. I had security deliver a few things from the market." He placed the dishes filled with eggs, bacon, and toast on the small table. Jared put butter and jam next to the toast, then sat across from her.

They ate in silence, too hungry to make conversational small talk. When nary a crumb of bacon remained, Jared sat back, full but not overstuffed.

He pulled out his cell phone, scrolled down the contacts, and pushed the phone across the table. "You'd better talk to the police so they realize you're safe."

Lara picked up the phone, tapped the screen, and brought it to her ear.

While she did that, Jared cleared the table.

"Hello? No, I'm using his phone. My name? Lara Adams. Yes, I'm with him."

She handed him the phone. "He wants to speak with you."

Jared tucked the phone between ear and shoulder while he put things away. "Hello?"

"You assisted Miss Adams?" Detective Alejandro asked.

Jared didn't want to expose Cyn and her activities. "In a manner of speaking, the Elite are on the case. She's under my protection."

"I'll make sure the paperwork is taken care of."

"What about her apartment?" While he knew she'd prefer to be in her own space, it wasn't secure. He'd like to get a few of her things to make her feel more comfortable here.

"It'll be ready in a few days. I'll let you know."

"Thanks," Jared replied and ended the call.

Lara yawned. "I can't believe I'm so tired."

"You've been through a lot in the last couple of days. Let your body rest."

Jared stood, grabbing Lara's hand and leading her into the living room. He helped her sit on the couch, then swung her feet up before covering her with the throw. "Take a nap. We'll talk more when you wake."

Lara yawned again. "Okay," she said as she snuggled into a throw pillow. In a voice slurred with sleep. "Tell me one thing."

"Yes?"

"How did you know I liked tea?"

"It came to me in a dream."

Soft snores brought a smile to his face. He returned to the kitchen and cleaned up the dishes from breakfast.

It was mid-afternoon before Lara began stirring on the couch. Jared had spent the time blowing up pixelated bad guys on his computer. He'd used headphones so as not to disturb her rest, with one earbud out so he could hear if she woke.

Lara opened her eyes and stretched with a groan that made him want to cuddle her. She sat up, the throw pooling in her lap. "Did I sleep long?"

"A couple of hours." Jared quit the game and spun in his office chair. "Do you want something to drink?"

"Water, but I can get it."

Jared held up his hand. "Stay there." He went into the kitchen, got her a glass of water, and handed it to her as he sat next to her on the couch.

"Do other shape changers exist?" Lara asked, taking a sip of water.

Jared leaned back. "I shouldn't tell you, but yes."

"Why can't you tell me?"

"Because regular people aren't supposed to know about us."

"What happens if they find out?"

"They either have their memories erased, or they're killed."

Lara's eyes widened in horror. "I want to keep my memories, and I don't want to die!"

He rubbed her back. "That's why it's critical that you don't share this knowledge with anyone. Can you keep a secret?"

"Yes."

"Then ask."

"Are there other shape changers like werewolves?"

"They get pissy when you call them weres. They prefer shifters."

"Got it. Shifter Wolves. Anything else?"

"There are tigers, lions, and bears."

"Oh my. Thank goodness, I'm not from Kansas."

"Funny." He pulled her onto his lap, and she rested her head on his shoulder. It felt right, natural, as if she was meant for him. Jared cleared his throat. "The predators are shifters."

"Except for you."

"Except for me."

"Is it hard to be prey?" she asked.

His hands clenched into fists, and he struggled to keep the anger from his voice. "It's a fight, every single day."

Lara stroked his nape. "I'm sorry I didn't mean to upset you. What about Dragons?"

"Yes, the doctor from yesterday."

"The older lady in the office?"

"Yeah, she's a dragon."

Lara tried to sit up, but he held her against his chest. "Really? That's so cool. What else exists?"

"Many things."

"Vampires?"

"Yes."

"I'll bet those two goons who interrogated me were vampires."

"Why do you think that?"

"There's something undead-ish about them."

"I'll let them know."

"Are they blood suckers?"

"Yep."

"I guess that Legolas look-a-like is really an elf?"

"Yes, but don't call him Legolas. He doesn't have much of a sense of humor."

"No Lord of the Rings jokes, got it. What about wizards and witches?" she asked, eyes alight with curiosity.

"Not in the form you're thinking. They're called mages."

"They can work spells?"

Jared nodded. "Funny thing about mages. They guard against magical attack, but never physical."

"Is that a bad thing?"

Jared shrugged. "It depends on whether they're helping or attacking. The best way to fight a mage is to break their concentration by distracting them with a physical stimulus. Depending on the type of spell, it'll rebound on them, and the fight is over."

"Wow, this is so neat," she said.

"Neat?"

"Yeah. All the creatures from fable and myth really exist."

"It's not all fairy tales," he cautioned.

"You've not read many fables, have you?"

"No, why?"

"The originals aren't the light and fluffy versions cartoons lead people to believe. They're pretty brutal." Lara started playing with the buttons on his shirt, focusing on her fingers instead of his face. "I have another question."

"Ask."

A faint pink blush painted her cheeks. "The dream thing."

"It was real."

"So last night when we… and then you… and I…"

Jared squeezed her. "Yeah, I had a great time."

"But it was a dream."

"It's called the Dreamscape, and according to sources, it's a place where souls meet."

"Spiritual bodies versus physical?"

"That's the best description I've heard so far. Want to dream again?"

Lara ducked her head, in a soft whisper she said, "Maybe."

Jared's mouth popped open. That wasn't the answer he was expecting. It was best to switch the conversation to a not so inflammatory topic, otherwise he'd recreate their dream right here on the couch.

"What about ghosts?" Lara asked.

"They're not typical dead people. They're killed by magical objects and are forced to haunt the area until the object releases them."

"Strange," Lara said.

Jared glanced at the time. "Speaking of strange, I'd love to take you to dinner, but since we're in danger, would you mind if we ordered in?"

Lara breathed a sigh of relief. "That wouldn't be strange, that'd be perfect."

Jared pulled out his phone and brought up a menu from his favorite steak place. "I'm hungry for steak. Make your choice, and I'll order it."

Lara stared at the screen and her tummy rumbled. "I deserve a treat, I've suffered an ordeal," she muttered, "A nice steak and a baked potato sounds good." She lifted her gaze away from the menu. "What happens if the bunny eats meat?"

"I get sick, really sick." Jared took the phone from her and placed the order, adding a piece of cheesecake for dessert. "The food should be here soon."

Lara leaned her head back against his shoulder and toyed with the buttons on his shirt. He put his arm around her shoulders and watched the fog roll in. For the first time since he'd began this hellish existence, he felt at peace, until the harsh ringing of the phone broke the mood.

§

Cyn left her apartment to meet with Hans and Megan. She exited her building and rounded the corner before popping into Shadow. She climbed up to the rooftop and over to the next building. While a curious part of her wanted to look over the edge to see if anyone watched, she couldn't let her curiosity about a tracker keep her from her appointment.

Sliding down the fire escape on the far side of the building, she popped back into Real. The ruse was meant to confuse anyone tracking her. While spells could track in both Real and Shadow, those tracking her would spend extra time trying to figure out where she'd gone. She'd evaded James on more than one occasion doing this. Numerous shifts between realities and it'd take them an hour or more to figure out her location. Up buildings, over rooftops and down again, she arrived at Hans' rooftop. A dark shape crouched by the low wall surrounding the roof's edge.

On silent feet she approached. "Hans?" she hissed in a near silent whisper.

The figure stood and stepped into a s grinned. Hans was dressed in a black pirate shirt tucked into black leather pants. On top was a black leather vest—his working clothes.

"Any new victims?" she asked.

"Not yet." His shoulder length white hair blew in the breeze and his head tilted to the side. "You've been tagged with a tracking spell."

"I figured. Do you have anything to get rid of it?"

He reached into one of the many pockets of the vest, pulled out a charm, and tossed it to her.

Cyn caught the small metal object the size of a quarter. A slight brown glow flowed from her body and drained into the disc.

Hans held out his hand. "I'll have Megan drive it around the city for a while. That should keep the Elite off your back. Was it James?"

She blinked back tears at the bastard's name. "Not this time. Elite Mage Randall Jennings. He's threatened to Recondition me."

Red flames flared to life in Hans' eyes. "Leave town, go stay with Dante. I'll take care of him."

Cyn shook her head. "Not until the current situation is resolved. Then I'll head to Oregon and check in with Dante. As for the mage? I think Jared will take care of him."

"Are you sure about Williams?"

"Yes."

"If he doesn't take care of the problem, I'll let Megs practice on Jennings."

Cyn grinned. She almost hoped Jared wouldn't take care of the problem since Megs had so few opportunities to practice her torture skills.

Hans reached out and pulled her into a hug. Cyn wrapped her arms around him and let him hold her. He, Casmier, Dante, and Mason were her mentors, surrogate fathers, and everything she'd ever needed, helping her through the roughest time of her life, when she'd been converted into a vampire against her will.

"What did James do?"

She couldn't help the tears. "He's two-timing me with a human."

"Shall I host him for a while?"

"No, I don't want to bring the Elite here. They'll monitor the area, which will make it harder to work, and at worst they'll shut you down."

"Are you sure?"

"Yes. Please don't do anything, not yet."

"All right. I'll be patient, for now."

Another voice intruded on them. "What are you doing with my man?"

Cyn pulled away, glance over her shoulder, and smiled. "Don't worry, Megs, he's not my type."

"I know." The self-proclaimed dark elf, Megan, stared at her with a penetrating gaze. "Are you okay?"

"No, but work always helps."

Megan wore her dark hair long, covering her pointed ears. Her mini skirt was paired with ripped leggings and knee-high boots. On top, she wore a crop sweater in deep purple that showed off her sparkly belly ring. "Let us know if we have to mess someone up."

Cyn smiled. "I love that you're as bloodthirsty as Hans. Right now, I want everyone to cut back on work. I don't want anyone to run afoul of the Elite. I'll take care of the bastard myself."

Hans tossed the coin to Megs who caught it and looked it over and sneered. "A mage put this on you?" Cyn nodded. "Shoddy work. Don't they craft their spells anymore?" Megs complained.

"It was probably a spur of the moment thing," Cyn replied.

Megs tossed the coin in the air and caught it in her fist. "I feel a shopping trip coming on."

Cyn chuckled and wished she could join the dark elf. But that would defeat the purpose of Megs leading the mage all over the city.

Megs approached Hans and gave him a steamy kiss. "I'm off. See you later darling."

Cyn averted her gaze not only to give them privacy, but because a dagger of jealously stabbed her heart. They had what she craved, a loving relationship with a partner who supported her.

With a heavy sigh she turned back to find Hans' penetrating gaze on her.

"What?" Cyn asked, nervously fiddling with a zipper pull. Hans always had a way of seeing to her heart. Thankfully he moved onto the job he wanted her to do. "I have a location for the van. Let's go." He led her down off the roof and into an unremarkable car, driving to the southeastern edge of Golden Gate park.

"Did you locate the entrance of the lair?" Cyn asked. She'd reported her findings to him when she tracked the van into the park, but that was the northwestern corner, and there was plenty of park between the two locations.

"No." Hans pointed to the prestigious medical school. "The van has been seen leaving the employee parking garage of the school."

Cyn's eyes widened. "Holy shit, this is sanctioned?"

Hans shrugged. "There's no way to know for sure. Find out what you can."

He handed her a small device no bigger than a dime. Cyn attached the collar cam to the neck of her black sneaky-suit. It would transmit images to the receiver at Han's warehouse A flash drive recorded for the stream in case the connection was lost.

He pulled out a small figurine in a hooded cloak and mumbled a phrase before handing it to her.

"What is this for?" Cyn asked.

"It's a sneak charm. It will hide you from security, both human and technical. That way you won't exhaust yourself using your talents."

Cyn tucked the activated figure into a pocket and got out of the car. Anticipation surged through her. She wanted to find out what happened to Uncle Jack and the others, and she wasn't leaving without answers.

§

Randall sat in his car with a specialized unit ready to track the vamp. An experimental system the Elite were field testing, it merged magic and technology. He wasn't sure how it worked, but the upshot was he was able to track his spell using GPS.

The sun set, painting the clouds with shades of pink fading into purple before going dark. A ping on the screen showed him the bitch vamp left her apartment. She exited the building, and he started the car. After gaining a visual, he verified the tracker was sending the correct coordinates to the map. A few blocks later and he lost the contact. Tapping the screen, the blip from the spell didn't reappear. Shit.

Finding a place to park, he disconnected the unit from the car mount and continued on foot. Hmm, perhaps she'd gone into Shadow? It seemed the most logical thing for her to do. In an alley he popped into Shadow with the device, which pinged right away. Good.

He made a voice note. "Need to track in Real and Shadow simultaneously."

Randall followed on foot before the device went dead again. "Bitch!"

Popping back into Real, he followed her trail. A few more shifts between Real and Shadow and he was ready to kill her himself. She'd led him on a chase all over the city.

Finally, the bitch's location stayed constant. She was in Shadow in the shopping district. He waited outside a high-end store. She was in the store for more than an hour. Glancing at the items in the windows, the vamp had expensive tastes. Which made him wonder, where did she get her money?

Randall made another note. "Financial check on Vampire Cyn Madison."

A group of women left the store. Three were fae, two were shifters and an elf. His screen pinged as the elf strode away from the group, laden with shopping bags.

Randall glanced at the GPS then back to the elf who stowed her items in the trunk of a sporty car. She waved to the shifters, got behind the wheel, and drove off. The tracking dot moved.

FUCK!

How the hell had that stupid bitch managed to give him the slip? He glanced at the time. Shit, he had an important meeting back at HQ in a few minutes. If it were with anyone else, he'd reschedule, but he couldn't miss a meeting with Captain DúSan.

Randall saved the GPS path. He'd follow it later, and figure out where she'd managed to slip by him and transfer the spell to someone else. He made it to the meeting with minutes to spare. There were many things on his to-do list, but first was getting that bitch vamp into Reconditioning.

Chapter 15

Lara ate the last bite of steak, savoring the flavor. She patted her tummy, pleasantly full. "That was delicious."

"It's my favorite restaurant." Jared polished off the last of his potato, and cleared the table.

Lara got up and rinsed her plate and placed it in the sink. She opened the cabinet under the sink looking for dishwashing liquid to tidy up the dishes.

"Go sit down in the living room. I've got this."

"Are you sure?" Lara asked, dubious. Her ex had been more than willing to have her clean up after a meal. The jerk went so far as to demand it even when she was ill.

"I'm a grown man, I know how to do the dishes. Go relax."

Lara took a seat on the couch, her brain questioning. Was he doing this to impress her? Was he trying to lure her in before showing his true colors? *STOP IT*. He wasn't her ex, and maybe he was exactly as presented. Lara rubbed her temples, trying to halt her thoughts from tumbling around.

Jared walked back into the room with a fork in one hand and the other hidden behind his back. When he reached the couch, he pulled his hand from behind his back with a flourish.

Her eyes widened.

"I hope you like chocolate cheesecake," Jared said.

"I love chocolate cheesecake." She tried not to drool.

Jared sat down next to her.

"Don't I get a fork?" Lara asked.

He grinned and shook his head. "Sorry, you'll have to let me feed you."

Lara narrowed her eyes at him. "Are you trying to seduce me?"

He held the first bite up to her lips. "Maybe."

She couldn't help but open her mouth and accept the sinful offering. Her eyes closed as the rich flavor hit her tongue. Oh, this was good. The best she'd ever tasted.

A groan from him made her eyes pop open. She lost focus on the flavor as she caught the pained expression on his face.

"What's wrong?"

"Feeding you chocolate."

Huh? "What?"

"You're too damned sexy."

She scoffed. "Yeah, right."

"Excuse me?"

"I know myself and sexy is the last word that would be used to describe me."

"What words would you use?" The bite in his tone was unexpected, but it didn't stop her from responding.

"Plain, unassuming, and dull, I guess."

With great care he put the plate on the coffee table. Jared grabbed her shoulders in a tight but not painful grip.

"You listen to me. You're sexy and sensual. Do not you put yourself down again, understand?"

Lara's jaw dropped. Sexy and sensual? Where was he getting these ideas? "Um, sure," she replied, not believing him for an instant.

Jared pulled her close, kissing each corner of her mouth. "We'll work on it."

Jared leaned back and reached for the chocolate cake, and turned feeding her into a sensual dance that heightened each touch, each kiss, until she was ready to tumble him to the couch and have her wicked way with him. Jared took small bites in between feeding her.

"Last piece," he said, bringing the laden fork toward her.

Lara opened her mouth, tasting the sweet delicacy. Chocolate coated her tongue. Once again with eyes closed, she savored the treat. A soft caress on her lips, and her eyes popped open, and caught him leaning away from her.

She licked her lips, tasting chocolate and Jared. Lara leaned over to kiss him again, and a loud ring startled her into jumping back.

Heat filled her face at the surprise. What was she doing?

Jared glared at his cell phone as he answered. "What?"

To give him space, she picked up the plate. He captured her wrist, shaking his head. He removed the plate from her hands and walked to the kitchen. She heard him speaking in a quiet voice but couldn't make out the words.

Jared sighed when Bar'ella placed him on hold. He rinsed the plate while listening to the decent music. The singer had just killed a man, and put a gun against his head when she came back on the line.

"How's our patient today?" Bar'ella asked.

"Fine. She's fully recovered."

"How are you?"

"Okay. No side effects."

She paused for a moment. "What's going on? Why are you so testy?"

"You're interrupting dessert."

Golden laughter filled the line. "Poor Jared. Oh, and remember, she's not to know about Shadow."

"Okay."

"I'm serious, Jared. She's not to know."

"I got that."

"What are you going to tell her when she asks what happened to the rabbit?"

Jared rolled his eyes. There was no way he'd deny Lara the knowledge, but he wasn't going to tell the healer that.

"I wasn't going to tell her anything."

Bar'ella paused. "She's probably curious. If you need to, tell her it's classified."

"Or I could tell her I don't know, and leave it at that."

"I suppose," Bar'ella admitted. "I want the both of you in the clinic tomorrow at nine."

"We'll be there."

Jared slid his phone into his pocket and returned to the living room.

"Anything wrong?" she asked

"That was the doc. She wanted to check and see how we were."

"That upset you?"

"It was something else she said."

"What?"

He sat down on the couch and put his arm around her. "It's important that you don't say anything to anyone about what I told you."

"Okay. But really, who would believe me?"

"You'd be surprised," Jared muttered.

Lara took his hand. "It'll be okay. I won't say anything to get you in trouble."

She was so damned sweet. Jared leaned toward her. "Now where were we before we were interrupted?"

A teasing smile crossed Lara's face. "You were about to carry me into the bedroom, hero style, then spend all night worshiping me."

Her eyes got big and her mouth popped open. Her cheeks flushed red and she put her free hand over her eyes. "I can't believe I said that."

Jared suppressed a chuckle and drew her to her feet and swept her up into his arms.

"Jared what are you doing?"

"Carrying you into the bedroom, hero style, as you commanded."

"I don't... I mean..."

"Shh. Let me."

"But..."

Jared bent his head and kissed her. He missed a step when she put her arms around his shoulders and leaned up into the kiss.

She tasted of chocolate and sin and woman, a dangerous, thrilling combination.

He entered the bedroom, placed her on the bed, and broke the kiss. While his body was ready and more than willing, he wanted to make sure she was on board with the plan. He pulled back from the kiss and gazed down at her. She looked delightfully mussed. "Lara."

Her eyes slid open and her smile was a seduction.

"You want this, right?"

"Oh yes." A frown crossed her face. "You're not having second thoughts, are you?"

"No. I want to make sure you're one hundred percent with me."

"I am. Please, I ache."

He needed no more permission than that. His hands roamed the side of her body from breast to hip. She arched into his touch.

Lara loved the sensation of his hands on her body. They slipped under her shirt and the heat of his hand on her skin felt decadent. The rasp of his fingers ignited sensation.

Jared massaged her breasts through her bra and while playing with her breasts didn't stimulate her, knowing that it excited him, fed her arousal. She thought being clothed would inhibit the pleasure, but it heightened it.

Jared rained kisses on her face and jaw while his hand played over her breasts.

Jared tugged her upright and pulled the shirt up and over her head. Lara reached over and brushed his chest, reaching for the buttons of his shirt. She slipped the buttons from the holes and spread the sides of his shirt, caressing the heated skin below.

His breath hitched and grabbed her hands. "Stop that."

"But I want to touch."

Jared took a deep breath and held it for a long moment. "Okay." Jared shrugged out of his shirt and threw it off the bed, then laid supine on the bed next to her. He threaded his fingers and put them behind his neck. "Please, be gentle," he whispered.

Startled, Lara looked down at his face and giggled. "Maybe".

Lara took advantage of the opportunity. Who knew the next time she'd have a smokin' hot man spread before her? His eyes closed when she began her exploration of his body. Lara's hands roamed his chest, finger tracing every dip and bulge. His skin was rough with hair that tickled her palm. She flicked her nail across his nipple and his body jolted. *Hmm interesting.*

Leaning over she flicked her tongue over the nub. His eyes popped open. "What are you doing?"

"Playing."

Where she got the courage from, she didn't know, but Lara reached up and caressed his eyes closed. "Lie there and take it."

"Whatever you say."

She played with his nipples before moving down his body. Fingers traced over sculpted abs, stroking nearer to her goal.

While she could spend hours petting him, what fascinated her was the hard length bulging below his belt. Quick hands opened the buckle and at the rasp of the zipper, his eyes popped open. "What are you doing?"

"Exploring," Lara said. Her courage drained away. What if he didn't want to be touched and fondled. "Is that all right?"

"Give me strength," he groaned. "It's fine."

"Good." She unbuttoned and unzipped the jeans. Tapping the side of his hip, she said, "Up."

Jared lifted his hips and she pulled the jeans down. "No underwear?"

"Didn't have any clean," he muttered.

Relief filled Lara. He forgot to do laundry. Regardless of how well they clicked, he was still human, still flawed. Though looking at his beautiful body before her, she couldn't find a single area he needed to work on. His physique was all hard strength and muscle.

"Keep your eyes closed," Lara instructed.

"Yes, ma'am."

Lara sat next to his hip and traced a finger over his penis, up one vein and down another. She'd read of silk-covered steel in various books, not knowing what it meant. But this was it. The skin was smooth, soft. The muscle beneath, hard and throbbing.

"Is it supposed to do that?" she asked as it pulsed up and down.

"It does that when stroked."

"Interesting." Did it do any other tricks? She wrapped her hand around the length, and caressed up and down, her thumb brushing the tip.

"Harder," he said.

"I don't want to hurt you."

"Do it like you did in the dream," he instructed.

Heat filled her face. His eyes were still closed so he didn't witness her acute embarrassment. "Like I did in the dream, got it."

Lara squeezed her hand tight and remembered how he'd guided her. A few strokes later, her curiosity got the better of her. What would he taste like? Without waiting for nerves and doubts to make her second guess herself, she licked the head of his erection.

"What…"

"Shh, I'm playing. Keep your eyes closed."

"All right, but I get a turn."

"Maybe."

"Definitely."

To stop him from speaking, she twirled her tongue over the slit. He tasted of salt and musk and Jared. A flavor she could become addicted to if she weren't careful. A further step on the slippery slope to loving him. Lara shied away from that thought, not ready to face heartbreak yet. If she didn't acknowledge it, it didn't exist. *Don't go there, not yet, not ever. Play and explore, don't think of anything deeper.*

A lick here, a suck there, and she settled in to have some fun.

"Stop," he groaned.

Glancing at his face revealed his teeth clenched and eyes squeezed shut. His hands were clamped into fists and the muscles in his arms flexed, showing ridges and veins.

"What's wrong?" Lara asked.

"You're too damned good at this. I'm going to lose control if you don't cease."

Lara thought about it. "Would that be bad?"

Jared opened one eye. "No, but then we'd have to find something to do while I recover."

She knew what that something was. Giving him a frown, she scooted to the edge of the bed and removed her shoes and socks.

Jared rolled toward the nightstand, pulled open the drawer, and removed a box. He placed it on the side of the bed. "Don't forget these."

He rolled back into position, a small smile playing over his lips.

Lara opened the box and took out a packet. She removed the condom and glanced at him, then back to the small circle of prophylactic. "I don't think this is large enough."

"It'll fit." His hands covered hers and they smoothed the condom down his shaft together.

"Okay, you can close your eyes now," she ordered.

"Are you sure?"

Lara bit her lip. "This time, please?"

"I'll do it for a kiss."

Lara placed a soft kiss on his lips. He leaned up as she retreated.

"That's it?" he asked, his voice filled with disappointment.

"That was the appe-teaser. Are you ready for more?"

"Starving."

Covering his mouth, she licked his lips. He parted them for her and flavor hit her body like a shot of strong alcohol. He tasted of chocolate, decadence, and strong male. She couldn't get enough.

A long moment later and Lara broke the kiss. Not that she wanted to. She could kiss him for a long time and it wouldn't be enough. Her body craved more. she wanted skin and she was overdressed for the occasion. Removing her bra, jeans, and panties, Lara was grateful she didn't have to worry about him seeing her naked.

She slid along his body, magnifying her desire. At his groan, she nibbled his bottom lip.

One leg drifted over his lap and she eased into a kneeling position over him.

Lara ran a finger up and down his sheathed erection and wrapped both hands around him, pumping once, twice.

Jared gasped and bit his bottom lip. "Stop. Too much."

"Okay."

Lara held his erection steady, then lowered her body onto his. The intrusion felt awkward at first. She'd never done this before.

"Let me help," Jared whispered.

"Please."

Jared unclasped his hands and gripped her hips, thrusting his pelvis up. He was all the way in. Oh God, it felt even better than in her dreams.

Lara's eyes closed at the sensation. Heat and warmth and fullness. Her body stilled, absorbing the sensation.

"Ride me," he instructed.

Lara rolled her hips forward and back, concentrating on how each tilt of her pelvis heightened the sensations. If she moved this way, he hit a spot that had her catching her breath. Other angles were nice, but this one, this one was magic.

His hands gripped her hips, tilting them to hit that spot. Too soon a starburst lit the inside of her eyelids. Her entire body clenched in one long orgasm. Muscles feeling like wet paper she collapsed on his chest. A shiver of delight shook her as he continued to pulse inside her.

"Did you like that?" he asked.

"Mmm, that was nice," she responded, floating on a sea of relaxation.

"Nice? We're going for sublime."

Jared rolled her beneath him. "Let's try this, shall we?"

Lara opened one eye and waved a hand. "Go right ahead. I'm done."

Jared placed a quick kiss on her lips. "I don't think so."

Long, slow thrusts built her pleasure with each stroke and soon she was tilting her hips into each surge. Her nails dug into his shoulders. Was it possible to die from an overload of pleasure? She didn't know but was more than willing to sacrifice her body to find out.

"Darn it, faster! Please, I need…" she ordered.

"As my lady desires." He lifted her leg over his shoulder and hit that spot. Fireworks burst forth showering her with intense pleasure. She was hurled into the heart of a supernova and it was glorious.

Her eyes opened as her body slid into delightful lethargy. His face above her was harsh with lines of strain.

Lara reached up and cupped his cheek. "That was... I've never... thank you."

"You don't think you're done yet, do you?"

"I'm not?"

"Oh no, darling, you have a few more in you."

"Nope, I'm done."

Jared nipped at her bottom lip. "There's a challenge if I've ever heard one."

His hips thrust against hers, and she began the journey to the heart of an exploding sun again.

After what seemed like hours, he collapsed, rolling over and pulling her against his side.

Lara was nothing more than a noodle doll. Her arms and legs refused to obey her commands. Summoning a burst of energy from who knew where, she placed her hand over his heart.

"Sublime?" he asked.

"How can you have the energy to talk?"

He squeezed her. "I feel invigorated."

"Well I'm done," she said with a yawn

A featherlight touch brushed her forehead. "Sleep."

Lara's eyes drifted closed and she succumbed to comforting darkness.

§

After Hans dropped Cyn off, she studied the various medical buildings and began her trudge up the hill in the icy cold breeze. She loved her job, freezing her ass off in the cold San Francisco night. The slog up the hill wasn't enough to keep the ward off the effects of the wind slicing through her. When she got home it'd be a hot bath and warm blood to relax her into day sleep.

Once she reached the campus, a handy map let her know the what the main buildings studied. She discounted the satellite locations in other areas of the city. If she were experimenting on someone and didn't want others to find out what she was doing, which department would be the most useful?

Psychiatric Medicine might be a good place to start. She stayed in Real, not wanting to alert anyone in Shadow to what she was doing until it was too late. Entering the building she studied the directory and headed to the basement level. She kept to the sides of the hallways, staying out of the way of patients, students, staff, and security.

Cyn fingered the chameleon charm and activated it before following various badged technicians to the lowest level of the facility.

As soon as she cleared the large, soundproofed doors, she heard the screams. Adrenaline surged and she instinct urged her to save whoever was in pain. But she forced herself to skulk through the facility, giving the charm a chance to blend her into the background.

Cyn peered into a window. An operating table stood in the center of the room while three people dressed in white coats recorded data on tablets. Two individuals in scrubs and face masks performed surgery on a patient who screamed with every incision. Shit. There wasn't anything she could do. To interrupt without knowing what was going on would be suicide for her and kill the person on the table.

Cyn moved on. This was, after all, a recon visit, not a rescue. But if the opportunity presented itself, she'd take it.

She prowled down the hallways, peeking into rooms as she passed. Many were empty, and the ones that were occupied held people wrapped in blankets, lying on cots. It was hard to tell if they were asleep or dead, but the shallow rise and fall of the covers assured her they were breathing.

Around the corner, she found an occupied room and her luck held; the person was awake. Taking the risk, she checked the door for alarms or other security. Nothing. She depressed the handle and pushed the door inward. As soon as there was enough space, she slid inside and held the handle so there wasn't noise.

"Who's there?" a raspy voice asked.

Cyn tiptoed to the bed and knelt beside it. "I'm a friend. Who are you? What's going on?"

"Name's Charlie. Some weirdos picked me up and brought me here."

"Where are you from, Charlie?"

"Me and a couple of others live on the streets over by Van Ness."

His face was weather worn and wrinkled. Gnarled hands gripped the edges of his blanket and the skin was embedded with smears of dirt. The good news was, she found the disappearing homeless. She needed to find out why they were here "Do you know why they brought you here?"

"Nope. They ain't chatty while they poke and prod a body. Hurts like a motherfucker.

Cyn reached for his hand and he jolted at the contact. "Come with me, I'll get you out." She hoped the charm would cover them both.

"Nah, leave me here. Fuckers blinded me." He turned his head her direction, but his eyes didn't focus.

"I'll stop them." Cyn promised as he relaxed into sleep.

She left using the same care as when she entered.

Cyn continued skulking, twisting at times to make sure the camera feed caught everything she was seeing. The labs were set up like a maze and she identified with the poor mouse searching for cheese. She passed labs, storage areas, and subject rooms but learned nothing about what was type of research was being conducted.

After what felt like hours of searching, she found the record room. Filing cabinets lined the walls and a desk in the middle held two monitors. She slipped into the room and went to the nearest filing cabinet, checking for security cameras and spells. Nothing. Pretty lax of them, except she was deep within the facility. The people in charge thought the information was safe because any intruders would be caught before now.

She opened the first drawer and grabbed a file. The information was all geek to her, but she flipped through each page. Pull file, flip pages, record, and repeat.

The computer was password protected, but the genius who'd set it up, taped it to the side of the monitor. A few keystrokes later and she was searching through the hard drive. A map of the facility popped up and she quickly memorized it before inserting a thumb drive into the port. She downloaded the data.

A sound from the hallway had her jerking from the chair. On quiet feet she snuck to the door and listened. Two security personnel passed in front of the door and she held her breath until they were out of hearing range. Her watch vibrated against the back of her wrist. Shit, it was nearing dawn. Time to journey home.

Download complete, she removed the drive and tucked it into a secured pocket. According to the recently memorized map, there was less distance to the end than go back.

A half hour later she located the exit staircase. Climbing it, she found herself in a small garage with a ramp that led toward the ceiling.

Engines rumbled to life and the roof slid up. Counting on the charm to obscure her, she darted up the ramp, avoiding the dark van coming down. Hiding behind a tree, she waited for the ramp to close and then walked down the dirt path to the golf course.

Cyn pulled out her cell. "I need a pick up."

Twenty minutes later Hans arrived and she reported what she'd found as he drove toward her apartment.

"The underground lab system isn't something our group can deal with. We're going to need help."

Hans glanced at her. "Can you contact your ex?"

Cyn glared at him. "No way in hell." But there was someone she could call. "I was told to contact Jared Williams if I need help."

Hans nodded. "I've followed his career. He's good, for an Elite. I'm tempted to bring him in, but not sure if he'd agree."

Cyn considered it. "He might. Be careful before revealing too much. Just in case."

Hans gave her a look. "I know what I'm doing."

She grinned at him. "Sorry."

"Call him and arrange a meet at the warehouse. We'll take his measure there."

Cyn texted, and after a short conversation, faced Hans. "He wants to meet at his place. He doesn't want to leave Lara alone."

"Is it secure?"

Cyn laughed. "More than your warehouse."

Interest lit his expression. "Is it sunlight secure?"

"No."

"Set it up for tonight." Hans pulled in front of her building.

Cyn leaned over and kissed his cheek. "See you later."

Chapter 16

Lara felt deliciously lethargic and toasty warm. Her body ached in a good way. Movement caused twinges of soreness in little used muscles. She floated on a cloud of bliss, not wanting any of this to end.

Until the pillow beneath her cheek moved and her eyes popped open. Hard firm flesh pillowed her head and a male nipple was within licking range. Oh lord, she was plastered against Jared! Her leg was thrown over his hip and her hand gripped the opposite shoulder, keeping him in place.

His chest resonated with his voice. "You don't have to hold me down. I want to be here." Amusement laced his tone.

"Um, sorry." Heat filled her cheeks, where was that hole in the universe when you needed one? Heck she'd even settle for the cartoon version at this point. It was one of her standard avoidance wishes. Uncomfortable or embarrassing situation, wish for a black hole.

Jared reached over and tilted her chin, lifting her head so she met his gaze. "It's okay. I admire a woman who hangs on to what she wants."

And she felt his 'want' swelling beneath her leg. The seductress within purred at the hardening flesh. Her leg rubbed over his erection and her hip pressed into his side.

Jared placed his hand on her knee keeping her leg in place.

"Are you sore?" he asked.

"A little, but I'm up for it if you are," she teased.

"I think we both know I'm 'up' for it." He reached over to the bedside table and retrieved the box. "Damn, we were busy last night."

"Are you out?"

"Nope, but there's only two left." He shifted her leg and rolled the condom on.

Jared turned so she was beneath him and grinned down at her. "We'll have to make them count."

His entrance was slow and delightful. A gentle ride and soft peak that left her wallowing in golden afterglow. Last night had been real, not a dream. Jared had serious moves and her body was loving all the attention bestowed by the maestro.

"We should pace ourselves. Once a day and twice on weekends," Lara babbled.

"Why?"

"I won't get anything done if my limbs are nothing but overcooked spaghetti all the time."

"I'll help." Jared left the bed and walked into the bathroom. That man's backside should be illegal. He returned accompanied the sound of water running.

"How can you move?" Lara complained.

"Stamina. Let's get you into the bath before my energy gives out."

He picked her up and carried her to an overly large tub. "No bubbles?" she asked.

"No." He stepped into the tub and sank into the hot water, arranging her on his lap. She leaned against his chest.

"After the bath, we'll have lunch, then I'll run to the store and stock up on supplies."

Hmm, running out to the store. "Could you get me a couple of things?" Lara's thoughts tumbled like clothes in a dryer, pondering what she'd need... oh! She sat up straight. "Don't forget, we're meeting Doreen for tea today."

"We? Tea?" He raised an eyebrow.

"Coffee, whatever." Lara waved a wet hand. "And yes, we. You're going to come with."

Jared grabbed it and brought it to his mouth, nibbling on the base of her fingers. "I'm not sure that's a good idea."

212

"We've got to go. I've to reassure Doreen that I'm okay." Lara's breath caught and she struggled to focus.

"She didn't believe you?" He pressed kisses into her palm.

"She wants visual proof, and won't take no for an answer." Lara leaned against his shoulder letting the heat of the bath seep into her muscles.

"Okay. Where's the tea shop?"

"Angelini's Coffee Roasters. Know where that is?"

"Yeah, a couple of friends hang out there."

The water cooled, forcing them from the bath. It was nice talking about everything and nothing while petting him. But it was getting late, and they needed to hurry if they were going to meet Doreen on time.

Lara dressed in layers, short sleeved shirt, long sleeved over shirt. Jeans and comfortable shoes completed the outfit. Jared was dressed, and in the kitchen making French Toast by the time she was ready. A quick clean up later and they were ready to go.

They left the building and walked the few blocks to the coffee shop. During the walk, Jared kept glancing to either side and stopping in front of window displays to look behind them.

"Anyone following us?" Lara asked.

"Not that I can see."

She glanced at the crowds of people on the sidewalk. "Do you think you're in danger?"

Jared shrugged.

"You are not invincible, you know," she said.

"I know. But the area is too populated for them to grab me."

Jared took her arm again and led her halfway down the next block to Angelini's.

They entered the popular coffee shop. Conversation, the whir of coffee grinders, and hisses of steam filled the air.

After the stress of the past couple of days, the crowd overwhelmed her. There wasn't enough air in the room. Her heart began to race, she flushed hot then cold and she wanted to scream at everyone. Jared placed his hand on her lower back. "Inhale slowly. That's good. Hold it." He counted to five under his breath. "Now exhale slowly. Focus on me. Ignore everything else."

It was difficult, but she managed to tune everyone else out and focus on what Jared was saying. It was a bunch of nonsense really, mismatched phrases that didn't make sense. She focused on his voice and after a few minutes, a measure of calm and peace replaced her panic.

"Steady?" he asked.

Lara took a deep breath. "Thank you."

"What would you like?"

Lara glanced at the menu. "A medium chai please."

Jared raised an eyebrow. "Nothing fancy?"

"You're waiting for the half-caf, half-soy, half almond milk, light sugar type of order?"

Jared shrugged. "Maybe."

"I'm just me," she scanned the rest of the menu as they stepped forward in line. "Okay, I'm changing my mind. A medium London Fog."

"Now you're messing with me."

She couldn't help laughing and pointing at the menu. "No, it's a drink."

"Don't we have enough fog here? Why do you need to import more from London?" he said with a wink.

Jared tried to keep her amused, because his senses were twitching. He was certain they were being watched. He'd been truthful when he'd told her a more populated area would keep them safe. They needed to remain among a crowd.

It was their turn to place an order. Jared pulled out his wallet and put the cash on the counter. Lara put her hand on his arm. "What are you doing?"

"Paying for our drinks, why?" He nodded at the barista behind the bar and took Lara's arm, steering her toward the pick-up point.

"I can get my own." Lara protested.

"It's my treat." Jared nudged her shoulder with his arm. "If you ask nicely, maybe I'll let you pay for our next meal."

214

Lara giggled and he took that as a sign her panic had cleared. He kept up the teasing banter while they got their drinks and headed to one of the occupied tables near the wall. A woman stood as they wound their way through the tables. From her attitude and bearing she appeared to be one of those protective types. She narrowed her eyes and scowled at him.

"Doreen, I'd like you to meet Jared Williams. Jared, this is Doreen, my boss and friend." Lara said.

Jared shook Doreen's hand. "It's a pleasure to meet you."

"I wouldn't be too sure about that if I were you," Doreen retorted.

"Doreen! Jared owns the bunny we found."

"And that gives him the right to become your lover?"

Lara's face turned bright red. Damn, now she was embarrassed. She was adorable when flustered but he knew better than to say anything.

Lara stood, arms akimbo. "I can't believe you said that," she hissed.

"I have a whole lot more to say," Doreen glared at him.

Jared cleared his throat. "Perhaps we'd better sit down and stop drawing attention?"

Doreen grudgingly resumed her seat. Lara sat next to her, leaving the seat across from Doreen open. It left his back to the rest of the café, not the best position to be in. Lara was exchanging fast whispers with Doreen. He was poised and ready to defend himself if necessary, however, Lara was doing an excellent job of politely telling Doreen to butt out of their business.

There was a distinctive vibration from his phone, letting him know the call was from the Captain.

"Excuse me, I've got to take this." Jared strode to a section of the coffee shop empty of tables and held up the wall while he took the call. There wasn't anyone near to overhear, but he kept his voice low just in case.

"Williams here."

"Sorry to disturb you, but you need to come into the office and verify a couple of reports. It's urgent."

"I'll be there soon. I need someone to protect Lara."

"She'll be fine in your apartment." Captain Jor'dan remarked.

"We're meeting one of her friends at Angelini's."

"What? Hmm, I'll see if Deidre's able to stop by and keep an eye on her until you're done."

"Thanks."

Jared hung up and went back to the table where an earnest conversation was taking place. Doreen was attempting to talk Lara out of a relationship with him, and while he'd love to stay and plead his case, the Captain wouldn't ask him to come in unless it was important.

"I'm sorry ladies, but I have to go."

Lara glanced up at him. "What's wrong?"

"There's an urgent matter at the office that I have to clear up."

She got out of her chair and hugged him. "What about the bad guys?" she whispered.

He leaned down and spoke in her ear. "A friend is coming to watch out for you."

"But what about you?" Lara asked, concern filling her voice.

"I'll be careful, I promise. When I get to the office, I'll text you."

Lara didn't like it, but there wasn't much she could say. "What does your friend look like?"

"She's 5'7", brown hair, and purple eyes."

A sting of jealousy bit her. "Ex-girlfriend?"

Jared laughed. "Hell no, she's dating a friend of mine. You're the one I want complicating my life."

Lara arched an eyebrow. "Am I a complication?"

"Yeah, and I'd have it no other way. Stay safe."

He pressed a kiss on her mouth and nibbled on her lower lip. "I'll be done soon."

Lara watched bemused, as he left the shop and jogged past the window.

"Well, that was an eyeful," Doreen said.

Lara sighed and sat down and took a swallow of tea. "What can I say? He's good."

"Seems to me, he's too good, like what's-his-face was."

Lara bit her lip. "There's a marked difference between the two."

Doreen drank her latte. "And what's that?"

"Jared takes care of me. He bought me tea, fixed me meals, and cleaned up afterward."

"It could be that he's just trying to get some."

Lara studied Doreen's suspicious expression and hurried to reassure her. Lara didn't know the right words to explain how she knew Jared was different. "But that's just it. He did all this after we had sex."

"Hmm."

"And he wasn't trying to impress me. It was a habit, something he's done over and over again. Unlike when the jerk tried to impress me and didn't know you weren't supposed to put dishwashing liquid into the dishwasher."

"I laughed my ass off when that happened."

"Me, too. But even on our first date, something was off about the jerk. None of those niggly little voices are saying anything about Jared."

"I reserve the right to withhold judgement. I think he's trying to scam you."

"What would he gain from it?" Lara wondered out loud.

"I don't know," Doreen admitted, "but until we find out, you need to be careful."

Her phone beeped, and she read the text. *At office. May take a while. XO*

"He texted me." She flipped the phone to show Doreen, then texted him back. *Thanks.*

"That's a point in his favor. What's-his-face never contacted you when he said he would." Doreen commented.

Lara's ex gave her excuses when she called him on his poor communication skills. She should have recognized him for the user he was. Jared's actions were encouraging. She was hopefully optimistic that this thing between them might last.

Doreen leaned forward. "What the hell happened to you? I haven't been able to get ahold of you."

What happened? Everything and anything had happened. She'd promised Jared she wouldn't share what he'd told her of Shadow Earth, but she needed to appease Doreen's curiosity with something.

Her mouth opened and closed, and Lara was aware she resembled a fish. "I... I was caught up in something involving my friend's work. I can't tell you anything other than that."

Doreen's eyes narrowed. "You can tell me anything, even secret stuff."

Lara shook her head. "Not this." Lara's mind replayed the events of the past couple of days. The more she thought about it, the more her hands shook, and the more anxiety grabbed her with angry claws. She wrapped both hands around the warmth of the tea cup. She focused on the heat of the ceramic and breathed through the rising panic. She had to take her mind off things, which led her in a roundabout manner to Cyn.

Wait a minute. Cyn had extreme photosensitivity and she knew the dragon doctor and Jared. Could she be one of the vampires? It would explain some of her behavior.

"Tell me what you can." Doreen's demand drew her from her tumbled thoughts.

"I can't." *It's too much.* "Drop it."

Doreen sat back and drank her coffee. "I'll leave it for now, but we'll be discussing this later."

Not if I can help it.

"Did you at least let the police know where you were?"

Lara nodded. "I called on of the detectives, I think it was Alejandro."

"Are you sure you called?" Disbelief filled Doreen's tone.

Lara set down her tea. "I called. A lot has happened to me over the past few days. Right now, you're stressing me out and need to back off."

Doreen sat back, a myriad of expressions crossing her face. Shock was followed by disbelief and before a smile lit her face.

"I'm impressed. You'd never talked back to me like that before."

Lara sipped her tea. "Last time you pushed me. I ended up on the bathroom floor, shivering for the entire weekend and I don't want that to happen now. I'm slowly learning to recognize and, if possible, stop things that stress me."

Doreen opened her mouth to speak but was interrupted by a commotion at the front door. A stunningly beautiful woman walked into the coffee shop, and both women and men jumped up, offering her a seat.

"Who do you suppose that is?" Doreen asked.

The woman had bright violet eyes, alight with mischief. "I believe that's my babysitter." Lara said.

"Babysitter? Why do you need a babysitter?"

The woman approached and overheard the comment. "Because Jared is concerned the bad guys are still around. Hi, I'm Deidre."

Lara shook her hand. "I'm Lara, and this is Doreen."

Doreen shook her hand. "No offense, but you look like a cream puff. What can you do against bad guys?"

Deidre grinned. "I'd tell you, but then I'd have to kill you." She winked at Lara.

Oh man, Deidre must be one of the magical creatures. Which one? Conversation at the table was polite, weather type of stuff, until Deidre asked where they worked.

"The main branch of the San Francisco Public Library." Doreen replied.

"Oh." Deidre smiled at the barista who brought her a steaming cup of coffee. "Put it on my tab, Jon."

"Of course, Miss Deidre."

"Come here often?" Lara asked.

"Every day." The violet eyed woman said. "The library. Isn't that where you found Jared?"

Lara nodded. "How did you know about that?"

Deidre waved her hand. "Oh, my bestie told me all about it. You might know her. Cyn? On the lookout for night classes at the Supervillain School of Villainy?"

Lara laughed. "I'm the one who told her about the school."

"Where can I go to take classes?" Deidre asked.

"I don't know if there's such a place. But it would be fun, wouldn't it?"

Doreen shook her head. "You're both talking nonsense."

Deidre and Doreen debated some point, but Lara didn't pay attention. All her life she'd been told that the things she thought of, her imagination, was nonsense.

A total stranger had validated her silly idea of the Supervillain School. But not even her imagination could compare to all the stuff she'd seen in the last couple of days. While it'd been terrifying at times, it was also amazing.

A different barista brought over a plate of pastries. "Here you go, Miss Deidre, for you and your guests."

Deidre grinned up at him. "Thank you, sugar."

The young man blushed and headed back to the counter, turning to look at Deidre every few steps.

That's when Lara knew. "Succubus!" Shoot, she said that out loud. Doreen frowned at her. "What do you mean?"

"Sorry," she mumbled to Deidre. "It's just their reactions to you put me in mind of the mythical creature."

"Some myths are truer than others," Deidre replied with a smirk.

"If you two are going to talk mythology, I'm leaving."

Lara covered Doreen's hand with hers. "No, please stay. Doreen isn't a big fan of mythology. She's more interested in current events."

"That's all right. I'm a fan of both myself," Deidre said.

The topic of discussion became general, and they polished off the pastries as the afternoon waned.

Doreen glanced at her watch. "Thanks for catching up, but I've got to go."

Lara stood and they hugged goodbye. She watched Doreen leave and sat back down.

"Sorry about the succubus comment earlier. Sometimes brain to mouth doesn't work well."

Deidre shook her head. "Don't worry about it. I still have a hard time getting used to the whole secrecy thing as well."

Lara was confused. "But you're a succubus, and a member of the group?"

"Yes, I'm a succubus. But I've existed outside of Shadow and never adhered to their rules. Now that I'm dating my honey, I'm forced to comply."

Lara's mouth opened and closed. There were so many things she wanted to ask, but where to start? "Are the myths about succubae true?"

"I'm not sure what myths you've heard." Deidre sat back finishing off a scone. "But I live off male energy."

"And do you drain them dry, leaving husks?"

"Nah, I just nibble here and there." Deidre paused. "I'm nibbling a lot less since my honey is able to keep me full."

"Was it something like Jared, where you were forced into this?"

"Nope. I was created via the belief of man."

Lara was fascinated as Deidre told her tale.

"That's incredible. To think of all the places you've seen." Lara remarked.

"It not all fairytales and roses. Some of it was pure hell."

Lara covered the woman's, demon's?, hand and squeezed. "I'm sorry." Curiosity compelled Lara to ask, "How's the sex?" Both of Lara's hands covered her mouth. Dang it where was that black hole again? "Sorry didn't mean to ask that," she mumbled from beneath her palms.

Deidre laughed and it was infectious. People stared at her, making the heat in Lara's face flame hotter. "You're the only one to ask that. Others want to, but they don't have the courage."

"Neither do I. It's the mouth brain thing again." Lara sipped her tea trying to erase the past couple of minutes.

"In answer to your question, fabulous. Before Damien, it was like breathing. I needed it, but it was just another body function. I thought the screaming O was a myth. Fake it 'till you make it. Damien rocked my world, and I finally understood what all the fuss was about. If you want any tricks to drive your man crazy with lust, let me know."

Lara's mouth popped open, then closed, then opened again. Should she? Yes. But that's when courage left her. All she could do was nod. Deidre began a face-heating, panty-wetting explanation on how to drive Jared wild.

The light faded and conversation moved to less arousing topics.

A quick check of Lara's phone revealed no new messages. "I wonder what's taking Jared so long?" she wondered aloud.

"They're crossing every t and dotting every i. It's going to take a while."

Lara's stomach rumbled. "I'm getting hungry. Shall we go get dinner?"

"I know the perfect place," Deidre replied. "Let's go."

Lara texted Jared. *Going to dinner with Deidre.*

Deidre leaned over and read the text. "Tell him no men allowed."

Lara dutifully repeated that and got a laughing emoji back.

Let me know when you're done and I'll come get you, Jared replied.

She sent a thumbs-up and followed the succubus out into the cool evening. The cold air caused goose-bumps to pimple her skin. Huddling into the warmth of her jacket, she and Deidre hop-scotched from store window to store window.

They rounded the corner and Deidre stilled, grabbing Lara's arm.

"What's wrong?" Lara asked in a whisper.

"I don't know, but my spidey senses are tingling."

Lara looked around for the source of the threat and felt a sharp sting in her arm. "What's that?" In slow motion, Deidre spun to face her. Her mouth stretched wide like she had a flip top head. Lara wanted to ask if the other woman was okay, but stringing words together was beyond her.

The world started acting silly. Buildings waved and wobbled; streetlights tried to grab her; trees were doing the samba. She stepped out of their way, and the ground jerked from beneath her feet. Darkness swallowed her.

§

Jared slid the phone into his pocket and grinned. No men allowed. That meant he'd have to get dinner on his own. He glanced at the clock on the far wall of the conference room. It was getting late and there was a good chance the Elite would have food brought in.

When he'd arrived hours ago, he'd been directed to the penthouse conference room. It was heavily warded and used for top secret meetings. The fact he was the lowest ranking individual in the room meant it was serious business. Captain Jor'dan stood near the white board, where all of the evidence had been gathered and time-lined.

Sitting at the head of the table was High Chancellor Ashton Ignatio. To his right was Regina, Oracle of L'Dan.

Jared had been asked to provide proof of his reports to verify and corroborate incidents that happened since he'd become a member of the Elite. Other members of the Elite had been brought in throughout the afternoon, but Captain Jor'dan made it clear Jared was to sit in on each session of questioning.

His pocket vibrated. It was Cyn and though it was barely dark, she was waiting for him at Han's warehouse. Lara and Deidre should be sitting down to dinner about now, so he had time to meet with Cyn before collecting Lara from dinner.

At a lull in the conversation he stood. "Excuse me, Sir, but I have an appointment elsewhere."

Captain Jor'dan narrowed his eyes. "The other project?"

"Yes, Sir."

The fae glanced at the High Chancellor. "If you'll not be needing Elite Jared Williams anymore?"

"He's free to go," His Grace responded, attention focused on the file in front of him.

Jared bowed at the waist and left. A tingle of magic passed over his skin as he exited the room. He wasn't sure what the spell was, since he'd been able to send and receive text messages within, but he wasn't too concerned about that at the moment.

His phone buzzed again. *ETA?* Cyn messaged.

I'm at Elite HQ. Be there in twenty.

Jared drove to a sketchy neighborhood and parked behind an old, run down warehouse. Cyn and a man he assumed to be Hans were sitting on the loading dock.

Cyn jumped up. "You weren't followed, were you?"

Jared shook his head. "If you mean James, no. The vamp has been driving everyone nuts trying to find you, but I made sure that he and Damien were working on something else when I left."

"What about Randall?"

Jared raised an eyebrow. "You're a very popular individual. He was in his office working on a report when I left."

"Good."

The other man cleared his throat, and Cyn rolled her eyes. "Hans, this is Jared Williams, Jared this is Hans Drebin."

Jared exchanged a handshake with Hans. "Forgive me for asking, but what are you?" Jared asked. The aura that surrounded the man was one he'd not seen before. It was a slow-bubbling deep red, hypnotic, like a muted lava lamp.

"I'm half demon, half human. I've been following your career for quite some time. I want you to work for me."

"Will it interfere with my Elite duties?"

"No. It'd complement them."

"What is it that you do?"

Cyn stepped forward. "Hans runs an independent investigation network, helping those who can't or won't go to the Elite or human police, for various reasons."

It sounded good to him. Helping those who fell between worlds was one of the reasons he'd accepted the original offer of becoming an Elite. "I'm interested, but I've got to take care of this situation first."

Hans opened his mouth and Cyn butted in. "You can discuss him working for you later. Right now we need to focus on what I found last night."

A chill that had nothing to do with the night air raced up Jared's spine. This was going to be hell. He knew it.

Hans led the way into the warehouse and into a spacious office area. There were multiple monitors surrounding a high-tech workstation. Jared gazed at the equipment with envy. "Nice system."

Hans shrugged. "Keeps me out of trouble."

Cyn laughed. "As if anything could keep you out of trouble."

"Or anyone," came a voice from behind them.

Hans smiled and held his hand out to the elf entering the room. She was shorter than most elves Jared had seen and was dressed in fishnet stockings, high-heeled boots, a short skirt and a white shirt tied between her breasts, baring her belly.

She walked up to Hans and gave him a kiss. He grabbed her ass through her skirt. A wolf whistle from Cyn and the couple ended the steamy kiss.

Cyn exchanged a hug with the elf. "Jared, this is Megan, Hans' love muffin. Megs, this is Jared Williams."

"Hello Megan," Jared said, shaking her hand.

The elf eyed him up and down. "Well hello, handsome." She spun to Hans, fingers clasped in front of her chest. "May we keep him?"

Cyn shook her head. "Sorry, this is one of the few decent ones."

Megan pouted. "Damn. I really want to find one with stamina, and Mr. Williams looks like he'd last a long time."

Jared had no idea what they were talking about and thought it be better if he didn't ask. It had nothing to do with where his mind had gone. At least he hoped not.

Hans hugged Megan. "Don't worry, dearest, we'll find someone. In the meantime, let's go over the data from yesterday."

The demon sat at the workstation and brought up footage. "This is from Cyn's collar cam," he explained.

They watched her progress through a labyrinth of corridors and rooms. Another screen showed the building layout and a dot of color showing her location.

"Where did you get this technology?" Jared asked. This would be great for tailing someone.

Hans glanced over his shoulder. "Trade secret, though if you become a contractor, arrangements can be made."

"I look forward to furthering our negotiations."

Cyn shook her head, and they went back to watching the video. Jared's eyes were drawn to a section of the building plans. If he could figure out a way to isolate the labs from the main hospital building… What about there?

"Stop the tape."

Everyone stared at him. "What do you see?" Hans asked.

Jared squinted at the screen. "Can you zoom here?" He pointed to a location on the monitor.

Hans zoomed in and after a perusal of the plans Jared nodded. "Let's mark this area."

Hans flagged each point with a marker on the schematic and the recording resumed.

Jared made note of the doors Cyn passed through as she progressed through the building. There was a flash of something on the corner of the screen. "Stop. Can you zoom in there?"

Hans manipulated the image and the small spec was blown up on one screen.

"What is it?" Cyn asked.

Jared flushed hot then cold as Hans manipulated the image to show the distinctive beak of a gryphon.

"It looks like a gryphon," Hans said.

Cyn's jaw dropped as she leaned to get a closer look. "I can't believe I fucking missed that." She turned bleak eyes to Megan. "I would have gotten them out of there if I'd have known."

The elf engulfed the vampire in a hug and patted her back. "I know you would have, Cyn."

Jared couldn't believe what he was seeing. A quick search of the paranormal database the Elite kept showed that there were no gryphons currently in residence, or visiting the city. That meant one thing. Those bastards were doing it again. He'd hoped they were in the beginning stages, but seeing those creatures burst that bubble with a harsh dose of reality.

Jared drew in a deep breath, but the cold, clammy feeling was back and getting worse. Cursing under his breath, he jerked away from the monitors and gripped the edge of the table. Black dots swam before his eyes, and the pain of thousands of needles pricked his skin. *Hold on, breathe through it.*

Re-venge, breathe in, breathe out.

Calm.

A soft voice spoke at his side. "Here's some ice water and a cold cloth. Put it on the back of your neck." The elf held the items out.

"Please," he said. It was all he could do to keep the shaking at bay.

Without touching him, she placed the cloth on his nape. The cold was a welcome relief to his overheated skin. On his other side, Cyn grabbed the glass and held it up with a straw. "Take a sip."

He did, and the cool liquid absorbed into his parched throat. He sipped more, careful not to drink too much. His hands clenched and unclenched the edge of the table. Soft music filled the room. Ethereal and light, it helped him to focus outside his body. He finished the water and a fresh glass replaced it. Once he'd finished the second one, he straightened from the desk with a final deep breath.

"Okay now?" Cyn asked.

Compassion and something more filled her expression. "You've dealt with panic attacks before?" he asked.

"More times than I can count," Cyn admitted in a soft voice.

Hans was busy with the screens then swiveled in the chair. "What does it mean?"

"It means the Alliance has their shifter army," Jared replied.

Cyn leaned against the table, arms crossed over her chest. "Can you help me shut it down?"

Jared was hesitant. While he'd love to destroy that lab, going back there, subjecting himself to those memories, was impossible.

"I..."

His phone vibrated with a call. He checked the number and had to grin. Lara was ready to be picked up.

"How was dinner?" he asked.

"Hello, Mr. Williams. Your little friend never made it to dinner. She's my guest." Jared knew that voice. Chills raced over his skin, and sparkles filled his vision. Panic threatened to retake him.

"What do you want, Glendale?" he snarled. *Focus. Focus on Lara. The bastard has her. I can fall apart later.*

"Nothing yet. Her continued good health depends on you. Be at this address by eleven p.m. and your little friend will be released safe and unharmed. Miss the deadline, and she'll be my next experiment."

The call was terminated. In a fit of temper, Jared hurled the device at the wall, where it shattered on impact.

"What was that all about?" Cyn asked.

Jared clenched his fists. He was going to have to enter that fucking lab again. "Glendale has Lara, and I have until eleven to turn myself in."

Hans' fingers flew over the keys. "We have a couple of hours. We need a plan."

Chapter 17

Lara regained consciousness with a pounding headache. The throbbing in her skull pulsed in time with the beating of her heart. *Not again.* She shifted, and other aches and pains caused a moan to slip free. Being kidnapped was a pain in the neck, back, leg, and, oh, upper arm.

It wasn't as romantic as the silver screen had led her to believe.

She took deep breaths to calm the wave of dizziness and swallowed a couple times to fight the rising nausea. She tried to lift her hand to rub her temple, but the arm wouldn't move.

When Lara opened her eyes, she was treated to a blurry world. What the heck? Blinking rapidly cleared her vision but didn't improve her situation. Both wrists were secured to the arms of the chair with thick straps. There was a belt across her lap. Her ankles seemed to be strapped to the chair because she couldn't lift her legs.

From the feel of various bands constricting her movement, she was stuck wearing the chair like a freakin' backpack. The most uncomfortable one she'd ever worn. Now if only there was a way to escape its strappy clutches. The buckles holding the straps were on the outside of her wrists and weren't reachable by her fingers no matter how much she wiggled and contorted. Heaving a sigh, she checked out the room.

There was a desk in front of her within kicking distance if her legs hadn't been tied up. The wall behind it was made up of huge windows that looked down a row of empty cages on either side of a central walkway. Lara didn't want to know who or what they kept in those cages. She really didn't.

To her right was a white board with various writing that she couldn't decipher. It wasn't formulas or anything technical though there were diagrams. The words didn't make sense to her. It appeared to be another language written in recognizable Roman alphabet characters. Further along the wall was a framed poster of Da Vinci's Vitruvian Man. She couldn't see anything beyond that; her neck wouldn't turn that far. On her left was a door, flanked on either side by bookcases, filled with medical books and journals.

No way to escape that she could see. Now what?

The door slammed open and a handful of men dressed in dark fatigues rushed into the room. Black masks covered their features. Scary. They carried guns, like something out of a military, black ops movie. Moving through the space on silent feet, they checked every nook and cranny. Tension filled the area. What were they doing? A couple of hand signals between them and their shoulders eased. The room was secure. Two positioned themselves on either side of the window. The other two stood by the door. All came to attention when a fifth black clad person entered. He stopped in front of her, paused for a long moment, then reached up and pulled off his mask.

The click of the door handle had her fantasy crumbling around her.

An older man appeared. His brown hair was streaked gray. Overall, someone she'd pass on the street without a second look, except for the manic gleam in his brown eyes. It scared her worse than the vampires had.

"Good, you're awake," he said, taking a seat behind the desk.

She swallowed her nervousness. "Who are you, and why am I here?"

"I'm Dr. David Glendale. Perhaps you've heard of me?"

Wasn't he the creep who'd experimented on Jared? If so, she was in serious trouble, but she wouldn't let him know that.

Her forehead creased in a frown. "Sorry, I don't read many medical journals."

Anger flared in his expression before he smiled. "You misunderstand. I'm surprised that your friend, Mr. Williams, hasn't said anything about me."

"I didn't know he was sick."

"He's not," Dr. Glendale replied.

"Then why would he tell me the name of his doctor?" she asked, trying to stall him. By now Jared must know she'd been taken, right? And he'd formulate a plan to rescue her?

"I'm the lead researcher in a cancer study he participated in a few years ago."

"Jared has cancer?"

The doctor rolled his eyes. "I told you he's not sick."

Lara slumped in the chair, faking relief. "Huh, I didn't know he was a cancer survivor."

"He didn't have cancer. It was a genetic study to determine cancer rates in siblings," the doctor explained.

"I wasn't aware he had brothers or sisters."

The doctor gave her a look she interpreted as condescending. "You haven't asked?"

"Sorry, doc, we've only recently started seeing each other. There hasn't been time to exchange life stories." Not when they were too busy burning up the sheets. She kept that part to herself. "Regardless, why am I here?"

"Mr. Williams has been asked to return to the lab for follow-up visits. He's ignored each and every request. Your presence here will ensure he comes back."

"You think he'll come because of me?"

His smile sent a chill racing over her skin. "Yes."

"I think you overestimate our relationship," Lara replied. "Let's say he does show up. Once he's here, you'll let me go?"

"Of course."

And if she believed him, he had ocean front property in Nevada he'd sell her. Lara shifted in the chair, unable to move much.

"Uncomfortable?" the Doctor asked.

"A bit. Can you untie me?"

"No. You're fine where you are."

What did he think she'd do? Overpower him and escape? "How long am I going to be tied up like this?"

"As long as it takes Mr. Williams to get here."

A cell phone rang. From the ring, it wasn't hers. Which reminded her, where was her purse? She scanned the floor; no purse, no phone, nothing. Shoot.

"Excuse me." He grabbed the phone. "Yes?" A look of consternation crossed his face. "I'll be right there." He kept the phone to his ear and left the room.

"Hey, wait…" The door closed behind him.

Carp. *Okay concentrate.* Maybe she could save herself. All she had to do was free one wrist. She twisted both wrists and pulled her arms toward her. There wasn't much wiggle room, not enough to get her hand free. What if she straightened her fingers and folded her thumb into her palm to make her hand smaller?

Dang it, it didn't work. The straps around the wrists were too snug.

Time felt like it was passing slower than a receding fog bank in the city.

The door opened. Perhaps the mad scientist had returned? Nope. A man in a white coat with a small case entered. He placed it on the desk and flipped up the lid. Out came a small white packet, gauze, a long green band, exam gloves, three vials, and needle attached to a tube.

"What are you doing with that?" Lara asked, panic rising. She hated needles, hated, hated, HATED, them.

Ignoring her, he donned the gloves and tore open the packet that smelled strongly of alcohol.

"Stop! I don't consent to this. Stay away from me," Lara tried to hop in the chair, but it was too heavy to budge.

He stood on her left and tugged the sleeve of her jacket, but it was trapped beneath the wrist strap.

"That won't work. The strap is too tight," she advised.

The tech swabbed the back of her hand with the alcohol wipe.

Oh carp, a needle in the hand hurt worse than in the arm.

Son of a beehive! The burn of the needle piercing her skin overwhelmed her. Little white lights flashed in her vision, and the dark tunnel welcomed her into comforting oblivion.

§

Hans and Jared dropped Cyn off at the northwestern corner of the park. She had multiple rescues to perform and not much time to do them.

Hans arranged for his people to be waiting to give the victims help; they'd arrive within the hour.

Cyn, loaded with cloaking charms, crept into the compound, after fiddling with the entrance hatch. She snuck down the access stairs, senses alert for any guards. The smart watch she wore showed her location as a blue dot on the floorplan of the tunnel system. Super cool.

First on the to-do list was to rescue the guy she'd spoken with last time. She skulked her way to his room, keeping clear of security cameras and the occasional wandering rent-a-cop.

The room was empty, and the mattress was rolled up on the cot. *Fuck! Too late.*

Next item was to get the rest of the humans out.

She crept down the corridor, surprised at the empty halls. Last time she'd had to avoid techs and others wandering the area. What was going on? Were the guards alerted to her presence and waiting to trap her? Or was it a trap for Jared instead?

She approached a corner and peeked around it. Halfway down the hall was the door that held the human test subjects. Cyn tiptoed along the wall, and peeked through the window. A single guard was stationed before the cell bay doors. Taking a deep breath, she centered herself and pushed the door open and attacked. A quick choke-hold and the guy slumped to the floor, unconscious. She pulled him to the side and propped him against a metal cabinet. On the other side of the cell bay was a metal control panel.

Cyn started flipping switches and peering into the block to see which metal doors were sliding open. Entering the first cell, she approached the occupant, holding a finger to her lips. He nodded once and she sat next to him on the cot.

"How many of you are there?" she asked in a whisper.

"Twenty," he said.

"I'm getting you out." Taking out one of the charms, she affixed it to the top of his scrubs. "This will help you avoid security. Help me with the others."

He rose. She took the cells on one side of the room and he took the other.

Cyn recognized more than one of the men in the cells. Once they were free, she motioned them to silence and led them through the maze of corridors to the landing at the bottom of the stairs.

"Freedom is at the top of the stairs. Once you're out, there will be people to help you."

"Are you coming, too?" one of them asked.

"No, there are others trapped here. I need to get them out as well."

Her watch beeped, letting her know Jared had entered the facility. She was behind schedule. "Hurry," she urged.

The group climbed the stairs. Those who lagged were helped by their fellows.

Cyn texted Hans. *Humans free, gryphons next.*

§

Jared approached the address Glendale had given him. He'd gotten over the shakes by focusing on Lara. *Save her, fall apart later.*

They'd dropped Cyn off at the golf course to infiltrate from that end. If his plan didn't work, she was back-up. Unlike the rest of the Elite, he didn't discount her skills and knew she'd save both him and Lara if necessary.

With one last deep breath, Jared entered the building and walked up to reception. "I'm here to see Dr. Glendale."

The man at reception typed into a computer. "Oh yes, room LL37. Take the elevator over there."

"Thanks."

Jared walked to the elevator, aware he was under surveillance, both technological and magical.

He had a few tricks up his sleeve, charms given to him by Megan. Once he retrieved Lara, he'd activate them to blur their movements and cover their escape.

The elevator took him to the lower level and the doors opened on a barren hallway. He expected to meet a guard or some other escort. The fact no one was waiting for him meant they were confident in their security.

The sign on the wall directed him to the right. The sickly green painted hallway was broken up with windows, doors, and security cameras. Peeking into windows revealed empty lab rooms with glassware and various devices. Continuing his journey, he kept his eyes and ears open for threats. Other than the vague feeling of being watched, he didn't detect anything else.

Jared reached the door marked 37 without encountering anyone else. No one. In a lab this size there should have been researchers and other personnel going about their business. The halls were empty, which set his nerves on edge. Maybe there was a full security compliment waiting beyond the door?

It had to be a trap. But there wasn't anything he could do about it until he reached Lara.

Jared paused for a moment and took a deep breath. This was it. He opened the door, stepped in, and eased the door closed. His back was against a bookcase as he surveyed the room for possible threats. No obvious cameras, which worked in his favor. But no guards either, which began to worried him.

Lara was the sole person in the room, and she was slumped in a chair and bound by psychiatric restraints. Other than a small bandage on the back of her hand, she appeared injury-free.

The monitor on the desk showed Glendale was logged in. Perfect. Jared pulled the USB drive from his pocket and uploaded the program onto the network, shaking his head at how little security there was. The Alliance relied too much on magic rather than technology. In two days, the sleeper virus would infiltrate the entire system. When he activated a simple command, it would corrupt all their data. He pulled the thumb drive from the computer and returned the screen to how he'd found it.

Now to rescue the damsel. He knelt by her side, opposite the door, and examined the straps on the chair and their locking mechanisms. It was similar to a handcuff lock. He slid a piece of wire into the hole and twisted. The lock popped open and he loosened the strap, freeing her arm.

Jared released her from the rest of the restraints. As he eased the straps from around her shoulders, her head lifted.

"Are you a dream?" she asked.

"Didn't we have this conversation?"

"Did we?"

He leaned over and kissed her. "Does that feel like a dream?"

Lara smiled. "You know it does."

Jared couldn't help but grin. He'd walked into that one.

"I'm as real as you are." He helped her to stand, pulling her into his chest when she tipped sideways. "What's the last thing you remember?"

"One of those lab flunkies came at me with a needle." Lara lifted her hand showing off the bandage.

"Did they inject you with something?"

"I don't think so. I think he took blood."

"Then why were you unconscious?"

"You didn't see the size of the needle." Her body shuddered. "I really don't like needles."

Jared tilted her face up, looking into her beautiful eyes. Pupil response was normal.

She smiled up at him and his heart clenched. "You rescued me."

Jared cupped her cheek. "Always."

"I thought nothing could bring you back to the labs."

"Nothing, except you."

Her expression softened. "Oh"

Oh? What the hell kind of response was that? He'd ask, but they needed to leave.

Lara rubbed her forehead with the palm of one hand. "It's going to be a bad one."

"What?"

"We need to go soon, or my headache will morph into a full-blown migraine and I'll be sick."

Shit. While he could carry her out, it'd be easier if she were mobile. But first, he reached into a pocket and pulled out a charm, fastening it to her jacket and spoke the activation phrase.

"Now you see me, now you don't?" Lara said. "What kind of spell is that?"

"It's a charm from a dark elf with a sense of humor," Jared replied, "but it will help us to escape. We need to leave, now."

He grabbed her hand, shoving her behind him as the door open.

Dr. Glendale, the rat bastard, entered the room with a pleased expression. The smug look on his face begged to be removed by Jared's fist. Jared's free hand clenched, wanting more than anything to punch the bastard. A stroke on his back from Lara helped pull him from the edge of violence. *Save Lara.*

"I knew you'd come," the son of a bitch gloated.

"I'm here for Miss Adams. We're leaving. Where are the guards and other personnel?"

"They're on alert, ready to stop you should anything unforeseen happen. You're going to assist in our research."

"Over my dead body," Jared said.

"It would be my ultimate pleasure to arrange that." Glendale moved behind his desk. "But first, I need the information you carry."

Jared stared at him. "What information?"

"Don't play dumb. Two years ago, you overheard the techs and their solution to the control problem."

Yes, he'd heard it. He'd consulted with Bar'ella and according to the computer simulations, the solution wouldn't have worked.

"I heard their solution," Jared admitted.

Glendale bent over, palms flat on the desktop. "Well, what is it?"

Jared crossed his arms. "It doesn't matter, it wouldn't have worked."

"How do you know?"

"Because in order to effectively control your army, you have to take away their decision-making abilities. They'd be nothing but robots, unable to adapt to their environment or changing situations, incapable of independent thought.

"How do you know?"

"Because I'm not an idiot. I ran the simulations."

Glendale waved that away. "You're not a researcher. You don't know what you're talking about. Give me the specific control key."

"No."

Glendale smiled maliciously. "You'll give me the information I want. Now." He reached into the middle drawer, pulled out a filled syringe and a device. It was a small box with two buttons on top—one red, one green. Glendale pointed it at Jared, muttered a few words, and pushed the green button.

There was gasp from behind him. Lara released his belt. Jared stepped away, not wanting her to be hit by whatever Glendale was doing.

Jared tensed as a flash of gray light surrounded him.

A slight tingling on his skin was the extent of the light's effect. Was that it?

"What was that supposed to do?" Jared asked.

Glendale frowned at the device, shook it, then repeated the words and pressed the buttons. Another light flashed from the device, but instead of enveloping Jared, it splashed against him and rebounded onto Glendale, who froze. The device slipped from his hand and fell to the floor, shattering into pieces.

Glendale's eyes reflected his growing panic.

"Freezing spell?" Jared asked, grinning because there was no way for the bastard to answer him. "Too bad you forgot about the neat little shifter ability. Magic doesn't work on us, asshole."

Lara grabbed his arm and asked. "Then how did he turn you into a bunny?"

"A chemical cocktail that forced the shift."

"Now what do we do?"

"We get the hell out of here while we can."

He wanted to beat the hell out of Glendale, but he had to choose. Get Lara out or seek his revenge.

No contest. Lara came first. But there was something he could do.

He walked over to the desk and picked up the syringe, lifting it within Glendale's field of vision. "Let's see how you like being a lab experiment." Jared stuck the needle into a vein in Glendale's wrist and depressed the plunger. "Enjoy."

He grabbed Lara's hand, "Come on, we're getting out of here. Headache status?"

"Throbbing."

"Bad yet?"

"No, but getting there."

They left the room and he took her hand leading her down the hall. She tugged. "Aren't we leaving?"

"Not yet. We've got to make sure this doesn't happen again." He pulled her into a quick kiss. "Ready for an adventure?"

The skepticism on her face was cute. "Maybe?"

"It'll be fun." He tugged her to the first set of doors he remembered from the schematic.

Jared released her hand. "Can you get the other door?"

"Sure, why?"

"We need to get these closed so the damage doesn't reach the hospital above us." Jared released the fire door and it swung closed.

"Damage? We're going to do damage?" She looked at him with a shocked expression on her face.

"It'll be fun," he reassured. Jared placed two fingers on her temples, and rubbed gentle circles on her skin. "I know you hurt, but the lab must be destroyed."

Lara bit her lip, and damn, she revved his motor.

"I'm not sure…" she protested.

"I know. But if we don't do this, other people will be taken off the streets and used for experiments. I have to stop this."

She looked into his eyes. He didn't know what she saw, but she took a deep breath and squared her shoulders, "Okay, I'm ready."

Jared kissed her forehead, wanting to do so much more. "That's my heroine."

They both pulled the second door closed, and when the two came together he took out the specialized tool, Hans had given him. Inserting it into the lock, the magic imbued in the device melted the metal from the inside so the doors couldn't be opened.

He pulled out his cell and sent a quick message to Cyn. *Have Lara safe, starting phase two.*

"Ready to rock?" he asked Lara.

"Bring it," she said with a pained smile.

§

Cyn had to get the gryphons out. Hopefully they hadn't been turned to the Alliance side of the force. *Hurry, hurry, hurry.* The urgency pounded through her blood and she had no idea why. Horrible consequences ensued when she'd ignored her instincts.

Skulking as fast as she dared, she reached the wing where the gryphons were held. She snuck around the corner, darted across the doorway, and pressed her back to the wall. 007 could kiss her ass.

She reached the double doors that led to the lab and peeked inside. The area was clear.

Cyn opened the door wide enough to slip through and held the press bar as it closed, trying to be as quiet as possible.

In the small room, two gurneys were pushed against the left wall, with other machines stacked alongside. To her right were medical waste bins, linen bins, and a control panel. Straight ahead was long hallway that ended in a door.

Creeping to the wall with the control panel, she peeked through the doorway at a barred cell across from her position. The sound rustling of. wings brought a small breeze scented with musty, wet feathers. A large gryphon paced within the cell. Head cocked to the side, it stared at her. *Hope it's not looking for a snack.*

Cyn faced the control panel. Based on the instructions, it held the release mechanisms for the entire cell block. She flipped the first four switches. The doors behind her burst open, and two guards rushed in.

The guards were dressed in gray pants and matching shirts with Elaine Pharmaceuticals emblem on the left shirt pocket. They each held a taser pointed at her. Ordinary humans from their auras. Easy.

"Step away from the panel. This is a restricted area, and you're under arrest," the first guard said.

Cyn smiled and flipped a few more switches.

"Stop!"

Cyn dove out of the way, avoiding the barbs from both tasers. *Missed!* Rolling to her feet she attacked the guard closest to her. Punches and a well-placed kick put him out of commission. The other one tried to install a second cartridge in his taser. She kicked his knee and down he went, taser falling from his hand. She flung it to the other side of the room where it slid under the gurney, and tossed the spent taser from the first guard's hand into the medical waste bin.

She dusted her hands together and flipped a few more switches on the control panel. Four additional guards entered the room. The two idiots must have summoned reinforcements.

Without speaking, they rushed her as a group. No matter how well she fought, their numbers overwhelmed her in the small space. One of the guards managed to pin her arms to her sides and lifted her from the floor, removing her leverage.

A loud squawk was followed by crunching sounds. The arms around her fell away and she dropped to the floor. Cyn tucked and rolled away. A large gryphon picked bits of brain matter from the skull of the guard who'd held her prisoner. The other guards were in similar straits as the gryphons crowded into the small space, wings rustling as they fed.

Cyn's jaw dropped. She hadn't expected the gryphons to be quite so huge. Their bodies, back legs, and tails were of a lion, with the front claws and head of an eagle. The final touch was the wings on their backs. They were both majestic and utterly terrifying.

She remained still, not wanting to trigger their hunting instincts. The one who'd chomped on her guard looked at her.

"Can you understand me?" she asked in a soft voice, not wanting to startle it.

It gave a loud cry. Cyn winced, the noise piercing her brain. The hunting cry of an eagle, amplified beyond normal levels. The effect on the others was immediate. The other gryphons stopped what they were doing and faced the one in charge.

The leader cawed softly. *"Thank you for freeing us,"* a masculine voice spoke in her mind.

"Are there any others in a different location?" Cyn asked, standing and dusting off her butt.

The leader shook his head. *"We were told the others died."*

The double doors were jerked open and a mage wearing a white lab coat entered. He was followed by four more rent-a-cops with tasers. They stood in the doorway, as it was too cramped in the space with the gryphons taking up the room.

"Return to your cells at once," the mage ordered.

The leader opened his beak. *"Cover your ears,"* he warned Cyn.

She put her fingers over her ears, pressing as tight as possible, but the piercing sound penetrated her brain.

"Down," the gryphon ordered.

Cyn hit the floor near the wall and rolled to her side, trying to stay out of the way. She tucked her body in a fetal position, facing the wall.

The hands over her ears muffled the screams and crunching sounds. Bits and pieces hit the wall in front of her and slid down, leaving bloody trails. It was a macabre work of art, horrific and beautiful.

A hard nudge on her shoulder and she squeaked. At least it wasn't a full-blown scream.

"You're safe," his voice assured.

"Thanks." Cyn uncurled from the floor and tried to avoid all the bloody bits. She was splattered as well. Damn it, she hated cold showers, but it was the best way to get blood off her and her clothing.

Cyn turned to face the double doors. Piles of blood-soaked fabric was interspersed with fleshy blobs and bone shards. Eww.

She didn't see any gryphons down.

"Are any of your people hurt?" she asked.

"No. Exit?"

Cyn reached into a pocket and pulled out a map. Opening it, she tiptoed over the gore to his side and pointed to the red line on the map. "If you follow this route, it will take you to the exit and into Golden Gate park. Keep to the cover of trees and someone will meet you."

"Will they lock us up again?"

"No, but you're going to need help adjusting to this new life," she stopped for a moment. "You were changed into this, right?"

"Yes, we are… were, human. What about you? Will you not be coming with us?"

Cyn glanced at her watch. "I'm waiting for the all clear, then I'm getting the hell out of here."

"There's something different about you."

"I'm a vampire."

Silence. None of the gryphons moved. Not a wing, not a breath.

"Vampire?"

"Yes." She allowed her fangs to drop and gave them a toothy grin. "There are many others who are different. When you get out, they'll brief you."

"It'll take some getting used to."

"It always does." Cyn smiled.

His wings shifted. *"My name is Captain Rafe Baldeva, on a special mission. On behalf of my men and I, thank you for the rescue. If you need anything, call."*

"Thanks, I'm Cyn. You need to go."

"Aren't you coming with us?"

Cyn checked her phone and shook her head. "I'm waiting for word from a friend."

"Josh, Cole, make sure she gets out."

Two gryphons nodded and waited out in the hall.

"I'll be fine." Cyn said.

"You're getting an escort," he ordered.

"Yes, Captain," she agreed, having met military types before. Arguing was a frustrating endeavor. Better to agree, then do what she needed to.

Cyn left the mess and stood in the hall, flanked by the two gryphons. Captain Rafe led the rest of the gryphons toward the exit, wings tucked tight to their backs. For such large creatures they walked with little noise. Their bloody tracks was easy to follow, but there was little she could do about it.

Pulling her phone from her pocket, she checked messages. No word from Jared yet. She'd give him a few more minutes, then run to his rescue. She sent a quick text to Captain Jor'dan letting him know there were gryphons loose in Golden Gate Park.

As soon as she sent the text, Jared contacted her. *Have Lara safe, starting phase two.*

"Let's go topside. My friend is going to blow this joint." Having memorized the route out, she followed the bloody trail until it faded after a couple of hallways. She led her bodyguards up the stairs, out into park, and the cold night air.

§

Jared and Lara walked at a brisk pace down the corridor past Glendale's office.

244

After many twists and turns down never-ending hallways, Jared found an empty room at the far end of one corridor. He opened the door, stepped inside, pulling her with him. There he put his arms around her, holding her close to his heart. Her arms wrapped around his waist and her head rested on his chest. It was what he needed after the worry and panic of the past few hours.

Jared had to go, but he also needed to assure both rabbit and man their mate was safe.

Mate?

While the thought should have sent him running, it had the opposite effect. If there was one person on the planet he could see himself settling down with, it was Lara. The more he thought about it, the more he wanted it, wanted her, in his life.

Too soon it was time to go. But after this was over, he'd hold her in his arms all night long. The trick would be convincing her to let him.

Jared pulled back. "I need you to stay here for a few minutes."

"Why?"

"Because you're in pain, and I want you to rest while I set things up. We'll need to move fast after that, so I want you to conserve your strength until then. Okay?"

The tension eased from Lara's shoulders and the dimple appeared in her smile. "I can do that."

Jared reached into his pocket and pulled out a small charm. "Keep this with you."

"Another trinket?"

"If something should happen, it'll allow me to find you."

"Okay." Lara rose onto her tiptoes and brushed his lips with a sweet kiss that hinted of passion. "Be safe and come back to me."

He winked. "I will. If I'm not back in thirty minutes, call Cyn, she'll get you out."

Lara bit her lip. "I don't know what happened to my purse or phone."

"Glendale had your phone, but I didn't see it in his office. Here." He pulled out the burner phone. "Cyn is programmed in."

She frowned at the device. "This isn't your phone."

"Mine broke. Someone threw it against a concrete wall."

"You?"

"Yeah." He leaned over and kissed her, trying to impart every feeling and emotion he couldn't verbally admit to. After a long moment, he pulled back and unwrapped his arms from around her. He didn't want to let her go.

She looked dazed, then licked her lips. If he stayed with her any longer, they'd be here for a while.

He went to the door, opened it and peeked into the hallway. Still clear.

Jared left the room, pulling the door closed behind him. He ran down the hallways, propping open doors as he went. Still no personnel or guards. While it could be due to the charms, he expected a few people to be working. No time to find out where they were. He had a complex to destroy.

Poking through a few cabinets, he found what he was looking for, and the other rooms he checked appeared to be similarly equipped. Starting at the room furthest away from Lara, Jared emptied the plastic trash can on the floor and threw crumbled pieces of aluminum into it, then poured hydrochloric acid over the top. A remote burner in a high location completed his prep. He repeated the process in three more labs.

Jared was on his way back to collect Lara, when his senses warned of danger up ahead.

Fuck.

Chapter 18

In the underground laboratory complex hidden beneath the streets of San Francisco, Randall left Dr. Mason Anderson's office. A security breach in the gryphon complex had forced Mason to go deal with the situation. Randall had offered his help, but his college friend had waved it off. "If I'm to get Glendale's job, I need to prove to the higher ups I can handle this on my own. We'll chat later."

Randall strode through the halls with feigned purpose. The security down here was strict and if he didn't have a reason to be here, he'd be escorted topside.

How had the Elite had uncovered his activities? An hour ago, while he'd been meeting with Mason, his cell phone vibrated. Reading the urgent message, he'd cursed. His cover had been blown. Fuck. The Elite intended to bring him in for questioning regarding Alliance connections. And there wasn't a way to hide his activities; Luesar would crack his mind open and all his secrets would be revealed.

A quick check of flights leaving SFO and he'd booked himself on the next flight out. Randall had set up an alternate identity for such an occasion, but he'd never thought he'd have to use it. While the Elite stationed newer recruits at the airports, they relied primarily on passenger data to catch their fugitives.

If he could convince the guards that he had business here, he'd be safe. The Alliance run labs would not open their doors to the Elite. Otherwise he'd be escorted from the premises.

The next other person he needed to check with was Dr. Glendale. Had the good doctor managed to get Williams into the lab? It surprised him that the incompetent ass had somehow managed to get funding for the project he'd fucked up the first time. But who knew the ways of those higher in the organization?

A single security guard stopped him and questioned his reasons for being in the area. "I'm on my way to a meeting with Dr. Glendale."

Randall was escorted to the office, and the man waited while Randall knocked on the door. Not hearing any response, he opened the door and stepped into the room, stopping in surprise.

"What the hell happened to you?" Randall asked. Glendale stood still as a statue behind his desk. Shattered pieces of plastic littered the floor. Slipping into mage-sight showed the specific spell surrounding Glendale. Basic freeze spell. Easy enough to get rid of, but it was oh so tempting to leave the other mage frozen.

Randall sighed and began muttering the counter-spell, having been familiar with this type of magic since he gained his mage level.

Glendale's breath whooshed out of him and he doubled over. "Thank you."

"What happened?" Randall asked.

"My fault," Glendale gasped. "I tried to use the device on Williams, and it backfired."

"You forgot that shifters are immune to magic."

Glendale straightened and glared at him. "Yes, I did, but I didn't expect it to splash back to me."

Randall frowned. "That's unusual."

"I wouldn't know. I avoid familiarity with shifters.."

"The magic dissipates. It doesn't rebound on the caster."

Glendale shrugged, dismissing the incident. "It doesn't matter. The important thing is that he escaped."

"He's not loose in the complex, is he?"

"Yes. He took the human with him. That should slow him down."

Randall pinched the bridge of his nose. This was all he needed, a human to be involved. "You'd better explain the human. Who is it? Why were they here?"

Glendale grabbed a glass of water and gulped it down. "I brought her here as bait to draw Williams here. It worked."

"No, it didn't. Now they're both running around the complex."

Glendale waved that away. "Security will apprehend them."

"I didn't see much security on my way over. Only one guard."

Glendale gave him a condescending look. "They're keeping an eye on the situation and awaiting orders. I didn't want Williams stopped on his way here. They're going to step in and capture him on the slim chance he escaped."

"Where is security now?"

"I don't know," Glendale admitted.

Randall gritted his teeth and counted to ten. Otherwise he'd be tempted to recast the freeze spell. Glendale must have greased palms to gain this position. There was no other excuse for this level of incompetence. "If Williams has something to repulse magic, what makes you think he'll be visible to security?"

"You worry too much."

"You don't worry enough. The last thing we need is an Elite roaming the halls unearthing secrets. Call security and have them locate him." Randall said.

Glendale picked up the phone and had a short conversation. From the rising panic in Glendale's voice, Randall knew the guards hadn't found Williams.

Fuck. Could this snafu get any worse?

"I'll take care of him, but I need to conserve my magic. Cast a tracking spell." Randall ordered as his phone buzzed. He glanced down at his messages. Damn it. The Elite were attempting to track his phone. He'd turned that feature off, but it alerted him every time someone tried to ping his location.

Glendale pulled out the appropriate paraphernalia from his desk. Four fat, white candles and a piece of chalk. He drew a complex pattern on the desktop with the chalk and placed the four candles at the specific points of the drawing.

He lit the candles with a lighter and muttered the words.

Something was wrong. What was it? Randall examined the drawing and the position of the candles. Everything was in the right place, each line of the drawing in the correct position. The words were said correctly with the right intonation, but they lacked power. There was no magic.

Glendale finished the spell with a swirling gesture and a quick snap. An image of Jared and his location should have shown up in the space between the candles.

It was an easy spell to perform for a person of Glendale's mage level. Glendale frowned and tried it again. Still no magic.

"Try lighting a candle," Randall suggested. It was the easiest spell possible and the first taught to children.

Glendale pulled another candle from his drawer and set it on his desk. Repeating the words and snapping his fingers should have caused the wick to burst into flame. But the wick remained unlit.

Randall did the spell and lit the candle.

"Magic works," Randall stated.

Glendale's shoulders slumped. "But not for me."

Randall shifted and saw the syringe. He picked it up from the desk. "What was in this?"

"The formula."

"You injected him? That'll make him easier to find."

"No, the bastard injected me," Glendale admitted.

Randall stopped. "Have any other Paranormals been tested with it?"

"No. It was specifically developed to use against shifters. There was no reason to experiment on the others. The goal is a shifter army, not a vampire or fae army."

"Congratulations, you're the first experiment. Your sacrifice will further science."

"Bullshit. I'll call Harold for the antidote."

Randall cast the location spell and found Jared, alone, nearing Dr. Anderson's office. "Williams is nearing the gryphon area. I'll bring him back."

"Wait. He should have the woman with him." Glendale said.

Randall studied the image. The doctor was correct. Williams was alone. What happened to the woman? Williams had been protective of her. That meant he'd stashed her somewhere while he went exploring. It was possible he was looking for the exit, but Randall had a difficult time believing that. The shifter was gathering information about the complex and needed to be stopped before he took his findings to the Elite.

"Have security locate the woman," Randall said, leaving the office at a brisk pace. He'd stop Williams and lock him up. That would take care of the abomination, permanently.

§

Jared rounded the corner to find Randall leaning against the wall, waiting for him. Crap.

"You should give yourself up and save yourself a beating," Randall advised.

"You know I've never been afraid of a fight."

Randall bowed his head in acknowledgement. "True." The mage glanced at the hallway. "Where is your little human?"

"Safe."

Randall stepped away from the wall. "I'll find her and take her back to Glendale for use as a test subject."

"I won't let you."

"It's amusing that you believe you have a choice in the matter."

Jared shrugged, knowing Randall was trying to make him mad. "Resorting to empty threats? I expected better of you."

"I don't make empty threats. I fulfill promises."

Jared fought not to roll his eyes. "You're not leaving the City. The Elite know about your nefarious activities."

"How did they find out?"

"That's an easy one." Jared said. "I told them."

"Bastard," Randall snarled. "If I want to leave, I'll leave. The Elite can't stop me, I'm untouchable."

"Keep telling yourself that. How's this going to work? I'm physically stronger and immune to magic," Jared said.

Randall smiled but didn't respond.

Jared recognized the slight sticky feeling in the air. Randall was about to cast a spell. With a circular gesture, glassware from the open lab across the hall flew toward Jared. The few pieces were easy to duck, and he rolled to avoid the glass shrapnel as it shattered against the cinderblock wall. Let the smug bastard think he'd caught Jared by surprise.

He dodged a few more instruments and a microscope, which shattered into pieces.

This was getting absurd. Time to go on the offensive. A tray filled with scalpels, syringes, and other sharp objects rested on nearby cart. Jared grabbed a handful and tossed them at Randall, who brought his arms up in an X pattern. A shimmering field of light surrounded the mage as the items bounced off the shield and clattered to the floor.

While Randall had been focused on the sharp items, Jared leapt into motion, sweeping the mage's legs and knocking him to the floor.

Punches and blows were exchanged, neither one able to gain the upper hand. They each knew the other's weaknesses. "You're going to pay for this," Randall threatened, wiping the blood from his nose.

"Try me," Jared taunted.

Another flurry of blows. His rabbit sensed the faint trace of chemicals in the air. Shit, time to go. Using a flurry of kicks and punches, Jared knocked Randall into the wall. The mage slid down into a sitting position, dazed. Jared ran to get Lara.

§

Jor'dan DúSan's cell phone chirped in the middle of a discussion with Bar'ella. He checked the message. *Gryphons loose in Real, Golden Gate Park. Don't harm them.*

"What is it?" Bar'ella asked.

Jor'dan turned the phone around. "From Cyn."

"Gryphons? I didn't know there were any visiting the City," Bar'ella said.

"I didn't get any notifications," Jor'dan replied. He logged onto the computer and verified there had been no visitors from the Gobi Desert in San Francisco.

They exchanged a look. "What if," Bar'ella remarked, "the Alliance started messing with magical creatures?"

"You think they have?" Jor'dan stood.

"Yes. I need to get my med kit. I'll meet you at Golden Gate Park, south entrance."

"It would be safer to remain here until we have the situation contained."

Bar'ella gave him a look. "What if they overwhelm you?"

"We'll deal with it."

"If that's your final word?"

"It is."

"In that case, I can wait at the clinic as well as I can here." Bar'ella left his office in a huff.

She'd given in too easily. Which meant she'd be meeting them at the park. Damn it. Short of having Ash order her away, there was nothing Jor'dan could do to stop her.

He summoned available agents into his office and outlined the situation. Within a short amount of time they were on route to Golden Gate Park.

They arrived in a clearing to the sharp retort of gunfire. "Find the idiot firing the gun." Jor'dan ordered. It endangered not only the gryphons, but any humans in the vicinity. The saving grace was that it was night and there weren't many people around.

A piercing cry of an eagle echoed through the park and two of the ten Elite ran toward the tree line.

Merrick stopped at Jor'dan's side. "We need to do something about the spectators." The mage pointed toward a small group of people milling around the paths. Civilians were recording the events on their phones. That was all Jor'dan needed. He pulled out his cell to text the special liaison between the Elite and the SFPD, but before he could finish the message, Detective Alejandro pushed through the crowd and jogged over.

Jor'dan had worked with Alejandro as liaison before. The man was competent and professional and fit in well with the Elite.

"What's going on?" Detective Alejandro asked.

"We need to disperse the onlookers. We've got gryphons on the loose."

The dark-haired detective turned to the crowd and with the help of fellow officers, dispersed the curious onlookers.

The whine of a drone filled the air. Damned humans. "Merrick, shut it down."

"Right boss."

The mage stepped away from the group and began to mutter while swirling his hands in arcane gestures. He ended by clapping his hands together and the drone fell from the sky, inoperable.

"Do you think they got any footage?" Damien asked as he and James joined him.

"I don't know," Jor'dan admitted.

"On it, boss." James collected the downed drone and checked it over. "No memory card." He did a quick technical check via his cell. "Nothing was uploaded to the web. Did you know it's illegal to fly a drone in the park?"

Jor'dan tilted his head and gave the vampire a look. "It's illegal to fire a gun within city limits, but it didn't stop those idiots from shooting at the gryphons."

Luesar emerged from the tree line and sprinted to their position. "There are twenty gryphons beyond the trees. They've killed the four humans who shot at them. Not sure if they're injured, but they're covered in blood."

"The humans or the gryphons?"

"It's a bloody mess—hard to tell."

"Damn it, she was right." Jor'dan muttered.

Merrick stumbled into their circle. His face pale and drawn. Luesar pulled out a protein bar and handed it to the flagging mage.

"Thanks. Who was right about what?" Merrick asked, devouring the bar in seconds.

"Bar'ella. We'll need her here to find out where they came from, but don't tell her," Jor'dan replied.

"Too late for that, boss. She's here." Damien pointed.

Jor'dan turned to see Bar'ella grinning. "Good thing, I disregarded your orders," she said.

"No one likes a smart ass," Jor'dan complained. Bar'ella patted him on the cheek.

"Good thing I'm a wiseass," she teased. Turning to the group of healers she began issuing orders. "Set up the tent over there. Make sure to remove your white coats. If they're anything like last bunch, they're not going to trust anyone in a lab coat."

Bar'ella strode across the clearing toward the tree line hiding the Gryphons. "Luesar and Merrick, make sure she's not harmed." Jor'dan ordered.

They grinned at him and jogged after the healer. What the hell was she thinking, confronting gryphons by herself?

Jor'dan shook his head and followed.

Chapter 19

Cyn and her two escorts ran through the trees at the first sound of gunfire. Fuck! Who was stupid enough to fire on a gryphon? The scent of blood filled the air, along with the screams of terrified humans. Wet, noisy ripping sounds followed. The gryphons were tearing the gunmen to shreds. It served the humans right for shooting at the gryphons.

A human stepped around the trunk of a tree and pointed a pistol at her. There was a flash of light and felt a sharp burn in her right hip. Instinct had her dropping to the ground. What the hell? Why was he shooting at her? Her two gryphons launched themselves at the shooter and made mincemeat out of him.

She touched the wound and her fingers came away bloody. Goddammed son of a bitch!

A rustle of wings and a soft touch on her back. *"He's dead."*

"Thanks." Cyn rolled over and winced at the radiating pain. With difficulty, she got to her feet. It wasn't too bad at the moment, but she'd be in agony later. She needed to make sure the gryphons didn't attack the Elite, then she'd limp off to see Bar'ella.

As if she'd been summoned, the dragon herself emerged from the trees. Within a flurry of wings, Cyn was surrounded by gryphon bodies.

"Cyn, is that you?" Bar'ella asked.

"Yeah, give me a sec, B," Cyn replied.

She put her hand on the back nearest her. The eagle head turned toward her, and she recognized the markings. It was one of her escorts. "I need to see Bar'ella. She'll help you."

"She's dangerous."

"I know. Please, can we move to the front?"

He ducked his head and slid from beneath her hand. In the space of a breath, another shoulder replaced his. *"Let us go and greet your friend."* Rafe said.

The wall of gryphons in front of her shifted until she and Rafe were standing in front of the group.

The feathers on Rafe's crest rose. *"Who are these people? They smell like enemies."*

Fuck.

§

Lara glanced around the room now that Jared was gone. It was a simple room with a chair, desk, and not much else.

While she'd been with Jared, the pain of her headache had taken a back seat to getting out of this rat's warren. Now it burst to life, in full technicolor sparkling flashes. Lara collapsed in the chair, careful not to jar her head. Closing her eyes, she rubbed her temples.

It helped calm the pain to tolerable levels for the moment.

Migraine in temporary abeyance, she leaned back in the chair, letting her mind drift.

The piercing cry of a bird jolted her out of her zoned-out state. Groggy, she glanced around, trying to find the source of the noise, but the room was empty. The call came again, a little weaker—the creature was in pain. Once that thought embedded itself into her brain, it wouldn't leave.

Carp. She needed to find what was in pain so she could help. While Jared would be mad that she left the room, this was too important to ignore. He could find her using the charm.

Lara walked to the door, cracked it open a smidge and peeked out. There weren't any guards waiting to capture her. She crept down the corridor, trying to channel Cyn's stealthy skills. *Go, go, super sneaky librarian.*

The cry sounded again, but it was much fainter. She pinpointed the room and opened the door. Stomach in knots from all the skulking, she slipped into the room, closing the door behind her.

In front of her was a creature straight out of mythology. A gryphon lay on its side, on the floor, with a large bulge in the stomach region. Blood was seeping from the rear end as well as from various cuts and wounds along the body

One eye opened at her presence. The beast panted.

"Are you okay? Ack, never mind, I can see you're not," Lara said and knelt at the creature's side.

Lara removed her jacket and tossed it aside. Dressed in layers, she removed her flannel shirt and the long-sleeved shirt below in case it was needed.

She started to rip the flannel, but the stubborn material wouldn't tear. She used her teeth to get a start and divided it into strips. When there were enough pieces, she wiped the blood away from some of the gryphon's more wicked looking wounds. "I don't know what to do," she confessed trying to staunch the flow of blood.

The worst was a large rip in the chest area. The amount of blood worried her. She wadded up her shirt and pressed it over the wound, wrapping one of the sleeves around the wing base and tucking the other under the gryphon's body.

The gryphon whimpered in pain, and the stomach rippled. Oh carp. As she didn't see any external genitalia, this was probably a female. The overly large bulge in her mid-section could indicate pregnancy and that would mean the muscle spasms... this wasn't good. Not at all.

"Are you giving birth?" *Please say no, please say no, please say no.*

The gryphon nodded.

Carp, carp, carp. She didn't know anything about birthing babies. A gush of liquid from the back end of the gryphon was followed by a whimper. Dang it, she was about to learn.

The distended belly rippled and the gryphon cried out, the sound piercing Lara's brain.

"You can do this, I'll help," Lara reassured her.

Soon a small head appeared from what Lara assumed to be the vagina. It was covered in blood and mucus. Another push and a tiny creature was halfway out of the mother's body. Lara put her hands around the small body, tugging it free. She grabbed one of her shirts and tried to clean the little one up as best as she could without water.

It was a cute little thing. A miniature gryphon.

A keening cry from the mother and the belly contract again. A second head appeared. "Another one? Okay we can do this."

She gently laid the first baby, bundled in her shirt, next to momma, who nuzzled the baby.

A second baby gryphon followed. She wrapped this one up in extra material, placing it beside the first. She wasn't sure if there were more babies inside. Lara rubbed her hand along the stomach, but had no idea what she was feeling for, so she turned to momma.

"Do you think there are anymore?"

The mom shook her head.

Lara crawled to the gryphon's head and pet the mom's neck feathers. "You have two beautiful babies." The gryphon cawed softly, expelling the last of her breath. Her head fell to the floor.

Tears gathered in Lara's eyes. "Please don't be dead. Please don't be dead."

She reached over the babies and burrowed her fingers beneath the feathers to check for a pulse. Lara watched the chest for breath, for any sign of life.

Nothing.

Lara picked up the two bundles and snuggled them close. "I'll take care of your babies, I promise," she whispered.

The door behind her burst open and she turned to face Jared, who held out his hand. "Come on, we need to leave." A quick glance around and he asked. "Are you hurt?"

"No." She swallowed a sob.

"We have to leave, now."

Lara bit her lip and tried not to panic. "Okay. Can I have your shirt?"

Jared quickly undid the buttons of his shirt and pulled it off his shoulders. His chest was so yummy she could stare for days. He held the shirt out to her and the bundles in her arms whimpered.

"What do you have?"

"Two beautiful babies. She died giving birth." She met his concerned gaze. "I promised her I'd take care of them."

Jared nodded. "We'll raise them as our own." He made a sling from his shirt, tying the sleeves around her neck using the body of the shirt as a pouch. He grabbed her jacket and held it as she slipped one arm into it while the other held the babies.

Once the babies were held secure, Lara leaned up and kissed Jared's cheek. "Thank you."

He reached out and tucked a lock of hair behind her ear. "You're welcome. Now let's go."

Jared led the way from the room and down the halls at a fast pace. Lara had to power walk to keep up. She didn't want to jostle the babies more than necessary. A growing pain in her side forced her to slow. "Jared," she panted. "I'm getting a stitch in my side."

Jared stopped, glancing back at her. "Shit, we need to move. I know you're tired, but their lives and yours depend on getting to the exit."

Lara took a shaky breath. "Okay."

He cupped her face, looking into her eyes. "You're their heroine. You can do this. I'll be right behind you."

"I'm their heroine," she repeated.

"Go to the end of the hall and turn right. Three flights of stairs and a door, and that's it. You've got this. You'll exit into Golden Gate Park. Run as fast as you can until you hit a clearing, okay?"

No, it's not okay. But there wasn't any other way. Lara took a deep breath. "Got it."

"You can do it, sweetheart," Jared gave her a quick kiss.

"Stop!" shouted the bad guys rounding the corner behind them.

"Go! Go! Go!" Jared ordered.

Holding her arms over her precious cargo, she ran.

Lara heard pop, pop, pop behind her and wanted to check, but she had to save the babies. Run... around the corner and to the stairs. *Come on, you can do it. One step at a time. Go!* And up the stairs she went. One foot in front of the other, the pain in her side was growing, her breath laboring. The stairs seemed never-ending until at last, she reached the door marked "Emergency Exit."

If there was ever a time for an emergency, this was it.

Lara slammed the door open wide and the sound of an alarm echoed up the stairwell.

She stumbled into the cool night, gasping for air. *Mental note. Run up the library stairs for cardio.* Urgency pounded through her system as she imagined the bad guys bursting through the door at any moment. *Run to the clearing.* She could have sworn she heard Jared's voice, but when she glanced behind her, he wasn't there. Pushed to her physical limits, she couldn't run anymore. Lara walked as quickly as the stitch in her side would allow.

Lara weaved between the trees and stopped when she heard voices. Peering around the trunk she saw a group of people milling around in a clearing. Lights had been set up, illuminating the area, but they were too far for her to see anyone's face clearly. Who were they? Good guys or bad?

§

Cyn stepped forward and doubled over at the intense pain. Without Rafe's support, she would have collapsed. Holy hell, the agony was insane.

"Cyn! Are you all right?" the healer demanded.

Cyn held up a hand, trying to breathe through it. "Not really. Give me a sec."

She took a deep breath, then another. Cyn leaned against the gryphon's side, using him to support her weight.

"Bar'ella, I'd like to introduce you to my new friends." Man, it was getting hard to breathe. Get through the meet and greet, then faint. "This is Rafe and his group. I found them in the labs. They need to be assimilated into Shadow."

She clenched Rafe's wing base, hoping she didn't offend him in some way. Fuck! Being shot sucked.

"Rafe, this is Bar'ella. She's a healer. The two next to her are," Crap how the hell to explain the Elite? "A specialized police force."

Captain Jor'dan appeared from the trees to stand next to Bar'ella. "That's Captain Jor'dan, head cop."

The world tilted to the left and her head felt full of cotton. Not good. The captain said something that Cyn didn't catch, concentrating on remaining upright. Gravity won the battle and Cyn hit the ground hard. Ouch. She rolled to her back to see the gryphons peering down at her. She empathized with the field mouse's fear of being surrounded by beaked predators.

"Let me through!" Bar'ella demanded.

Cyn could sense their reluctance to let anyone near her. "Please? She's not going to hurt me."

The gryphons on her right side backed off and Bar'ella knelt next to her. "Now what happened?"

"I got shot."

"Where?"

"Right hip. Ouch."

"Is this your first bullet wound?" Rafe asked.

"Yeah. Not going to repeat this experience."

He nodded.

"I need light," Bar'ella ordered.

Captain Jor'dan responded. "Damien and James are bringing it."

Cyn tried to sit up. "No. Not James." She couldn't deal with him now, not injured, not vulnerable. She pleaded with Bar'ella "Please."

Rafe cocked his head to the side. *"Is he a threat?"*

Bar'ella narrowed her eyes. "Only to her heart. They're having a lover's spat."

"No. We're done. He cheated."

"What? You didn't tell me that."

"No...time... chat," she panted. What the fuck happened to all the air?

"She's in shock. Jor'dan, keep James away. I need a blanket. Hurry."

"Let me assist," Rafe said, then laid down next to her uninjured side. The heat coming off him was incredible. "So warm," she said, her tone dreamy.

Between one blink and the next, the area was bathed in bright light, blinding Cyn for a moment. The top edge of a wing shielded her eyes. "Thanks," she mumbled.

And then the world went strange. Shouts and demands were muffled, and the pain seemed far away. She felt floaty, unreal. It was kinda nice. A warm soothing sensation chased the pain away. It was as comforting as a hug by a fire warmed blanket.

Her wonderful bubble of lassitude popped forcing her back to reality. Damn it. Bar'ella sat back, visibly pale and shaking.

Yelling filled the clearing. She knew that voice. James was demanding access to her.

Rafe left her side and stood between her and the vamp, tensed and ready for battle. *"Leave now."*

Captain Jor'dan spoke, but she couldn't make out what he was saying.

"Cyn, call me," James yelled.

"As if," she muttered.

Bar'ella packed away her med kit and smiled down at her. "A few days of rest and you'll be as good as new. The bullet deflected off the iliac crest and lodged under your muscle. I've removed the bullet and pumped you full of blood."

"Thanks, B."

"Now you rest for a bit and we'll see about your new friends."

"Don't lock 'em up."

"We won't. I think Captain Jor'dan and Captain Baldeva have come to an understanding."

With Bar'ella's help, Cyn sat up and looked around. James was gone. Relief warred with disappointment. She wanted him, yet he was poison.

"Everything set?" Cyn asked.

"Yes," Bar'ella answered.

Cyn got to her feet and dusted her hands. "My work here is done. Thanks for the healing." She gave Bar'ella a hug.

"You're welcome." Bar'ella returned the hug. "You're clear for travel tomorrow night, but you need at least three days of rest and pampering when you get to Portland."

"How did you know?"

Bar'ella winked at her. "A little birdie told me."

The earth beneath them shook with the rumbling force of a thousand jet engines. Cyn and others were knocked off their feet.

"What the hell was that? An earthquake?" Cyn asked.

§

One of the babies whimpered in Lara's arms, and she leaned down to rub her cheek over the feathery head. "Shhh, it's all right. I've got you. We're safe for now."

An arm came around her shoulders, and she glanced up at Jared. Relief was a drug that made her giddy. She leaned into him, letting him support her.

"Are these good guys or bad?" she whispered.

Jared peered around the tree. "Good guys."

He stepped from behind the trees, bringing her with him.

The ground rumbled beneath her. She fell to her knees, unable to brace herself because of the babies. Jared caught her and sat down, cradling her in his lap.

"Earthquake?" Lara asked.

"Nope. Lab destruction."

"What did you do?"

"Chemistry." He winked.

Which could mean so many different things that Lara didn't know where to begin questioning him. The bundles in her arms squirmed and she unwrapped them enough so they could take in the night air. They cawed softly back and forth, engaging in twin-speak.

The rumbling of the ground stopped. "Is it over?" she asked.

"I think so." Jared eased her from his lap, and helped her to her feet. "Stay here, I'll get the doctor to check you and the kids."

"I'm not hurt."

He cupped her cheek in his hand. "I know, but I want the doc to check to make sure they didn't inject you with something while you were unconscious."

"Oh, okay."

Jared placed a soft kiss on her lips that held a promise of passion. "I'll be right back."

"I'll be waiting," she teased.

Lara couldn't help but ogle his butt as he walked away. That man had a fine back end.

An arm circled her throat and she was yanked roughly against a body. "Make one sound and I'll kill Jared," a male voice threatened.

Carp, not again.

Chapter 20

Cyn observed the activities being conducted in the clearing. The gryphons were being examined by the Bar'ella's healers, and Rafe and Captain Jor'dan were engaged in a civil discussion. His Grace High Chancellor Ignatio joined the group. While there were a few raised crests, no attacks followed, and she released a sigh of relief when the tension in the gryphons relaxed. *Crisis averted.*

There was one thing left to do before she could head home. She didn't see Jared or Lara. Cyn pulled out her phone. A quick text to make sure they were okay, and she'd leave.

A familiar voice raised the hair on her arms. James, the rat bastard, insisted she be brought to him.

Nice try, asshole.

Cyn needed to get the hell out of here; exit stage right. She walked the opposite direction, away from James and his demands and commands, sidestepping other members of the Elite, who were smirking with amusement.

Elite Mage Merrick Kenelm stopped her. "Miss Madison? I believe you're wanted over there." he pointed in James' direction.

Her eyes narrowed. "Very funny. I have pressing business in that direction." She waved to the trees, away from James.

The mage stepped out of her way and grinned. "Good luck. You're going to need it."

"I'll take all the luck I can get."

Movement within the trees set off her 'all is not right' antennae. After leaving Mage Kenelm, she skulked around the edge of the lights and entered the tree line.

Why was Randall creeping along the trees instead of out with the rest of his Elite buddies? Had his nefarious activities been discovered? Please let it be true. *I hope they catch your lying ass, you condescending son of a bitch.* A chat with Jared and she'd find out. If not an anonymous call to the Elite tip line should take care of him.

Randall looked like he'd been through a war zone. His shirt was ripped, sleeves shredded. Soot covered all exposed skin, and his hair looked like it'd gotten an electric shock treatment. Suspicious, Cyn followed him.

She grinned when Jared led Lara into the clearing. They'd made it out, though Lara resembled a bloody rag doll, holding a bundle to her chest. Jared kissed her cheek and walked toward a group of milling Elite.

Lara wore bemused expression as she watched Jared speak with Bar'ella. Cyn paused behind a tree, ready to join Lara, when Randall darted out and grabbed Lara, holding her hostage in front of him.

Cyn skulked between the trees until she was behind them, out of Randall's line of sight. She crept out, about to jump him, when a tingle of magic slid over her skin. *Fuck, too late.*

Never interrupt a mage during a spell. It had been drummed into her years ago by her mentors when she'd first turned into a vampire and was learning the laws of Shadow Earth. It was dangerous for the mage and for everyone within a three-block radius. When mages lost control of their magic, bad things happened.

§

Lara swallowed and didn't make a sound. She couldn't, not with the arm pressing into her throat.

"Your lover ruined everything." The voice behind rasped, as if he had a two pack a day habit. Horrible hacking coughs shook them both, yet he maintained his tight hold on her.

"You'll both pay for that," he threatened.

More threats. Lovely. Lara didn't respond since it was difficult to breathe, let alone speak.

Jared emerged from the shadows. "Randall, release her."

"No. She's my final revenge," the man behind her said around a hacking cough.

Randall? Jared's partner? The one who'd been after Jared to force him back to the labs? Carp, she was dead for sure.

"What do you want?" Jared asked.

The men in the clearing noticed what was happening and approached. Reinforcements, but for whom?

Jared raised his arm to shoulder height, fist clenched.

The others halted at the command.

Randall drew in a gasping breath. "I want you back in the fucking lab, where an abomination like you belongs. You've destroyed this lab, so I'm going to destroy you."

Another coughing fit and Randall began to mutter.

The words were incomprehensible, sounding like magic words. Wait, magic? What had Jared told her? *Mages guard against magical attack, but never physical.*

Physical. His arm was in front of her, in biting range. Lara opened her mouth wide and bit down hard on the arm in front of her. *Blech.* The sooty taste of smoky skin filled her mouth, seasoned with the coppery tang of blood.

Randall yelled and jerked his arm, but she didn't let go. With his free hand he slapped the side of her face, forcing her to let go. She took three stumbling steps and fell to her knees. The two babies squawked.

A wall of heat enveloped her, followed by a roiling cloud of flame. Lara held her breath and squeezed eyes closed. She flopped on her side and curled around the babies hoping to protect them from the fire.

Pain, such burning pain. She wanted to scream but didn't have the breath. Dots danced in the blackness of her vision, and her body relaxed into unconsciousness.

§

Jared's heart stuttered when Randall began the spell. He raced toward them, hoping to yank Lara free before the spell took effect.

Two steps later he was tackled to the ground. Jared turned fought to push Merrick away, but the mage shook his head. "It's too late. She disrupted the spell!"

A large fireball roared from Randall's hand and spread outward, engulfing Lara and the kits.

"NO!"

Moisture leaked from his eyes, but he didn't care. She was gone. Her sweet smile, her strong compassion, her beautiful soul, gone.

"What the hell?" Merrick asked.

The fireball that surrounded Lara snapped back, contracting inward to Randall.

A sizzle, pop, and agonizing scream and Randall ceased to be; all that remained was a smoldering pile of ash.

Merrick released him, and Jared crawled to Lara, kneeling at her side.

There wasn't an area on her that wasn't burnt, though her skin was an angry red instead of charred black. A quick check assured him that she still breathed. "Thank you, God."

"Don't thank your deity just yet." Bar'ella slid to her knees on Lara's other side. Captain Jor'dan and High Chancellor Ignatio watched. He wasn't sure if they were here to help or take Lara into custody.

"She has a pulse," he reported.

"And I'd like to keep it that way," Bar'ella did a quick examination. "Remove the shirt. Let's see what's going on."

Jared lifted the knotted sleeves over Lara's head and supported the kits. "What about the babies?"

"Babies?" Bar'ella's started at the bundle in his hands. "What babies?"

As gently as he could he parted the folds of the shirt and tilted them toward Bar'ella. Two tiny beaked heads wobbled on weak necks, cawing softly. Jared pulled the bundle close to his chest, his inner rabbit wanting to keep the kits warm.

Bar'ella's mouth popped open along with the Captain and High Chancellor. "Where did you get them?" Bar'ella reached for one of the kits. It sniffed the air, growled, and snapped at her.

She jerked her hand back. "Shit, I forgot, I'm the enemy." Bar'ella glanced around the clearing. "Danelle!" she called.

The fae healer ran up. "What can I do?"

"Check to see if the kits are healthy," Bar'ella ordered, turning her attention back to Lara. With the Captain's help, they turned Lara onto her back and straightened her legs. Her coat was burnt and her skin was red, but it appeared the damage wasn't bad. The burns were limited to the backs of her hands, her neck where her clothing hadn't covered her, and her face.

Her jeans were scorched in places, but they weren't burned through.

Bar'ella touched Lara's skin, and the glow from Bar'ella's hands spread, covering Lara's body. "The good news is the fireball didn't last long enough to do severe damage. She has first degree burns on all exposed skin and minimal burning on the rest."

"She'll be okay?" Jared asked Bar'ella, around the lump in his throat.

The healer gave him a soft smile. "Yes, she'll be fine." Her expression turned stern. "She's had two healings in a short amount of time. She'll need extra food and plenty of rest over the next few days."

Jared's fear and worry drained from him at the news Lara would be okay. And he'd feed her steak and cheesecake and spoil her with breakfast in bed. He sat back breathing in the cool air, letting relief fill him.

The kits reacted by shifting and mumbling. His rabbit surged to the fore, showing him how to calm the babies. He made a soft hurring sound.

Danelle reached out and let the babies scent her. "Oh, aren't you adorable?" she cooed. "Let me check you over."

She peeled back the shirt. "Can you lift them out?"

Jared removed them one by one and held them close to his body.

Danelle smoothed the feathers on the top of the kit's heads. She held out her hands, and a soft glow enveloped them.

When the glow receded, she smiled, "Congratulations, they're both completely healthy for being human / gryphon hybrids. That one is a little girl," she said, pointing to the one in his right hand, "and the other is a boy."

"Thank you. Will they be able to shift into human children?"

Neither of the two had opened their eyes yet, content to snuggle into his chest. The feathers on their heads were soft and downy.

"I don't know. Doctor Bar'ella should be able to tell you," Danelle admitted.

Bar'ella spoke up. "I've got samples from the other gryphon and I'll work on trying to get them into human form, but I want to wait on these two."

"Why?" Jared wanted as much information as possible; Lara would want to know.

"I don't want to interfere with their development. Forcing the shift could be harmful to their health. I won't know that until I do an in-depth examination. And I'm not going to do that until I've got the adults squared away," Bar'ella said in a stern tone.

Jared bowed his head once, knowing better than to question her judgement. He snuggled with the kits while waiting for Lara to wake.

§

Lara opened her eyes and brought one hand to her head. A slight twinge was all that remained of her headache. "What happened?"

The doctor from before, Bar'ella, helped Lara sit up.

"You got caught in a Fire Death Spell," Doctor Bar'ella said.

Lara shuddered. Being engulfed in a large ball of flame wasn't her idea of a good time. "I remember the flames. But if it was a death spell, why am I still alive?"

"Mage Randall hadn't finished the spell. You broke his concentration and the magic rebounded into him," Doctor Bar'ella replied.

"Good, it worked." Lara slumped in relief.

"You meant to do that?" the Doctor asked, expression shocked.

"Yes. Jared told me mage people don't guard against physical attacks. And Randall said he'd kill Jared and make me pay for foiling some scheme. I couldn't let him kill Jared, I just couldn't."

"You're never supposed to stop a mage mid-spell. It's extraordinarily dangerous, and often fatal for anyone caught in the blast zone."

"Oh." Lara felt the blood drain from her face. "What should I have done?" It'd be good to know in case it happened again, though she hoped it wouldn't.

No one looked at her, nor gave her an answer. She couldn't let the bad guy go through with the spell, not if she could stop him.

Jared knelt next to her. "It worked, and that's what matters."

He placed the two adorable baby gryphons in her lap. She smiled down at them and stroked her finger over their tiny wings. "They're so cute," she whispered.

"Yes, they are." Doctor Bar'ella agreed.

"Hey Lara."

Lara pulled her gaze away from the two in her arms. Cyn approached the group. "Auntie Cyn, come look at my babies."

Cyn plopped down next to Jared. "Where did you find the gryphon kids? In the lab? Rafe told me there weren't any other gryphons down there."

"Who is Rafe?" Lara asked.

A strange expression crossed Jared's face. "Rafe Baldeva?" he asked.

Cyn nodded. "Yes, he's the leader of the group of gryphons I saved from the lab."

Jared nodded, but he didn't say anything else.

"I wonder if they know about the one I found." Lara mused, looking down at the babies. "It was so sad. The mom was in such pain. Bleeding from multiple wounds, and struggling to give birth. I tried to help, but I didn't know what to do. It was beyond my first aid skills."

The doctor jolted. "Wait…she had a live birth? These are newborns?"

Lara bit her lip. "They're an hour old, maybe? And yes, live birth. Very messy; blood and stuff everywhere."

"But gryphons lay eggs." A light-haired man in a gray suit crouched behind the doctor.

Something about the man frightened her, and while she tried not to show it, the babies on her lap cawed and squirmed. Jared placed a hand on each, doing a trill thing that calmed them back into sleep.

"Remain calm and you won't upset them," he suggested in a soft, soothing tone of voice.

Lara closed her eyes and took a deep breath. "Remain calm. Okay." She opened her eyes, stared at Cyn, and explained. If she couldn't see the scary man, he couldn't frighten her.

"The lady gryphon was in the middle of labor, contractions coming one right after the other. She died after giving birth and I promised I'd take care of them." Lara rubbed her cheek over one downy head.

Cyn patted Lara's leg. "Auntie Cyn will be right here to help, after I return from my trip."

"You're leaving?" Lara asked.

Cyn nodded. "There's an urgent situation that needs my expertise. I'm hoping it doesn't take long."

Lara grabbed Cyn's hand. "Thank you, for everything."

A hint of blush crept up Cyn's cheeks. "You're welcome."

"Call me when you get back?" Lara asked.

Cyn leaned in for a hug and a quick pet of the gryphons. "I promise." She disappeared into the trees at the same time a loud voice rang over the clearing. "Where the hell is Cyn?"

Lara shared a glance with the doctor. "I'm not going to tell. Are you?"

Doctor Bar'ella shook her head. "Nope."

Jared rubbed a finger along one of the babies' backs and its little tail twitched. "What will you name them?"

Lara opened her mouth then closed it. "I... don't know. I haven't thought that far ahead."

Jared smoothed the head feathers of the other, "There's no need to rush it."

Lara focused on the kits and two names popped into her head. "Thea and Raiden."

"Those are good names, strong names," Doctor Bar'ella said.

"Thanks. I just wish I knew where they came from," Lara admitted.

The scary man motioned to the Captain and they walked away from her small group. Lara's shoulders drooped in relief.

A few moments later the Captain came back and crouched down on Lara's other side. "I know it's late and you're tired. I'd like you to come by my office tomorrow at eleven and bring the kits."

"What's going on?" Jared asked, tension filling his tone.

They weren't going to take the kits from her, were they? She glanced at Jared, who must have seen the panic in her eyes.

"It'll be okay," he reassured her.

The Captain patted her shoulder. "It's nothing to worry about. No one here knows anything about gryphons, including the ones Jared rescued. We need to contact the natural group for information."

"Natural group?" Lara asked. "You mean there are wild gryphons, so to speak?"

Doctor Bar'ella nodded. "They live in the Gobi Desert."

Jared cleared his throat and corrected the Captain. "Miss Madison rescued the gryphons and the trapped humans, not me."

The Captain sighed. "We all know that, but the official report will say you did."

Lara frowned. "But why?"

Jared leaned over and whispered in her ear. "Women in Shadow Earth aren't allowed to do things like rescue people or endanger themselves in any way."

How absolutely asinine! She opened her mouth to give them what for, and Jared placed his finger over her lips. "Shhh, I'll explain later."

Eyes hot with temper, she took a deep breath to calm down. "Okay, later."

One of the healers brought over a large sling, padded with cotton balls and bandages. "For the kits."

Lara smiled. "Thanks."

The healer glanced at Jared. He didn't notice, his attention focused on transferring the kits into their travel nest. The woman walked away, a disappointed expression on her face.

Lara frowned at Doctor Bar'ella. "What was that about?"

The doctor grinned. "She had hopes. Many of them do."

"Hopes of what?" Jared asked.

"My healers want you."

Jared raised an eyebrow. "For what?"

"You're unique, hot, and a gentleman."

Lara nodded in agreement. Jared made her panties wet with a smile.

Jared shrugged. "I'm flattered but not interested."

"I'll let them know." Bar'ella grinned.

Lara opened and closed her mouth. "But…"

He settled the sling around her neck. "You're the only one I need. The others, they don't matter. They don't know me like you do." Jared stood and lifted her into his arms, and rubbed his nose against hers. "You're my sanctuary."

The doctor grinned. "I'm glad someone has tamed the rabbit."

Lara wasn't sure she'd tamed Jared, but she'd take him.

Doctor Bar'ella stood and took a stumbling step. Captain Jor'dan caught her under the arm, supporting her. "Damn it, B, you've done too much. You need to eat and rest."

"Don't you tell me what to do, Jor'dan. Or I'll be dining on chicken fried fae."

"Stubborn." The captain searched the clearing, "Ash! Code Gold."

The scary man in the grey suit approached. He and the Captain spoke in a language Lara didn't understand.

The Doctor's shoulder slumped. "Fine, but I will be seeing the kits tomorrow."

"As long as you rest of the remainder of the evening," the scary man said.

Jared carried Lara out of the clearing, to the street and waiting vehicles beyond. "Will she be okay?" Lara asked.

"She's just exhausted from all the healing."

Lara rested her head against his shoulder. "I can walk, you know."

"I know, but the mother of my kits is going to conserve her energy."

Lara's heart stuttered in her chest. He wasn't saying what she thought he was saying, was he? "What?"

"The mother of my kits is going to rest." He walked to one of the SUVs, opened the back door, and set her into the middle of the bench seat, then slid in beside her.

Jared turned to her and cupped her cheek, rubbing his thumb over her cheekbone. "I know things have happened fast and it's been one extreme adventure after another, but you're in my heart and I want you in my life. I'll always rescue you, whether it be from bad guys, anxiety, or even spiders."

Lara sat there stunned. She felt like a fish, with her mouth hanging open. "Um, thanks, but you're safe from spiders. It's cockroaches I'm scared of."

"Hmm, we may need to negotiate on those." He winked at her and Lara couldn't help but giggle.

She studied the sleeping kits. "Do you really think it'll work between us? You're a hero and I'm… I'm not. I'm just me."

"What do you mean? You helped the gryphon give birth, you saved the babies, and you're willing to raise them even though you don't know anything about them. That's a heroine in my book." He took a deep breath. "Give me a chance to be there for you and the kits. Please."

Lara couldn't stop her insecurities from rising. "But how long until you're bored?"

"I won't, but if you're worried about it, we try it for a year, then re-evaluate."

Lara rolled her lip between her teeth. "Okay. We'll try it for a year."

He gave her shoulders a squeeze. "Great. That means we'll stop by your place tomorrow and pack up your clothes and things."

"I can't, not everything," she protested. "It's too soon."

"What's wrong? My place is secure and sound proof. These two are going to be loud."

"I know, but..."

He stopped and considered. "What would make you more comfortable with this?"

"I don't know, but my ex did the same thing, then tried to take me over. I'm scared. I know it's the right thing to do, but it's happening too fast. You see that don't you?"

Jared sighed, and tucked her into his body. "I get it. Stay with me tonight. Tomorrow we'll see what we need to do for the kits. Okay?"

Lara nodded. "It's not that I don't want to. I do, but..."

"It's too important for you to decide right now."

"Yes. And I still have to process everything that's happened today."

"What do you need?"

"Right now? Just to go home."

"I'll get them to drive us." He rested his cheek on her head. "Once we're done tomorrow, we'll figure out a routine and life will calm down." One of the babies woke and wiggled around. "Well, at least as calm as having two kits can be."

The two vampires who'd questioned her got into the front seats. "Everything worked out?" the dark haired one, Damien, asked.

"For the moment." Lara replied, still mistrustful of the two.

It was a short trip to Jared's apartment. Traffic was light that time of night, or should she say that early in the morning. Was it really three a.m.? A yawn over took her and she snuggled into his embrace. She needed to stay awake for a few more minutes.

Chapter 21

Lara ran through a burnt landscape, dodging the twisted remnants of trees. She didn't know what she was running from, but if she didn't escape, she'd die.

A figure appeared in front of her.

She slid to a halt, kicking up ash. It tickled her nose and she sneezed five times in rapid succession.

Randall blocked her way, and the fire in his eyes expanded outward to engulf his body. He was one with the flame.

His burning hands reached for her. She tried to run, tried to leave, but her body didn't move. She was trapped!

He grabbed her shoulders, and she was thrust into the heart of the flame. Burning hair and skin with pain unlike anything she'd felt before. Her mouth opened; no sound emerged.

Lara was dying.

Lara jerked upright with a gasp. Her heart pounded with adrenaline; sweat dampened her hands and hair. Where was she this time?

The dim light showed a familiar room, Jared's bedroom. She was in Jared's bed.

Jared snored on the other side of the mattress. Between them he'd made a nest of pillows and blankets to keep the two baby gryphons protected.

Hand shaky from the dream, she reached for the nearest baby and stopped. Her sleeve was torn and bloody. The lingering scent of burned clothes and blood was too much. She needed to get clean, now.

Lara pushed back the covers, careful not to disturb the kits, and the blanket slithered to the floor. What the heck? She'd been placed on top of the bed, between two flat sheets. Judging by the dirt and yuck on the sheets, it was a brilliant idea.

She walked to the bathroom, thankful for the small amount of light that allowed her to maneuver around the furniture.

Lara closed the bathroom door and squeezed her eyes tight before turning on the light. When she was used to the brightness, she looked into the mirror. Dirt, soot, and blood created a smeary make-up that bordered on horrific.

Turning on the faucet, she gulped down two glasses of cold, refreshing water.

A knock on the door startled her. "Are you all right?" Jared opened the door, his face filled with concern.

"I had a nightmare," Lara confessed. "And I need to get clean."

"Take your time. If you want anything, including help washing any hard to reach areas, let me know, okay?" he said with a teasing grin.

"Thanks. For everything."

Jared stepped into the room and placed a soft kiss on her lips. "You're welcome."

He left, pulling the door closed behind him.

Lara showered, washing her hair and body multiple times to make sure no hint of yesterday remained.

While she rinsed, she considered Jared's offer. To move in with him for a year. Give them a chance to date. There was no way she'd be able to live with him and not be devastated when he left. It was already too late. Lara took a deep breath, realizing it was too late, she loved him.

Lara finished and wrapped a towel around her body. What to do about Jared? She needed to chat with someone, but didn't know anyone other than Cyn well enough to ask.

Cyn!

A quick check of her jeans confirmed the burner phone Jared had given her was still in the pocket.

She sent a text to her friend. *How long have you known Jared?*

We're not close, but I've met him a couple of times, why?

Darn, how to encapsulate all she wanted to ask in a text?

I'm worried he's a frog in prince's clothing.

He's not.

How can you be sure? Lara typed.

Do you know what he's most afraid of?

Lara bit her lip. *Going back into the lab, I think.*

Exactly. That's what he did. For you.

Thanks. Do you have time to visit before you leave?

I'm already gone. Managed to catch an earlier flight.

Good luck and be careful.

I will, take care of those kits and your man. □

Lara smiled and placed the phone on the counter, turned out the light, and walked into the bedroom. The sheets she'd slept in before had been removed, and a shirt was waiting on the bed.

"Thank you," she whispered.

"You're welcome. Get some rest. We've got a few hours before we're due at the clinic."

Lara pulled the shirt over her head and let the towel fall to the floor. She slid beneath cool sheets and rolled to her side, facing the middle of the bed. She stretched her arm on top of the covers near the nest and he covered her hand with his.

"Sleep well," he whispered.

§

Lara wore the sling with the kits beneath her coat, protecting them from the cool air. Jared held the door of the Luna Clinic open, and she stepped inside, nerves jangling.

Jared placed his hand her lower back. "It'll be okay. Think of it as a check-up."

"Check-up, right." The waiting room resembled others she'd been in. To one side there was an area with small chairs and brightly colored toys. The reception window was in front of them with a door to the left side of the window. The chairs on the right were empty. No one was around for an appointment.

The receptionist waved them to the door. "The doctor will see you now."

The click of the automatic lock disengaged and Jared put his hand on her low back and they walked through.

Three people met them. "May we see them?" the tall woman in the blue scrubs asked.

Lara unzipped her coat and pulled the sides back. She placed one hand under the sling and moved the material aside. The three assistants moved in closer, oohing and ahhing over the cute kits.

"I was wondering what happened to you," a familiar voice said.

Doctor Bar'ella walked toward the group. The assistants glanced up at her voice. "We've never seen kits before. It's a learning experience," the man explained.

Doctor Bar'ella rolled her eyes. "You've not seen a baby dragon or phoenix, either."

Blue scrubs grinned. "We're waiting for you to get pregnant."

"Impertinent." Doctor Bar'ella shooed them away. "Enough of the cooing. I need to check them out. Danelle, my office please." Danelle followed them into the room.

Tasteful artwork hung on the walls. To the left was a desk with two chairs in front of it. Overflowing bookcases completed the furniture.

"Please have a seat." Doctor Bar'ella motioned to the two chairs and sat behind her desk. "How are you feeling, Jared?"

"Fine," he answered.

"No adverse effects from the chemical cocktail? No elongated ears or other partial shifts?"

Lara raised an eyebrow. "Elongated ears?"

Doctor Bar'ella smiled. "Shifters can get caught partial shift."

Lara craned her neck to check Jared's backside.

"What are you doing?"

"Checking to see if you have your cute little tail."

A snicker from Danelle was quickly stifled at Jared's dark look.

"My tail is tucked away, where it belongs."

The doctor removed the stethoscope from around her neck and listened to his heart and lungs. She held her out her hands a few inches above his head. "Everything looks normal. Please shift."

Doctor Bar'ella stepped back, and Jared unbuttoned his shirt.

Lara cleared her throat. "What are you doing?"

"I don't want to get caught in my clothes." Jared shrugged out of his shirt and Lara enjoyed the sight of his shoulders and chest. From the sighs coming from the other two women, they also appreciated his assets.

He kicked off his shoes and socks, then stood, unsnapping his jeans. Jared raised an eyebrow. "I hope you're all enjoying the show?"

Danelle fanned her face with her hand. "Don't stop, please."

Jared winked at Lara and dropped his jeans. Oh man, he went commando. She had a single breath to enjoy the sight of him before he started to change.

Sparkles started in the center of his chest, moving outward to encompass his body. After a bright flash of light, resting on his clothes was Jared bunny.

Doctor Bar'ella leaned down and picked him up, putting him on her desk. He hopped over to the edge nearest to Lara, little nose sniffing.

"You want to check out the kits?" she asked.

He nodded.

"I don't think that's a good idea," the doctor warned. Lara pulled the sling open and held it out to Jared. Both gryphons turned to him and snapped their beaks.

Lara jerked back in her seat. "No kits, Jared isn't dinner."

She marveled. Their eyes weren't open, and yet they focused on him as prey. Two soft caws and they snuggled in.

Jared sniffed and hopped to the other end of the desk. The gryphon's heads followed the movement and Lara didn't know quite how. Sound or scent, or a combination of both? She was so focused on what the kits were doing, that she missed what the doctor did to Jared. "You can shift back," Bar'ella instructed.

A yawning black hole appeared over bunny Jared. Sparkles and streaks of light were sucked into the heart of the void. Another flash of light and Jared sat on the edge of the desk, naked.

He hopped off the table. Lara had to bite her lip to keep from reaching out to stroke his backside. Later, she'd do that later.

"Any adverse reactions?" Doctor Bar'ella asked.

Jared shook his head and began to dress. Lara shared a look with Danelle, who sighed. "Let's take a peek at those kits. May I?"

Lara helped the healer remove the sling and set the bundle in her lap.

Danelle picked up the girl and handed her to Lara. "This is Thea, yes?"

"Yes."

"She's such a pretty little lady."

Danelle drew Raiden from the sling. "Now let's check this little guy out." She held him in her arm and examined him, checking wings, claws, paws, beak and tail. Raiden didn't appreciate his tail being manipulated and snapped at Danelle. She held his beak between two fingers. "None of that, mister," she said, as he tried to flap his wings and jerk his beak away.

Danelle kept a hold of his head and beak with one hand and continued the exam with the other. "He's going to be a handful, but he's fine. Switch."

Lara grabbed Raiden and handed Thea over. Raiden huffed and settled his wings, content to snuggle in Lara's lap. She stroked the back of his head with one finger. "Such a horrible thing to endure, wasn't it?"

Raiden cawed softly.

Danelle performed the same assessment on Thea, who endured the indignities with poise and calm. "Both are well, no physical anomalies." She placed Thea next to Raiden.

They were interrupted by a knock at the door.

The doctor frowned. "Who could that be?"

Jared opened the door to a petite young woman with multiple piercings in her pointy elven ears. Her brown hair was streaked with dark red and tipped with black. She wore fishnet stockings, a leather mini skirt, and a deep ruby tank top. On top she wore a leather jacket.

Danelle and Bar'ella both stood. "Who are you and why have you barged into this office?" Doctor Bar'ella asked.

"It's okay, I know her," Jared said.

"Chill, dragon lady. I'm here to see the adorbs little tykes and to give them a pressie from Auntie Megs and Auntie Cyn."

At the mention of Cyn's name, the tension eased from the doctor's shoulders.

"You know Cyn?" Lara asked.

Megs nodded. "It's complicated, but she's a relation. Here you go." She handed the small wrapped package to Jared. "Can I see?"

Jared glanced at Lara. "She's not a threat to them."

"Okay."

Megs knelt at Lara's side. The kits tilted their heads toward her, but didn't have the same focus they'd had when Jared was a bunny.

"You're an elf?" Lara asked.

"Dark elf. I'm with Hans," Megs replied.

"Cyn's torturer friend, Hans?" Lara inquired.

"Got it in one. Oh, aren't they the cutest!" She held out her fingers, and both kits sniffed the air but didn't snap. Lara took that as a good sign. Megs gently rubbed their downy necks.

Jared had unwrapped the package. "Collars?" He lifted them up. One was pink and the other blue.

Megs stood. "There's a glamor imbedded in each collar that will hide their gryphon form. To humans they'll look like large kittens."

"Did Cyn asked you to make these?"

Megs shook her head. "Nope. I did it on my own. Once she told me about the babies, I couldn't resist." Megs grinned at Lara. "And you're more than welcome to bring them to the warehouse to play. Hans and I would be delighted to gryphon-sit anytime you need a break."

"Does Hans know anything about gryphons?" Doctor Bar'ella asked.

285

Megs shrugged. "He didn't say one way or the other. He instructed me to make the offer. Here." She held out a business card to Lara. "For you and Jared only."

Lara took the blank card. Megs pointed. "Put your thumb in that corner." Lara did as instructed and an address and phone number appeared in glowing silver on the card. When she removed her thumb, the image disappeared.

Both Megs and Jared stilled, then looked at the door.

"Ooops. I've overstayed my welcome. I'm out," Megs said and faster than a blink she was gone.

"What a strange woman," Doctor Bar'ella muttered.

"Are all dark elves like that?" Lara asked.

"Oh no," said Danelle, "most are very strait-laced and uptight."

"Interesting."

Jared nodded. "That she is. You should meet Hans."

"I'm looking forward to it."

"Hand me those charmed collars, will you?" Doctor Bar'ella asked.

Jared handed them over and the Doctor's eyes unfocused. "Hmm, there doesn't appear to be anything amiss. Please be careful if you decide to use them," she warned.

"You don't think she'd hurt the kits, do you?"

"No, but I've also never heard of a dark elf, so who knows what her motivations might be?"

Another knock on the door and when it opened, Captain Jor'dan entered the room followed by the scary man from yesterday, or was it this morning?

"Captain Jor'dan, Your Grace." Jared bowed from his waist.

Danelle curtseyed and with head bowed left the room. Lara wanted escape as well. The kits turned their heads toward His Scary Grace and bristled their wings.

"What are you two doing here?" Doctor Bar'ella asked.

His Scary Grace stood against the now closed door. "I'm here to lend weight to Jor'dan's request."

The doctor narrowed her eyes. "What request?"

Captain Jor'dan pulled out his cell phone, dialed and set it on the desk with the speaker on. "The one where I ask the natural gryphons for help."

Jared stood next to Lara, between her and His Scary Grace. He put his hand on her shoulder. "Remember, remain calm."

Remain calm, her left foot. She beckoned him with her finger. He leaned down so she could whisper in his ear. "I'll calm down when he stops being scary."

"That might take a long time."

Lara hid her head against Jared's side and suppressed a giggle.

The call was answered. "Hello, this is Noyon Nergüi Gerel's office. How can help you?"

"Hello, this is Captain Jor'dan from San Francisco, representing His Grace, High Chancellor Ashton Octavius Ignatio. I'd like to speak to the Noyon if possible."

"Noyon Gerel is in a meeting with his advisors. I'll have you him call you back as soon as it's over."

His Grace stepped forward and cleared his throat. "I'm afraid the matter is urgent and can't wait."

The assistant paused. "Yes, Your Grace. Allow me to put you on hold and let him know."

Beautiful haunting music came over the speaker.

Captain Jor'dan turned to His Scary Grace. "Why did you say it's urgent?"

"I've dealt with previous Noyons. If we want an answer this century, we need to chat with him now otherwise, they'll leave us waiting for decades."

During the hold music, Lara glanced up at Jared. "Does everyone speak English?"

Captain Jor'dan gave her a small smile. "No. they're speaking in their native language. I have an app that translates their speech into English."

Lara had a feeling that had been for her benefit, but she wouldn't quibble about it. "Thank you."

Captain Jor'dan gave a small smile. The music stopped and a stern male voice came over the line.

"Your Grace, you honor me with your call. Please forgive me, my advisors are here as well. How may I assist you?"

"Two kits have been found and need care. I would like a list of food preferences and knowledge about raising kits."

"Two kits?" Lara heard other voices in the room. The Noyon must have the call on speaker as well.

"Yes."

"Impossible. All of my people are accounted for, and none are in your part of the world."

His Scary Grace cleared his throat. "The two were born of a woman who'd been converted into a gryphon by the Alliance."

"Abominations!" It was the nicest word that was uttered. The voices were calling for the kits to be killed or left out in the elements. The Noyon called for calm in his office, and it took a few more minutes for the others to quiet.

Lara's heart sank. No one would hurt her babies. No one. She was on her own with these two. After comforting hug from Jared, she realized she wasn't alone. "I'm here," he whispered. That meant the world.

"I'm sorry, Your Grace, there's nothing _I_ can do."

"Thank you, Noyon Gerel."

The call disconnected, and Doctor Bar'ella stood. "Jor'dan and Ash, thank you for your help, but you need to leave. Now."

The two exchanged a glance. "I think she's kicking us out, Ash."

His Scary Grace nodded "I believe you're right. I wonder why?"

"I'm expecting a very important phone call." She went to the door and held it open. "Good day, gentleman."

Captain Jor'dan looked back at Jared. "Are you coming?"

"They need to stay," the doctor said, shoving the Captain out into the hall before closing the door behind him and leaning against it. "Stubborn males."

Lara looked at Jared. "What was that all about?"

Jared shrugged. "I have no idea."

Doctor Bar'ella resumed her seat and waved to the other chair. "Sit and stop hovering."

"Yes, ma'am."

The doctor glared at him. "That's enough out of you, or I'll banish you from the office and you'll miss the information."

"What information?" he asked.

"You'll see."

The telephone on her desk rang. Doctor Bar'ella pushed a couple of buttons then put it on speaker. "This is Doctor Bar'ella."

"This is Sernai. You got the message."

"Yes, I did."

"Are the Captain and High Chancellor still there?"

"No, I got rid of them as soon as I could."

"Good." The speaker sounded relieved.

"How much did you hear?" Doctor Bar'ella asked.

"Enough to know that the palace office is in an uproar over two abominations."

"Yes, but it's a bit more complex than that."

"In what way?"

Doctor Bar'ella shared information regarding the birth.

"Poor kits," Sernai said. "I can't speak for long." She quickly rattled off a list of things to do for the babies. Doctor Bar'ella jotted down notes. "I've got it. Thank you."

"Please let me know if I can help further."

Lara raised her hand. Doctor Bar'ella nodded. "Yes?"

"Is there someone else there?" Sernai asked.

"Yes, it's the woman who rescued the kits when their mom died."

"What question do you have for me, child?"

"Why are you willing to help when the Noyon was so upset?"

"Ah, I see I must explain. We've not had a new kit born to us in two centuries. For you to have two is a blessing from the Gods. However, the males have forgotten that we too once mixed with humans. While what was done was horrible, and your kits will not be accepted by our people, they are babies and not even the Noyon would countenance destroying babies."

"Thank you for your help."

"You're welcome. I only ask that I be permitted to visit."

Lara looked at Doctor Bar'ella, who nodded. "I think they'd like that, as would I. Thank you."

"Doctor Bar'ella, I'll make the arrangements through you to insure sure all the proprieties are maintained."

"That sounds good."

Through the phone they heard a knocking on the door. Then, "I must go. Goodbye," and the call was disconnected.

Doctor Bar'ella wrote out the instructions then handed the paper to Jared. "This is what you need to do for the short term."

He looked at the page before handing it to Lara. The first thing was to feed them like baby eagles.

"How do baby eagles eat?" Lara asked.

Jared researched it on his phone, but Bar'ella answered before he could. "They eat meat from fish, mice, squirrels, and bunnies."

"Ew." Lara wrinkled her nose. "I'm not sure I could do that."

Jared glared at the doctor. "Bunnies are not on the menu. Don't worry, I'll take care of feeding them." He grabbed Lara's hand and pulled her to her feet. He tucked the collars into a back pocket. "We'll get out of your way. We have some shopping to do."

"Keep me informed of their progress," Doctor Bar'ella said.

Lara smiled, "We will, thank you."

After a stop at the nearest pet store, they returned to Jared's place and set up an area for the babies. Lara placed them into their nest. With Jared's arm around her shoulders, she watched the kits settle in.

Jared cupped her cheeks, running his thumb over her cheek bones. "I love you, Lara Adams."

He bent his head and placed a steamy kiss on her lips. She wrapped her arms around his shoulders, pressing her body as close to his as their clothes would allow and a large squawk broke them apart.

"It's going to be an adventure," Lara said, as Thea tried to peck at her brother.

Laughter shook Jared's body. "That it will. There's no one I'd rather share it with than you."

Epilogue

Master Jenner Quaid stood in front of the windows in his penthouse suite, looking over the skyline.

"What is the status of the experiments in San Francisco? Did Glendale meet his deadline?" he asked Mateo, his executive assistant.

"I'm afraid there's bad news, sir." The terror in Mateo's voice was unmistakable. Jenner couldn't blame the man. He'd fired many aides in the last two years. He remained facing the window, aware Mateo became incoherent in a direct face to face conversation. Jenner kept him on because the man was brilliant at organizing.

"What happened?" Jenner let out a resigned breath. *How had Glendale fucked up this time?*

"From reports of an agent in the vicinity, Dr. David Glendale, Dr. Mason Anderson, and all lab personnel are dead. An explosion destroyed everything within the lab, but not the structure itself."

Burning anger rushed through his body. *Don't take it out on Mateo.* He counted magical elements, willing himself calm. Rage-fueled magic spelled disaster for all involved. "The facility itself is still intact?"

"Yes, sir."

"Was it Glendale's fault?"

"No. Shifter Jared Williams is responsible."

"Glendale manage to get him to the lab?"

"Yes, sir." There was a slight pause. "Do we retaliate against shifter Williams?"

The shifter was a member of the Elite and under DúSan's watchful eye. While it might feel good to get revenge, Williams had eliminated the problem of Glendale.

"No. We take no further action against him."

"Sir?"

"He's too well protected. Glendale's mistake was not letting him go. What of the others? Gryphons, I believe? Did they survive?"

Mateo hesitated. "I don't know. The agent didn't include that information."

"Find out if any survived." The reflection of the window showed his assistant scribbling on his tablet. "I want copies of all files regarding the experiments." Jenner said.

"All data regarding that location was corrupted," Mateo replied.

"How?"

"We don't know for sure. The computer mages said a virus corrupted the data. We have people working on it, but the servers were damaged and they're not able to recover the data."

"They didn't use off-site storage?"

"No, sir."

"Why not?"

"The decision was left to the site managers."

"Did any survive?"

"No." A chime rang from Mateo's tablet. "It's time for the meeting with the department heads."

"Tell them I'll be right there."

Mateo left the room. Jenner closed his eyes and centered himself, allowing the last of his anger to dissipate into the ether. Steps would be taken so a repeat of the San Francisco fiasco wouldn't happen again.

He walked into the boardroom. All department heads were present.

"Good afternoon, gentlemen. As some of you may have heard, the shifter project was destroyed."

The mages looked around at each other as Jenner briefly outlined what happened. "No further funds or research into this area of study will be approved. What else are we currently working on?"

The head of the Technology Department stood, clearing his throat. "We've made great strides in software development. We've been able to key it to humans and can nudge them into certain types of behaviors. We're releasing the beta version next month."

Jenner consulted his tablet for notes on the project. "Is it compatible with Paranormal brainwaves?"

"On those we've tested, yes. However, our sample size is limited to mages and shifters who were inclined to assist. We need to test it on a wider sample size to verify the magic kernel works."

"How do you propose to test this?" Jenner asked.

"We're hosting a writing retreat with a mix of humans and Paranormals. The programmers have imbedded the kernel into innocuous writing software. The plan is to activate the kernel in stages to test responses."

Jenner tapped his chin. "Writers tend to be more imaginative, more open to suggestion. They'll be the perfect test subjects. Keep me informed of your progress."

The End

About the Author

Stephanie has always had an overactive imagination. She often changed the endings of stories in her head, when books didn't end the way she thought they should. A friend convinced her to write her own stories, and the box that held all the wild and curious creatures in her head, exploded in a multi-hued, chaotic mass of light. Her fascination with mythology and space has fueled strange and interesting stories that she hopes you enjoy. She lives in San Jose with her husband and two fur babies, Mina and Vlad.

Other Titles by Stephanie Kayne

Demon's Desire

I Heart Geeks